CONQUEROR'S CITY

Graham
Porter

- Conqueror's City -

- Graham G Porter -

For my wife, Heidi

My best friend and most loyal fan

———————————

Conqueror's City: Histories of Asfáleia Book One by Graham G Porter

grahamgporter.com

Cover by Graham G Porter; Image(s) used under license from Shutterstock.com
Map of Asfáleia Copyright Dewi Hargreaves 2021 (dewihargreaves.com)

Additional Credits:

Ellie Hawkes at Elspells Writing Feedback (elspells.com)

Nathan Jones Beta Reading (theroadtonathan.com)

Many thanks to my proof-reader for putting up with endless questions!

Thanks also to all the published, publishing, querying, writing, and aspiring authors on Twitter @ #WritingCommunity, #WritersOfTwitter, #AmWriting and elsewhere for encouragement, support, suggestions, criticisms, and the benefit of your wide and varied experiences

And last but decidedly not least, my thanks to Heidi Kinsella and Madison Eastwood for reading the same story over and over again and never once complaining. Love you guys!

ISBN: 978-1-3999-2868-7 (print)

First Edition

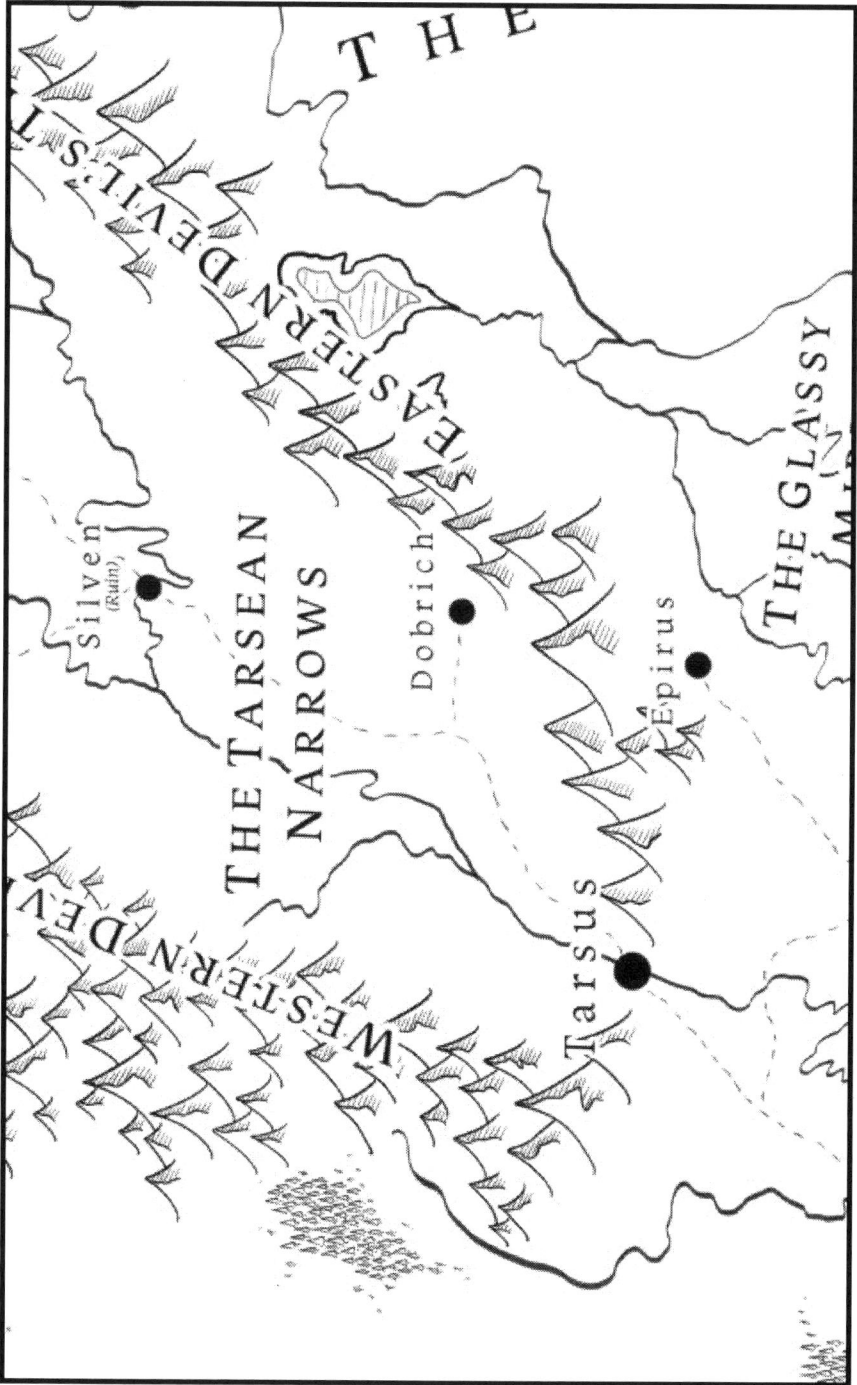

Hearken while I tell you the history of our land, in such terms as I have pieced it together through long years of study and thought. This tale may be true, or only partially so, I cannot genuinely be sure of which, but I do know that it is the best summation of what knowledge we have and thus, I believe, it constitutes a worthy narrative. I would give evidence for its accuracy by humble reference to my own credentials as perhaps the most eminent scholar of history in the modern world. Over the course of decades, I have devoted my considerable intellect and keen acumen to developing a comprehensive understanding of the story of this land. Few indeed, in this age or the last, can speak with such authority on these or many other matters.

Acusilaus "The Wise", royal historian, c. 850M

Few can speak with such authority on these matters. So few indeed, one might even say none, and not be far wrong. Certainly not the conceited lackey of a minor king, so blinded by the supposed brilliance of his own intellect that he would no longer recognise the truth if it hit him squarely on the nose. Beware, dear reader, of the man who names himself "the wise", not all is as he would have it to be.

Polemon of Chalcis, philosopher and cynic, c. 950M

CHAPTER ONE

Deep in the Drevenwood
6 of Hippodromos 868M - Mid Autumn
Two years before the siege of Tarsus

Warriors we / Comes our day
Warriors free / Lives for the Rutik!

Warriors we / On the march
Warriors free / Lives for the Rutik!

Warriors we / Off to fight
Warriors free / Lives for the Rutik!

Rutik marching chant, callouts with selected responses, date unknown

Chapter One

A wave of bone-deep fatigue swept over Mira as she scratched at the wound on her right forearm, breaking the newly formed scab. A trickle of fresh blood ran down her arm and dripped to the forest floor, the tiny splashes of crimson merging into the myriad shades of brown amongst the fallen leaves. The wound was shallow but painful, not debilitating but only one of a dozen others she had taken in the preceding hours. She sighed and allowed her shoulders to sink as she rested her elbows on her knees and removed her helm. Her long, fine hair was dark with sweat and fell limply onto her neck, so she pulled a leather cord from her pouch and tied it back carelessly. Long days in the saddle and a night without rest had left her drawn and pale, with dark haloes surrounding her eyes, purple and black like old bruises. A glancing blow from a spiked mace had torn a tattered rent in the chainmail on her left side and sliced into the leather beneath leaving a mangled scrap hanging loose that jingled merrily as she moved. Dried blood, some of it hers, had formed a brownish crust in a dozen places, and coated most of her right leg, mingling there with mud, sweat and rainwater.

Tutting, Mira set her helm aside and pulled a small knife from her belt, using its sharp tip to pry idly at the rotting log she was sitting on. Bits of green moss and crumbling bark dropped silently to settle amidst the detritus of fallen twigs and leaves that lay like a carpet around the trees. Autumn was now well-established in the Drevenwood, the weather was quickly turning colder, but the ground had yet to freeze. Streams and rivulets of snowmelt from further north still ran hither and thither across the wooded slopes, following old channels and carving new ones. A short distance away, Mira's soldiers were watering the horses in one such stream and she could hear their panting breaths between gulps. The horses were near exhausted too, she knew, and could not maintain this pace for much longer. The soldiers themselves were in little better shape, unsurprising after a day and a night of running and fighting, constantly on the alert, seeing danger in every shadow.

Mira's knife jarred as she hit a particularly sturdy knot in the wood and she cursed, far more loudly than was warranted. She felt rather than saw the soldiers' heads turning towards her and waved a hand dismissively before spitting on the ground in disgust. The soldiers went back to their work, understanding of her impulsive outburst. Constant tension had stretched everyone's nerves near to breaking point, and tempers were short throughout the troop.

"Fucking Baimoi aren't going to give in easy." Sergeant Teja's bass rumble interrupted her brooding. Teja was in his early thirties, twice Mira's age, and had more than a decade's military experience, dwarfing her meagre tally.

"Very well, sergeant. We'll chance an hour here before moving on. Try and rotate the sentries if you can, see that everyone gets some rest."

"Get some rest yourself, you look half dead."

Most officers would have regarded the sergeant's remark as insubordinate and reprimanded him accordingly, but Mira was unconcerned with her soldiers' manners, only that they could fight, and Teja was a demon in battle. He fought using a customised *bardiche*, a broad-headed axe with a long handle, somewhere between a battle-axe and a poleaxe. The weapon's head was an uneven crescent, extending three or four inches down the haft in a sharp curve, but sweeping out to a full ten inches in length above. With Teja's considerable weight behind it and swung with the full force of his broad shoulders and bulging biceps, the bardiche could chop through anything lighter than full plate armour and even put a serious dent in that. Mira had once seen him behead three charging warriors with a single powerful sweep – a feat that required a remarkable combination of timing, reflexes and that most valuable of a soldier's skills, luck. She wondered how he saw her, but quickly answered her own question: an experienced soldier, he resented taking orders from a junior officer, fresh from the College of War and with no experience at all to speak of.

The captain of their troop had died the previous day, in the first enemy attack. The Baimoi might have targeted him specifically, aiming to take out their commander. Alternatively, he might simply have been unlucky. Either way, a flying javelin had pierced his cheek as he turned his head to shout his orders to the troop. Thrown from ground level, the barbed point was angled upward on impact and plunged through his brain before bursting out of the right side of his skull. He was killed instantly and tumbled him from his saddle before his last words had faded from the air. Their First Lieutenant had died in the ensuing melee, her life snatched away by a Baimoi axe, along with most of her chest. The axeman had died a moment later, stabbed in both sides by Rutik spears but it was too late for the lieutenant. Despite having no practical command experience, Mira now found herself promoted to the senior officer in command of a troop of light cavalry, lost in unfriendly territory and running for their lives. A part of her delighted in the opportunity to prove her worth but another, more insidious part questioned and doubted her ability. She was their leader by default, but it remained to be seen whether the soldiers would follow where she led.

Even had there been the time to spare, Mira would not have shed a tear for either of her superiors. Upon arriving at the Rutik outpost, she had found a Captain well past his prime who treated this, his last posting before retirement, as a task to be endured with as little exertion as possible. A second Lieutenant, fresh-faced and innocent, was an additional complication he neither wanted nor needed. For her part, his Lieutenant had her eyes firmly upon promotion, seeing herself as the natural successor to the command of the troop. Mira was potentially a competitor, and the other Lieutenant was keen to make sure that she remembered her place. The common soldiers of the troop were bored and neglected but comfortable with their Captain's lethargy since it meant less work and less danger for them too. Even now they watched Mira sullenly and whispered amongst themselves as she passed, almost daring her to call them out or issue a command.

In all, including the officers, the troop had lost eight in the fighting so far and their three scouts had never returned, leaving Mira to assume that they were dead or dying somewhere out in the woods. That left them with a headcount of just nineteen soldiers, seventeen in any shape to fight, and twenty-three horses. In a fair fight, Mira would bet on her fellow Rutik over almost any opponent, but they were wildly outnumbered, and the enemy ranks were swelling all the time. Teja had come through it all with hardly a scratch however and showed no sign of strain. That, to Mira, was far more valuable than stiff and formal respect for rank.

"Dismissed sergeant," she replied, more formally than she had intended but Teja nodded and turned to relay her orders to the troops. Mira returned to picking at the log but the brief interlude with the sergeant had focused her mind on the present and she dismissed the obvious hostility of her soldiers in favour of more pressing concerns. Once they got back to safety, there would be time enough to make friends, or at the least instil some discipline. And if they never got back? Well, in that case, she too would be lying dead on the forest floor somewhere, and all the enemies she had ever made would no longer bother her in the slightest.

The Baimoi were a large and warlike tribe that had abandoned their homelands far to the north and embarked on the long, perilous journey through the Drevenwood to reach the land of Asfáleia. The geography of the land was such that the mountains and rivers formed a natural funnel out of the western woods and into Rutik territory. In truth, it was more of a migration than an invasion – great, trailing caravans of men, women, and children, heavily laden mules, and carefully shepherded livestock. This was not the first of such migrations, nor was it likely to be the last, for it seemed the north held an inexhaustible supply of peoples. Those lands were a patchwork of rival tribes, all constantly at war with one another. Borders and boundaries shifted and changed as one tribe or another got the upper hand for a while, then shifted back a year, a month, or even just a week later. Every so often a smaller tribe would get pushed out altogether and would decide to travel south in search of new lands and plunder.

When those smaller parties arrived, the Rutik would talk, bribe, or coerce them into service as foot soldiers in one of the Kingdom's numerous wars. New arrivals would either be turned against the next tribe in line to invade or else attached as auxiliaries to one of the Rutik armies fighting the Achaeans. Unfortunately for the Baimoi, they were too proud to be persuaded and far too numerous to be paid off or intimidated into anything. Interrogated captives had told the Rutik of a great battle with some foreign empire in the east. That empire had expanded their territory, pushing the tribes to the west, and creating a far larger exodus than would normally have occurred. The Baimoi caravans were well-supplied and heavily defended and that left only one option: the Baimoi would die so that the Rutik could continue to thrive. It was, Mira felt, the way of things. and a task the Northern Army had performed before and would inevitably perform again in the future.

In another unfortunate turn of fate, the Baimoi had proven both more stubborn and more determined than anticipated and what was planned to be a quick, punitive, action had dragged out for three long years and become a war of attrition and slow, grinding slaughter. The Baimoi would filter out of the woods in small groups, attacking and killing Rutik patrols and looting caravans before fading away, back into the trees. Every so often their raids would become intolerable, and the Rutik commanders would order a large-scale sweep, hundreds or sometimes thousands of soldiers filing into the woods to kill anyone they found. The Baimoi would respond by meeting the Rutik head-on, and the mulchy ground of the Drevenwood would be fertilised with the dead of both sides. Eventually, the Rutik would triumph, their superior equipment and organisation strengthening their hand. The Baimoi would retreat deeper into the woods to lick their wounds and the Rutik would return to quarters, happy with a job well done but within weeks the Baimoi would launch a raid or two, and the whole cycle would begin again.

Summer was the season of war in the north, and things had already quietened down considerably when orders came down the line for Mira's troop to ride three days into the Drevenwood before coming around in a wide curve and returning to camp. It was a scouting mission, designed to get the lie of the land before the winter snow and ice arrived in force and their Captain had not been best pleased with the assignment, nor the prospect of spending a week in the cold, damp woods. There was always the possibility of meeting the enemy, of course, but a troop of thirty Rutik light cavalry was still a force to be reckoned with and it was unlikely that the Baimoi would be present in sufficient numbers to hazard an attack. If they were, Mira was confident she and her comrades could fight their way out.

Each of her soldiers carried a long spear and a falchion, relatively short in length, with a straight edge and distinctive curve at the point. They wore green tunics under chainmail vests, steel barbutes protected their heads and each horse had a circular shield slung on its flank, crafted from solid poplar wood, covered with leather, and embossed with the black wolf's head of the Kingdom of the Rutik. She had been so proud of them as they rode out of camp that morning, with the bright spring sun glinting off their polished armour. They were less pristine now, their armour scratched and dented, some carrying hurriedly dressed wounds, others having lost a helm or shield. All of them were coated in dried blood and dirt. Unsure of their true mettle, Mira worried that they might have little taste for further action. She felt a little guilty for even thinking that her fellow Rutik might run from a fight but in the circumstances, it would be difficult to blame them if they did.

Mira's spear was leaning against a tree nearby, within easy reach should the alarm be sounded. As a Second Lieutenant, she was issued with a breastplate but otherwise attired identically to her soldiers. Even at that, the breastplate was plain and unadorned since she represented the lowest rank of a commissioned officer. She had eschewed the standard falchion in favour of a heavier longsword, however, which had convinced her of its worth once more during the first chaotic attack of the Baimoi, the previous day. A shout from the trees, followed by a short, sharp scream snapped her attention back to the present. Firmly suppressing her exhaustion, she grabbed her helm and jumped to her feet, to see a contingent of Baimoi burst from the cover of a large thicket that had grown up around the trunks of a few mighty old beech trees. The edge of the thicket was about thirty yards from where she sat and even as she bellowed orders to her soldiers, the Baimoi were almost upon them. At that moment, a second band of enemies emerged from the trees to their rear, equally close and just as numerous, and the air was filled with war cries, arrows and thrown spears.

Still shouting, Mira took up her spear, flung it at the nearest enemy and pulled her sword free of its scabbard. Had they been facing Achaeans or another force of Rutik she would have held on to the spear since a sword is less effective against heavy armour, but the Baimoi wore leather vests, thick padded jerkins or nothing at all and her blade would be equally effective against all three.

"Form up around the horses. Defensive lines, now!"

A short distance away, Sergeant Teja echoed her orders and the Rutik soldiers responded without hesitation. They divided quickly and efficiently into two lines, one to either side of their mounts, spears resting on the rims of their shields, and preparing to repel their attackers. A corner of Mira's mind was pleased to note that whatever resentment they harboured against her, her soldiers knew their business. She suspected that was down to the first lieutenant's influence, rather than the captain's but either way, in the face of an enemy assault, it was a reassuring discovery.

The Baimoi were screaming now, charging in two disorderly masses, rage and bloodlust overcoming what little discipline they possessed. Truth be told, it was a terrifying sight, but Mira was nothing if not pragmatic – there was nowhere to run and nowhere to hide, so no matter how numerous or frightening the enemy, there was nothing else to do but fight. Her shield was still strapped to her horse, too far away to reach easily. The strap of her helm was hanging loose, the brass buckle slapping against her neck as she moved but it was too late to do anything about it. Taking a two-handed grip on her longsword, she assumed a fighting stance and prepared to do battle.

"Hold the lines! Hold the lines and kill the fuckers!" All around her the Rutik soldiers roared their defiance. "Rutik! Rutik!"

CHAPTER TWO

Deep in the Drevenwood
7 of Hippodromos 868M - Mid Autumn
Two years before the siege of Tarsus

Drevenwood — from the old Bulǵha *dreven* or древен, meaning ancient. The name is used by Rutik and Achaean alike, and few ever stop to ponder its meaning or origins. Like the sad remnants of the Bulǵha people, scraps of their language remain here and there, lingering like half-heard echoes of a forgotten past.

Acusilaus, "Peoples of Asfáleia", c. 900M

Chapter Two

Twenty minutes of fierce battle followed as rabid Baimoi fervour met steely Rutik resolve. The Baimoi poured into the attack, heedless of their own safety and determined only to break the hated enemy. The Rutik stood firm, meeting the first attackers with the points of their spears, then leaning into their shields to repel the next. Mira anchored one end of the two lines, Teja the other and although their fighting styles could hardly have been more different, they were both equally effective in the role. Teja was frighteningly strong, and fast for a man his size, cutting enemies down and then tossing them aside to send their comrades crashing into a heap. Mira was considerably quicker even than the sergeant and fought with the precise economy of effort born of long and dedicated practice.

Her orders issued, Mira now fought in silence, darting in and out of her enemies' reach, killing or maiming with almost every strike. She skewered one Baimoi warrior with a quick thrust through his left eye and into the back of his head. Pulling her sword clear, she blocked a spear coming in from her left, then twisted to push the weapon aside before running her opponent through with a single thrust to the solar plexus. The razor-sharp longsword punched through the Baimoi's rough leather armour and slid smoothly into his gut. Mira's balance was near perfect, but the point of her blade grazed the man's spine, slowing her withdrawal long enough for suction to form around the wound. Another enemy was upon her before she could recover her stance, and it might have gone badly had not the next Rutik in line hamstrung her attacker, causing her to stumble and fall. Mira saw the shock and pain in the woman's eyes, momentarily sympathised and then swept her blade across her filthy throat. The sharp edge cut through a necklace made from braided horsehair, sending coloured beads tumbling in all directions before blood spurted from the wound and coated Mira's leg from hip to shin. Without so much as a gurgle, the Baimoi fell, and Mira turned to look for her next opponent.

The remaining Baimoi pressed the attack with remarkable determination but now the scattered bodies were impeding their progress, tangling their feet in broken limbs, and stealing their footing with slicks of blood and gory viscera. Mira saw one of her soldiers go down, a wild strike from a Baimoi spear piercing his thigh even as an axe thudded hard into his shield. In the chaos of battle, cruel fate killed as easily as ineptitude. His attackers roared in triumph and his life might have ended at that moment, had not the next Rutik in line stepped smartly sideways, planting her feet to either side of his chest and hunkering behind her shield to deflect the enemy's blows. Mira watched with pride as the rest of the Rutik line reacted in smooth unison, each soldier taking a step to their left, closing the gap, and smartly denying the enemy their opening. Another Baimoi charged in at that moment but out of the corner of her eye, she registered the fallen Rutik soldier crawling out from under his comrade and regaining his feet in the relative safety behind the line. By the time she had dealt with her attacker, the soldier was back in the line, bleeding but alive and, more importantly, still fighting.

Moments seemed to stretch into hours as Mira blocked, hacked, stabbed, and slashed but the battle was soon over. Dismayed by their losses and the ferocity of the defence, the Baimoi attack faltered and failed. The Rutik soldiers cheered and shouted crude insults as their enemy slowly backed away. They had won but Mira could see several Rutik bodies bleeding out onto the forest floor. She knew then that she had only moments before she lost her soldiers to their thirst for vengeance. If they took to pursuing the Baimoi through the trees then all was lost, for they were too few for such escapades. Sooner or later the enemy would regroup, find their courage, and turn back to pick off the scattered Rutik one by one.

"Mount up!" she bellowed, as loudly as she could. "Mount up! We ride!" Mira swung back into her saddle, aware that her soldiers were wavering, unsure of her authority and unwilling to retreat in the face of a defeated enemy.

"Mount up or stay and fucking die!" She pulled her horse around as she spoke and glared at the first soldier she set eyes upon. Under her stern gaze, that soldier faltered and then climbed back onto his horse. Another soldier, perhaps a friend or particularly close comrade, followed and that was enough to tip the balance. Moments later, all the soldiers who were still alive were back on their horses and waiting for direction.

The hours following the Baimoi attack were a blur of leafy branches rushing past in the gathering dusk and the crunch of galloping hooves on the forest floor. They rode hard, continuing to head west and determined to put distance between themselves and the remainder of the Baimoi. East would have been the more prudent direction of travel, taking them closer to home and safety. However, reporting back to her commander that she met the enemy, defeated them, and then promptly ran away was unlikely to be well received. There was no sign of their scouts, but Mira was still hopeful that at least some of them would return eventually. After three hours, when Mira deemed that the Baimoi threat was far enough behind, they slowed to a canter and then a walk until they found a suitable place to make camp. When they arrived in a large clearing, with good lines of sight in all directions, she called a halt, assigned half a dozen soldiers to sentry duty, and ordered the remainder to rest.

Mira had barely settled onto the ground when one of the sentries called out an alert and two bedraggled figures staggered into the clearing, leading a single exhausted horse. She recognised one of them as the scout Beuca and rose to meet him. Beuca was around her age but had learned his trade hunting in these same woods with his parents and grandparents. He was by far and away their best scout and Mira was pleased to see him return. The second figure was unrecognisable for a moment, a gaping wound to her scalp having coated her features with thick, dried blood. Beuca handed her off to another soldier and limped over to Mira to report.

"Beuca, what happened out there? How did the Baimoi manage to surprise us? Where was our warning?" The scout paused for a minute, looking around for a more senior officer but finding none.

"They're dead, Beuca. You report to me now."

"Sorry, Lieutenant. We tried to get back to the troop, but the woods are crawling with Baimoi, the fuckers are everywhere. Every time we made some progress, we'd hit another batch of 'em and have to turn back. I found Arika by pure chance and we joined forces, but I haven't seen any sign of Asbad."

Teja arrived as the scout trailed off. His face was grim as he nodded to Mira and made his report.

"Arika's in rough shape, Lieutenant. The head wound is bloody and not that deep, but she has a fucking dart stuck in her gut that we can't get out."

Beuca shuddered and rubbed at a large tear in his jerkin, below his ribs where he had taken a hit powerful enough to do damage but that somehow had not penetrated his leather armour.

"Big group of the bastards surprised us a few miles back. Darts and arrows coming from all directions. I was lucky: got behind a tree just in time. Arika wasn't quick enough, but I was able to drag her out of there."

"You've done well, Beuca," Mira said, recognising the man's anguish. Even allowing for exhaustion and strain, he seemed stricken with grief, and she wondered momentarily if he and Arika were perhaps closer than simple comrades-in-arms.

"What's our position?"

"Frankly? We're fucked. The gang you met were outriders, probably scouting or just hunting. I've seen two or three of those, as well as some bigger and some smaller but they're not the real problem. There's a whole army out there, approaching from the south and west. Hundreds of the fuckers. I didn't get too close, or close enough to count anyway but it's a proper horde and they're headed this way. We need to move. Now."

"There must be a major attack planned," put in Teja, with a deep frown as he worked out the implications. "Might be they'll press on and just ignore us if they're after bigger game?"

"Respect sergeant, but no. The Baimoi are settled north of here in the deeper woods. If they're coming from the south and headed for our lines, that means they've gone a long way out of their way to attack where they're not expected. They won't want to take a chance on us making it back with a warning."

Mira's mind raced as she absorbed the stark facts of the matter. Her duty was clear, and it was exactly as Beuca had suggested: at all costs, they had to make it back to the lines with news of the Baimoi attack. All other concerns were secondary but unless they could evade their pursuers, there would be no chance of warning anyone. She made a series of decisions quickly and without hesitation, knowing that swift action was their only hope of survival. She reached for her helm and spear and addressed the sergeant.

"Round up the troops and get them mounted. We move out as soon as we're ready."

"Aye, lieutenant." Teja acknowledged her orders without question and with no hint of panic in his voice. Mira felt immensely grateful for the capable and unflappable sergeant. Was there a thaw in his attitude towards her since the battle, she wondered. She was the only one who had come close to matching his score of kills amongst the Baimoi. Perhaps that had earned her a modicum of grudging respect. He was by no means friendly of course, he would not be that easily won over, but maybe he had decided to give her the benefit of the doubt. Time would tell whether it lasted.

"What's our course?" Mira looked at Beuca, but the scout had nothing further to add. She paused for a moment, thinking.

"We head north. If we can get enough distance between us and them, we can loop back around to the east and head for camp." Teja nodded and once again turned to relay her orders to the soldiers. Mira looked at Beuca sympathetically and then ordered him to find a fresh horse. Since the Baimoi attack, they had several spares, so that at least was not a concern. Within fifteen minutes, Mira's troop was assembled and moving out of the clearing.

Mira and her soldiers rode north for about three hours before meeting opposition. They were re-forming after negotiating a particularly dense patch of woodland when missiles began dropping from the night sky without warning. A roughly fletched arrow glanced off a soldier's helm and another of the vicious little darts hit a horse in the flank, driving it wild with pain and causing it to almost throw its rider. Strangely, the deadly rain stopped almost as quickly as it had started but Mira knew they were out of time. The enemy, in whatever numbers, were directly to her north meaning that she would have to change course if she was to avoid another battle. She turned to the east and motioned for the troop to follow but they got less than three miles before another hail of arrows, darts and stones came shooting out of the trees ahead. She made to turn back north but emerged into a clearing, on the far side of which a large band of Baimoi warriors stood waiting. Mira knew that her Rutik could take them on if need be but the incontrovertible equations that governed the mathematics of war meant that they could not do it without taking casualties, and without it taking long enough for more of the enemy to arrive.

Mira knew that they could not afford to be bogged down so, reluctantly, she turned back towards the south and west.

"We ride hard and fast. Hard and fast like there's no tomorrow and be damned the filthy Baimoi. We'll outpace them, get around behind them, and then turn back north."

They got about five miles to the south before being turned aside again, this time driven west and deeper into the Drevenwood. Six times over the course of the night, Mira tried to break out of the encircling enemy and six times they were driven back on course. Twice she tried stopping at a defensible spot and digging in, hoping to at least take control over the terrain on which they would fight. The Baimoi were having none of it though and drove them onward with storms of arrows, darts, and spears before they could even find cover. Shortly before dawn, the pursuit seemed to slacken somewhat, and Mira took the opportunity to rest. With that, she found herself trapped once more in the same perilous corner she had started from but no closer to finding a way out. She rolled her eyes. *Good job with your first command, Mira*

Throughout the night the Baimoi opposition had grown steadily stronger, the barrages of missiles steadily heavier and their chances of escape steadily slimmer. As morning approached, the enemy was not so much hunting them as herding them, driving them steadily westward into what was, in all likelihood, their doom. The scout Arika had passed away silently shortly after midnight, still strapped behind Beuca on a spare horse. Beuca's face had turned stony when a soldier gently pointed out that his passenger was dead. Without saying a single word, he turned in the saddle and cut Arika's ties, letting her cold body gently tilt sideways and drop to the ground with a dull thud. That was the Rutik way, stoical to the last, but Beuca had not spoken since and when Mira caught his eye, there was nothing there but pain.

Another soldier had also succumbed to his injuries during the night, his wounds turning septic and poisoning his blood. Two more were caught by arrows, one pierced through the throat, the other, lacking a helmet, through the top of his head. Yet another was killed when her galloping horse trapped a hoof in a deep hole, hidden by the darkness and fallen branches. The horse fell hard, twisting as it fell, crushing its hapless rider against a protruding tree root and breaking her neck instantly. Her mount broke both its front legs, one in multiple places and its piercing screams of agony were almost human-sounding and rang through the quiet woods like a banshee's wails until Teja stepped up with a spiked hammer to put it out of its misery. By morning, Mira's troop was down to less than half-strength and none of them were unscathed.

As the first shafts of bright autumn sun filtered through the branches, incongruously beautiful to the beleaguered Rutik, Mira ordered the troop to mount up once more and set off towards the west. She had not abandoned hope of shaking their pursuers but for the moment there was little option but to follow the path set for them. One of two things would happen, she figured: either the Baimoi would eventually make a mistake, leaving an opening or a weakness that she could exploit to break through and escape; or else they would eventually reach a point where the Baimoi would pull the noose tight around their throats in which case they would try to fight their way out, and probably fail.

In truth, Mira had little choice in the matter since the Baimoi were now fully in control of the narrative. She contemplated another attempt at turning – north, south, or even back to the east but reluctantly dismissed the idea. She had fourteen soldiers left, and any attempt to break free would leave yet more of her charges injured or dead. The wiser choice now was to conserve what little strength she had left and await her moment – whether that was to escape or to die. Either way, she needed to have enough able bodies left to at least make one last show of Rutik honour and might. With that singularly forlorn hope in mind, she rode on, keeping the troop in close formation as best they were able, taking the lead with Beuca by her side and Teja bringing up the rear with two of their most able fighters. Every so often they could see the enemy amongst the trees, watching them and waiting for whatever came next.

Shortly before noon, Mira's diminished troop emerged into a large clearing and the final ambush was sprung. As they reached the centre of the open area, large numbers of Baimoi appeared from amidst the trees on all sides, hemming them in, waving their weapons and roaring curses and insults. Mira knew she had only moments to act. If they remained where they were, the mob would descend upon them with fury and tear them to pieces. Her only viable option was to break out somehow and hope to flee before the enemy could catch them. Mira knew her chances were slim, but her scant advantage lay in two facts. One, the enemy was without mounts, as was the way of fighting in the old country: that gave her the advantage of the speed and the ability to strike fast and hard at a particular spot and be away and gone before the enemy could bring numbers to bear. Secondly, now that the Baimoi had decided to attack, it would be in their nature to all pile into the fight: no proud warrior could stand for being left out, so if she could once break through their line, there was a solid chance that they would have an open passage back to safety.

Standing up in her stirrups, Mira scanned the gathering Baimoi. At a quick tot, she guessed there were fifty or sixty of them in total, and possibly more hidden from sight in the trees. There were two spots in the line that appeared weak – one an opening between two trees where the concentration of enemy warriors was noticeably lower, the other a slight gap in the line between two large clusters of Baimoi. Both were tempting targets, and Mira immediately discounted them. The Baimoi were savages but not stupid. If there were obvious weak points in their formation, they were there for a reason. Mira had been herded and steered for days, and instinctively knew that the supposed weak points were only one more such tactic, intended to corral them into one final bloody ambush.

Instead, Mira selected one of the spots that appeared more heavily defended, but in an area where the forest was somewhat thinner, and her troop could gallop at full speed to safety if they could but break the enemy. Without hesitation, Mira called her soldiers into a tight formation, and they followed her lead as she charged full pelt into the enemy. Overconfident, and still jostling for position, the Baimoi were taken by surprise and Mira's charge hit them hard, throwing them into disorder. Half a dozen of the Baimoi were killed in the first clash, two by Mira herself. A half dozen more were thrown aside by the impact of the sturdy Rutik horses and trampled under steel-shod hooves. More of the enemy quickly closed in, however, and a fierce, close-quarters battle ensued. Mira knew their only hope lay in maintaining momentum and continuing to move forward: if they got bogged down, if their charge stalled, the Baimoi would gather in sufficient numbers to drag them down and kill them. Their survival depended on being more savage than their savage enemy, but those of Mira's soldiers that remained were the iron-hard core of the troop, the ones that were too tough or too stubborn to have given in already. They were the best of the troop, fighters and Rutik to their core. They would deliver the Baimoi a masterclass in savagery that would not be quickly forgotten.

For a few long minutes, all was shouts of anger, screams of pain, the wet thud of steel impacting flesh, the smell of fresh blood and viscera and the strange clarity that came to Mira in such moments. All her life and all her being were distilled down to a matter of moments when nothing in the wider world mattered even a jot and her only option and desire was to fight and to kill. With a grunt of effort, Mira drove her spear deep into the sternum of a Baimoi warrior, a tall woman with flaming red hair, tied into a long plait that swung wildly back and forth as she writhed on the point of the weapon, squealing in agony. Before she could follow up though, another enemy warrior barrelled in from her left. Wounded and half-crazed he collided with the haft of Mira's spear, dragging the weapon from her hands, before collapsing into a bloody tangle with the hapless redhead. The weapon was lost but it no longer mattered, for with the fall of the Baimoi warrior, Mira's troop saw an opening and, as one, renewed their charge for freedom. A moment later they were past and galloping through the trees, curving slightly to the left to plot a course eastward and home.

CHAPTER THREE

Outskirts of the Drevenwood
10 of Laphraois 868M - Late Autumn
Two years before the siege of Tarsus

Asfáleia – the cradle of civilisation, the place where it all began. Aeons of history, power existing from eternity. Humanity are the interlopers here, feeding on the shattered remnants of forgotten lives, like bloated flies on rotting corpses. Mindless, they breed and multiply, live and die, neither knowing nor caring of the past. Their petty nations war and squabble, their final arguments ever settled with destruction and genocide. Humanity is an infestation, a lingering disease of blood-filled lesions and festering sores – may Asfáleia be the place where it all ends.

Polemon of Chalcis, "The Ancients Weep", c. 975M

Chapter Three

The journey back to camp was a nightmare of riding, fighting and hiding as Mira's troop raced to outpace the pursuing Baimoi. The enemy was slower, following on foot, but Mira knew that if they pushed the already exhausted horses too much harder, the loyal beasts would fail sooner rather than later, and their advantage would be lost. The Rutik had to pace themselves, keeping their formation tight and their weapons ready. They rested when they could, fought when they had to, and tried to defend the remaining packhorses, and their precious cargo of supplies. It seemed to Mira as though a lifetime had passed amongst the trees but eventually, they emerged onto the plain and finally their dogged pursuers dropped back as the Rutik lines approached. The Baimoi hurled raucous jeers and ribald insults at the Rutik troop but knew that their prey had now escaped their clutches. Mira imagined that they were not too put out by their failure, having delayed her long enough to blunt the impact of her warning and besides, they had taken a terrible toll along the way: Mira had entered the woods with twenty-nine other men and women of the Rutik and returned with only nine.

Mira had not expected a hero's welcome but her return from the Drevenwood presented something of a problem for her superiors. An untested officer, she had assumed command under difficult circumstances, triumphed over their enemy and survived to tell the tale. She also brought home a respectable proportion of her soldiers, along with actionable intelligence on the enemy's movements. Had she been another officer, they might have rewarded her with a decoration and a promotion, probably without a second's thought. Mira, however, was not another officer and therein lay their conundrum. In theory, the Rutik army awarded promotions based strictly on merit and seniority. The tradition dated from ancient times, when the Rutik were a tribe rather than a nation and a person's value was judged solely by their deeds. In more recent times, however, little more than lip service was paid to the tradition and promotions were awarded to the rich and the well-connected and Mira was neither of those things.

The mission was a black eye for the commander, since it had been carried out on his direct orders, so he was keen to blame someone for the fallout. Mira's captain, despite his attitude, had been a well-regarded man and a decorated hero, so accusing him of dereliction was not an option. The first lieutenant was of minor noble stock, vaguely related to the queen and hence also above reproach. Teja and the others were, of course, too inconsequential to shoulder any significant portion of responsibility and that just left Mira. She reported to the commander immediately upon her return, detailing the events of the mission carefully and without embellishment. When she finished, he stared at her in cold silence for a minute, and then dismissed her with a wave. She was deeply irritated by his attitude but kept her feelings to herself, marching out without a word. On balance, she supposed, it could have been a lot worse, but it was not until a few days later that the other shoe dropped, and she realised that she had effectively been blackballed. The officers' mess fell silent when she entered. Around the camp former friends and allies greeted her shortly, then walked away, not wanting to be seen in her company. Her requests for resupply and reinforcements were declined or ignored.

Disregarded by her commanders and ignored by her fellow officers, Mira had taken to spending her evenings at the campfires of the common soldiers. They at least seemed not to resent her presence, even if they were still a little cautious around her. For Mira, the whole situation was depressingly reminiscent of her time in training, far away in the capital city of Rutiksborg. Her father, Valamir, was descended from a line of ancient Rutik chieftains. Her mother, Alwina was the youngest daughter of a family of minor Rutik nobility. Both were of good stock then, but neither had much in the way of fortune or connections. Mira was the fifth of seven children, five of whom survived into adulthood – three brothers and two sisters. Valamir doted on his children but was obsessed with raising them in the true traditions of the Rutik people.

From the age of six, Mira was taught to fight with sword, bow, and spear, and by the age of ten was competent with them all, and more besides. Valamir trained his children in the forms and theory of combat, then set them against each other in duels and brawls for more practical lessons. A true Rutik, he also placed great value on education and taught them their letters, the secrets of mathematics that the Rutik had learned from invaders of the old country, even straying into history and philosophy at times. One by one, as they came of age, commissions in the Rutik army were purchased for Mira's older siblings and they were sent off to fight for the glory of the Rutik. One by one, they died.

When Mira's turn came, her father was already a broken man – most of his family gone, along with the small fortune that had been their birth right. The best he could do for his one surviving daughter was to get her a place in the College of War, to train and study for a year before being assigned a position as a junior officer somewhere. Where her siblings had entered the College with a suitable post already purchased, Mira would start her training with no guarantees of anything except what she could earn for herself. At fifteen, she left home with only her sword and the clothes on her back and her father did not emerge from his rooms to see her off. Still, she was excited to join the College and confident that her abilities would gain her glory and fortune in short order, and she travelled the short distance to the Rutik capital in good spirits. Life at the College was not to live up to her expectations, however.

From the start, Mira excelled at pursuits both academic and practical. Her father had trained her well and she regularly beat all comers in fencing, archery, and horse riding. Determined to pull her family name out of obscurity by rising in the ranks, she absorbed her lessons in military tactics and strategy like a dry field absorbs sudden rain. At times she even startled her tutors with her insight and analysis and her understanding of mathematics and logistics seemed almost instinctual. Every morning before breakfast she would rise silently and go for a run around the campus perimeter, almost six miles, and then practice her forms alone on the parade ground, oblivious to the slow stirring into life of the rest of the facility. The only areas in which she struggled were the mandatory lessons in etiquette and politics, neither of which held her attention for long. She struggled through, however, and passed the requisite exams with passable if not exceptional grades. In short, Mira was almost a model student, but her achievements made her unpopular with her fellow cadets, especially those long on gold but short on merit. They ostracised her, mocked her and went out of their way to see her fail. Mira bore it all in stoical silence, rarely rising to their bait, but that did not satisfy their envious hatred. One evening five of her fellow cadets cornered her in a storeroom, having lured her there under false pretences. They intended to beat her soundly, perhaps even to injure her sufficiently to effectively remove her as competition, but Mira's stoicism was not without limits. Twenty minutes later, one of the would-be bullies was unconscious with a fractured skull, another had a broken arm and a third had no less than four cracked ribs. The other two got off with scrapes and bruises but all learned their lesson equally well and Mira was not troubled again.

By any measure, Mira was top of her class and yet, when the time came for graduation, she found herself at the bottom of the list of assignments. As it turned out, the mother of one of her former bullies was a decorated veteran of high rank and sat on the Board of Governors for the College of War. Another had an uncle who commanded the Royal Legion and was more of a politician than a soldier. Between them, those two worthies saw to it that, whatever Mira's qualities as a soldier, she would start her career in the lowliest possible position. A month later she arrived at the Rutik camp near the Drevenwood to a decidedly lukewarm welcome. She told herself that it did not matter, that she could rise above their spite to keep her eyes on her goals, but it was never entirely true. To have worked so hard and go unrecognised stung her pride far more than she was willing to admit.

Now, once again, Mira was caught in a tangled mess that was not of her making. The solution to her superiors' problem was, for a while, to pretend that Mira did not exist, to ignore the problem in the hope that it would eventually go away. Mira and the remainder of her troop found themselves abandoned in quarters, with neither new leadership nor new orders. For weeks they languished in neglect, licking their wounds, resting, drinking, and lazing around. To add insult to injury, the weather was worsening as winter rapidly approached. Somehow, no matter how high they stacked the logs, the warmth of the fire never seemed to drive away the dampness and the cold.

On one such miserable evening, Teja was perched on a stool that seemed ludicrously undersized for his massive bulk, slowly working his way through a flagon of cheap wine. Beuca sat cross-legged on the ground, half-heartedly whittling.

"Bugger!" The unfinished carving sprang out of the scout's hand as his knife slipped, its point stabbing into the side of his thumb. Teja gave an amused grunt as Beuca stuck his thumb in his mouth and muttered more muffled curses. Dropping the knife, he fumbled for the fallen wood with his free hand and tossed it angrily into the fire.

"Fucking stupid thing," he said, withdrawing his thumb and turning it towards the light of the fire to inspect the damage.

"What was it supposed to be anyway?" Mira asked. He looked up at her and rolled his eyes.

"A stag's head," he replied with a shrug. "Never was much good at this though."

Mira nodded sympathetically. They were all looking for something to do these days, and there were few enough options.

"Maybe try something a little less ambitious?"

"He's doing a good job of whittling his own thumb," offered Teja straight-faced. Beuca scowled at him as Mira laughed at the sergeant's rare show of humour.

"Was that a joke, sergeant?" she asked, still laughing. Teja shrugged and hefted his flagon in a wry toast.

"Damn poor one if you ask me," snapped Beuca but Teja toasted him too, then squirmed uncomfortably on the tiny stool.

"If you could whittle up some furniture, that'd be more helpful."

Beuca clicked his tongue in disgust, retrieved his knife and wiped the blade on his trouser leg.

Beuca looked about to respond, no doubt with further heartfelt expletives but was interrupted by the arrival of two men at the edge of their campsite. One was tall and bulky, his features concealed by the dark hood of a long cloak. The other was a man of late middle age, slightly balding, with sharp blue eyes and a narrow mouth. The taller man hung back as the second stepped closer to the fire.

"Lieutenant Mira of Norderhofschlag, daughter of Valamir and Alwina?" Mira looked at him in surprise, wondering how he knew of her origins. She was sure that he did not get the information from her commander, who had never expressed even a passing interest in getting to know her. Mira resolved to keep her cards close to her chest until she could get a handle on the situation. Beuca was watching with interest, but she noticed that Teja was glaring at the shadowy figure of the second man in the background.

"Yes. Who's asking?"

"I am Lord Ohtrad, Baron of Astnide, humble representative of the League for the Restoration of Rutik Glory. At your service." Mira raised an eyebrow at that. She knew of the League from her father, who had some peripheral involvement in the local chapter back home. She had pegged them as a collection of old soldiers, determined to relive their glory days but otherwise not of any great significance. She was surprised to hear that the League still existed, and even more surprised to find them in a military camp, represented by someone of such high status.

"Mira then, at yours," she replied with a nod. "How can I assist you, my lord?" The baron looked around at Teja and Beuca before responding.

"Is there perhaps somewhere that we could speak in private?" Mira's gaze drifted to his associate in the shadows. Although the other man had not moved so much as a muscle since arriving at the campfire, she somehow felt intimidated by his presence – something in his posture or his mere presence raising the hairs on the back of her neck. She felt the urge to reach for her sword, to fight or perhaps to run away. Glancing at Teja she saw the same conflicting feelings playing out on the sergeant's normally impassive face. Something was wrong here, and although she had no idea what it was, it reinforced her resolve to proceed with caution.

"You may speak freely in front of these men," she replied. "I trust them with my life."

"Very well. You are familiar with the work of the League?" Mira nodded, though in truth she had no real idea of their methods or intentions.

"The restoration of Rutik glory presumably," she said, belatedly realising how sarcastic the response sounded. Ohtrad seemed unoffended however and chuckled softly, nodding.

"Indeed so. We work to ensure that the old ways are remembered, and that the Kingdom does not fall into degeneracy and dishonour. Like your own father, we are concerned that the venerable traditions that brought the Rutik to power and glory, have been *diluted* by our own lack of moral fibre. We have become less than we were, and the League would reverse that process, with whatever tools necessary." Mira nodded cautiously. Despite his habit of hesitating before emphasising certain words, it seemed a practised speech. If Ohtrad was being allowed access to military encampments, he or the League must have considerable authority somewhere within the Kingdom's leadership. Ohtrad smiled and continued.

"You are wondering what all of this has to do with you. The League has a need for *representation* in the army. We have objectives that require a more direct approach than is available to *diplomats* such as me. Your commanders have offered your troop to our service, but I would prefer that you joined our cause willingly, rather than just because you are following orders." Mira looked around at Teja and Beuca. Ohtrad had their full attention now and she could see their minds turning the offer over and over, looking for the catch that had to be there somewhere. In the army, there was always a catch.

"Very generous, my lord, and much appreciated but what would our service involve? We are soldiers, after all, not historians. We worry more about the future than the past, no matter how glorious it was."

"Much the same as you would be doing otherwise," Ohtrad replied with a shrug. "Scouting. Combat missions. Other more *specialised* activities but nothing that would test the resolve of a troop such as yours. Events in the Drevenwood may not have impressed your commanders but there are those of us that take a more *charitable* view. In simple terms, you have the skills that we need, and we are prepared to reward you appropriately for the application of those skills to our problems.

"For you to lead, promotion to Captain would be required, of course. You would be allowed access to funds for equipment and supplies, with a generous amount of leeway for... incidentals. You would also be allowed to operate with some impunity, outside of the normal chain of command, so to speak."

Mira stared at him, a little stunned by the sudden prospect of such a dramatic change to her fortunes. She looked over at Teja, who shrugged, then at Beuca, who nodded. She decided to push her luck a little, just to see what would happen.

"We would need permission to recruit," she said carefully. "Our numbers are somewhat depleted."

Ohtrad smiled broadly, probably knowing full well that he had already won the day.

"Appropriate orders will be provided to your commander. You may have your pick of reinforcements from anywhere within the Northern Army. Have we reached an accord then?"

"I believe so, Lord Ohtrad. Where do we start?"

"It will take a day or two to make arrangements, get formal orders drawn up and so on. Your instructions will follow shortly thereafter. In the meantime, here is a little something to *pass the time* more easily." He pulled a small leather bag from under his cloak, tossing it at Mira's feet, where it landed with a promising jingle of coin. "For now, I bid you good night… Captain Mira. I believe we will meet again soon though now that we are *all on the same side*."

Mira got to her feet and saluted, wondering which side precisely she was now on, and Ohtrad turned to go. He took a couple of steps, and the second man moved forward to meet him. As Ohtrad continued walking, the other man's hood turned slowly as he looked around at Mira and her soldiers. The sense of danger became almost palpable, as though the man had somehow become more intimidating by having moved a little closer. Mira swallowed and resolved to hold her ground but somewhere in the back of her mind, the primitive voice of a small creature under the glare of a fearsome predator screamed at her to run. The man spoke, his voice low and gravelly.

"The League rewards its faithful servants." He gestured at the bag of coins with a gloved hand. "But we tolerate neither failure nor disloyalty. Be sure that you earn our gratitude, and not our ire, Captain, and remain faithful. Always."

Without waiting for a response, the man turned and followed Ohtrad away from the campfire. As they disappeared into the night, Mira released a breath she had not known she was holding and sank back down into her seat, staring at the bag of coin and wondering what, exactly, she had signed them up for.

"Well, that was fucking strange," muttered Beuca.

"You think I should have refused?" Mira looked up at him and raised an eyebrow, but Beuca just shrugged and looked at Teja. The sergeant scratched at his stubbled chin for a moment or two before speaking.

"Not sure we had all that much of a choice, to be honest. Captain though, eh? Suppose we'll have to curtsey real nice every time we see you now?"

Mira snorted with laughter at the sudden image of the hugely muscled soldier before her genuflecting daintily.

"A simple salute will do, sergeant," she replied with a smile, reaching for the coin purse. "Now, how about we put some of this to good use? I suspect we can do better than that flagon of sour ale, for a start."

The two men got quickly to their feet, needing no further convincing, the thought of good wine and good food banishing their more immediate doubts, and went to retrieve their horses from the corral. There was an old, cosy inn about three miles down the road that served some decent wine. Mira planned to have a couple of cups with Teja and Beuca, before heading back to camp with a supply for the rest of the troop. Along the way she replayed the evening's events in her head: one moment feeling pleased with the sudden upturn in their fortunes, the next worried about the parting threat. She was excited about the prospect of action and even more excited about the prospect of escaping the suffocating bonds of the regular army. The strange man's last words cast a pall over her happiness, however, as dark and menacing as a thunderous raincloud. No matter how often she dismissed them and tried to focus on the positives, she could not shake the lingering shadow. Then she thought about her treatment at the hands of her commander, her fellow officers and her so-called classmates in the College and frustrated rage pushed all other concerns from her mind. If she was ever going to escape the grubby shackles of her modest origins, she needed a chance to show the world what she could do. Whatever the risks, her chances of doing that seemed immeasurably higher out in the field than sitting in camp, kicking her heels in the dirt.

The next year and a half passed quickly for Mira and her troop, moving from one place to another, carrying out the orders of the League and enjoying their sudden elevation to relative prosperity. Ohtrad had proven as good as his word and a couple of days after their conversation at the campfire, a courier arrived with their orders and confirmation of her promotion to full Captain. Supplies and funding were duly made available, and Mira set Teja and Beuca to the task of recruitment. She ordered Beuca to expand their contingent of scouts to ten, instructing him to find men and women of experience and capability. Teja, she ordered to recruit amongst some of the more renowned divisions of the Northern Army to find reliable soldiers of quality. Their efforts proved fruitful, since as it turned out Mira was far from the only person in the army keen to escape the endless grind of war against the Baimoi. A month, almost to the day, after Ohtrad had made his proposition, the troop was up to a strength of forty in total and their first orders arrived by courier.

Their first mission was straightforward and unchallenging: escort a group of Baimoi prisoners south and east to the city of Magdeburg and there turn them over to the local representatives of the League. What the League wanted with Baimoi prisoners was not explained to her and she decided not to ask. With the prisoners delivered, they camped a short distance outside the city and waited for their next assignment, which was not long in coming. From Magdeburg, they turned south towards Harbrook, where they met up with a large division of infantry, preparing for an assault on a small town that had rebelled against the crown. Mira's troop was assigned to infiltrate the town before the main assault and when the infantry struck, they were to decapitate the opposition by immediately assassinating the mayor and his subordinates. Again, they succeeded in their objectives and again they waited a short time before the next set of orders arrived. And so it went, one mission following another, always brief and with specific objectives.

Over time, Mira's troop grew adept at finding creative solutions to the problems that the League placed before them. Mira lived by her father's maxim: 'no warriors in the world can beat the Rutik, but if you have to resort to brute force, you're already losing'. Leaning heavily on Beuca's knowledge and experience, she trained the entire troop to operate in silence, in the dark, alone or in small groups, using whatever means they found at their disposal to achieve their aims. Meanwhile, Teja drilled them relentlessly in hand-to-hand combat, armed and unarmed, with swords, spears, and long knives. Between them, the captain, the sergeant, and the scout turned the troop into a well-oiled fighting machine. For their part, most of the soldiers rose to the challenge, encouraged by Mira's relentless determination to turn them into the best unit in the Rutik army. Those few that did not were quietly persuaded to find employment elsewhere and resigned or were transferred to other parts of the army.

The League was pleased with their successes and as promised, rewarded them handsomely. Mira found herself authorised to requisition whoever or whatever she needed from local commanders and with a stipend of petty cash to do with as she pleased. She saw to it that her soldiers had the best of everything – weapons and armour, food, and drink. For those eighteen months they saw neither hide nor hair of Ohtrad however, their orders were delivered by courier, their direct contact with the League limited to occasional

- Graham G Porter -

inspections by lowly functionaries. Once or twice, they cooperated with other units that had been given a similar remit to her own and served the League as they did. Mira wondered how far the League's tentacles reached, and how much power they had amassed in the Kingdom. Those were concerns far higher than her rank allowed her to consider, however, and as soon as they arose, she pushed them aside to concentrate on the here and now. The truth was that she enjoyed her role, and the freedom it came with, even if it was backed by threats. She relished the adventure and the thrill of operating independently and unencumbered by layers of senior officers. One thing she was not about to do was put all of that in danger by asking too many questions. As she was fond of saying, fate would bring fresh sorrow soon enough.

CHAPTER FOUR

Rutik city of Harbrook
1 of Athanaios 869M - Late Winter
A year before the siege of Tarsus

Happiness is not meant to last
If it was enduring
There would be more of it around

The poet Epinicus, c. 815M

Chapter Four

Corraidhín grimaced and huddled closer into the meagre cover of a doorway and pulled his drab cloak more tightly around his small, wiry frame. The night was bleak and murky with fog, not a star to be seen in the sky, and a piercing wind was blowing in from the north chilling everything it touched. A short distance away, his companion looked over at the small movement and grunted.

"Sorcerer's wind," he growled, and he spat on the ground in disgust. Despite the comment Radomir seemed immune to the cold, and his cloak hung loose from his broad, muscular shoulders, the hood dangling down his back. He stood out in the open, perfectly still except for his sharp, pale blue eyes, which were constantly on the move, peering into every shadow and covering every point of access to the grubby alley in which they stood. Constant vigilance was something else the Bulġha learned at a young age, or at least they did if they wanted to live to be any older. Radomir's people were the remnants of an older age, hunted now everywhere they lived and surrounded by enemies, human and otherwise.

"Come closer, my friend, step out of the breeze for a while."

"Nah. Rather have room to move." In stark contrast to Corraidhín, Radomir was a massive hulk of a man, well over six feet tall and built like a well-fed bear. His prematurely greying hair was cropped close to his scalp and intricate, winding tattoos in an ancient, angular script emerged from his hauberk and snaked around his neck and wrists. Every inch the wild man of the north, he looked utterly out of place in the dreary, urban environment of the alley. Corraidhín watched him for a minute or two, then shrugged.

"Suit yourself," he said, his mind already elsewhere. Truth be told the city did not suit him greatly either. He had grown up on the Illyan Isles, in the oceans to the west of Asfáleia – a territory as untamed as the far north, if a lot less perilous. The Illyans benefited from the constant caress of a warm southern current and were almost completely covered with ancient, leafy forests. Thinking of the majestic trees and sheltered glades sent a pang of homesickness through Corraidhín's heart but he quashed it ruthlessly. The Isles would no longer welcome him, not after all he had done, and not done, since leaving.

"You really think the Rutik are coming this time?" asked Radomir. Corraidhín glanced around reflexively to confirm that the alley was empty before answering. They were, after all, right in the middle of Harbrook, one of the most heavily fortified Rutik cities, save perhaps their capital city itself, Rutiksborg. Even the backstreets saw occasional patrols and most of the citizens were merchants, blacksmiths or curriers, horse traders or saddlers, all beholden to the army in some way or other. The wrong word reaching the wrong ear at the wrong time could lead to serious trouble for trespassers such as they.

"That's what we're here to find out, so I suppose we'll see, won't we? There's no doubt that the Rutik drums are beating for war again, but where they're marching to is a closely held secret."

"Always fucking marching somewhere though," replied Radomir. "Like bloody ants."

Corraidhín laughed, amused at the image of Rutik-ant-soldiers marching off to war, but the comment was true enough for all that. The uneasy truce between east and west had become less and less reliable of recent years as the newly resurgent Kingdom of the Rutik flexed its military muscles and turned its greedy gaze on the Achaean cities.

Corraidhín was about to reply again when he was cut short by the arrival of a new figure in the mouth of the alley. Bracing himself, he stepped out of the doorway and lowered his hood, raising a hand in greeting. The cold wind hit his face more forcefully now that it was exposed, carrying with it the smell of lime, faeces, and fish oil. He recalled passing a tannery on the way to the alley, which explained the robust odour but failed to make it any more pleasant. The newcomer moved further into the alley, stopping about ten feet from where Radomir stood watch, looking around nervously before reaching up to pull back its own hood to reveal a pinched-featured woman of middle years. Her nose that had appeared to have been broken and badly reset at some point in the past, and now sported an unsightly lump of cartilage across the bridge.

"You have my coin?" she said, uninterested in casual conversation.

"I do," replied Corraidhín, producing a small but heavy bag from beneath his cloak. "You have the documents I requested?"

She nodded and Corraidhín struggled to supress a sigh of relief. The woman was a senior officer in the headquarters of the Western Rutik Army and a highly decorated veteran. He had received word that she would be amenable to trade information for gold through a mutual acquaintance in Eresos, a man he knew well but trusted very little. Reasons had been given for her willingness to betray queen and country – a gambling addiction, a poor turn of luck, overwhelming debts to the wrong people but still it had seemed an obvious trap. Nevertheless, the documents on offer – copies of strategic maps, records of logistical arrangements and so on – were too tempting and Corraidhín had agreed to the meet.

The Rutik officer produced a thick package from beneath her own cloak and Corraidhín was about to hand over the gold when Radomir stiffened and spun around to stare fixedly at the far end of the alley.

"Somethings not…" he began, before being interrupted by a shout from the darkness.

"Halt! Surrender in the name of the Kingdom and the League!" The booming voice echoed off the grimy stone walls and Corraidhín turned quickly, seeing movement in the shadows at either end of the alley. The officer tossed the package of documents at him, laughing, and pulled out her sword.

"Nothing in there but old tally sheets anyway. Now: you heard the man – surrender!"

Corraidhín froze, thinking quickly. Only Rutik soldiers were allowed to carry weapons within the city walls, so he and Radomir had been forced to hide theirs before entering. Neither of them were armed with anything more than a short knife, which would not serve much use against the armoured soldiers filtering into the alley. It seemed unlikely that they would be able to bargain their way out of the situation, but it was the only hand he had left to play. He raised both hands, palms out.

"Now just wait, please, wait," he said, trying to strike a note of panicked innocence. "There's obviously been some sort of mistake, let's talk about this for a moment…"

One of the reasons why Corraidhín and Radomir had made such an effective team for years was that they trusted each other implicitly, and both knew when to follow the other's lead. Most times, Corraidhín could have relied upon Radomir to hold his peace while the islander tried to negotiate with the Rutik. This, however, was not one of those times. The Bulġha had carried out his own assessment of their predicament and reached an entirely different conclusion.

"Let's not!" he roared, already moving. The Rutik officer turned her attention from Corraidhín only take the full force of Radomir's charge, his meaty left shoulder hitting her in the chest, sending her flying across the alley and into a wall. He skidded to a halt beside her and, while she was still dazed from the impact, he reached down to grab her chainmail hauberk with both hands, hefted her above his head with a grunt of effort and flung her at the approaching soldiers. The unfortunate officer recovered her wits in mid-air, and barely had time to give a strangled squawk before she collided with three other soldiers, and they all went down in a tangled heap. Once again, Radomir was right behind her and, stooping to pick up a fallen spear, he cleared the fallen bodies in a single leap and launched himself into the crowd of soldiers behind.

"For fuck's sakes, Radomir!" Corraidhín muttered, rolling his eyes in disgust. *Sometimes I despair of that man,* he thought to himself, but since the die was now clearly cast there was nothing else to do but back his companion's play. The Rutik officer's sword was lying on the ground nearby where it had fallen from her grasp when Radomir hit her. Flicking it neatly into the air with one foot, he caught it neatly by the grip and tested the weight for a moment before running after his friend. The blade was heavier than he was used to but would have to do. Corraidhín preferred to use a short spear in battle but also habitually carried a rapier as backup and was an accomplished swordsman.

By the time Corraidhín caught up with Radomir, the Bulǵha had taken down three more Rutik soldiers with his newly acquired spear and was holding a half-dozen others at bay. Corraidhín used the other man's body as a shield to conceal his approach before darting to one side at the last moment and crippling a Rutik soldier with a darting thrust to the back of her knee. Two of the remaining soldiers turned angrily towards him as she fell, and he knew that if they managed to get their spearpoints around quickly enough he would find it hard to strike another blow, given the much shorter reach of the sword. There was no time for fancy swordplay either, or the carefully manoeuvring into position that sometimes allowed a sword to get past a spear. More Rutik were rushing up from the far end of the alley and if they could reinforce their comrades before Radomir and Corraidhín broke free, they would find themselves surrounded and heavily outnumbered. As soon as the two soldiers turned to face Corraidhín, however, Radomir saw his opportunity and drove forward, skewering one soldier before swinging to the left and catching a second with the butt end of the spear. The two facing Corraidhín half turned back at his approach, blindsided, and starting to panic, giving the islander the opportunity to dart in and slash his blade across one man's throat, before reversing his grip and driving the point downward into the back of the other's calf. The last of the Rutik soldiers staggered back in shock, her spear held defensively in front of her, but they ignored her and took off at a run, moments ahead of the arrival of the reinforcements.

"We'll never make the gate!" shouted Radomir as they ran. He was an exceptionally strong man: fit and hale from years spent in the field, but he was not built for sprinting and not much of a long-distance runner either. Corraidhín was better suited to the task but not about to leave the other man behind.

"Find somewhere to lay low, I can hide us," he shouted in response. They could clearly hear the Rutik soldiers following, slowed by their armour and weapons but determined to catch up, and knew they had not long to escape. They could happen onto a patrol at any time, and it was likely that their pursuers had sent a runner to the nearest barracks as well, so the city would soon be crawling with angry soldiers out for vengeance. Corraidhín might have been isolated from the islands for decades, but he still retained a certain amount of the ancient power that had been gifted to him on his departure. All they needed was a few seconds, moments even, to duck into a doorway, behind a stall, or into an empty building and he could pull the shadows in around them. That done, he could blur the lines of reality until there was no way short of a stronger power still that anyone in this world or any other could find them. Strictly speaking, they would not be invisible, his power did not stretch that far. It was more that anyone passing by would suddenly find their attention diverted elsewhere. Playing with people's minds was far easier than altering reality.

One of the pursuing soldiers shouted a challenge as they rounded a corner, but they ignored him and kept running. A short distance ahead Corraidhín spotted a stack of barrels outside of an inn, clearly awaiting pick up the following morning. Placing a hand on Radomir's shoulder he steered him towards them. Moments later they were safely behind the pile, pressed up hard against the damp oak of the barrels and breathing in the stale alcoholic fumes that drifted from the open bungholes. Corraidhín had his moment, and in a moment his work was done. The Rutik soldiers thundered past, noticing neither the barrels nor the men hiding behind them.

A month later, Radomir and Corraidhín were back in Tarsus and freshly returned from an audience with the king. Radomir was one of the King's Rangers, an elite force that reported directly to the monarch. Corraidhín's role was more nebulous since he carried no official credentials and technically answered to no one. However, the years of his long association with Radomir and useful services to the crown, as well as his long personal friendship with the king had had bestowed a *de facto* status upon him at least equal to the

Rangers'. The pair had entered the mess hall in the main barracks on the southern side of the city when they spotted two more Rangers at a table near the back. Raising a hand in greeting, they collected some food and settled onto the hard wooden bench on the far side of the table from their comrades. A half hour had passed since the changing of the guard on the city walls and the mess hall was crowded and noisy, filled with the chatter and rowdy banter of soldiers at ease.

"Good to see you both," said Corraidhín as he seated himself, nodding to the two other Rangers. Radomir added a grunt by way of his own greeting and dug into his food without further acknowledgement of his company.

"How're ye, Corr? Been a while," one of the Rangers replied, setting down her fork to study the two newcomers. The Rangers' duties were various, and regularly carried them to all corners of Asfáleia. It was not that often that their paths crossed and usually only when there was an urgent mission that required more than a single pair of Rangers. Time to sit and chat was a luxury not often afforded them.

"I am well, Ombly. What news from the north?"

"Same news as always really. Bandits, wild animals, the odd Vedi wandering around to keep things interesting," Ombly shrugged dismissively, glancing at her partner for confirmation. A standing duty of the Rangers was to maintain order in the Tarsean Narrows, far to the north, tracking down and neutralising anyone or anything that might pose a threat to the farmlands closer to the city.

"Same old shit," agreed the other Ranger. Ombly, whose proper name was Bilyana, was of the Bulġha, like Radomir, though of a different tribe. She was built much like Radomir too but a good two feet his lesser in height. The nickname came from her deformed right hand, shrunken and curled almost into a claw in an accident of birth. The damaged appendage was little impairment to her fighting abilities though, and she could wield a long spear as well as any of the other Rangers. Her partner was known as Red, the obvious nickname coming from of his tangled mop of flaming red hair and unkempt beard. Red was even shorter again in stature but equally well built, and carried a reputation for brute ferocity that barely stopped short of berserker status.

"Heard you got an audience with the big man himself," added Ombly, referring to the king. "What form is he in?" In his youth, King Achaeus of Tarsus had earned his princely spurs amongst the Rangers and had acquitted himself admirably, earning both their respect and their trust. The Rangers that remembered those days still thought of him as a friend and comrade, more so than the ruler he had eventually become. Corraidhín nodded, popping a lump of stewed meat into his mouth, chewing and swallowing before responding.

"Good. You know Achaeus: always hoping for the best but expecting the worst. Worried about the Rutik making noise over in the west."

"Fucking greenshirts," put in Red, referring to the Rutik by their emerald-coloured tunics. All four of them had clashed with the Rutik on various occasions in the past, usually when the Rangers were on scouting missions or assigned to assist one of the other Achaean cities in a border dispute, or some sort of raid.

"They're buzzing like flies on shit around Harbrook," added Radomir, through a mouthful of potato and gravy. He and Corraidhín had been forced to take a circuitous route back to Tarsus after leaving the Rutik city and along the way had observed large movements of troops on the roads.

"Achaeus thinks we'll see a major campaign launched before the year's out," said Corraidhín. "No solid intelligence, but far too many signs of it to ignore."

"Won't be this year, I reckon," said Ombly, running her good hand through her greasy black hair. "Summer's nearly over and they won't start campaigning in the autumn. The Rutik aren't stupid."

"Worse if that's true," grunted Radomir. "This busy a year ahead of time? Hit's going to come harder when it comes."

"You might be right there," agreed Red. "Whatever. This year, next year, who gives a shit? We'll kick their Rutik arses back the way they came whenever they like. Where you boys headed next then?"

"Epirus," replied Corraidhín with a shrug. "Achaeus has a cousin there that sent word. Seems he has some information for the king that can't wait. Should be an easy run, there and back."

Epirus was the last of the other Achaean cities that still swore fealty to the Tarsean crown. Once every Achaean in Asfáleia had bowed their heads to the descendants of Arrias the Conqueror, and Tarsus had ruled the land from east to west and everywhere in between. Long years of decline and neglect had seen the western half of the country lost to the Rutik however, and the other Achaean cities drifting away one by one into self-sufficiency and eventually independence.

"That's what you said about Harbrook," said Radomir, deadpan. Corraidhín widened his eyes and made a passable attempt at feigning innocence.

"I don't recall saying anything of the sort!"

"Easy run, you said. In and out. Remember it clearly."

"Perhaps you misheard then? I'm quite sure I would never have underplayed the risks of such a mission."

Radomir snorted, and Red and Ombly both laughed. Corraidhín's ability to lead the Rangers into complicated and dangerous situations was almost legendary.

"Perish the thought!" said Ombly, still laughing. Corraidhín smiled in return and waved a hand dismissively.

"Indeed so," replied Corraidhín, then the smile faded from his face and his look turned thoughtful and worried. "Joking aside, that mission should have been easy. We should have been in and out before the Rutik even knew we were there. Instead, it all went sideways, and we ended up running for our lives. Not the most satisfactory of outcomes."

"Putting it lightly, Corraidhín," said Radomir. "They set us up, knew exactly where we'd be, and closed the trap at the right moment. Ever since the fucking League took over, the greenshirts have been running rings around us."

The League, or more properly "The League for the Restoration of Rutik Glory" was said to be the power behind the Rutik queen and the driving force behind decades of reform that had turned the kingdom into a highly organised and frighteningly effective war machine. Depending on who you listened to the League was either a clandestine society; agents and assassins for the Queen; a collection of demagogues and firebrands; an integral part of the Kingdom of the Rutik's hierarchy; guardians of ancient secrets; or practitioners of the darkest of alchemical and even magical arts. There were stories of the League stealing babies from their beds and spiriting them away for gruesome experimentation. Others spoke of League members on the battlefield, fighting side by side with regular soldiers but possessed of horrific strength and speed. Another tall tale claimed that the Rutik Queen herself was a member of the League, or that if she was not, she was their thrall, their prisoner, or their slave.

The League generated such a volume of rumours that it had become impossible to tell fact from fiction, even for the Rangers, who had more information on Rutik affairs than most in Tarsus.

"Fucking hate those creepy fuckers," said Red, spitting the words out between clenched jaws. He and Ombly had clashed with the League on a trip to Eresos in the south, about a year previously, and come off much the worse in the encounter. Red was not a man to let such an insult pass lightly.

"On that we can agree, my friend," said Corraidhín, nodding. "And yet Achaeus will not allow us to tackle them directly. He fears… escalation if we cross them too badly. He believes diplomacy will yield better results."

"Take the high path, rise above it, all that shite," added Radomir, sarcasm dripping from his voice. "Like they're eventually going to learn to play nice or something."

"More likely they'll eventually rise up and pull us off the damn high path, drag us right down into the shite with them," said Ombly, shaking her head in disgust.

"Something else we can all agree upon, I think," replied Corraidhín. "They have no interest in diplomacy, and every interest in killing every last one of us."

"Let 'em try," growled Radomir. His bravado raised an ironic cheer from the other Rangers, but their faces remained grim. Whatever the League was planning, and whatever the eventual outcome was, it was a certain bet that the end result would be suffering and death for any who opposed them and the Tarsean King's Rangers were likely to be right in the thick of things, doing exactly that. Corraidhín raised his tankard of water and spoke solemnly.

"Tarsus and the king." The others joined him in the toast, then settled back down before Red added the traditional rejoinder amongst the Rangers.

"Honour and glory and no peace this side of the grave." And the others raised their drinks again.

CHAPTER FIVE

The Royal Palace, City of Tarsus
28 of Athanaios 870M - Late Winter
Three months before the siege of Tarsus

Arrias The Conqueror; Arrias the Second; Achaeus the Wise; Arrias the Third; Araros; Archelaus the Younger and the Elder; Aegeran the Good; Aenas the Brave. Generation after generation of kings and queens, though all following the strange Tarsean tradition of given names in the male form regardless of gender. Names carefully recorded to trace the history of a nation. The trail of lineage goes cold at the founding of Tarsus, however. Prior to that, only one is known, and that neither Achaean nor much spoken of. *Chavdar* the first and last emperor of Menos. May curses be upon his name.

Acusilaus, "The Eternal Glory of Tarsus", c. 850M

Chapter Five

Spring was finally in the offing, but winter was proving reluctant to relinquish its chilly hold on the Royal Palace of Tarsus and the coarse sand of the training ring was damp and clammy against Arion's cheek. He lay still for a moment, waiting for the pain to subside, listening to the sounds of the north wind whistling around the palace towers above and the steady, droning murmur of the huge city itself, muffled by the palace walls. The first blow had cracked smartly off his wrist, sending his sword tumbling into the air and across the ring. The second came only a moment later, hitting him in the back of his knee as his opponent stepped neatly past him and struck downward. Mastering himself, he struggled onto his hands and knees, spitting sand from his mouth, and trying not to put too much weight on his injured limbs. Their weapons were blunted, of course, with neither tip nor edge but a solid hit from a three feet long piece of metal was always going to hurt. Sweat-dampened locks of Arion's curly brown hair dangled before his steely grey eyes; he brushed them aside in irritation as a shadow fell and he looked up to find Radomir standing over him.

Arion was tall for his years, but Radomir towered over him as he struggled back to his feet. At six and a half feet tall, the taciturn Bulğha towered over pretty much everyone. He was a massive hulk of a man, built like a well-fed bear and he came from a tiny Bulğha village far to the north in the Narrows, where life was cold and hard all year round. The Bulğha were a near-forgotten people, displaced and almost wiped out be the Achaeans, long before Tarsus was even built. Their remaining settlements were scattered between the most distant and least habitable corners of Asfáleia, where they scraped a living hunting meagre game and occasionally raiding into more affluent areas. Young Bulğha often choose to leave, and rumour had it that Radomir had come south at an early age, seeking adventure, fortune, or better weather. He had enlisted in the Tarsean army following a night's heavy drinking and an ill-considered fistfight with a group of nobles. The story was that the fight left one man dead, another permanently incapacitated and half a dozen more with broken bones and Radomir's choices had been reduced to the army or the gallows.

His skills made him a formidable warrior, and once he learned to control his temper, an exceptional soldier. Now he served in the King's Rangers and was a favourite of Arion's father, having served him well and loyally over the years. Arion was not entirely sure what those services involved but he knew that, in addition to their normal duties, the Rangers were often tasked with resolving all manner of problematic situations, within the Kingdom and further afield. Permitted far more freedom of action than the regular army, the Rangers were the King's elite, and by reputation, Radomir was amongst the best of them. He usually passed through the city three or four times a year and had standing orders to attend the palace for training sessions with Arion. In addition to his size and prodigious strength, Radomir was frighteningly fast and equally proficient with all manner of weapons. After their first sessions, Arion had complained to his father that the Bulġha seemed more interested in delivering beatings than delivering lessons. King Achaeus had merely smiled, however, and replied that Radomir's role was to teach Arion how to survive in battle and if he was making it hurt, that probably meant that he was doing a good job.

Retrieving his sword, Arion returned to the starting line, checked his footing, and then attacked for what seemed the hundredth time that morning. His arms ached from holding the heavy training weapon and he was covered in bruises from Radomir's "lessons". Darting forward, he swung at Radomir's right shoulder but twisted mid-strike and swung down towards his leg instead. Radomir was not fooled for a moment and ignored the feint, stepping back casually to allow Arion's sword to pass, before moving back in and blocking Arion's recovery with his knee. A moment later, Arion was prodded none too gently in the stomach, almost winding him.

"Your guts are in the dirt, boy," said Radomir, turning his sword point to the ground and leaning on the pommel. "It'll take a while, but you'll die screaming in the end."

Arion struggled to recover his breath before responding.

"My armour would have stopped it. I'd have had you on the backswing."

Radomir barked a dismissive laugh.

"Your armour might have stopped it alright: if you had armour. It would still have hurt though, and still have knocked you back on your heels. Then I'd have battered your silly head in so what brains you have would have joined your guts on the ground."

Arion winced stood a little straighter and tried, but failed, to face Radomir on a level.

"I am a prince you know," he snapped. The words had sounded better in his head. Spoken aloud, they seemed petty, childish, and rather pathetic. Radomir raised a mocking brow before replying.

"Will that save you from a sword to the belly? No? Then shut up and try again – from the high guard this time." Dragging his feet, a little theatrically, Arion returned to his starting position and prepared to strike again. Apart from the King himself, there were few people in the palace hierarchy with the authority to show such a blatant disregard for the niceties of protocol and Radomir was not one of them. Arion suspected that the Bulġha did not care and wondered whether he could report him to his commanding officers, perhaps cause him a little trouble in return for the bruises. The thought of anyone giving Radomir a dressing down made Arion smile and his fit of pique quickly passed. He would probably pick the officer up mid-sentence and fling him through the nearest window.

Arion stopped smiling and looked up to examine his opponent carefully. Radomir stood waiting, not even bothering to assume a guard position, his training sword wrapped in one meaty fist, the other protected by a small buckler fastened to his wrist. He still wore the uniform of the King's Rangers, a studded leather hauberk rather than chainmail or breastplate, as was standard in the Tarsean army. The Rangers were primary was patrolling the Tarsean Narrows far to the north of the city. Working alone or in pairs, they tracked and killed bandits, wild animals and anything that might threaten the Tarsean farmlands. Most importantly, they were charged with eliminating the Vedi, the hideously deformed monsters that occasionally dragged themselves down out of the mountains. The Rangers were expected to move quickly when needed and for that reason travelled light, not wanting to burden their mounts with the additional weight of full armour. They spent the greater part of their lives in the field, as evidenced by the sun-darkened and almost leathery skin that showed on his craggy, scarred face and massive hands. Lacking a helm, his hair was cropped close to his scalp – black but greying around the edges causing Arion to wonder what age he was. Intricate, winding tattoos in the Northern style emerged from his hauberk and snaked around his neck and wrists, giving a wild, almost feral look to his face where they reached his temples and accented his sharp, pale blue eyes.

"Pay attention, boy!"

Arion blinked and ceased his examination, moving forward more warily this time. If he could stay in the game, drag the battle out for a while, perhaps he could find a way past the man's guard and finally land a blow himself. Less than a minute later, however, he was on his bottom on the ground with his ears ringing as the flat of Radomir's blade caught him solidly in the side of his head.

"Most swordfights are over in moments. Whatever you're going to do, do it with your first strike or you won't live long enough to get another." He reached down and grasped a handful of the back of Arion's jerkin, pulling him to his feet seemingly without effort. Arion left his sword on the ground and staggered a little before regaining his feet. He shook his head to try and clear the ringing.

"Corraidhín says that sword fighting is a matter of strategy, timing and finesse." Corraidhín was another of his father's favourites though, again, his exact role was something of a mystery to Arion. He was not a Ranger but seemed to be closely associated with them, and most particularly with Radomir. Arion harboured a suspicion that he was a spy of some sort, but with little evidence other than a lack of any other explanation for the man's behaviour. Corraidhín's favoured weapons were a rapier and a short spear and although he was no match for Radomir in size or strength, Arion would have loved to see the two facing off in the ring. Radomir replied with another dismissive grunt, before moving to lean his sword against the low wooden railing that surrounded the training ring.

"Corraidhín says a lot of things." Radomir yawned and stretched, looking for all the world like an old bear stirring from hibernation, a little too soon to be properly awake. Arion smiled, knowing well that even though the two men were perfect opposites in almost every way, they were a lot closer friends than either of them liked to let on. He was seized by a mischievous urge to poke the old bear.

"Don't you think he makes a lot of sense though?" He delivered the comment in the most innocent tone he could muster, delighting in the glare he earned from Radomir in return. The echoing sound of the noon bell tolled across the city, signalling the end of their practice session. Radomir retrieved his sword and tossed it to Arion, hilt first.

"Clean those before you go."

"Yes, Radomir." Arion made his reply as meek as possible and earned himself yet another irritated scowl. Radomir left without another word, heading back to the walls to resume his regular duties. Despite his tiredness and his bruises, Arion left the ring with a smile on his face, feeling as though he had managed to pull a small victory from the jaws of defeat.

Once the practice swords were cleaned and returned to their proper place in the armoury, Arion headed back to his rooms for a change of clothes, accompanied by the two burly soldiers assigned to be his bodyguard for the day. Along the way, he stopped to chat with a couple of the palace servants, and they laughed and joked with him as though he were an old friend, rather than the son of their King, who would one day be their ruler. An easy-going and friendly youth, Arion was popular amongst the palace staff, most of whom had spent their lives in the palace and watched him grow over the years. His permanently tousled hair was a frequent subject of their friendly teasing and Arion took it in good spirits, always ready with a witty comeback or clever response.

He left the two servants laughing in his wake and detoured to the kitchens to prevail upon the head cook to make him a pre-lunch snack. The cook, who Arion always felt was inexplicably skinny for a man who spent his life surrounded by food, could usually be relied upon for a heel of bread and some honey, or a taste of whatever was stewing in the massive pots that hung above the kitchen fires. The cook was duly generous, and Arion seated himself at one of the high, wooden preparation counters to do battle with a meal of freshly baked bread and soft, salty butter. Beka, one of the junior chambermaids arrived as he was eating, and he smiled in greeting before hurriedly wiping crumbs from his mouth with the back of his sleeve. Beka was only a few months younger than he and, to his eyes at least, very pretty indeed – black-haired and dark-skinned with deep, soulful brown eyes. She returned the smile and propped herself on the counter next to him.

"Greetings, my prince," she said, giving a rather perfunctory bow. Arion wondered if she was mocking him somehow but decided that studied nonchalance was the best response and waved away the formality.

"How goes it, Beka?"

The chambermaid shrugged and then frowned.

"Well enough, I suppose, but all we hear now is war, war, war. Do you really think the Rutik are coming?" She stared at him intently. He found himself momentarily lost in the depths of her eyes but then remembered that he was the Prince of Tarsus. He could not be seen to be mooning after a servant girl, no matter how pretty she was.

"Ahem," he said, adopting the manner of one of his father's generals tasked with reporting on a situation. "It can't be denied that the Rutik have the numbers to launch an attack at any time. On the other hand, as you know, Tarsus has never been captured in a thousand years and we have sufficient forces to repel any such attack so there's not really…"

He was interrupted by a snort from across the kitchen and looked around in surprise as the cook approached.

"Hark at the young general!" he cried, laughing, and waving a wooden spoon dramatically. "He has the enemy all but routed and they haven't even left Rutiksborg yet!" Stunned by the unexpected assault on his flank, Arion turned back to Beka only to find that she too was now smiling.

"Well, I mean, I'm not a general of course but…" He trailed off, utterly thrown by Beka's amusement, opened his mouth to speak again and then immediately shut it, looking glum. The cook laughed even harder and clapped a meaty hand onto his shoulder.

"Don't be downcast, lad, I'm only making fun of you. He's not wrong Beka, the Rutik would be mad to come here, and they might be a lot of things but mad isn't one of them."

"There have been reports of a large army gathering near Harbrook," put in Arion, feeling the need to reassert his authority a little. The cook nodded and smiled.

"Aye, I've heard that too. Likely headed for Larissa, I'd say, maybe even Chalcis if they're brave but they won't come this way. They're not crazy, lad." Larissa was the smallest of the remaining Achaean cities, situated on the southern coast of the land.

"You're right I suppose," replied Arion. "Larissa would seem the most likely target."

"So, we're safe then?" asked Beka, before realising how heartless that sounded and covering her mouth with her hand, her eyes widening. "Not that I want Larissa to suffer, of course, it's just…"

"Aye lass," said the cook gently. "We know what you meant and there's nothing wrong with worrying about you and yours first."

"If the Rutik attack Larissa, we'll send soldiers to help them defend," added Arion. "We won't leave them to fight alone, don't worry." Beka nodded and looked thoughtful for a moment.

"Maybe I should sign up. I mean, I don't know much about soldiering, but it seems the Rutik are determined to make a fight of it one way or another.

Maybe it's time I did my part?" Arion stared at her in surprise, then realised that he should have expected her to harbour such sentiments. For as long as he had known her, Beka had always been one to stand her ground in a fight. He remembered when they were both small children, running around the palace in an unruly pack, Beka had always been in the lead, cheering the others on to ever greater heights of mischief. Still, joining the army and going off to fight the Rutik seemed a wholly different matter.

"Would you really do it? Wouldn't you rather stay here and…"

"Stay here and what? Serve your meals and tidy your rooms?" She rolled her eyes and stuck out her tongue and Arion could not help but laugh.

"He'd probably like you to tuck him in at night too," added the cook, also laughing. "Maybe read him a bedtime story!"

"Actually, that sounds quite nice. Can you read the one about the pirates from the Reaver Kingdoms tonight? I'm in the mood for a bit of swashbuckling!"

"As my prince commands," laughed Beka. "But if you don't mind, I'd better get on with my chores now, else they won't be finished in time." Arion rose to his feet and bowed courteously.

"As you wish!"

"Aye," added the cook. "I'd better be on my way too I suppose. Dinner won't look after itself." As the two servants turned and headed off to their respective tasks, Arion returned to his meal and reflected on the conversation.

The two servants' attitude to their prince was common amongst the palace staff, who had almost all known him since he was a small baby and treated him more as a brother than a future ruler. His father encouraged it too: one of his favourite axioms was that a king should be a servant to his people, not the other way around. There were plenty in Tarsus who took the opposite approach, of course, even amongst the younger generations. Tarsus was an ancient city with wealthy families whose lineage stretched back into antiquity, some of them almost as powerful as the king himself and egalitarianism was a dirty word amongst them. The elders amongst them were even more stuffy and set in their ways, enforcing the strict codes of social hierarchy that had been set down centuries before when Tarsus ruled over all of Asfáleia.

Arion wondered what things were like in the Rutik cities now. He had heard that in the barbarian tribes far to the north, from whence the Rutik originally hailed, any man or woman, no matter their heritage, could hope to be a chieftain one day, as long as they were willing and able to bind followers to their cause. The Rutik were a kingdom now though, so perhaps that had changed. Thinking of the Rutik made him think of the war again, which led him to think of Beka's desire to sign up. He was struck with a vision of her lovely face smashed and broken as she lay killed on a filthy battlefield somewhere. He shuddered at the thought and pushed away the remains of his small meal, his appetite departed. Beka would do as she pleased, of course, but he hoped she would decide against it in the end. Despite her being a servant and he a would-be king, he rather liked the girl. Wondering if perhaps she liked him too, he took his plate across to the washing up pile, waved to the cook and departed for his rooms.

CHAPTER SIX

The Tarsean Narrows
6 of Boukatios 870M - Early Spring
Two months before the siege of Tarsus

To fund his own extravagant excesses, Archinus the Second of Tarsus had increased taxes on the vassal cities by astronomical proportions. After a while, the city governors objected, struggling to pay for necessary public works and essential defences on the meagre crumbs that Archinus left uneaten, but they were easily silenced or replaced. Archinus ruled for forty years, dying by poison at the hand of his own son in the year 588M, at the age of fifty-eight. Rarely was patricide a more noble deed, and his son became known as Arion the Brave for his efforts to repair his father's legacy but the impact of the venality and greed of Archinus ran deep, and the damage to the kingdom was beyond repair.

Polemon of Chalcis, "The Ancients Weep", c. 975M

Chapter Six

A week or so later, Arion and his father, Achaeus King of Tarsus, were riding north along the Tarsean Narrows, setting a brisk pace for the thirty light cavalry that followed. It was early morning, and the sun was still only barely rising over the eastern range of the Devil's Teeth Mountains, turning the towering peaks into dark, sinister silhouettes against the light beyond. Looking in the opposite direction, the western range was more distinct and detailed, with rough, scrubby foothills rapidly turning to much steeper slopes and sheer cliff faces. Higher still the mountain tops were white with snow and ice, seeming so barren and forlorn it almost made him shiver to look at them. Their path followed that of the Bisaltes River that ran the full length of the Narrows from the cursed city of Menos in the north to Tarsus in the south. The river was narrow but deep and fast running in the spring with snowmelt from the lower mountains. Further along, it was joined by the Inachos River, which flowed down from the ruins of Pleven but that was as far as Arion had ever been.

Immediately north of the city sat the breadbasket of Tarsus – thousands of acres of pasture and crop fields. The farms were neatly laid out on the open flat plain, rectangular fields with narrow lanes between, the odd square of orchard breaking the monotony. They were also bustling with life: animals grazing or being moved from one place to another, farmhands going about their business and so on. In some ways, it seemed more an extension of the city than the proper countryside. Here, a couple of days further north they had passed all of that already and the more open grazing areas that were spotted with cattle and horses too. Now there was only grass to be seen in all directions – a smooth, flat, slightly undulating plain that stretched east to west between the mountains. Yesterday, Arion had spotted a herd of deer in the distance and the occasional hare could be seen sprinting from cover to cover. There were wolves too, he knew, and even the odd bear, but neither would trouble such a large party of humans.

Somewhat embarrassingly, Arion's stomach rumbled loudly enough to be heard and Achaeus looked over and smiled at him indulgently. They had set off before sunrise with only a few minutes spared for breakfast and Arion was used to better fare than dried meat and road biscuits.

"Another hour and we should be able to take a break," said the king, turning back to stare into the distance. Achaeus had been king for almost fourteen years and the responsibility weighed heavy upon his shoulders. He was still strong and fit though and an excellent rider, his upright posture reminding Arion to correct his own.

"What are you looking for, father?"

"The Rangers," Achaeus replied, without looking at him. "If we do not soon come upon them, that likely means they have been forced to bring the creature down themselves and it would be a shame to have ridden all this way for nothing."

The Vedi, sometimes known to the common folk as Hillmen were strange, twisted creatures that seemed almost a mockery of humankind. As they rode on in silence, Arion's mind drifted back to his lessons with Corraidhín, a few years previously. He remembered being fascinated by the islander's description of Vedi he had seen and tackled in his years with Radomir.

"But if they're all different, how do you even know they're even all the same things?" he had asked, with a ten-year old's delight at the thought of catching an adult in a mistake, eagerly grasping the opportunity to drag a dull lesson into more interesting territory. As was his habit when the weather was fine, Corraidhín had chosen to conduct his lesson in the palace gardens and the sat cross legged on the neatly trimmed lawn, with the smell of freshly bloomed flowers strong in the air and the susurrating hum of happy bees in the background.

"I don't *know* anything, Arion, but remember what I taught you about the balance of probabilities and the preponderance of evidence? The Vedi that we see in the Narrows are the most warped of their kind, physically and mentally. They are rogues or outcasts, forced into exile by their own kind.

Deep in the mountains there are entire communities of those less altered, where you will see far more commonality. There the Vedi live together, work together and breed together, the last perhaps being the most convincing indication that they are all of a kind."

"But look," interrupted Arion, determined to press home his point. "People are all the same, I mean basically, we've all got two arms, two legs and so on, right? We can all walk and talk, we all have two eyes and two ears. Radomir told me about a Vedi with two heads! And another that had snakes coming out of its shoulders! Don't tell me those two were the same species, it doesn't make any sense!"

"Radomir has many stories," the islander replied with a smile. "Some of them are even true. Regardless of that though, what of the man who loses an arm in battle, is he no longer human? Or the woman born misshapen of feature or weak of mind? Is she not a person, just as you are?"

Arion had missed the slight smile that crossed Corraidhín's face as his features wrinkled in thought, unwilling to let go of his premise but unable to marshal a convincing counter argument.

"Those are all accidents of one sort or another though," he said eventually, determined to press on. "It's not like people are naturally that different from each other."

"I would caution you to think carefully about the path upon which you are setting your feet, young prince. Denial of a person's humanity is the first step towards denying them of the rights and privileges we are all entitled to, and a

- Graham G Porter -

short walk from denial of more tangible possessions. A king must rule for the benefit of all his subjects, not just those he deems normal or useful."

"Well, I know that! Father says that all the time, but we're talking about the Vedi now, and they're definitely not people!" Arion remembered thinking furiously, determined to find a way to circumvent his tutor's logic. He loved Corraidhín dearly, and lived in awe of Radomir, but sometimes they treated him like such a child!

"Those of the Vedi less afflicted by the *change* live, learn and love like anyone else, Arion. If you cross their territory or otherwise offend them, they will attack but they're not wild animals."

"The change?" asked Arion, distracted by the emphasis Corraidhín had placed on the words, and sensing a greater significance behind them than their simplest meaning.

"It is my belief that the Vedi as we know them today are the product of a great catastrophe generations past, Arion: one that began with your own ancestors in the cursed city of Menos to the north. But we digress from the topic at hand, and your father will not thank me if we do not complete your lessons. Let us return to the subject of geography then – list for me the six largest rivers that pass through Asfáleia, where each begins and where they end."

Back atop his horse in the Narrows, Arion smiled at the memory. Although he had done his share of moaning at the need for such lessons, he remembered those times fondly, and had a great affection for both of his tutors. The Vedi had been a topic to which he had returned at every possible opportunity, much to the occasional frustration of Corraidhín. Hunting them down before they reached the more populated areas of the Narrows was one of the most essential tasks of the King's Rangers but occasionally the king himself would decide to take a hunting party out to assist. He believed it was good training for the soldiers, teaching them to act in unison and to keep formation as they attacked. This was the first time he had asked Arion to join them, and the young prince was in equal parts excited and anxious.

"Do we know what sort of creature it is, father?" asked Arion.

"Little enough, Arion. Scouts reported it as being between eight and ten feet tall and hairy but could provide little more information than that. I think they saw it from a distance and declined to get any closer. Decided prudently, you might say!" They rode on in quiet contemplation for a while, Arion listening to the rushing water in the nearby river and trying not to think about food.

"Do we have enough soldiers, father?" he asked finally, looking a little worried. Achaeus gave a short laugh and looked back at their followers.

"Are there enough of us?" he called cheerily, and the soldiers responded with a resounding chorus.

"Yes, your majesty".

Achaeus was well-liked amongst the ranks, known to be a tough but fair ruler, and more importantly, one who would not spend soldiers' lives needlessly, nor shy from sharing their risks alongside them. The King laughed and acknowledged their reply with a wave before turning back to Arion.

"They seem to think so. In truth though, as with any battle, one never knows until the fighting begins. We are thirty-two including you and me. By now the Rangers will have gathered to at least half a dozen strong. Unless this beast has some hidden power that we are unaware of or is not alone, it should be more than enough."

Arion thought about that, less than reassured by his father's last statement. There were stories of Vedi with magical powers, superhuman strength and all sorts of other alarming abilities. Still, the mention of the Rangers helped calm his nerves a little. Normally the Rangers operated alone, or in small groups depending on the task before them. It was rare for six of them to come together at once and with Radomir amongst their number, Arion could almost be confident that they were ready for the task ahead. The Rangers would herd the Vedi into the King's path, and then the two forces would crush the creature between them. Arion shifted uncomfortably in his saddle. Despite having longed to join the hunt for years, now that they were getting close to their prey, he found himself thinking that perhaps he should have stayed at home a little longer. Here in the Narrows, far from civilisation, and far from the security of the palace, the thought of tackling a monster of unknown but undoubtedly fearsome capability seemed markedly less glorious and far more dangerous.

Arion's worrying was interrupted by a shout from one of the soldiers, and he turned to see her standing in her stirrups, pointing to the northwest. He followed her gesture and saw, in the distance, the faint silhouette of a mounted man, riding towards them at some speed. Without needing to be told, the Tarsean soldiers fanned out protectively around their charges but as the rider came closer it became clear that he was of the Rangers and their guard relaxed somewhat. Achaeus gave the order to ride out to meet the approaching man and soon he was amongst them. The Ranger was almost as tall as Radomir, Arion noted with surprise, though of far slighter build. A long, jagged scar ran the length of his face and down his neck before disappearing into the collar of his jerkin. He looked hard, Arion thought, almost like he was chiselled out of rock. It was impossible to imagine such a man ever yielding. Other than Radomir, Arion had not met many of the Rangers but surely, they were not all like this? Once again, he felt nervous and a little afraid. The knowledge that such doughty warriors were out there, and on their side, was comforting when one was a long way away, behind walls and with a warm, cosy fire to sit in front of. Out here on the plains they were intimidating, to say the least.

Despite his rough and ready appearance, the Ranger saluted smartly as he approached the king and gave his report quickly and concisely.

"The Rangers are a half day's ride north of here, my king. They trail the Vedi at a distance, but it slows now. Radomir believes that it will soon turn and fight and requests that you… ahem… hurry your arse up, my King. Sorry."

Arion was shocked to see a faint flush come into the man's cheeks as he spoke. The shock quickly passed, however, and he found himself relieved to see a sign of humanity in his leathery face. Achaeus threw back his head and laughed.

"Very good, Ranger. If you would be so kind as to lead the way, we shall make all haste to the north. Aika?" He turned to address one of the soldiers by the diminutive of her given name, Aikaterine. His father's aptitude for remembering names had always astonished Arion, sometimes it seemed he knew every servant in the palace and every soldier in the army. "Fetch this man a fresh horse, double-time if you please."

A few minutes later, they were riding north at a fast trot. Having left two soldiers to guard the supplies and spare horses they were travelling light now. The horses could have easily managed a much faster pace, but Arion assumed that his father was husbanding their strength, keeping some in reserve for a final charge. Now that they were moving, his nerves settled somewhat, enthusiasm and anticipation beginning to take over.

A couple of hours later they were continuing north at a steady pace when an ear-splitting roar reverberated across the plain, loud enough to startle the horses and send small creatures scattering to cover for miles around. As the echoes faded, Radomir's rumbling bellow could be heard, shouting orders. Achaeus forsook his caution and ordered them into a gallop. Arion's excitement mounted as the air, now filled with the sounds of angry combat, rushed past his ears. He pulled loose his spear, holding it tightly in his right hand and angled it slightly upward to reduce the possibility of inadvertently catching the point on the ground. He slid his left hand through the enarmes of his shield until the straps were tight around his forearm, and he could safely loosen the leather cords that bound it to his saddle. Beside him, his father made his own preparations, though in place of Arion's plain hunting spear he carried the famous War Spear of Arrias – a family heirloom of numerous generations and a fearsome weapon.

As the sounds of battle grew closer, their view of the scene was blocked by a copse of ancient-looking fir trees. The trees themselves were straggly and weather-beaten but holly bushes had sprung up around them, taking advantage of the meagre cover they provided, and it was impossible to see through to the other side. Achaeus called a halt and then quickly split their forces in two before proceeding. Arion was to take half of the soldiers and curve out to the left and pass the trees from that side, whilst Achaeus would take the remainder and go to the right. Arion had not expected the privilege of leading his own force, but his blood was up now, and he was so caught up in the moment that the responsibility of it did not faze him. With a wave to his father, he led his soldiers off to the northwest and quickly rounded the trees.

Achaeus had intended that the two wings of cavalry would sweep in upon the beast from either side, hitting it in separate waves, moments apart, with spears driven by the momentum of galloping horses. All being well, the creature would die almost immediately and with no casualties to the Tarseans. As soon as Arion rounded the trees, however, he knew at once that the plan was not going to work. The Vedi was far taller than had been reported for a start, towering over the plains at almost fifteen feet high, and of extremely stocky build with long, heavily muscled arms. Its skin was dappled grey and looked as tough as old leather. From about waist height down, its body was covered in metallic-looking scales, thick enough to withstand even the most solid of blows. Its head appeared sunken into its shoulders, with no neck to be seen in between, making its face seem almost to be growing out of its chest. Its gaping mouth gaped open to reveal a forest of yellowed fangs that were inches long. Then it roared deafeningly, an awful, bone-chilling sound, like no animal Arion had ever heard.

Tackling it from horseback would be folly: if one of its fists connected with a rider they would surely be killed. They stood a far better chance on foot, where at least they could duck and dodge with more freedom. A more immediate problem was that the Rangers were already engaged and fighting a losing battle, with two down and out of the fight. One lay still on the ground, his back twisted into an impossible curve. The other was conscious but bleeding from a massive head wound and unable to stand. She was desperately trying to drag herself away from the creature's feet but risked being trampled at any moment. Radomir shouted an order and a third Ranger rushed to her aid, pulling her back towards the trees.

Radomir and a single other Ranger now faced the Vedi. Both were fearsome fighters, but it was obvious that even they could not hold out against such an enemy for long. Radomir was doggedly standing his ground, having moved to place himself between the creature and the injured Ranger. He was wielding a massive, double-headed war axe and knocking chunks out of the creature's flanks with each mighty swing. The other ranger was moving quickly, darting in, stabbing with his spear, and then darting back out again before it could get turned towards him. Watching closely, Arion saw that the two were working in perfect coordination. Radomir would strike a blow with his axe, and the beast would swing around to face him, roaring in pain and rage. Even as it completed its turn, the other ranger would press forward on its other side, driving his spearpoint deep into its back, causing it to immediately lumber back around to face that threat instead. It was a dangerous game, requiring impeccable timing and not a little luck but the two men were masters, keeping the Vedi constantly off balance.

Arion saw his father ordering his men to dismount and hurried to give a matching order. The soldiers spread out into a rough semicircle, lowered their spears, and charged into battle. Arion and his band did the same and the creature was quickly surrounded by spears on all sides. Within moments, a dozen spears had lodged in its thick, hairy hide and it threw back its head and roared in rage and frustration, revealing a gaping maw filled with long, tusk-like teeth. Two more spears connected, and the beast swung around, dragging the soldiers off their feet as they released their grip on their spears a fraction of a second too late. Both men were flung through the air, each taking down two or three of their comrades as they flew. None of the soldiers were seriously hurt but the Vedi took advantage of the chaos to try and break free of its tormentors. Still roaring, it lowered its left shoulder and charged forward, sending half a dozen more soldiers tumbling to the left and right. It was bleeding in a score of places; a large strip of flesh was hanging off its right arm and there were still two spears embedded in its skin but none of that seemed to slow it in the slightest. Before the Tarseans could recover it was through their cordon and barrelling off across the plain at immense speed.

Arion heard Radomir cursing as he watched the Vedi go, his jaw dropping open at the suddenness of it all. One of the fallen soldiers was screaming, the beast having trodden on his leg in passing, crushing it horribly. Others were moaning or shouting at each other, trying to disentangle themselves from the heaps into which they had fallen or simply trying to recover their wits. The voice of Achaeus cut through the cacophony:

"Anyone still able – we ride, now!" With that, he set off at a run towards his mount, three soldiers hurriedly following, along with Radomir. Arion headed for his horse and swung up into the saddle before pulling it around to see who had followed. Just four were now mounting up alongside

"Get a move on, boy!" snapped Radomir, kicking his horse into a gallop.

Soon the Tarseans were galloping across the plain in a pack, riding as hard as the horses could bear. They gained on the Vedi slowly but lost a soldier along the way when her mount took fright at its continuing roars, stalled and reared, throwing its rider to the hard ground below. Radomir shouted at one of the others to stop and help, and everyone else kept going and they were about a hundred yards behind their quarry when the Vedi managed to surprise them once more. Without warning, it skidded to a halt and spun around, staring at them with angry, bloodshot eyes. Achaeus roared at the others to keep moving, and the gap rapidly closed but when they were a little under fifty yards away it crouched and then sprang forward at an incredible pace. It covered the distance between them in mere moments, far too quickly for the Tarseans to change course and it barrelled into them at full speed, knocking soldiers and horses in all directions, swinging with its massive arms as it passed. Arion was thrown from his horse as it reared and tried to avoid the flying fists. He landed on his back, bounced and then tumbled a short distance further, hitting his head sharply on a rock. A million tiny stars burst across his vision and then everything turned to blackness and silence for a moment.

As soon as he was able, Arion struggled to his feet and looked around. What remained of his father's hunting party was in complete disorder. Two of the soldiers were dead, one crushed beneath his mount, another with his neck bent to an unnatural angle. Radomir was on the ground nearby, on his hands and knees but unable to rise further. A short distance away he could see another soldier struggling to regain control of her terrified horse. Arion's head was pounding, and everything was a little fuzzy around the edges. He felt as though he was struggling to wake from a dream and for a moment he wondered if his father would wake him this morning or one of the servants. The thought jarred his memory, however, and he looked around frantically for his father, finally spotting him lying on his face a short distance away. Arion staggered over to him but even as he bent to try and help, an almighty bellow ripped through the air.

Arion straightened up and spun around to see the Vedi heading straight for them, its huge feet hitting the ground so hard that the ground itself seemed to shudder with the impact. Fear gripped Arion so tightly that he found he could hardly breathe, and the pain in his head was only getting worse. Struggling to focus, he knew that he only had moments before the beast arrived. He had lost his spear when he fell from his horse and his sword seemed a desperately feeble weapon to fend off a creature the size of the Vedi, but Achaeus too had lost his spear and it now lay an arm's length away on the grass. The War Spear of Arrias was almost eight feet long, the shaft made of ancient oak from the Drevenwood, far to the west, and reinforced with bands of steel along its length. Writing in a strange, curling script was engraved into the wood and highlighted in silver and gold. The head alone was eighteen inches long, forged in the partisan pattern and almost three inches across at its widest point. The blade razor-sharp all along its length and rumour had it that it had never seen a whetstone since Arrias was presented with it as a gift by his brother, centuries before. Every Tarsean king for generations since had carried it into war.

Arion grabbed the spear with both hands and turned to face the charging creature. The spear was longer and heavier than anything he had ever practised with but somehow it seemed to rest easily in his hands and the weight felt reassuring rather than tiring. It might have been his addled mind but later he swore that he had seen the carved words glimmer and glow for a moment as he swung the spear up and into position. Either way, with the weapon raised and ready, he felt energised, his fatigue and various aches and pains from the fall fading into the background. He felt as though he could take on anyone or anything and he almost laughed out loud with the sheer, potent vitality that flowed through his veins. Setting the butt of the spear on the ground behind him, he looked up to see the Vedi now only yards away, close enough to see the spittle flying from its mouth as it roared and howled.

Seconds passed when Arion could have taken his shot but knew, somehow, that the moment was just not right. The Vedi was almost upon him now, perhaps ten feet away, not more. Its bellows were making Arion's ears hurt, and his teeth were clamped together tight enough to crack. One more step, and the moment would be right. If he waited for the beast to take one more step, he could end its miserable life. He had no idea how he knew this but there was no time to second guess himself and he waited for that last step, every nerve in his body screaming at him to run, to hide, to somehow get himself away from this terrible danger. The Vedi took another step, and a stray gust of wind carried its musky, sickening scent over him. He could see directly into its eyes as it bore down upon him and was surprised to see intelligence there, a calculating wit that was planning its own attack, even as he was planning his.

The moment came and Arion struck, driving the spear forward and up with all his strength, burying the leaf-shaped head deep into its throat, entering above its collarbone. Arion's knees buckled with the immense force of the impact, and he might have fallen, had not the butt of the spear hit the ground, driving itself inches into the soft loam. The Vedi's crazed charge had given it too much momentum to stop or even change course, and as it barrelled forward, the spearhead was forced back until the weapon stood upon its end. Almost vertical now, the sharp blade travelled upwards, glancing off the creature's spine and piercing its brain. Even then the Spear of Tarsus was not finished with its foe, seeming to twist of its own accord in Arion's hands, liquidising the inside of the creature's skull before bursting out through the top of its head in a triumphant spray of blood, gore, and shattered bone.

With the Vedi now pinned at the top of the spear, the immense weight of its suddenly limp body dragged Arion down before pulling the weapon from his hands. He fell to his knees, even as the massive creature fell beside him, and all his exhaustion came flooding back in a rush. His ears were ringing, his head aching furiously. He knelt there on the grass, unable to find the energy even to turn and check on his father. Somewhere, distantly, he heard voices. Someone was calling his name. He tried to turn his head, but his muscles would not obey, and his vision was blurring anyway. He reached down blindly, his hand feeling around until it found the haft of the spear. Touching the carved wood with his fingertips, Arion remembered the moment he had thrust at the Vedi. He had been the one to make the move, but he now believed that the spear itself had been guiding his hand. He had wanted to stop the beast, to defend his father and himself but the spear had only wanted blood. He felt an echo of that desire now, as his fingers brushed across the mysterious lettering. The spear wanted him to take it up again, to rise and fight and kill and keep killing until all before him were dead. Past reason, Arion tried desperately to comply but had not the will. The world began to spin before his eyes, and he was having difficulty forming even the simplest of thoughts. Still gripping the spear's haft, he crumpled to the ground and fell into blessed unconsciousness.

CHAPTER SEVEN

Rutik city of Magdeborg
15 of Boukatios 870M - Early Spring
Two months before the siege of Tarsus

At the height of its power, Tarsus reigned supreme over the Achaean city states and the entirety of Asfáleia was within its domain. Levies, taxes, and generous tributes arrived by the cartload, and the royal coffers swelled to bursting. Arrias was a conqueror, but also a builder and from the ashes of the old Menosan Empire, he raised a mighty kingdom. His children and grandchildren followed in his footsteps and, in the year 136M, Arrias the Third was crowned in a glorious palace, built of gleaming marble amidst a city of polished granite.

Acusilaus, "The Eternal Glory of Tarsus", c. 850M

Chapter Seven

Orders from the League arrived one cold spring morning in the month of Athanaios, 870M. Mira and her troop were back in the city of Magdeburg, resting and recuperating after a brief return to the glades of the Drevenwood. It had not been a pleasant mission, but Mira had carried it out without question, as always. According to the League, a particular major in the Northern Army was fomenting rebellion, bitter at the seemingly never-ending conflict in the woods. Mira's troop had followed the major's command into the woods, trailing them at a day's distance until they set up camp at the banks of a small river. Teja had led the bulk of her soldiers in from the east, firing off arrows and shouting Baimoi war cries, whilst Mira had waited with Beuca and the other scouts, concealed in a gully to the west. The Major's forces had mustered impressively quickly, moving out to meet the enemy in good order. Teja and his followers continued to make as much noise as possible feigning resistance but retreating rapidly.

Once the main force of the Rutik had been drawn away, Mira and her contingent moved in towards the camp, cutting the sentries' throats with hardly a sound and slipping into the camp like shadows. The Major stood close to a campfire, with half a dozen guards around him, waiting for the other soldiers to return. Mira's scouts killed three of them with arrows and wounded a fourth, then they charged from the trees as a pack and attacked. The wounded woman fell quickly, the arrow protruding from her shoulder hindering her movement. The other two guards put up more of a fight, but Mira's scouts met them with equal ferocity and determination. Mira herself ran right past them, dodging a wild swipe from a sabre, and moved quickly to engage the Major. He was a middle-aged man, in good shape for his years and as Mira approached, he swept a long, curved sword from its scabbard and stood his ground, his face showing no sign of fear. He was capable with the sword too, giving Mira pause for a moment or two as she tried to get the measure of him. It was over in minutes, however, as she found a gap in his defence and swept her blade across his face. He staggered back, howling in sudden agony and she finished him with a slash across the throat. The scouts had finished with the guards by that time and Mira did not hesitate, ordering them back into the trees without further ado. Mira travelled a distance to the west, then circled around and rendezvoused with Teja's contingent, continuing to the east to get out from under the trees and onto the road to Magdeburg. Neither Mira nor Teja had lost a single soldier in the brief action and that, to Mira, meant that it was a job well done.

Upon reaching the city some days later, she used some of the League's funds to book out an entire boarding house for the troop and allow them a few days of much-needed leisure time. It was an indulgence, of course, and not one which army command would have approved but Mira knew that the League would not object. Their first night in the boarding house rapidly descended into drunken chaos as weeks of danger and tension were released in a single burst. They drank, then ate, then drank some more. They sang old soldier's songs and argued over the words, almost came to blows and then made up with enthusiastic embraces. Mira, as their commanding officer, stayed somewhat aloof from the most raucous outbursts of the troop but drank more than her share of the innkeeper's best wine and laughed dutifully at the antics of her followers.

As the evening wore on, one by one the lighter drinkers wandered off to bed or dozed off where they sat, and the crowd of revellers grew smaller and quieter. By the time the midnight bell tolled, only half a dozen remained – Mira, Beuca, Teja and three solid veterans. The songs faded into tired reminiscing: battles won, battles lost and the friends that had died along the way.

"I always liked Wala," Mira said, interrupting one of the veterans as she recalled a former comrade. Wala had caught an arrow during a short, sharp battle with an expeditionary force from the city of Chalcis. The arrow had ricocheted off a stone on the ground catching Wala under his chin and pinning his tongue to the roof of his mouth before continuing into his brain. The

Chalceans had been lingering within a day's ride of the Rutik city of Harbrook, gateway to the heart of the Kingdom of the Rutik, attacking merchant caravans, capturing couriers and generally causing trouble. Mira and her troop had been despatched to put an end to the problem, which they had, though not without losses.

"Aye, Captain," replied the veteran. She was a sturdily built woman by the name of Gelvira. Teja had recruited her from a heavy infantry regiment of the Northern Army, and she had proven her worth to the troop on multiple occasions since. "Shame really. Had a bit of a fling with him one time and to be honest, his tongue was the longest part of him." Mira snorted with laughter and was joined by the others. None of them were strangers to death and the laughter helped, for a while at least. Mira rose to her feet, a little unsteadily she had to admit.

"To Wala," she cried, raising her cup. The others joined in the toast before lapsing into silence. They continued in that vein for another hour or more, by turns jovial and melancholy until one by one they wandered off to bed.

Mira was the last to go, as was her duty as the senior officer. She finished her drink and was about to leave when the innkeeper caught her eye. He was behind the bar cleaning mugs with a tattered looking cloth and looked boyishly handsome. He had a twinkle in his eye and had been particularly diligent in attending to her needs throughout the evening. He saw her looking and smiled warmly before returning to his task. Mira watched him work for a moment, noticing the thick, black hair that covered his muscled arms and a small scar above his right eye that marred his youthful perfection, and somehow made him appear older than he probably was. She weighed up how tired she was, how drunk she was, how late it was, and how quickly the morning would come. The sensible thing to do would be to ignore the man and retire to her bed alone. *Fuck it,* she thought, *life's too short.* Straightening her hair and wiping her mouth with the back of her hand she rose to her feet and sauntered towards the bar, determined to find out exactly how twinkly those eyes could get.

A couple of exceedingly pleasant hours later, Mira finally fell asleep. She was woken a short time later, however, when her newfound lover clambered out of bed before dawn to begin the task of preparing breakfast for his guests. It was only when she sleepily rolled over to bid him farewell that Mira realised that she had forgotten to ask the man his name. She mumbled something unintelligible instead but was rewarded with a friendly chuckle and a slightly mocking bow. The innkeeper left and she tried to go back to sleep but found that despite her exhaustion, the mood had left her. and she eventually gave up, struggled out from beneath the covers to pull on her clothes. Her head was pounding, and her mouth tasted as though something had crawled inside and died during the night. She bent to retrieve a hastily cast-off boot and groaned as the movement seemed to throw her brain around inside of her skull. She almost returned to bed at that but managed to master herself and headed for the barroom instead. Perhaps a bit of something to eat would ease her woes. Maybe even a trickle of something to drink.

Entering the barroom, Mira saw the innkeeper once more at his station and flashed him a smile, then frowned as he failed to return the gesture. He glanced up almost furtively and blanched a little before looking back down sharply. Mira followed his line of sight across the room to find herself looking at not one but two tall, hooded men in dark green cloaks, one to either side of the outer door, menace exuding from every fibre of their being. Seated at a table in the middle of the room was none other than Lord Ohtrad of the League for the Restoration of Rutik Glory, watching her entrance with keen interest.

"Captain Mira, do join me." She marched over as stiffly as she was able and pulled up a stool, now regretting her choices of the previous night.

"Greetings, Lord Ohtrad."

"Greetings indeed, Captain. It has been some time since last we met but I hear great things about your service to the League."

"We do our best." Mira winced, knowing that her words hardly qualified as sparkling conversation. The pain in her head seemed to be gathering its strength now, focusing on a point behind her left eye. It was all she could do not to slump onto the table

"Your best. Indeed, you do, and your best is *impressive*. There are those amongst our number who now believe you may be destined for *great* things. Great things indeed." Accepting a compliment graciously was not Mira's strongest talent at the best of times and this was far from the best of times, so she chose to ignore it.

"What brings you here at this early hour, my lord? I doubt we'll see much of my troop for another hour yet."

"Early bird catches the worm, Captain," he replied with a shrug. "A strange turn of phrase really. If one looks at it from another perspective, the early worm gets eaten, doesn't it? I suppose that's not so likely to inspire early rising in the listener though, eh?" He laughed a short bark of a laugh, sharply at odds with his measured, almost musical speaking voice. Mira found herself staring at him in bemusement, and promptly busied herself fixing the buttons on her shirt.

"Anyway," he continued. "You and I have been assigned a mission together, working hand in glove so to speak. You as the representative of the martial strength of the Kingdom of the Rutik, me of its more *transcendental* power.

I will brief you in a moment, but I thought it best that we get to know each other a little better first, so as to ensure that we present a *unity* of purpose, and without any misunderstandings."

"Misunderstandings?" repeated Mira, raising an eyebrow. "I'm not sure what you mean, my lord."

"What I mean to emphasise is the *absolute* necessity for everyone on this mission to understand their allotted role and to remain within the boundaries that have been set for them. The consequences of failure here could be catastrophic for the Kingdom. There is a great, great deal riding on our success, which will only be achieved by complete and unwavering adherence to the plan.

"As I have said, you represent the physical strength of the nation, the brute force if you will, saving of course your own markedly un-brutish demeanour. If you prefer a more flattering metaphor, you are the spear in our hand. A spear that is beautifully crafted and exceptionally deadly but a spear that doesn't decide where to strike of its own volition. The spear strikes wherever it is pointed, or along the path it is thrown. Similarly, we expect you, and your soldiers, to follow our path and to go exactly where we point you. Deviation from the plan will not be tolerated. Independent action will not be tolerated. Failure will not be tolerated. To extend the metaphor: a spear that does not fly true is useless and must be discarded."

Ohtrad paused at that, staring fixedly at Mira, as though waiting for her to respond but she held her tongue for a moment, struggling to get her alcohol-fumed thoughts into order. She could not see the point of Ohtrad's speech.

For the last year and a half, she and her troop had done nothing but follow orders. Never once had they refused or even questioned them. So why had Ohtrad chosen this moment to exert his authority? Why this sudden doubt as to her loyalty? It was nothing she had done, or not done – of that she was sure, which left only one reasonable conclusion: this next mission was of such difficulty, or such importance, or both, that Ohtrad himself was worried. Whatever he was about to ask of her, she was probably better off refusing but that was almost certainly not an option.

"I am at your command, my lord," she said finally. She did not feel comfortable addressing him by his name despite his permission to do so, certainly not after he had only finished putting her so very clearly in her place.

"Are we united in purpose and understanding then, Captain?" Ohtrad insisted.

"Yes, my lord, I believe we are," replied Mira, with her most innocent smile. "Perhaps you would like to fill me in on the details of your plan?"

"Not my plan, Captain Mira – the plan. The only plan that matters at this point," corrected Ohtrad, with what Mira suspected was an insincere smile. He continued:

"You will be aware of course that the army is mustering at Harbrook?" Mira nodded. There had been no formal notification but like all armies, the Rutik army was sustained by gossip. Most of a soldier's life was spent in boredom, and bored people talked – it was human nature.

"Rumour around the camps is that we march on Tarsus, my lord."

"Indeed so, Captain. The Queen has decreed that the time has come for the Kingdom of the Rutik to finally destroy its ancient enemy. And yet there is a problem. We have gathered at Harbrook in such numbers as you would not believe. Infantry in their tens of thousands, cavalry in their thousands. Once they are upon the march, the siege train alone will stretch a day's march in either direction. The Kingdom is roaring, Captain, and the Tarseans would do well to cower." Ohtrad's eyes were shining as he described the might of the Rutik army, or perhaps he was envisioning the destruction of Tarsus. The Rutik and the Tarseans had been enemies for centuries and fought on opposite sides in a dozen major wars and a thousand minor conflicts. Tarsus was the lynchpin in the axle of eastern cities that thwarted Rutik ambitions: defiant and powerful, they kept the alliance together. Mira wondered though whether even such a mighty army would be enough. The defences of Tarsus were legendary, and it had never fallen in recorded history. The glory of Tarsus was perhaps diminished in recent times but still, they were a formidable enemy. She looked up to see that Ohtrad was nodding in agreement, as though following her train of thought exactly.

"Now you see the crux of the problem, Captain. Tarsus is, as they say, a difficult nut to crack. We have the numbers, and we have the strength but if we cannot force an entry, we will be tied into a siege that might last for years. Meanwhile, our enemies elsewhere will seize their moment to rise, and we might well find ourselves beset on all sides and unable to respond.

It is for that reason that we of the League have made arrangements to *place a finger* upon the scale. A second army has been prepared, in absolute secrecy, at a fortified encampment east of Magdeburg. Ten thousand of our strongest and bravest cavalry wait there for our arrival and for their orders to move out. You and I, Captain Mira, will accompany them on their journey across the Devil's Teeth Mountains and onto the grassy plains of the Tarsean Narrows. From there we will have a straight run to the city itself, to take the Tarseans from the rear and throw the game in favour of the Queen. What do you think of that?"

"My lord, I…" Mira trailed off. Ohtrad had only just warned her of the consequences of questioning his orders but crossing the Devil's Teeth, especially in such numbers, was nothing short of madness. The Teeth were well known to be virtually impassable: almost impossibly high, towering over the plains below, wracked with foul weather and rumoured to be populated with terrifying creatures. The idea of taking a huge number of horses through that terrain was a special form of insanity. Ohtrad, however, nodded.

"I see you appreciate the scale of the task before us, Captain, but never fear: a way has been prepared. The League has spent years, a fortune in treasure and ten thousand lives preparing a path through the mountains. Rest assured, we will make it through, but it will not be easy and that is where you and I come in. There will be cold, there will be pain and there will be suffering. Our brave warriors will be tested. Sorely tested, and some may falter. My associates and I," he gestured towards the cloaked men standing beside the door. Mira had almost forgotten them as she listened to Ohtrad but now, as she glanced in their direction, they somehow seemed more solid than anything else in the room. Although neither of them moved, she knew in that moment that both were staring at her from beneath their hoods. She could feel their eyes boring into her, even from across the room.

"My associates and I will ensure that the will of the Expeditionary Army does not waver. We will stand behind them so that whatever they may face along the road, turning back remains always the less *attractive* option." Mira glanced at the two men by the door again, feeling their gaze upon her, even though their eyes were hidden within their hoods. Somehow, she did not doubt Ohtrad's words.

"And what about me, my lord?" she asked, returning her attention to Ohtrad by an effort of sheer will. "What role am I to play in this?"

"My associates are powerful, Captain, but they are few and I? I am only one man. We cannot watch ten thousand all by ourselves. And even if we could, we are *different*. We are not soldiers; the men and women of the expeditionary force will not trust us. They will hide their fears from us, conceal their doubts and disguise their intentions. You and your troop will fill that gap. You will watch where we cannot, you will listen to what is said beyond our hearing, and you will take the measure of the troops when they are not within our influence. You will be our eyes and our ears and if necessary, our knife in the dark."

"You want me to kill Rutik soldiers, my lord?"

"I want you to do what's necessary, Captain. Do you take issue with that order?" Mira had never killed another Rutik, but she supposed that if it came down to it, killing a person of one kingdom, as opposed to a person of another, was merely a matter of perspective. The task before her was not a particularly pleasant one but she and her troop had carried out unpleasant missions before. What was one more?

"No, my lord."

"Outside of that, you will act as our protection detail. You will defend our lives with your own if necessary and ensure that nothing and no one gets the chance to interfere with our work."

For the next half hour, they ran through the basic details of the mission, step by step, Ohtrad patiently filling in some of the blanks in Mira's understanding. When it came to assaulting the northern gate of Tarsus, however, Ohtrad's explanation was less than satisfactory.

"That, Captain Mira, is one of those parts of the mission that you need not concern yourself with. Suffice it to say that we, meaning the League, of course, have in hand. For your purposes, it is sufficient to know that the gates will open. You may be assured of that as a fact, and plan accordingly."

"I'm not sure I like that idea, my lord," replied Mira, frowning. "How can I know if we are on track to succeed if I don't know when this help is coming, or where it's coming from?"

"Faith, Captain Mira, you must have faith. All will be revealed at the appropriate time." As a statement, Mira felt, that was resoundingly unhelpful but again there seemed to be little to be gained by pressing the point, so she moved on.

Ohtrad left an hour later, seemingly satisfied with Mira's responses and leaving directions to the encampment. Mira sat quietly for a while, as the barroom slowly came to life around her, her soldiers arriving in varying states of disarray and seating themselves around the room. Teja arrived shortly after Ohtrad left and took the seat he had vacated, sitting opposite Mira and studying her levelly with scarcely a hint of fatigue and no sign at all of a hangover.

"Trouble, Captain?" he asked after a moment. Mira continued to stare at the scarred surface of the barroom table for a while before glancing up at him.

"Isn't there always, sergeant?" she replied, looking around for the innkeeper, feeling the need to fill her belly. Teja scratched his beard and belched before replying.

"Aye, Captain. Seems like that's our lot alright."

"You don't know the fucking half of it, sergeant," she replied.

A few hours later, as the troop passed through the city gates, a shiver ran through Mira's body. She was missing the embrace of the heavy blankets the boarding house had provided but suspected that the lack of a warm bed would prove the least of her troubles in the days to come. Mira liked certainty in her life, a certain clarity, and the League's vague orders had unsettled her. As they rode, the Devil's Teeth loomed in the distance, colossal ramparts resolutely braced against her approach. The highest of the peaks were wreathed in dark clouds, the lower reaches wrapped in snow. The mountains seemed to exude a brooding menace, mocking Mira's petty force, daring her to stand against them. Mira firmly suppressed a shiver and steadied herself for whatever travails lay ahead. The League commanded, and she obeyed, that was their agreement. Whatever duties awaited them; she did not doubt that her troop would prevail.

CHAPTER EIGHT

Foothills of the Devil's Teeth Mountains
25 of Dios 870M - Mid Spring
One month before the siege of Tarsus

Almost four centuries of Tarsean hegemony passed before the first of the Rutik set foot in Asfáleia. They emerged from the Drevenwood in small numbers at first, fleeing some unspecified, or at least now-forgotten, threat to the north. Secure in their supremacy, the Tarseans did not see the newcomers as a threat – granting them lands in return for fealty and servitude. The Rutik as savages but Tarsus recognised their value as mercenaries and auxiliaries. Coming from a warrior tradition, the Rutik accepted their allotted fate without complaint and became a fearsome weapon to be pointed wherever their masters willed it.

Acusilaus, "Peoples of Asfáleia", c. 900M

Chapter Eight

Mira and her troop arrived at the camp a week later. It turned out to be of substantial enough construction, with a heavy rampart of tightly bound logs topping a mortared stone wall and enclosing a large enough area to accommodate a significant number of troops. As they approached, Mira noted three flags flying over the gatehouse – one bearing the black wolf's head of the Kingdom of the Rutik, a second the insignia of the Northern Army and the third showing the strange, angular script of the old country – the mark of the League for the Restoration of Rutik Glory. The presence of a League flag on a military base was highly unusual. Mira knew better than most that the League had its own force of soldiery but had not imagined that it was of any significant size. She had assumed that their interests were managed by small troops such as her own but showing their colours openly alongside Kingdom and division suggested a much more substantial, and overt, level of involvement.

Upon reaching the gate, she found their arrival anticipated and they were immediately led to quarters on the south side of the camp, a position that Mira noted was almost as far away from the command tents as it was possible to get whilst remaining within the walls. There was a political game being played, and she was little more than a pawn. The feeling did not sit well with her, and she resolved that until she had a clearer understanding of the rules, she would have to be cautious in her moves. As was the habit of the Rutik army in the field, their tents were clustered around an open space, where the troops could light their campfires, repair their gear, and pass the time at cards or dice until they were required for duty. She had Teja uproot them all and move them closer together, reducing the amount of space in the central area but creating a gap that was about five feet wide between their encampment, and those of neighbouring units. That done, she set pickets at each of the four corners and organised a rotation of the guard through the night and into the next day.

The morning after their arrival, Mira rose early and headed for the stables to saddle her horse, intending to watch the morning parade and keen to take the measure of the garrison. The camp itself was neatly organised, as was the habit of the Northern Army but the so-called yard was little more than a large clear space, outside the gates. It was unsurfaced but large amounts of gravel had been dumped onto it, mined from the nearby mountains. Weeks and months of cavalry drills had compacted the gravel and earth into a near-solid layer, but it was still very much in keeping with the style of a temporary encampment, and nothing like the grandiose plazas Mira had paraded across in Rutiksborg.

Inside the yard, twenty thousand men and women of the Rutik mounted on strong Rutik mares were on parade in a perfectly lined out formation that was four hundred wide, and fifty deep. Even at a glance, Mira could tell these were no common soldiers. The riders were tall and strong with cropped hair and hard, stern eyes. Rounded helms dangled from their saddles, and polished breastplates shone against green tunics. Each soldier carried a long spear in one hand and the other a round shield. On each shield was painted in black a horse's head on a green field. In place of his or her spear, one soldier in twenty held aloft a silver trimmed, green pennant, again marked with the horse's head. The pennants waved and flapped in the wind, but otherwise, the formation was completely motionless. Not a soldier stirred as Mira stood and stared.

In a separate line, facing the others, a group of about forty officers were mounted and inspecting the formation. The officers were mostly older and more experienced looking than the fresh-faced regulars but equally well turned-out, and their horses were stunning. She trotted towards them and gave them her compliments on the parade performance. A colonel looked down his nose at her from atop a perfectly groomed bay mare that sported a saddle and tack of clearly expensive manufacture.

"Captain Mira, I presume? We were expecting you a week ago." Mira shrugged. She had travelled as quickly as possible after receiving her orders – if she was late, it was not of her doing. Her lack of a response did not endear her to the colonel, however, and he continued to glare at her for a moment before turning back toward the other officers.

"Lieutenant Adalwolf, take Captain Mira to get the lie of the land. I expect she will be impressed with our progress here."

"Yes, Colonel." A young officer spoke up. He was tall, well-built, and not unhandsome Mira thought and she smiled as he introduced himself and saluted.

"At your service, Captain. I am Adalwolf, First Lieutenant, nineteenth company."

"At ease, Lieutenant." She looked around him to make sure that the colonel had moved on, but his attention was entirely elsewhere, seemingly having immediately dismissed the problem that was Mira as beneath his notice.

"Sorry, you drew the short twig, Lieutenant. What did you do to piss off the colonel?" Adalwolf laughed a warm, heartfelt chuckle that endeared him to Mira still further.

"I couldn't possibly say, Captain," he replied. Like all Rutik cavalry horses, his mount was a mare, this one chestnut brown with a splash of white across the forehead. Adalwolf looked extremely comfortable in the saddle and Mira complimented him on his riding.

"My father bred horses. I have been riding since before I could walk. Gamanhilte here is a good horse though, strong, and obedient. She will carry me across the mountains, I believe."

"I believe she will," replied Mira with a smile. They rode on in silence for a while, then chatted in a friendly manner about inconsequential things whilst Adalwolf led them roughly east towards the foothills of the Devil's Teeth. Adalwolf seemed happy in his position and eager for the trials ahead, but Mira was curious.

"Tell me, Lieutenant," she said. "How do you feel about the task our Queen has placed before us?"

"How do I feel?" Adalwolf asked, looking confused. "I would not presume to think that the Queen is concerned with my feelings, Captain. We have our orders."

"Of course," replied Mira. "But you are a soldier and an officer. You must have some experience; else you would not have been selected for this mission. So, let me put it another way: give me your professional assessment of our mission, Lieutenant."

"Immediately, Captain," Adalwolf laughed. He seemed unperturbed by Mira's sudden switch from casual conversation to formal orders and Mira found herself liking the young officer more and more. "So, basic mission details first: twenty thousand cavalry travel approximately sixty miles across the western Devil's Teeth Mountains, to reach the Tarsean Narrows within three weeks, there to turn south and assault the walled city of Tarsus, catching the enemy by surprise and opening the city to assault by our main army to the south. How am I doing so far?"

"Tell me something I don't know, Lieutenant," replied Mira, without rancour. The road became rougher as they continued east. By that time, it was little more than a wide, well-trampled trail. The omnipresent mountains seemed to loom ever higher as they approached, which Mira could not understand, since they had only travelled a few miles.

"Yes ma'am. On the positive side, we have been in this camp for a little over six months and for all that time, there has been a constant stream of traffic into the mountains. Scouts first, followed by sappers, followed by multiple trains of wagons and livestock, all protected by scores of foot soldiers. A way has been prepared for us, built, supplied, and secured by the full might of the Rutik army.

"On the negative, the Devil's Teeth are widely believed to be impassable. No matter the preparations, we will face the harshest possible terrain, freezing rain and snow, winds funnelled through the passes and in places air so thin we will struggle to breathe. There are stories of wild men in the mountains, I don't know how true they are. There are stories of other things too, things left over from the old days. Frankly, I doubt the truth of those entirely but who knows? Either way, the journey across the mountains will by no means be easy."

Adalwolf glanced across at Mira, perhaps trying to gauge how she was taking his assessment. She waved at him to continue. Their ride had taken them to a point on the trail where the ground began to rise sharply, and their progress slowed as the horses adjusted to the incline.

"Assuming we survive the mountains with enough soldiers in fighting shape, the short trip down the Narrows should be uneventful. The Tarseans will be fully occupied with the army at their southern gate. The only danger is that we are spotted by some shepherd or crop farmer, who takes it into his head to run for the city, warning them of our arrival. If the northern gates are held against our assault in any great force, our chances of success reduce dramatically. We must reach the gates quickly, that part seems relatively easy. To be honest, though, I'm not entirely clear on how we achieve the next part. It's not like we can ride over the walls and there's not been any talk of us bringing siege engines across the mountains. Not sure that would even be possible.

"Anyway, leaving that aside, once we're inside the city, again much depends on how far news travels ahead of us. If we can move quickly enough, I'd rate our chances of reaching the far gate as reasonable to good. The last link in the chain is opening the southern gate. We must assume they'll have mustered some sort of defence by then, once we breach the north gate the alarm will be raised immediately. All being well though, they'll still be in shock at finding us inside the walls and struggling to re-orient themselves. We hit them hard, keep moving and break through. We don't have to hold the gatehouse forever, just long enough for the rest of the army to get through and reinforce us. It'll be tough but I think it's doable. Once the army arrives, we sit back, watch the fun and wait for our medals," he finished with a smile. "I think that's about it?"

"Not a bad summation," conceded Mira. "But still little in the way of information that is new to me. Tell me something else – where is the League in all of this?"

Adalwolf did not answer. Instead, he rode off to the side of the track, pushing through some scraggly bushes and gesturing for Mira to follow. Wary, Mira followed slowly, one hand on the hilt of her sword. She need not have worried, however, for on the far side of the bushes, Adalwolf had already dismounted, and now stood a short distance away, a few feet back from a jagged cliff edge, staring out across a stunning vista. The cliff curved around a narrow spur of flat land, jutting out from the side of the mountain. By turning in place, Mira found that she could see for miles in almost all directions, her vision only blocked by the mountains themselves. It was stunning and for a few minutes, neither of them spoke as they stood silenced by the view.

Finally, Mira stirred herself and, without turning away from the view, gently but firmly reminded Adalwolf of her question.

"The League, Lieutenant."

Adalwolf hesitated again but eventually answered.

"My apologies, Captain. We are encouraged to keep all information relating to the League within our own congregation. It goes against the grain to speak of them to an… outsider, Captain. Even one as well-connected as yourself."

"You are one of them, then?" asked Mira, frowning. She found herself put out at Adalwolf's response. She and her troop had spent a year and a half following the League's orders, doing their bidding, and winning their battles one after another. Surely at the very least, that should have earned her their trust?

"Yes, ma'am. Many of us in the expedition are. I'd even hazard a guess to say the majority, though of course not all of them are devout, or even fully initiated. Still, we shall all be together for the next while, plenty of time to introduce them to the deeper mysteries." Mira could only stare at the man, who a moment ago had seemed so sensible and pleasant. Speaking of the League seemed to energise him, and his eyes now gleamed with an almost feverish intensity. It appeared that the League's adherents carried no obvious identification, no badges, or other marks to show their allegiance. Naively, Mira had assumed that they would be easy to spot and, hence, easy to avoid, or at least to treat with additional discretion. She had ridden with Adalwolf for hours, chatted with him on a range of subjects and was only now realising that he was probably a fanatic.

"I think we've gone far enough for today, Lieutenant," she said, as he followed her onto the road. "Let's head back. And I'd like you to keep today's conversation to yourself, for now, thank you."

"Yes, Captain," replied Adalwolf. "On your order." He saluted, pulled his horse around and headed back down the steep path. Mira followed, still thinking furiously, one thought chasing another around her head. Whatever the truth about the League was, it was clear that they would need to be considered in her assessment of the situation and accommodated in whatever plans she had to make. They passed the return journey in silence and parted company at the gates to the camp: he to put the horses away, she to return to her tent and think about what she had learned.

The Expeditionary Army departed from camp about a week after Mira's arrival. Spring had given way to summer by that time and the weather was pleasant enough as they set out, but threatening clouds still masked most of the higher slopes ahead of them. Perhaps by virtue of their singularly unusual geographical features, the Devil's Teeth were also possessed of unique and most unconventional weather patterns. One of the Rutik scouts had described the crossing as being "like passing through one season in the morning, another in the afternoon, and a third as soon as you turn a corner". One face of a mountain might be bathed in summer sunlight, and relatively warm if you did not venture too much higher in altitude; whilst another face of the same mountain was in the midst of a blizzard-driven snowstorm, with temperatures well below freezing. One valley might offer protection from the wind, and be quiet and calm, whilst the next might offer only its services as a funnel, corralling the mountain gales and goading them to ever greater displays of strength. All in all, Mira reflected grimly, this might be the last taste of true summer they had for a while.

Mira's troop took up their allotted position in the column and left the camp shortly before eleven, the first units having left almost five hours earlier. Only so many horses could fit across the road at any one time, of course, and a space had to be left to one side to allow for the transport of messages and so on. Ohtrad was riding at her side, with four other adherents to the League accompanying him. Two of them he referred to as his bodyguards: they were grizzled and tough-looking, clearly veterans and heavily armed. A third man, shorter and slighter of build, with a mop of unkempt, straw-coloured hair, Ohtrad introduced as his scribe, Waldebert. Waldebert looked to be a man deeply unhappy with life and barely nodded in response to Mira's greeting.

The final member of Ohtrad's entourage might have been one of the two shadowy figures that had accompanied him to their meeting in the inn in Magdeborg. He wore the same long, green cloak and a similar deep, dark hood so it was difficult to be sure but he exuded the same menacing, slightly disturbing aura. He rode stiffly, staring straight ahead and Mira found it difficult to force her gaze to linger upon him for more than a moment or two. Ohtrad did not introduce him, as such, and referred to him in passing as "the Avatar", without making any attempt to explain the significance of the name or elaborate on his reason for being there. The Avatar himself offered no greeting and did nothing to acknowledge Mira's presence. He appeared to be unarmed at least, which was of some comfort to her, though who knew what he had concealed beneath that cloak? She supposed that his purpose would become clearer as time passed, or maybe once they arrived in Tarsus and in the meantime resolved to keep a close eye on his behaviour.

The first two days passed pleasantly; the altitude was still low enough for the summer sun to warm the air as they rode. The soaring peaks of the mountains loomed up before them and all around them, casting long, cold shadows but so regally beautiful that Mira's breath caught in her throat every time a new aspect caught her eye. On the second day, they lost their first soldier when her mount stumbled on a hidden rock and fell heavily, crushing her beneath its bulk. She survived the fall but was in no fit state to continue her mission, so Mira assigned one of the support staff to ferry her back to base camp on a small cart, distributing the supplies it had previously held amongst the remaining carts. She told herself it was merely an unfortunate accident and not a worrying omen for the long journey ahead but even she was not convinced. At the end of the second day, on schedule, they reached the first fortified encampment that had been prepared for their arrival.

There were four such camps along the route, set at intervals of three days' travel, strung out along the road like pearls on a necklace. Once they got into the mountains, the more supplies they had to carry with them, the slower would be their progress so the depots were essential to completing their journey within the allotted time. This one was intended less for resupply, since they brought with them more than enough supplies to make it further, and more as a waypoint, to mark the boundary between the gentle foothills and the Devil's Teeth proper. The resupply points had been established in the months prior to the Expeditionary Army setting out. The first one, being easily reached and within striking distance of the base camp, was used as a forward station. From there, an area within three days ride had been extensively scouted before selecting the next resupply and the most viable route between the two. Next, large numbers of Rutik soldiers had been despatched to secure the route and the next supply point. Once the way forward was deemed relatively safe, the sappers and engineers were despatched, along with a veritable army of slaves. For a month or more groups of such workers worked long hours in freezing conditions, clearing paths, levelling obstacles, and securing cliff faces, whilst others laboured to turn the frozen trail into something resembling a road. Meanwhile, at the designated second resupply point, a third group cleared land and fortified the area with wooden palisades, made from logs carted and dragged all the way from the lowlands. Once the resupply point was secure, the carriage of supplies began, not for the expedition itself at that stage, but to feed the soldiers and workers as they continued with their efforts. More soldiers were brought in to patrol the newly cleared route, and more workers began the process of constant maintenance required to keep the new road in usable condition. Even as the second resupply was being properly established, the forward scouts had already moved on to the next phase, exploring a further three days' ride ahead, seeking the next route and the next resupply point.

On their fourth day out of the first camp, Mira began to see evidence of how difficult the pathfinding process had been. The frozen bodies of slaves and craftsmen could be seen by the sides of the road, first a few here and there, later in ever greater numbers. The cold, the extreme weather, rockslides, and wild beasts had all taken their toll on the hapless workers, and no one had felt it worth the effort to reward their labour with anything more than being tossed aside like broken tools. The dead slaves were poorly dressed to resist the elements, though Mira assumed that they had been stripped of their outer garments by their fellows, once it became clear that the previous occupants no longer required protection from the cold. Some were horribly maimed, flesh torn to shreds by savage teeth and claws. Others had become a food source after dying, their emaciated bodies gnawed and torn by much smaller incisors. At one point Mira led her soldiers over a narrow stone bridge, stretched across a deep crevasse. Looking down as she passed, Mira noticed that the rocks far below were littered with corpses, twisted, and broken into impossible poses by their impact with the icy stone. She imagined the slaves toiling away to clear rocks and level the path, then the ground beneath their feet opening to swallow them and send them screaming to their doom. Mira shivered from more than the cold at the thought, and a traitorous voice in her head wondered whether their mission was worth such sacrifice, unwilling as it probably was.

A day out from the second resupply point, despite the best efforts of the work crews, the going became increasingly difficult. They rode steadily while daylight lasted, fording fast-running mountain rivers, and detouring around obstacles that no amount of forced labour could remove. There were more forgotten bodies to see too, and now they were not just slaves. Many of the discarded corpses were clearly Rutik soldiers, some even officers. Most were still armed and armoured where their bodies had fallen entirely out of reach. Mira wondered why her fellow soldiers would abandon her comrades so but reasoned that they had not seen any such bodies earlier because in the earlier stages of the route it was still feasible to collect the deceased and transport them home, or at least to a more suitable burial site. This high into the mountains, every man and woman, scout or soldier, craftsman or slave, was fighting for survival, every ounce of their energy devoted towards battling the freezing wind and avoiding the hidden pitfalls of the treacherous terrain. There was neither time nor resources to collect bodies, and so the soldiers, like their enslaved charges, were left on display for all to see — frozen monuments to a thousand doomed struggles.

By the third resupply point, the expedition had slowed to a crawl. Conditions were horrendous from dawn to dusk, and still worse through the night. The sun still shone but the air was so thin that it held no warmth at all, and the Rutik soldiers shivered and froze. Each night, dozens would lose fingers and toes to frostbite, sometimes even noses and ears. Each day they rode on wrapped up like ancient mummies, frost glittering on their cloaks and headscarves, their horses blanketed and blanketed again against the cold. Every morning, a handful did not rise at all, the biting cold having claimed them while they slept. At first, their commander ordered such casualties properly buried but soon, as had the patrols and slave masters before him, he surrendered to the inevitable and accepted that time spent burying the dead was only leading to still more deaths, and further casualties were mournfully left where they lay, frozen in sleep forever. Others were lost when cliff edges crumbled, or they stepped in the wrong place, or missed their footing and tumbled to their deaths in the rocky valleys far below. The mountains lost none of their grandeur and the views were no less startling, but their mounting toll cast them in a less majestic and far more sinister light.

After their column had passed, the Kingdom would have no further use for the hard-won passage, so they were gathering up the scouts and patrols along the way and adding the most able-bodied to their number. Those men brought tales of further horrors – soldiers carried off in the night by creatures that were almost human, but larger, stronger, and utterly terrifying. Casualties amongst the support train, following dutifully behind the main column, were even higher since the soldiers were in peak physical condition and equipped with the best protection against the cold that the Kingdom could muster. The followers were equipped with whatever they could find, and often were older or weaker than the soldiers and they died in their droves.

Ten days out from camp, their journey was interrupted by a drawn-out and extremely ominous rumbling, that echoed around the surrounding peaks, making it difficult to trace the origin. Reining in, Mira, turned this way and that, trying to identify the source of the disturbing sound. As she looked around, the sound grew louder and deeper, a deep grating rumble that soon became almost overwhelming. Mira realised it was an earthquake. Somewhere amidst the mountains that surrounded them, the ground was moving and settling. However, it was only when she saw the slopes nearest to them begin visibly shaking that Mira recognised the true danger. As she continued watching, the shaking grew more apparent, and the drifts of snow turned to heavier, deeper flows. Transfixed, knowing she was in terrible danger but with nowhere to go and nowhere to hide, Mira watched as massive chunks of rock and ice broke loose and tumbled towards the Rutik expedition. Boulders the size of barns bounced and rolled freely, carried on a current of smaller debris, mixed with equally gigantic chunks of ice and earth. In moments, the rumbling had risen to a thunderous crescendo as thousands of tons of mountainside shuddered itself loose and tumbled inexorably towards lower ground. Mira quickly lost sight of her troop, barely able to see even those immediately next to her as a cloud of swirling snow and bitterly cold vapour.

For a few minutes, everything was noise and movement as the entire world disappeared into chaos then, slowly, the sound began to die down and the air began to clear. As the road behind her began to reappear, Mira stared in horror to find that a huge swath of the column had disappeared. They had been

- Conqueror's City -

passing through what they thought was a relatively safe section of road, wide enough to ride five abreast, but still, the column of soldiers stretched over seven miles into the distance. For about half a mile directly behind her position, everyone seemed fine – shaken and battered by the sudden violence but otherwise intact. Beyond that though, for almost another half mile again the column was just gone. An entire section of road and everyone on it had been entirely swept up, crushed, and carried away by the falling mountainside, leaving only filthy rubble and settling snow behind. Ten days into their journey, Mira had the logistics engrained upon her mind and doing a quick calculation, she estimated that they had probably lost around fifteen hundred soldiers to the landslide. Adding back in those already lost to the cold and the environment, they had already lost perhaps a tenth of their number and they were not even halfway to their destination.

The remainder of the distance to the fourth resupply point was a slow, painful grind through appalling weather conditions and frequent small disasters. More soldiers and followers were lost as the Devil's Teeth did their best to bite. Those that remained were beaten down by the cold and the constant danger, tired, demoralised and struggling just to continue moving forward. The only people that seemed unphased by their journey were the representatives of the League for the Restoration of Rutik Glory. Ohtrad and his companions seemed almost to travel in a bubble of splendid isolation, as though the dangers of the mountain were something occurring elsewhere and not something they need concern themselves with. Normally they rode at the head of the column with the commander and his guard, with Mira and her troop a short distance behind. Occasionally Waldebert would drop back and attempt to engage her in conversation, but Mira was cold and miserable, and mostly ignored his overtures or dismissed him with a monosyllabic response. At other times, Ohtrad took his retinue further back in the column, lingering towards the rear and at times they strayed even further, riding out ahead or deliberately falling behind for reasons Mira did not care to guess at.

CHAPTER NINE

Achaean city of Tarsus
25 of Dios 870M - Mid Spring
One month before the siege of Tarsus

It is an accepted truth that nature prefers to remain true to certain fundamental principles. A stream springs forth in the mountains and the water flows downhill. A sparked flame springs upward without exception. The ground is beneath our feet, the sky above our heads. If it were not so, we might wake in the morning and find the world so utterly changed as to be unrecognisable. In such a realm, there would be no fixed outcome for any particular action, and a step forward could just as easily take a person backwards instead. Life absolutely requires a degree of certainty.

Cleitarchus, "The Natural Wonders of Asfáleia", c. 675M

Chapter Nine

The throne room in the Royal Palace of Tarsus was abuzz with excited chatter as the great and good of Tarsean society awaited the arrival of envoys from the Kingdom of the Rutik. Their war with the west had rumbled on for almost three years by that time, and the Tarseans were tired of the fighting, tired of their sons and daughters not returning home, tired of the constant mental attrition of news from the field, bad or good, it scarcely even mattered any more. Battles were won and ground was gained, battles were lost, and ground was forfeited. To the ordinary people of the city, those little twists and turns of fate were almost meaningless since few of them had even been to those places. At a deeper level, however, they knew that a battle lost on the banks of the Spercheios, ten miles south of Chalcis and eighty miles from Tarsus itself, brought the Rutik invaders that much closer to their own walls. Thus, the arrival of Rutik envoys was greeted with excited anticipation as the citizens of Tarsus hoped and wished for a peace treaty, an armistice, or even a lull in the fighting.

The throne room itself was breath-taking in its grandeur and beauty. Some thirty feet above, the ceiling sloped delicately towards a central peak, decorated with a series of intricately carved bosses, each the symbol of an enemy defeated, or an ally gained. The ceiling panels were ancient works of art, beautifully painted and edged in gilded carvings but darkened and almost obscured by centuries of torch smoke. Along either side of the room, forty feet apart, matching rows of soaring marble columns and half pilasters, supporting an upper level of smaller arches that in turn supported the ceiling. The side aisles beneath were narrow and bare, leaving nowhere for ne'er do wells to lurk unseen. The openings in the arcade above appeared to lead off to another level of the palace but were, in reality, blind and inaccessible, to prevent the throne room from being overlooked from above by spies or assassins. The floor beneath Arion's feet was set in luminous and chromatic marble, white as fresh snow, run through with geometric patterns in brilliant blue. A plush, velvet carpet in matching blue ran along the centre of the hall, drawing the eye immediately to the raised dais at the far end and the imposing golden throne thereon.

As was practice and tradition on such occasions, two hundred wooden chairs had been brought in and arranged in four rows of twenty-five, to either side of the centre aisle. The chairs ran from the front of the hall and almost halfway along its length and seated the thickest cream of the Tarsean nobility – the high lords and ladies that inhabited the palatial mansions on the northern side of the city. Between them, those two hundred owned most of the land in and around the city and controlled most of the wealth that flowed through it. Most were the progeny of eminent lineages stretching back into far antiquity. A few even boasted of ancestors that fought alongside Arrias the Conqueror, in his battles to establish the kingdom. Flowing robes, velvet and fur were much in evidence, and sparkling gems embedded in shining gold weighed down their necks, wrists, and fingers. A few of the older ladies wore delicate coronets but most wore their hair long, loose, and unadorned, as had been the fashion for the last few seasons. They sat and talked quietly amongst themselves, contributing little to the general furore but exchanging the piquant morsels of gossip and titbits of information that fed their endless machinations. Before the day was out, subtle but significant changes would have been made to the balance of power in the city. The lords and ladies would discuss who was in favour with the king, and who was not; who was amassing wealth and who was losing it; who was cheating on his wife, and who was cuckolding her husband. In their minds, the delicate balancing of such trivialities dictated the course of future alliances and drove decisions much more far-reaching than simple matters of state.

Larger and far louder crowds of people filled the remaining space between the seated area and the end of the throne room. Those further away were left to stand, not having earned the privilege of being seated, but they did not seem to resent the slight. Having arrived only recently, many were still pushing through the crowds to reach family, friends or a better vantage point. There was much shuffling and jostling, accompanied by the occasional sharp word and more than a few none-too-delicate curses. Those already settled talked loudly, laughing, joking, and paying little attention to their solemn surroundings. The majority were lesser nobility of one sort or another – minor lords, holders of untitled land or the younger sons and daughters of more illustrious parentage. A smattering were of a lower class still: bankers, merchants and the like, whose accumulated wealth afforded them a stature in society that their family name could not purchase. The atmosphere at the far end of the throne room was like that of a county fair, or the aftermath of some feast of celebration. Most of their number rarely had the opportunity to attend court, and the proximity of their betters, as well as the imminent arrival of their king, was the cause of much excitement. Some had begun their celebrations much earlier in the day and were now far louder and more raucous than strict protocol would have preferred.

Arion entered the throne room, preceded by two burly guards, and followed by his father's Lord Chancellor, the Commander of the Royal Legions and the Master of the Royal Mint, in strict order of precedence. Half a dozen lesser dignitaries followed: diplomats, strategists, and other such functionaries. A short distance behind them walked a clutch of nervous-looking scribes, translators, and clerks, followed finally by a second pair of guards. It was not the first time Arion had led such a procession, of course, but even so, when the doors opened and the wave of heat and sound washed over him, he faltered momentarily and almost stumbled. The Lord Chancellor reached out a liver-spotted hand to steady him, but Arion shook it off, straightened himself, raised his chin and marched solemnly into the room. The rear of the hall rang in a spontaneous ovation as he entered, accompanied by cheers, and shouted praise. The worthies towards the front fell silent instead but did allow him a small measure of carefully restrained applause.

Arion tried not to catch anyone's eye, knowing that his place was to appear aloof and untouched by such vulgar appreciation. Still, as he moved around the dais and turned towards the throne, he could only barely restrain a silly grin. His place was on a smaller throne, a short distance to the right of his father's and he carefully arranged his ceremonial robe before seating himself. Once he was settled, the three leading dignitaries positioned themselves to stand behind and a little to the right, so that they were almost directly behind Arion. The functionaries of state retreated further onto the dais and moved to the left, whilst the various forms of clerk continued past the dais entirely and took their places at a few small desks that had been placed off to one side. Arion's amusement deepened as he watched them all slot mechanically into their appointed positions. It reminded him of the cunning clockwork toys his father had once returned with following a trip to the Achaemenid Empire years before. He almost giggled as he remembered one of the toys falling apart after long use, scattering small cogs and wheels all over the nursery floor. Perhaps the same would happen if the Lord Chancellor were to fall over someday!

The two guards that had led Arion in took up their posts at the front corners of the dais, one to either side and, at some unseen signal, both snapped to attention and crashed the hafts of their halberds onto the floor – once, twice, three times. The noise in the hall subsided rapidly as the two guards cried out in unison:

"Order and silence for the arrival of your king! His Royal Highness, King Achaeus of Tarsus, Epirus, the united cities, and all the territories of Tarsus and beyond, Knight of the Order of Arrias, Defender of the Realm and Keeper of the Sacred Pact!" As the guard's words echoed around the hall, the lords and ladies rose as one to their feet and placed their right hands on their hearts, whilst those lesser mortals present fell to one knee and bowed their heads in supplication. The guards banged their halberds once more, the doors swung open again and Arion's father walked in. Achaeus wore a luxurious, pale blue robe that cut off exactly at floor-length, almost giving the impression that he was floating into the room rather than walking. A heavy golden chain hung around his neck, with a pendant in the shape of a lion's head, the eyes picked out in large, glinting sapphires. He also wore a golden crown, beautifully worked, and set with diamonds and sapphires but it was not the true Crown of Tarsus. The true crown was a much heavier and even more ostentatious affair and Achaeus was in the habit of not wearing it unless he had to, preferring the lighter, more delicate crown that he now wore. His empty, unadorned hands were clasped at waist height and his head turned neither left nor right as he took his place on the throne.

Once the King was seated, the guards banged their halberds one final time. Those standing were seated, and those kneeling rose to their feet to stare curiously at their ruler. Achaeus raised his right hand in greeting, then placed it across his heart, mirroring the gesture his higher nobles had made a moment before. As he lowered his hand once more, he stole a quick glance across at Arion, smiled subtly and winked. Still thinking about the clockwork toys, Arion almost forgot himself and winked back but managed to restrain himself. His father noticed his struggles, however, and his eyes glinted with amusement for a moment. Shifting slightly in his chair, Arion returned his gaze to the crowd as his father gestured to the Lord Chancellor, who in turn signalled the guards at the far end of the hall. One of the guards saluted in response and turned to knock sharply on the main doors. Nothing happened for a minute or two, and scattered murmuring and shuffling broke out amongst the crowd, though they quickly fell silent once again as the doors opened to admit the king's visitors.

Once again, the first through the doors were guards but this time they wore the emerald green of the Kingdom of the Rutik, rather than the pale blue of Tarsus. Also, unlike their Tarsean counterparts, they were unarmed, for no one save the Palace Guard were permitted to carry a weapon in the throne room. The two entered the room turned sharply to the left and right, and then moved to stand beside the Tarseans at the door. Next to enter was the Rutik consul and her husband. The ambassador was not well known to Arion, but he had been introduced to her before. She was an older woman, with greying hair with a hard face and narrow, suspicious eyes. Arion had not cared for her when they met, finding her tone abrasive and unpleasant. Her husband was taller and somewhat younger, dressed in a black leather tunic, sporting a silver badge in the shape of the Rutik wolf on his right breast. His face was blank and fixed as he matched his wife's steps, but Arion noticed his eyes moving around the room, taking in everything that was to be seen. The pair continued until they were approximately two-thirds of the way along the aisle then stopped, bowed stiffly to the King, and then stood to one side.

"Achaeus of Tarsus," the consul said loudly. "May I introduce His Grace Videric, Principal Counsellor to her Majesty the Queen of the Rutik, Keeper of the Royal Seal and Higher Master of The League for the Preservation of Rutik Glory." The consul's last words were almost drowned out by outraged murmurs at the disrespectful form of address for the King of Tarsus. One of the guards banged his halberd for silence but the murmurs quickly became loud conversation as the Rutik envoy's titles were pronounced. Few amongst the crowd had any real idea of what The League for the Restoration of Rutik Glory was, or what it stood for, but all had heard the rumours. Considering the stories, Arion was not sure what he had expected from this representative of the League but a part of him was disappointed when a rather ordinary-looking man walked through the doors and into the throne room.

His Grace Videric was of average height, and his head was completely shaven, his skin smooth and unwrinkled, making his age hard to judge. His face resembled a diving hawk, utterly focused on its prey, and he walked into the throne room as though in no rush, utterly unphased by the gilded surroundings, the large crowd or the king that was waiting for him on the throne. A heavy, golden chain of office dangled from his neck, a massive pendant in the shape of a wolf's head resting on his chest and he carried a long staff of black wood, topped with a spherical knob of solid gold, the end of which clicked rhythmically against the pristine floor tiles as he walked. Arion noticed that both the Consul and her husband had bowed their heads as he entered, their eyes fixed firmly on their feet, and Videric made no acknowledgement of their presence. He glanced at the King to find him staring fixedly at the newcomer. Arion noticed a slight curl in the corner of his father's mouth, as though distaste or irritation warred for control of his features.

The two figures that followed Videric into the throne room, however, were anything but ordinary in their appearance. Both were tall and of sturdy build, looming over the assembled crowd like outsized statues somehow come to life. Their exact features were impossible to discern, for they wore long, forest green cloaks, held tightly around their bodies, with deep hoods that hid their faces in shadow. The hoods were yet another breach of protocol, for it was forbidden for anyone to approach the king with their head covered. From the angle of their hoods, the pair were looking straight ahead and although he could not see their eyes, Arion felt as though they were both staring directly at him. A feeling of immense unease struck him, unfocused and without obvious cause but deeply rooted and almost palpable in its intensity. It was as though he were trapped in a most terrible nightmare, knowing that some horrific danger approached from somewhere out of sight. Tearing his gaze from the two men, he realised that the entire crowd of Tarsean nobility had fallen silent. Several of the higher lords were gripping the arms of their chairs, their knuckles tight and straining. Those further down the room were wide-eyed, and a number appeared to be shaking. Turning back to his father, Arion saw that although the colour had drained from King Achaeus's face, his expression was now definitely one of barely restrained anger. Like Videric, however, the two cloaked men seemed oblivious to the effect they were having on the watching crowd, and the three continued to advance until they were close to the throne and then stopped, Videric slightly ahead, the other two positioned to his either shoulder.

Videric looked up and opened his mouth as though to speak but Achaeus raised a hand to warn him into silence.

"Commander," he said, turning to address the leader of the Palace Guard. "Clear the room. Only your own guards are to remain."

"Yes, your majesty." The Commander snapped to attention and moved quickly to order the sudden evacuation. Normally, Arion would have expected the onlookers to object to being denied their opportunity for entertainment but on this occasion, they seemed more than happy to be leaving. The guards' main difficulty appeared to be in preventing their retreat from turning into a rout as they struggled to empty the room in an orderly manner. Achaeus watched silently until the last of the onlookers were evicted, and the doors were closed once more before turning back to look at Videric.

"What is the meaning of this? We were expecting diplomats and negotiators, not some… cultists, and whatever these two are. How dare you?" The colour flooded back into Achaeus's face as he spoke, his anger getting the better of him.

At that moment, Arion noticed that the Commander had not returned to the dais but now stood with his men, his hand on the hilt of his sword, watching the Rutik party closely. Nor had the guards returned to their previous positions at the doors, or along the sides of the room. They were now clustered into three groups: one behind the Rutik, spread to either side of their Commander, and the other two to either side of the dais itself. Their halberds were not lowered but were gripped tightly with both hands and Arion could see the tension in their stances as they readied themselves for sudden movement. Surely his father did not expect actual violence to follow. Who were these people to command such an extreme response? Feeling exposed, he squirmed in his chair as these, and other questions chased each other around his head. He felt his panic rising and swallowed deeply, trying to force down his fear but unable to master it entirely. By contrast, Videric seemed entirely at ease with developments and paid no attention at all to the manoeuvring of the guards, or the king's obvious anger.

"King Achaeus," he said finally. A small smile flickered across his face as he spoke, twisting the corners of his mouth slightly but never reaching his eyes, as though he found something vaguely humorous in the title.

"Your majesty, we are not a diplomatic mission, there will be no negotiation, and the Kingdom of the Rutik has no interest in flattering your ego. Her Royal Majesty, Malasintha, Queen of the Rutik, has charged me with delivering a message." He gestured to the men behind him, one of whom reached beneath his cloak and produced a short but intricately carved hatchet. For a moment, the room rang with the scrape of metal as the Tarsean guards lowered their halberds and inched forward, and the Commander's sword swept from its sheath in one smooth, practised movement. Videric seemed unperturbed, however, and merely reached for the small axe, and then turned back to hold it before the king, resting on his upturned palms like a platter of sweetmeats offered to a guest.

"It is traditional in Rutik society, King Achaeus, for the death of an enemy to be bought with the shedding of blood – normally through the ceremonial sacrifice of hostages, or those of the enemy's citizens resident in a Rutik settlement. However, since we have neither of those things at this moment, I am to present you with this weapon as a token of our intentions." He bent slowly to place the hatchet on the steps of the dais, without taking his eyes off the king.

"In the interests of preserving tradition, however, which is amongst the highest callings of the League, I am also to inform you that by the time our audience is complete, your outpost on the shores of the Köningssee Lake will lie in ruins, every man, woman, and child therein sacrificed to the glory of the Kingdom of the Rutik. Finally, I am to inform you that Tarsus will meet the same fate. The Rutik are coming, *King* Achaeus, and death follows with us." Achaeus sprang to his feet at the man's words, his face a mask of fury.

"How dare you?" he repeated, his voice a cracked roar of outrage. "How dare you? I should have you cut down where you stand for this insult!" The Commander and his guards had reacted slowly, as shocked by the Rutik announcement as their leader but now they levelled their weapons and made to advance. Videric did not spare them so much as a glance.

"That would be ill-advised," he said and as he spoke, the two men at his shoulders turned slowly, each raising their right hand, palms outward, fingers splayed wide.

Arion groaned and clutched his head as a tremendous throbbing pain swelled into life behind his eyes and his ears popped painfully as though from a sudden increase in air pressure. Achaeus appeared similarly afflicted, staggering back but managing to steady himself with a shaking hand on the arm of the throne. Three of the guards closest to the Rutik party dropped to the floor with a discordant, jangling crash of armour and dropped weapons. Two more fell to their knees, tearing off their helms to snatch gasping, laboured breaths, ruby-red blood pouring from their noses and ears. The Commander and most of the other guards cried out in pain and fell back, colliding blindly with each other and seemingly unable to control their movements. The fallen guards lay unmoving, save for the occasional twitch of a hand or foot. Blood was now pouring out from beneath their helms, pooling on the floor around their heads. The two Rutik completed their turns and returned to their previous positions, as though never having stirred at all, unmoved by the chaos they had inflicted upon the Tarseans.

"Ill-advised, indeed," Videric continued, his tone even and lacking in emotion. He seemed almost bored by the audience now, evidently satisfied with having said his piece.

"We were provided with rooms upon our arrival in your city. They are small, but adequate for our needs. We will rest there for the night and set out for Rutiksborg at dawn. I strongly suggest that my associates be permitted a peaceful night. Any disturbance of their rest is unlikely to be well received." With that, and without even waiting for any response from Achaeus, he turned and walked unhurriedly out of the room, followed by the two other Rutik.

Back in the throne room, the pain in Arion's head was gradually receding and he watched as his father sank into the throne, rubbing at his face with his hands. The Commander gritted his teeth and moved to check on the fallen guards.

"They're dead, your majesty," he reported a moment later. "What in the name of Arrias was that?" The other guards were moaning and moving gingerly but mostly back on their feet. The Commander despatched one of them to fetch assistance and more guards, then sent the rest to positions around the room. When he turned back to the throne his face was strained and pale, his eyes bloodshot and slightly wild looking.

"Compose yourself, Commander. Arion, are you alright?" Looking up slowly, Achaeus now turned to his son, his movements tight and carefully controlled. He was retaining his composure only by sheer force of will, but his fortitude was comforting to Arion, and he almost managed a smile before responding.

"Yes father, I'm fine." Achaeus stared at him for a moment, clearly concerned, before turning back to the Commander.

"See to it that these men are buried with honours, Commander. And see to it that neither you nor your guards speak of what happened here to anyone outside of this room. Is that entirely clear?" Still shaky, the Commander took a deep breath and bowed in acknowledgement.

"Good. The quarters assigned to the Rutik are to be isolated and watched closely but no one is to interfere with them unless they attempt to break out into the palace. I also want a scouting party despatched to Köningssee Lake immediately. Their orders are to evaluate the situation and return here with all haste." Arion marvelled at his father's rapid recovery as the king rattled off his orders, scarcely seeming to pause for a breath. His thoughts were jumbled, and he was finding it difficult to process what was going on around him. The throne room seemed to be coming back to life, however, as a pack of servants arrived to attend to the fallen, accompanied by a fresh company of guards.

"And summon my generals, Commander – three hours from now, I want them assembled in my chambers for a council of war."

That night, when the rest of the palace was silent and sleeping, a large contingent of the Palace Guard remained awake and watchful, a human cordon thrown around the Rutik quarters. None of those present had been in the throne room earlier in the day but they had been well warned of the danger presented by their charges and were determined to fulfil their duty. A long corridor led past the other guest rooms, all of which had been vacated and the doors locked and barred. At either end, a full dozen Guards were stationed, deemed to be a safe distance away but also with a full view of anything that moved in the corridor. Guards had also been posted outside in the gardens, watching the windows, and more were patrolling the other areas of the palace. Nothing was being left to chance: if the Rutik so much as stirred in their sleep, the Guards would know about it and the alarm would be raised. What would happen next was anyone's guess but if it required them to sell their lives dearly to protect their king, the Guards were prepared to do so.

Shortly before midnight, two figures emerged from the room. The dark green of their cloaks appeared even darker in the torchlight and their outlines were blurred and wavering, as though slipping in and out of shadow. Nevertheless, it seemed impossible that the guards would not see them. The corridor was only six feet wide, and all ornaments and furniture that might have served for cover had been carefully removed. At either end of the corridor, a dozen pairs of eyes were open and watchful. And yet, somehow, the guards did not see them. Exiting the room, one figure turned to the right and the other to the left and both proceeded to their respective ends of the corridor without the guards so much as twitching. From there, they slipped through the silent palace, brushing past guard stations and ignoring patrols, the one headed deeper into the palace and into the tunnels and caves that ran far below, the other remaining above the surface, calling at the throne room, the king's quarters, and a handful of other locations.

By the time dawn broke over the city, both figures had returned to their room and still, the guards did not register their movements. Nothing obvious had changed to mark their passage but in the shadows behind the Tarsean throne, under the king's bed and in dozens of other places in the palace and beneath the wider city, purple gems flashed and winked. The gems had been carefully hidden, so as not to be visible to passers-by or any others who might come looking and their light was dim, sickly looking, and unlikely to draw any attention. They were the size of a large raspberry, and perfectly smooth on the surface but deep within they were filled with roiling, churning clouds of oily black smoke. Where there was air around them, it seemed to shiver somewhat, rippling like the heat above a fire.

Achaeus turned over in his sleep and woke with a moan as the snaking tendrils of a dark nightmare slowly unwound from his mind. The room was dark, the heavy curtains and outer shutters blocking out most of the moonlight and he sat up in bed blinking around in near blindness. He was not prone to nightmares and generally slept soundly so being awake in the night was unusual for him. He tried to remember the details of it, or even why he had been so frightened, but it was slipping away in chunks that slowly disappeared below the surface of his mind like rocks dropped into a bog. All he was left with was a vague sense of anguish and loss, the memory of unmanageable fear, and a raging headache. Settling back under the covers, he closed his eyes and waited for sleep to return. It took a while, and when he finally dropped off, the nightmare was there waiting for him.

Under the bed, the tiny purple gem grew dark when Achaeus awoke, and sparked back into life as soon as he returned to sleep.

CHAPTER TEN

Achaean city of Tarsus
26 of Dios 870M - Mid Spring
A month before the siege of Tarsus

The twin mountain ranges known as "The Devil's Teeth" are unique in that their very existence defies any conventional explanation. Moreover, amidst their soaring peaks the most uncompromising laws of nature are reduced to mere suggestions, to be disregarded at a whim. How did such a place come to be? By what power is it permitted to endure? To a man of science, the Devil's Teeth mountains are a series of riddles without plausible solutions.

Cleitarchus, "The Natural Wonders of Asfáleia", c. 675M

Chapter Ten

Hippotas the Younger, son of Hippotas the Elder lived a blameless life, causing little trouble to anyone and making few if any enemies. He was short and not particularly handsome, but he kept himself clean and tidy, his greying black hair cropped tightly, and his robes of office always carefully pressed. Along with his name, he had inherited a position in the Tarsean bureaucracy and there he carried out a small but vital function in the transfer of legal ownership between buyers and sellers of property. His job was to check the copy of the deeds that the city kept on file, against the copy submitted by the seller. If everything was in order, he would use his stamp marked

'Approved' and send both documents to the city magistrate's office. If there was some issue with the signature, the seal, or some other discrepancy between the two documents, he would use his stamp marked 'For Review' and send both documents to the city magistrate's office.

The work required him to have a good eye for detail but was otherwise unchallenging. Most people would have found it boring and repetitive, but Hippotas knew that an orderly and trusted system of property transfer was fundamental to the city's economy, and he was proud to play his part in it. His pay was meagre enough, but since he had neither a spouse nor a family, and little in the way of hobbies or interests, it was enough for him to live on. The city required Hippotas to work six days a week, from early in the morning until the six o'clock bell. Upon hearing the bell, he would gather up his things, wish a polite farewell to his fellow clerks and walk a short distance through the city to the King's Arms tavern. The King's Arms was a quiet spot, and the owners kept it meticulously clean, which Hippotas appreciated. He would stay long enough to consume a meal and a small cup of wine before heading home to retire early to his bed. Normally, he found the brief sojourn calming after a hard day's work but as he left that night his mind was restless and he walked home with his head down, lost in thought.

The problem, he believed, was that he had not been getting enough sleep lately. What little sleep he was getting was shallow and unsatisfying. Different variations of the same dream seemed determined to interrupt his rest. Sometimes the dream took place in the offices where he worked. Other times, in the boarding house where he lived. Once or twice, it had taken him to other places entirely, places he neither knew nor recognised. Wherever the setting, the dream would invariably begin with him surrounded by people, all chatting happily and courteously exchanging niceties. Hippotas did not recognise the other people, but he knew somehow that they were significant to him, and that he craved their approval. They would discuss the weather, his work, his health, and other such mundanities, punctuated with friendly smiles and warm laughter. Sometimes there would be wine passed around, and sweet cakes or savoury titbits.

After a while though, the dream's day would wear on and the shadows in the room would begin to grow. One after another, the other people would wander into the shadows. There they would linger for a while, deep in conversation with some unseen other party. When they re-emerged into the light, their smiles were gone, and they were silent and sullen. They watched Hippotas from the corners of their eyes and would turn away if he approached, ignoring his greetings. Offended, he would turn to some other person and strike up a conversation but eventually, all the other people had visited the shadows at some point or other, and there was no one left for him to talk to. Try as he might, he could never hear what was being said in the shadows, and all he could make out were whispers. Nor had he the courage to enter the shadows himself. Something lurked in there, something dark, he could feel it in his bones, and the whispers sent anxious shivers through his body.

As more people emerged from the shadows, the atmosphere in the room became progressively less congenial. Those who Hippotas approached greeted him with frosty disdain, or outright hostility. Those he passed by were talking amongst themselves and Hippotas could hear them deprecating his work, his personality, and his appearance. They called him a jobsworth, a scroll-shuffler, and a dogsbody. They would say he was boring, uncouth, and ill-mannered. They would remark upon his height, the uneven set of his ears, or some stain or tear in his clothing that he could not see. The chorus of complaints and insults would rise and rise, fuelled, and encouraged by more whispers from the shadows. Eventually, someone would throw something, a piece of food usually, and it would bounce off his head, scattering crumbs in a shower across his robe. He would try and brush off the remains, but more would follow, hitting him from in front and behind. Heavier objects were thrown – cups and plates, followed by books, ornaments and whatever else came to hand. The crowd would begin to jeer at every impact, laughing as he was knocked one way or the other, cheering when he stumbled or threw up an arm to protect his face. They would begin to jostle and push him roughly, their sneering faces looming close for a moment. Something would strike him hard on the back of the head, a small statue perhaps, or some other weighty object. His vision would go black, and he would fall to the floor with a cry.

The crowd would gather around and begin kicking him, viciously hard: in the back, the stomach, and the head. Some of them had sticks now, heavy canes with solid brass handles and they beat him without mercy until he could feel bones fracture and break. Usually, his ribs broke first, followed by an arm perhaps, and then his nose. The beatings would continue until Hippotas was barely alive and still his attackers would not relent. Blood was in his eyes; he could no longer see. His teeth were smashed, and he could not even cry out anymore. The voices around him faded and became hollow, as though heard from a distance or through a thick pane of glass. As the final blow crashed down, however, cracking his skull and crushing his brain, he could still hear the whispering from the shadows. Now it was laughing though. Laughing at him, revelling in his pain, celebrating his imminent death.

Hippotas invariably woke from his dreams drenched in sweat and shivering, regardless of the temperature in his room. He felt as though he had not slept at all and somehow his body still ached from the beatings. There were no obvious bruises or other marks, but the pain stayed with him during the day, making him uncomfortable no matter what position he tried to adopt. He would find himself sitting at his desk staring at some document or other, seeing nothing, lost in his head with voices swirling around in his mind, mocking him, insulting him, taunting him. His work was suffering, he knew that for a fact. Just that very morning, the Senior Clerk had pulled him aside to let him know that the lawyers had complained about documents not being stamped correctly. The Senior Clerk had not been angry with him, he was a kindly old man who had grown up with his father and Hippotas was a good worker. He spoke gently, but Hippotas recognised the scorn beneath his tone: it was well hidden, but he could hear it. If this continued, he would face censure, perhaps lose his job, bringing shame and destitution. Why was this happening to him? It wasn't fair. All those people laughing at him – what had he ever done to deserve that? He had turned and walked away from the Senior Clerk without a word, blood pounding in his ears.

Reaching his lodgings, he gave a heavy sigh and lifted the latch, pulling the creaky door open and slipping inside. He had hoped to avoid his elderly landlady, but she was sitting at the table as he entered, going through her accounts. She looked up as he entered, and said something innocuous, a greeting perhaps but Hippotas could not hear her. The whispering was back, louder now, and impossible to ignore. It was grating on his nerves, setting his teeth on edge. His landlady spoke again, tilting her head and frowning as though looking at a particularly complicated mathematical equation. Hippotas could only hear the whispering, but he caught the look in her eyes – all feigned concern and shallow friendliness. She was laughing at him too, underneath her kindly exterior. Hippotas was not fooled. The whispering became more insistent still: taunting him again, goading him. The Senior Clerk, his landlady, the bartender at the tavern, those young men he had passed in the street, they were all mocking him. His ears were thumping again, and a sudden, vicious headache was making it hard to think. Sparks began to dance in front of his eyes and still, the whispering continued. Why was this happening to him? It was unbearable. Soon the jostling would start, and then the sticks would surely follow. He just couldn't stand it anymore. Not again.

"And who is going to stop it?" the whispers asked. Then, laughing: "You? You're nothing. Worse than nothing. Pond scum. Animal excrement. A filthy stain on humanity."

"Leave me alone!" Hippotas shouted, staggering into the room and almost falling as his left foot caught on the leg of a stool. His landlady was on her feet, staring at him, wide-eyed. She looked scared. He had frightened her. Good. She would not be so quick to disrespect him next time. She spoke, but her words were little more than a jumble of noisy nonsense. Was she mocking him again? The whispers agreed that she was, laughing at her scornful abuse. Hippotas spotted a heavy, cast-iron saucepan on a hook beside the water basin, washed and ready for use in the morning.

As he turned around with the pan in his hand, the old lady screamed in terror and tried to dart around the table, heading for the door. The whispers were quicker, however, and at their prompting, Hippotas cut off her path. As she cast about looking for some other avenue of escape, Hippotas stepped closer, swung the iron pan over his head and brought it down as hard as he could manage. He was not a strong man, but the blow caught her just above her left ear, cracking her skull and sending her crumpling to the floor. He swung the pan again, bending to reach her fallen body. The pan hit her in the face this time, smashing her nose and cheekbones. He swung again, and again, and again, and again until blood spattered the walls, and broken teeth, bits of bone and even lumps of flesh and hair were scattered across the floor. Finally, he dropped the pan, battered, and dented now and covered in gore. The old lady's head was essentially gone – crushed into a pulpy mess of blood and brains. Hippotas stared for a moment, looking slightly baffled, then carefully replaced the pan on its hook and pottered off to bed. That night, for the first time in weeks, he slept soundly.

The story of Hippotas was that of madness and senseless tragedy. Had it happened in isolation, it would have been forgotten as soon as the clerk was arrested, tried, and convicted. Hippotas would have been sentenced to death, or if the judges were feeling lenient, to live out the remainder of his years in a penal colony. Either way, it would have been a tragic and meaningless ending to a tragic and meaningless story. Neither Hippotas nor his landlady was of much importance in the scheme of things, and neither left behind a family to grieve, and Tarsus was a large city, housing almost three-quarters of a million souls within her walls, and a quarter more in the slums outside the walls. Such things were uncommon but not unheard of. The story of Hippotas, however, was only one tragedy amongst a multitude that befell the people of Tarsus at that time.

That same night, one of the palace guards leapt from his cot in the barracks and began roaring nonsensical threats and battle cries at unseen assailants, before grabbing his sword and turning on his newly awakened comrades. One guard was killed, and four others were injured before the remainder managed to put the man down. Much like Hippotas, the guard had never previously shown any signs of madness. The following night, a mother in the lower city strangled her five children, one of whom was only a newborn, still wrapped in swaddling cloth. The deed done, she laid them out neatly on the bed that they shared, and then threw herself from a window, falling five stories to meet her death on the paved street below. A cobbler returned from work and stabbed his wife; a tavernkeeper poisoned her ale supply and twelve people died in agony; a child pushed her playmate off the top of a high wall, laughing as the other girl fell; an elderly couple somehow armed themselves with crossbows, barricaded their house and began shooting passers-by from the upper windows; and so on, and on and on. Heartbreak and calamity were everywhere, spreading across the city like a most virulent disease.

After a week of such happenings, Corraidhín found a trail at one of the gory scenes. Upon hearing of the first such incident, and even the second, he had, like everyone else, put the killings down to freak occurrences brought on by the stress of the siege, or perhaps the work of Rutik spies or sympathisers. He heard of the third and fourth simultaneously, from a reliable contact in the merchant district. The contact was a man in his mid-fifties, moderately successful and not given to flights of fancy. Thus, when he described the extreme carnage wrought in two separate places, almost at the same time, wide-eyed and in graphic detail, Corraidhín began to suspect that something more sinister was occurring. He visited the two scenes, but the bodies had been removed by that time and any traces obliterated by the Sheriff's or the cleaners. He missed the next killing too, only hearing of it almost twenty-four hours later. Then he got lucky, for a certain definition of lucky, and the next murder occurred close enough to where he happened to be at the time, that he heard the screams and was able to reach the scene whilst it was still fresh and undisturbed.

The trail was nothing so simple as bloody footprints, or a scrap of torn clothing, but he had learned his craft in the woods of the Illyan Isles, tracking nymphs and faeries through the leafy glades. There were other types of spoors to be found and less mundane trails to be followed and Corraidhín knew their secrets well. He was only in the city at all, of course, because Radomir was there, called to duty on the walls in anticipation of the Rutik invasion. Where Radomir travelled, Corraidhín followed, or often the other way around, so it was natural that upon finding the mysterious trail, his first move was to find the burly Bulġha and recruit him to the cause. As ever, Radomir had listened to his explanations, rolled his eyes, and gathered up his kit without a word. And so it was that the two men found themselves pushing their way through dusty cobwebs in the tunnels and caves far beneath the Palace of Tarsus. The trail had led to a house in the upper city and from there to the cellars below. From the cellars, they made their way down a narrow brick-lined passageway until they were directly underneath the palace gates. There the path forked, then forked again and it was some time before Corraidhín could pick up the trail once more. Now they were tired and filthy from crawling through gaps and pushing past rubble and debris to get to long-abandoned spaces and still the trail continued.

"This is a waste of time." Radomir's customary snarl was low-pitched and gravelly but still somehow shockingly loud in the confined space and Corraidhín turned quickly to raise a shushing finger to his lips. After a moment's silence, he turned back and whispered over his shoulder.

"Patience, my friend, we are close now – I can feel it."

Radomir grunted in disgust but obediently lowered his voice a little further.

"You said that an hour ago."

"An hour ago, we were close, now we are closer."

"I should be on the walls. King's orders." In the flickering torchlight, Corraidhín grinned. He and Radomir had known each other for almost a decade and had spent years of that time travelling the length and breadth of Asfáleia, as often following their instincts as following the king's commands. He knew the bigger man well enough to know that his discomfort was more a product of their claustrophobic surroundings than any imperative to be obedient.

"It seems to me that the King's Rangers are wont to follow the spirit of his orders, rather than the letter. The king commanded you, commanded all of us, to defend the city and that is exactly what we're doing. Albeit not exactly as he intended it, I accept."

Radomir grunted again and shrugged, turning the movement into a groaning stretch, his broad shoulders almost touching both sides of the tunnel simultaneously. He seemed about to respond but Corraidhín froze, raising his right hand into the Ranger's sign to hold fast. Radomir had his massive axe slung across his back but held the torch in one hand and the weapon was unsuitable for use in such close quarters anyway. Silently, he pulled a heavy, long-bladed knife from its scabbard on his leg and waited in perfect stillness, like a canny mountain lion, waiting on the sight of its prey. The smaller man whispered without moving, continuing to stare forward into the darkness.

"Twenty feet ahead the tunnel opens out into a larger space. There is something there. I don't know what it is, but it hears us and is waiting." Radomir did not question his comrade's statement. Over the years he had gotten used to trusting Corraidhín's extraordinary senses that had alerted both to danger often in the past. Corraidhín unstrapped his short stabbing spear and held it two-handed, pointing the way. He had brought the spear with him from his island home and the shaft was narrow and light, looking almost flimsy. Radomir could not identify the dark, seemingly ungrained wood from which it was made but knew that it was far stronger than it looked. The point of the spear was black: meteoric iron, Corraidhín had once said. There were no natural sources of metal on the Isles, and they were a reclusive people, shunning all trade with the other nations of Asfáleia so perhaps iron that fell from the sky was the only kind they could get. Corraidhín glanced back over his shoulder and gestured to his right and Radomir nodded, tacitly understanding the plan.

As quietly as possible, the two moved along the passage and out into the space beyond, Corraidhín immediately moving to the left of the entrance to allow Radomir to follow and move to the right. They found themselves in a large, high-ceilinged room, the far corners of which were cluttered with battered crates, broken shelves, and discarded bric-a-brac of one sort or another. The Tarsean palace had grown over the centuries and as new wings were added, older areas were neglected and closed off. Even the original palace had been built atop far older structures, some of which remained intact, albeit forgotten and lost beneath the deepest cellars. Below that again were the natural tunnels and caves that, it was said, could be followed all the way to the city of Menos in the far north, if one could only find their way. Rooms such as the one they now entered were a common discovery, former storerooms that were no longer required or no longer useful. Radomir's torch guttered and almost died out as he slotted it into a convenient bracket on the wall. Dark shadows leapt in all directions by the light of the moving flame and then settled, seeming to merge into a single black silhouette in the centre of the room. The two men kept their weapons raised and continued to circle to either side as the shadow coalesced into a vaguely human shape, its features indistinguishable save for two glowing red eyes and a mouthful of long fangs that glinted orange in the torchlight.

Neither man needed the other to shout orders or telegraph their next moves. Radomir was the battering ram, smashing their enemies' defences, or he was the bulwark blunting their attack. Either way, Corraidhín was the light cavalry, dashing in as soon as the other man provided an opening, attacking with lightning speed, the tip of his spear stabbing and slicing, finding the smallest chinks in the target's armour. Radomir buried his knife deep into the creature's neck and twisted it as he withdrew, aiming to cause maximum damage. However, it seemed unphased by the gaping wound and scarcely seemed to notice the impact of Corraidhín's spear in its lower back. Raising a clawed hand slowly, it swept around almost casually and caught Radomir in the chest at a speed that defied the weirdly languid movement. Radomir's studded leather armour protected him from serious harm, but the impact knocked him from his feet, sending him flying backwards to crash into a stack of old crates that immediately collapsed, cushioning his landing but filling the air with choking dust and splinters.

As the creature turned its attention to Corraidhín, the islander began moving faster, his spearpoint a dark blur. Moments later, the creature was wounded in a dozen places but still apparently unimpaired. Over and again, Corraidhín ducked and weaved, avoiding its vicious swings, and striking back with astonishing precision and control. The creature seemed unable to catch him as he danced around it, stepping to one side, then the other, then past it to strike again from the rear. It howled in anger at that, frustrated rage adding a new speed to its movements and in minutes, Corraidhín was having to devote all his attention to dodging its blows. As a demonstration of ability and control, his was a masterful performance but it would have been clear to anyone watching that it could not go on forever. Sooner or later, Corraidhín would tire, or make a mistake, one of those blows would connect and that would be the end of the matter. It was clear to Corraidhín too, but he also knew something that no other could: he did not have to hold forever, only for long enough.

With a roar, Radomir surged out of the darkness, draped in cobwebs, and coated in dust, his battle-axe now freed of its straps and grasped tightly in both hands above. The creature had no time to react as the axe descended upon it like a crash of thunder dropping from the heavens, catching it on its right, between shoulder and neck, where its collarbone would have been, had it been any natural animal. The impact was soundless and seemed to have little effect on the creature, but the momentum of the heavy blade carried it downward, through its chest and out again above its left hip. Cut clean through, the creature's top half slid sideways onto the floor, whilst its legs remained upright and in place, bizarrely unaffected. Radomir swung his axe back up as the creature's torso began pulling itself towards him and with two swift blows, he removed both its arms at the shoulders. Corraidhín stepped back in to drive his spear into its lower back once more, vertically from above, pinning it to the rough planks of the floor. The creature screeched in frustration, the sound painful and grating to the two men, and then was quickly silenced as Radomir struck twice more – removing its head from its shoulders, and then stepping around its dismembered body to split the head in half along its length. No longer able to screech and unable to move, the creature gave a single, lingering gurgle before sighing into collapse.

As the two men watched, the creature's body parts began to smoke and dissolve leaving little behind a moment later but a stinking grey residue. Radomir planted the head of his axe on the ground and rested on the haft, watching as it soaked into the floor. Exhausted, Corraidhín looked around and then moved to sit on a nearby crate, his spear across his knees.

"What," said Radomir. "The five kinds of fucking fuck was that?" Corraidhín shrugged wearily.

"I don't know. Nothing good." Radomir tore his eyes away from their defeated enemy and looked at him, his now tender expression seeming out of place on his harsh, craggy features.

"Are you hurt?"

"No, my friend. Not hurt – just winded. Give me a moment to catch my breath." Corraidhín looked up and smiled but Radomir grunted, and his face reassumed its habitual scowl. Reaching for a nearby piece of broken wood, he lowered himself to a crouch and poked at the creature's remains. Where the tip touched the residue, it began to blacken and Radomir quickly dropped the wood and rose to step back.

"Never seen that before." He shrugged and looked around for something to clean his blade with. Pulling a tattered canvas off a nearby pile of old furniture he began industriously scrubbing at the sticky ichor that coated the steel axe head. The blade was deeply engraved with angular symbols, marking his Bulǵha ancestry. Radomir's people now dwelt in the furthest reaches of Asfáleia, living hard brutal lives in the shadows of the frozen mountains. Once they had roamed across the plains in large numbers but the arrival of the Achaeans, millennia before, had seen an end to their dominance. The remaining Bulǵha clans were reclusive but forced to constantly defend their homes from the ravages of the Achaeans, the Rutik, wild animals, and the far worse creatures that descended from the mountains. Their travails had produced a warrior people, men and women who learned to fight as soon as they could walk and feared almost nothing, having already seen the worst the world could throw at them.

The Bulǵha also tended to be pragmatic in outlook and not given to pondering mysteries. Hence, Radomir disregarded the creature's remains almost as soon as his blade was cleaned. Corraidhín was more interested but seemed unwilling to approach what was now little more than a dark stain on the floor.

"Yours was a blow well struck, my friend," he said finally. "Whatever that was, there is little doubt that the world is better off without it."

"Ha. Well, if you want something killed, I'm your man. Can we go now?"

"Yes, of course – lead the way." Corraidhín's tone was light, but his brow was creased with worry. Radomir slung his axe and retrieved his knife and the torch before leaving the room to return to the cramped tunnels. Corraidhín lingered for a moment after, staring at the patch on the floor, his mind racing, then turned to go. He was deeply unsettled, as though the strange creature had left a dark shadow on his mind. Feeling the darkness that closed around him, he hurried into the passage to catch up with Radomir and the warm, comforting light of his torch.

CHAPTER ELEVEN

The Royal Palace, City of Tarsus
3 of Euthaios 870M - Late Spring
Three days before the siege of Tarsus

The venerable philosophers and distinguished theologists of the Achaemenid Empire posit that religion is essential to our understanding of the world. Without gods, they say, how will the sun rise in the morning, or set at night? Without gods, what will become of our immortal souls when our frail vessels of flesh and bone are exhausted and done? However, the very nature of their questions reveals the weakness of their position. Their gods are nothing but an easy solution to intractable problems, a way to explain the inexplicable. Their adherence to religion is a form of intellectual weakness – an inability to simply say "I do not know".

Polemon of Chalcis, "Religion and philosophy in Asfáleia", c. 965M

Chapter Eleven

Achaeus the Third, King of Tarsus, ruler of the greatest city in Asfáleia, mighty in battle and wise in judgement, fell to his knees, clasped his hands to his breast and keeled over onto his side on the floor, with a long, gurgling groan. He froze as he hit the floor, not moving a muscle for a good twenty seconds before slowly opening one eye to see his three young sons all staring at him with doubtful expressions.

"Stop opening your eyes father, you're supposed to be dead!"

With a dramatic sigh, Achaeus closed his eyes and feigned death once more. Arion was not so easily fooled, however, and poked him sharply in the ribs with his wooden sword, just to be sure. In the background, Achaeus could hear his other sons, the twin boys Athilas and Epilas giggling quietly. The twins were almost four years younger than Arion, scarcely more than toddlers at the time. Dark-haired and pale-skinned, small for their age, the twins rarely spoke, and a quiet giggle was the closest they ever came to outright mirth. The twins were introverted, whereas Arion was a friend to all and would happily chat with anyone who came within earshot. Where Arion loved to be taken outside in the fresh air, riding his ponies, or exploring the castle grounds, Athilas and Epilas were content to remain indoors, often sitting quietly with each other, oblivious to the world around them.

Such an underhanded assault on a defenceless man was not to be borne, of course, and Achaeus leapt to his feet with a ferocious roar, sending the three boys scattering in all directions. Achaeus almost caught Arion, but the prince dodged sharply, almost stumbling, before darting towards the far side of the room. Achaeus treated him to another loud bellow and made to give chase when there was a sharp rapping at the door. Stirred from his daydream of happier times, Achaeus started and then called his permission to enter. The door opened to reveal one of the liveried servants that inhabited the palace.

"My liege," she said politely. "Master Corraidhín of The Illyan Isles is here seeking an audience."

Achaeus frowned. He had known Corraidhín for what seemed to have been most of his adult life, and the man had been of service to the crown on many an occasion, bringing news from faraway places, offering counsel, and employing his vast network of contacts and spies that stretched even further than Achaeus's own. On a personal level, Achaeus liked the man – there was an unflappable grace and calm about him that seemed to spread when he was present in a room. Still, when Corraidhín arrived unsummoned, it usually meant that there was a problem, and Achaeus had more than his fill of problems at that moment.

"Send him in," he replied wearily, waving the servant away. While he waited, Achaeus allowed his mind to slip back to that day years before and smiled as he remembered, Arion groaning and sitting down on a nearby blanket box, his face red from exertion and sulky looking. Achaeus looked at him fondly for a moment before stepping across the room to take a seat beside him. There was no sign of the twins, their flight having taken them into the next room, or perhaps even further.

"Duty calls, my son," he said gently. "As much as I would prefer to stay, you know I must go."

"Just a little longer? Please, father!" Achaeus shook his head as kindly as he could.

"Another time, Arion," he replied. "Perhaps tomorrow?" Arion shrugged and then nodded, leaning across to hug his father's muscled arm.

"Good boy," said Achaeus with a smile, tussling Arion's curly black hair with his free hand. After a moment, he carefully pried the small fingers off his arm and got up to leave. Arion watched him go without speaking, then picked up his sword and ran off to look for his brothers.

When Corraidhín arrived in the throne room, Achaeus was pacing back and forth in front of the throne. The islander waited patiently as the king returned to his throne and took a moment to compose himself. The Tarsean throne was almost as ancient as the city itself, tall-backed and etched in gold. Over the years, Achaeus liked to think that the seat had moulded itself to his form, but perhaps the truth was that the throne, and the spirits of its previous occupants, had moulded him instead. Either way, it was a comfortable enough spot and Achaeus settled himself back and greeted Corraidhín with a nod.

"What news, Corraidhín of Illyan?" Corraidhín looked around before replying, checking for servants and others who might overhear. Satisfied that they were alone, he turned back to the throne and bowed deeply. Achaeus examined him closely, taking in the scuffs and tears that marred his usually exceptionally neat clothing and the fresh stitching that closed a nasty gash on his forehead. His frown deepened.

"Lord King, my apologies but there is a matter I must bring to your attention." Unable to restrain himself, Achaeus sighed and gestured for him to continue.

"You will be aware, no doubt, of the rumours that have been circulating in the city? People disappearing without a trace, others brutally murdered in their homes, strange creatures lurking in shadows?" Achaeus nodded. The City Sheriff had briefed him on the matter only days previously as part of his regular report. Achaeus had listened with concern at first, but the sheriff's report was so vague and light on detail or actionable intelligence that he had eventually dropped it into the metaphorical pile designated "problems to be dealt with later". With events progressing in rapid succession, Achaeus had been forced to adopt a ruthless triage process.

"There are as many rumours as there are frightened citizens," he replied with a shrug. "What of it?"

"That is true, Lord King, and to be expected in the circumstances but as you know, rumours are my stock and trade, and some are more concerning than others. One such rumour caught my attention and with the permission of his Captain, Radomir and I undertook to follow its trail. From a scene of terrible slaughter in the merchants' district, we tracked the faintest of signs down into the tunnels beneath the palace itself."

"Beneath the palace, you say?" Achaeus was more concerned now, thinking immediately of his sons and the potential risk to their safety. The involvement of Radomir in Corraidhín's adventures did not surprise the king in the least. Much like the diminutive islander, Radomir was an outsider, one of the wild Bulġha from the north and not of the Achaean people at all but he too had been of service to the crown over long years, fighting the king's enemies wherever they raised their heads. Unlike Corraidhín, Radomir was not one to give advice or listen to whispers, but Achaeus knew the two men were close. Wherever one, the other as Achaeus's poor, deceased wife had once said.

"And? Don't be coy man, clearly, you found something of concern. Saboteurs? A Vedi down from the Narrows? What?" In normal times, it would be highly unusual for one of the warped beasts that haunted the Narrows to have found its way so far south. The King's Rangers were diligent in their duties, usually tracking and killing them long before they reached civilised lands. In anticipation of the Rutik assault, however, most of the Rangers had been recalled to the walls and the northern passage was largely unguarded, Achaeus having reluctantly left the peasant farmers to fend for themselves.

"What we found Lord King, was neither man nor beast. It was something else, something not of this world perhaps. It is difficult to explain in the language of the Achaeans, you have no words for such things. Without wanting to be dramatic, one might call it a demon, though that would only capture half of the truth of it. Regardless, it was something that should not have been there, and something extremely dangerous."

"A demon?" Achaeus's frown deepened still further. The Achaeans were not a superstitious people and demons were largely considered the fanciful inventions of children's storytellers. Momentarily, he wondered if perhaps Corraidhín was making a joke, but he dismissed the notion immediately. The little man was not one for frivolity.

"You killed it?"

"We did. Well, I should better say that we destroyed it, perhaps. I am not sure such a thing can truly be killed. My concern lord is that where we found one, there might be others lurking and I suspect that bloody murder is but the least troubling of their proclivities. With your permission, Lord King, I would like your permission to do what I can to mitigate this threat."

"Yes, yes, of course. Whatever you need is yours, Corraidhín. I shall give the order that you are to be given full access to the city stores and a troop of guards if that will help."

"Alas, Lord King, this is not a problem that your guards or supplies can solve. However, it is my hope that if we cannot banish this enemy entirely, we can at least reduce the amount of damage it can accomplish."

"Very good, Corraidhín. And my gratitude, as ever, for your service. The crown and the people of Tarsus thank you." Corraidhín nodded and being thus dismissed, he bowed once more before turning to go. He got halfway to the door before the king called out his name and he turned back.

"Demons, Corraidhín? Were the thousands of Rutik at our gates not enough of a problem that we must have yet another?" Corraidhín looked at the king, concerned at the dark rings around his eyes and heavy bags beneath. Achaeus looked exhausted and Corraidhín knew that his labours were far from over. There was something else too, however, something that he had not noticed until then, and something that vanished almost as soon as it caught his attention. Perhaps it was a trick of the light or a manifestation of his concerns but at that moment it appeared to Corraidhín as though a dark, nebulous shadow lay across the throne and the man seated therein. It had traces of the demon's shadow about it, though fainter and without an obvious source. For a moment he continued to stare, willing the shadow to reappear so that he could examine it more closely but whatever he had seen, whether he had truly even seen it at all, was now gone and the throne room was brightly lit by the afternoon sun streaming in from the western-facing windows. He knew there was little light of comfort he could impart to the king himself, however.

"In the forests of my home, Lord King, they say that problems arrive like a pack of wolves, one after another and from all directions. The trick is to isolate each from its fellows and defeat them one by one. Concern yourself with the enemy at the gates, Lord King, and let those of us with the necessary talents worry about the enemy within."

With that, Corraidhín turned once more and walked from the room, leaving Achaeus alone to ponder the fate of his realm. Leaning back on the throne, he laced his fingers behind his head and stared around the vast throne room wondering how Arrias had felt when he looked upon the same scene. Achaeus had done his best to live up to his renowned ancestor's example, though by nature he was more of a strategist than a hard charger. When the time came to charge, Achaeus had never hesitated, of that he was proud, but he preferred that all other options were exhausted first before putting men's lives on the line. Perhaps had he followed more closely in the footsteps of Arrias, Tarsus would not have come to these current, most dire of straits. On the other hand, if Achaeus's father had bequeathed him a large, well-trained, and highly experienced fighting force as did Chavdar, the father of Arrias, perhaps Achaeus could have been a conqueror too. Perhaps, perhaps, if, but maybe. Achaeus had seen over fifty winters all told, fourteen as King. He could not for the life of him see where he could have done things differently, that the outcome might also have been different. Born into a world where the Rutik were already firmly ensconced in the west, and only growing in number by the year, conflict was inevitable. Perhaps it could have been provoked sooner, and the Rutik nation tackled whilst it was still relatively weak. If Achaeus had managed to rebuild his army more quickly, or to a greater scale perhaps, then perhaps the war could have been delayed. But for how long? A year? Ten? Perhaps, perhaps. If he had not waited so long to marry, perhaps he would now have a bevy of strong full-grown sons to fight by his side, each with their following of mighty warriors. There had always been so much to do but perhaps if he had done more.

Ever since his father died, Achaeus had seen his kingship as a vocation and a privilege and devoted himself to it entirely, and to the exclusion of all frivolous and personal interests. He had married Arion's mother, the only true love of his life, only because she had landed in his lap, and he had fallen for her completely. When she died, he had turned to his second wife in a desperate bid to fill the jagged gulf of grief that seemed almost about to split him in two. He loved Arion and the twins dearly, of course, but that gulf had never been truly filled, and to his everlasting shame, when the twins' mother had died in childbirth, he was unmoved. After all, he barely knew the woman. The marriage had been arranged between his courtiers and their counterparts in Epirus, to cement relations between the two cities. They were married less than a year and Achaeus had spent much of that time away from the city – hunting in the north, fighting to the west, or visiting the southern cities, cementing alliances, and pressing the claims of his kingdom to their rulers.

Achaeus shifted uneasily on the throne, painful memories vying for attention with his immediate concerns. As the afternoon turned to evening and the light started to fade, the servants lit the torches and Achaeus sat and brooded over the glorious past, the wretched present and the violent future. Alone again in the throne room, he felt an unshakeable sense of foreboding, as though a black doom was settling upon his heart. The longer he sat, and the more he thought, the more convinced he became that the line of kings that began with Arrias so long ago would end with him. It was time, he decided, to send the twins away, and get them somewhere safe for the duration of the siege. Chalcis was the safest of the free cities, the closest in strength to Tarsus itself, but Epirus was the last that remained wholly loyal to the crown, and Achaeus knew that his relatives in the city would take good care of his sons. Arion would have to stay, of course. The twins were little more than babies and putting them out of harm's way was only prudent. Arion was the Crown Prince and heir to the throne, however, and though he was still a boy, the people would expect him to share in their suffering. If Arion was to one day lead the kingdom, a reputation as a coward could not be risked. It was not a decision that Achaeus was happy with, but he suspected that there would be more such in the days to come.

Meanwhile, in the shadow of the throne's tall back, the tiny purple stone pulsed and glinted.

After meeting with the King, Corraidhín returned to his lodgings and closed the door carefully behind him. Upon returning to Tarsus two months previously, he had taken a room above an inn, near the docks, as was his habit. Had he asked, he probably could have procured rooms at the palace, the barracks or at the home of one of his friends and associates in the city. Any of those options would at least have been more salubrious but he preferred the inn despite the closeness of the walls, the constant noise from below, the smell of unwashed bodies and stale ale, and the somewhat tatty furnishings. When he lay in bed at night, he could hear the waves lapping against the harbour wall, and in the morning the cries of gulls and other sea birds stirred him to wakefulness. The noises were soothing to him, reminding him of the islands where he was born, allowing him the illusion that home was just over the horizon.

His surroundings, therefore, were not the source of his distraction. Instead, a part of his mind was on the walls, with Radomir, waiting for that one wayward arrow or lucky spear thrust that might find a chink in his armour, a gap in his defence. Radomir gave the impression of being utterly indomitable, but

Corraidhín was under no illusions at all in that regard. Out on the wall, a person, any person, could die in an instant and Radomir was no different. He would have felt better, perhaps, if he could have joined him there to fight at his side. He and Radomir were always stronger together, their different skillsets complementing each other, and merging to produce a more rounded whole. Unfortunately, Corraidhín knew that his duty lay elsewhere at that moment. He had made a commitment to the king and, moreover, was convinced that the creature in the tunnels implied the presence of a grave and immediate danger that could not go unaddressed.

Frowning, Corraidhín pushed his concern for the other man to the back of his mind and drew in a slow, deep breath. Breathing out, he gently allowed all thought to drift from his mind, leaving him with a tranquil feeling of floating in perfect emptiness. Slowly opening his eyes, he found the room around him had faded to grey, with all sharp edges blurred and all hard surfaces dull and insubstantial. On the room's small single bed sat the figure of a woman, tall and slim but wrapped in a long, hooded cloak, pinned at the collar with a single shining jewel. The stone was a perfect match for the one that hung upon a golden chain around his neck, except that where his was of amber, hers was a perfect diamond. Her hands were resting on her lap, her skin pale and flawlessly smooth, her face mostly hidden by the hood. She sat comfortably at ease, as though she belonged in the small room, almost as though she had always been there. The lines of the furniture faded further into the background, but Corraidhín scarcely noticed, his attention wholly fixed on the figure before him.

Corraidhín dropped to one knee and bowed his head deeply. An aura of peace and tranquillity filled the room, accompanied by a faint smell of cherry blossoms. He remained bowed in silence for a long moment until finally, the woman spoke.

"Corraidhín," she said, without raising her head. "My little spear. My most wayward son. It warms my heart to see you."

"My lady Oracle, my apologies. It has been some time."

"Years, Corraidhín. Decades perhaps." Corraidhín knew that time meant little to the Oracle. To one who has seen millennia come and go, a year passes in a moment. Still, he was filled with remorse.

"There is always so much to do, my lady, but I make no excuses and can only offer my apologies once again." She looked up at that, fixing him with eyes that glinted in silver, piercing and brilliant. As he met her gaze, he knew that she could, if she so chose, see his every thought and feeling and was reminded that there could be no secrets from this woman. She saw all of him, knew all of him, and above all understood him in his entirety. He found himself speechless under her examination. The feeling was not unpleasant, for the lady was ever gentle, but after so many years it was strange to feel so utterly exposed. He wondered what she saw there, inside his mind, and how she would judge him for it.

The moment seemed to stretch into eternity and Corraidhín's anxiety grew but then, to his surprise, the Oracle arched a single elegant eyebrow and laughed. Her laughter was musical, all Corraidhín's doubts, and fears were assuaged in an instant, and he found himself smiling.

"Oh Corraidhín, my love, you have not changed. Still trying to save that little bird with the broken wing. If the cliché was not so apt, it would almost be humorous." Corraidhín continued smiling, accepting the friendly teasing without rancour.

"Someone has to, my lady," he replied. The Oracle shrugged delicately, her shoulders barely moving.

"Perhaps, but sometimes a cause cannot be redeemed. I suspect you know that, and yet it will still not stop you from trying. Such has always been the way of your family; it is one of the reasons they are beloved by all upon the Isles. Your brothers have been worried about you, by the way. I shall let them know that you are in good health; unless there is a message you would like me to pass on?" Corraidhín thought for a moment, then shook his head sadly.

"What I need to say to my brothers is best said in person. But thank you, my lady, for your kind and generous offer."

"The people of the Illyan Isles are my servants, but I am equally theirs, you know this. I will help where I can. which brings us nicely to the crux of the matter. You did not call upon for me for the exchange of niceties." It was a statement rather than a question and Corraidhín bowed his head apologetically and proceeded to tell the Oracle about the creature he and Radomir had encountered in the tunnels beneath the palace and his fear that there might be others lurking elsewhere in the dark, lonely places. The Oracle listened carefully and without interrupting, her expression slowly adopting a deep frown. When he had finished his tale, she stared at him for a moment, perhaps processing what she had heard, and then closed her eyes. She remained standing, perfectly still, shining and beautiful in the shabby room but Corraidhín felt her presence withdraw, leaving him struck by sudden, bitter loneliness and longing for her return.

Minutes passed before the Oracle's presence returned and she opened her eyes, her frown now deeper still. She appeared less luminescent now, the warmth of her aura somewhat cooled.

"I have done what I can, my son. I cannot reveal myself openly in this place, there are too many eyes watching, but my power is now yours to utilise as you will. I cannot fight this battle for you, but I have made it so that the creatures can no longer manifest themselves in this world. Their whispers and the foul pollution of their sark souls will continue to work its evil on peoples' minds but now you can take the battle to the ether and fight them where they are most vulnerable."

"My lady, there are no words to express my thanks. I am in your debt once more. Can you tell me what they are? I felt their evil, but their nature is hidden from me somehow."

"I cannot tell you exactly. I feared to look too deep lest I find something looking back. They are evil, it is true, but I believe that they were not always so. Once they were something else, something good, but corruption has overtaken them somehow. And they are but the vanguard, my son – a dark shadow falls across this place, my son and hard times lie ahead." Her colour was slowly returning as she spoke, but Corraidhín recognised the weariness in her words and a feeling of endless sorrow. They stood in silence for a moment, both lost in thought before the Oracle spoke again.

"When will you return to us, my wayward son? Your home awaits, and your brothers await. You can even bring your young man if you wish. We can find a place for him too, though we may perhaps have to enlarge some of the doors." She smiled sweetly, and Corraidhín recognised the gentle jibe as an attempt to lighten the mood.

"Nothing would bring me greater pleasure my lady, but I fear he is not ready to settle down just yet. The quiet peace of our leafy groves would be as a slow death to a man such as he. Perhaps one day."

The Oracle inclined her head and smiled kindly.

"I do hope so, my son, with all my heart. Do not wait too long though, the lives of his kind are short and often brutal, and you may not have as much time as you hope for. Now I must leave you, for other matters require my attention. I shall carry your memory with me until we meet again in happier times."

"And I yours, my lady," Corraidhín replied, bowing as she slowly faded away and the room around him began to harden back into reality. The loneliness seized him once more as her presence departed, almost swamping him but held back by the memory of her words and her touch. The sound of drunken singing filtered up through the floor, off-key and jarring. The fishy smell of a fresh catch being offloaded on the docks drifted through the open window, and Corraidhín wrinkled his nose and blinked. The feeling of loneliness faded gradually into a more familiar but more distant sense of absence. No matter how far he travelled and for how long, a part of Corraidhín would always remain at the Oracle's feet. For all her kind words, however, their conversation had left him less certain that he would ever return home. Whatever was coming, he now believed that Radomir's time on the wall might well be the least of the trials to be overcome.

CHAPTER TWELVE

Western Devil's Teeth Mountains
15 of Boukatios 870M - Early Spring
Day ten of the siege of Tarsus

Truly, little is known and understood about the beings that we now call the Protótokos, the Firstborn. The legends would have us believe that they all emerged from the same original seed but as time passed, they separated into clusters and communities of the like-minded. Over the millennia, similarly oriented communities merged and amalgamated and gradually the clans coalesced into being. The clans thus formed were five in number: the Tis Thálassas, of the sea; the Tis Erímou, of the desert; the Tou Págou, of the ice; the Tou Dásous, of the forest; and the Tou Vounoú, of the mountain.

Meton, "The Ancient World", c. 700M

Chapter Twelve

The next morning, Mira awoke to find that her charges were nowhere to be seen and after some rather frantic conversations with the sentries, she determined that they had broken camp and left almost an hour previously, shortly before dawn. The sentries pointed her to the east, and she thanked them before hurrying back into the camp to rouse her troop. Half an hour later they were mounted and moving out, far more quickly than most other units would have been able to manage but still far too slowly for Mira's comfort. Heading down the mountain road at a fast trot, to conserve the horses' energy should a sudden sprint or charge be required, her mind ran through all the terrible fates that might have befallen Lord Ohtrad and his followers. She wondered how she would be judged if she failed in her duty to protect him and suspected strongly that it would not end well for her. The League did not present themselves as forgiving in such matters.

"Scouts returning, Captain," a soldier called from behind her, and she looked up sharply. She had sent Beuca and another scout on ahead at the camp, leaving their share of camp-breaking duties to be divided amongst their fellows.

"What news, Beuca?" she called as they drew close. The scout reined in a short distance away and saluted smartly.

"Got 'em, Captain. They're about a mile ahead."

"Doing what, for fuck's sakes?"

"Seems like they're looking for something, Captain, not sure what though – it's just more mountains and more snow as far as the eye can see out there."

"Fuck's sakes," she repeated shaking her head. "We'd best get after them then, I suppose." She waved the troop forward and set a harder pace, cursing some more under her breath.

Almost an hour later, they rounded a rocky outcrop to find Ohtrad and the Avatar standing close together on side of the road, staring at the upper slopes, with the two bodyguards and Waldebert waiting quietly a short distance further ahead. Mira called a halt and dismounted, marching angrily towards Ohtrad with a fierce expression set firmly upon her face. One of the bodyguards looked up and nodded as she approached and Waldebert waved cheerily, apparently oblivious to her mood. She ignored them both and stomped to a halt a few feet from the target of her ire.

"Lord Ohtrad! I must protest! How am I supposed to protect you if you leave camp without even telling me?" Ohtrad turned sharply as she spoke, as if surprised by her presence. She glared at him, but he stared right back at her, unperturbed, before turning back to his study of the mountainside. She followed his gaze, squinting her eyes against the wind and the light rain that it whipped into her face. The stretch of road on which they stood curved slightly to the left to avoid another outcropping of rock, and whilst the slope below was steep and treacherous, the incline above was shallower and covered in a thick layer of compacted snow. A few large boulders broke up the white monotony of it but other than that there was nothing to be seen. She turned back.

"Lord Ohtrad, I…"

"Wait." The word was not a request but a command and despite her anger, Mira had to obey. She turned again to look at the slope, still seeing nothing of note and began to wonder if perhaps the cold had gotten into the man's brain somehow. She was about to look away once more when something caught her eye.

About five hundred yards up the slope, there was movement on the surface of the snow. Mira's first thought was "Fuck! Avalanche!", especially since the movement seemed to be spreading across the slope as she watched. The odd thing though was that the source of the movement seemed to be centred on a score of specific spots on the snow. It was not one single, massive movement of the surface, it was dozens or even hundreds of smaller ones, many of which were close together but few that overlapped. Stranger still, as she kept watching with macabre fascination, the centre of each disturbance began to swell upwards, stippling the snow with a multitude of tiny hills. The hills grew higher and steeper, snow beginning to roll down the sides to encircle each with a tiny wall. Mira glanced at Ohtrad, but he seemed transfixed by the phenomenon and did not appear to notice her attention. She looked back up the slope to see the little hills become much bigger mounds, but it was not until the first head broke the surface that she understood what was truly happening.

"Ambush!" shouted Mira, drawing her sword and waving frantically to Teja and the rest of her troop. "Form a defensive line before me! Now! Protect the Lord Ohtrad!"

"Belay that order, Captain," said Ohtrad, calmly but firmly. Mira stared at him in confusion and then looked back up the slope to see dozens of figures now forcing their way to the surface. They had been hiding beneath the snow, waiting for the Rutik column to pass. Was this what Ohtrad had come to find? She glanced back at Teja, raising her hand in the signal to hold. Teja drew to a halt, and the troop with him, looking as baffled as she did. Some of the ambushers had now emerged fully from their concealment and Mira was horrified to realise that whatever they were, they were certainly not human.

Even at that distance, Mira could tell that their attackers stood far taller than any normal person. It was hard to gauge exactly but some of them looked as though they were eight or ten feet tall and that was only the most immediately obvious of their deformities. Height and vague build aside, however, each of the creatures was as different from the next as they were from Mira herself. Some appeared to be covered in long, straggly fur whilst others were entirely hairless, surely a major disadvantage in the freezing mountain climate. Some were even covered in what appeared to be long, bony spikes, protruding at all angles directly from their flesh. Their skin and hair showed a myriad of wild combinations of colour and texture, some so garish and bright that she wondered if it was natural or some type of body art, perhaps a dye or tattoo. Their limbs were of all shapes and sizes too, some extraordinarily long and others ending in what looked to be large protrusions of bone. The creatures now bellowed and roared as they stumbled into shambling, loping runs, some on two feet, some on four. Some stooped to scoop up rocks and flung them at the waiting humans. Most flew wild, but one landed with a crash on the hard surface of the road only ten feet from where they stood.

Regardless of their method of locomotion, the creatures were now barrelling across the packed snow at frightening speeds, and the distance between them and the road closed rapidly. Mira pulled her sword free, certain they were about to die. Even with Teja and the others by her side, she doubted they would be able to resist the oncoming horde: the creatures would roll right over them without even stopping, and she was glad that Ohtrad had ordered the troop halted. The creatures' charge was targeted at Ohtrad and the Avatar and by extension Mira herself. With a little luck, Teja and the others might have time to get back to their horses and escape. She tightened her hold on the sword, the leather wrapping on the grip cold and solidly comforting in her palm. The creatures were closer still now and she could see the strange and unnatural details of their bodies. She wondered if her sword would even penetrate their hides and almost laughed, bitterly reflecting that it would make little difference to the outcome either way. Still, she thought, it would be nice to at least hurt the bastards before they tore her to pieces. If nothing else, she would go down fighting.

"Now would be the appropriate time, I believe," said Ohtrad, raising his voice to be heard over the approaching clamour. Mira looked at him in surprise, wondering if he was addressing her and what, exactly, it was he expected her to do at that moment. His comment was meant for his other companion, however, and the cloaked and hooded man moved forward in response. He seemed to study the approaching monsters for a moment longer, before slowly raising both of his hands into the air, and bringing them sharply down again, palms turned flat towards the ground. There was a clap of sudden thunder and for an instant, Mira thought they were about to be enveloped in yet another landslide, but the effect was more targeted, if equally dramatic and horrifying. As the creatures continued to charge wildly towards them, the ground beneath their feet cracked, crumbled, and flew into the air, tossing the astonished creatures skyward in a cloud of snow and mud. Then, the Avatar's hands came down once more, bringing the landscape with them, smashing it back down to earth with a colossal, ear-splitting crash, burying the monsters beneath tonnes of earth, rock, ice, and snow. As the Avatar returned to his position beside Ohtrad, it was almost as though the attackers had never existed, and the mountain had swallowed them whole.

Ohtrad turned to Mira, an expression of supremely smug satisfaction on his face. As he caught her eye, a horrifying feeling of panic and fear swept over her and she wondered if she too was to be buried in the mountains. Was that why they had left the camp early? Was this something that no one was supposed to see? She caught herself about to take a step backwards and stood stock still instead, returning the man's gaze as calmly as she could. Ohtrad stared at her for a moment, then smiled.

"Do you understand now, Captain?" Mira gave a small shrug, unsure of what answer was expected from her. Her mind was racing – what could you say, after something like that?

"I'm a little stunned, my lord," she managed finally. Ohtrad nodded and his smile widened.

"Everyone is when they first witness the true power of an Avatar. They are… magnificent, yes? Awe-inspiring, you might say. And believe you me, Captain, what you saw today is only the beginning. Thanks to the Avatars, we of the League are powerful beyond your *wildest* imaginings – the power to move mountains." Mira nodded and forced a smile. Best to appear impressed, she reasoned, since he seemed so immensely proud. She stole a glance at the Avatar, half expecting him to have grown gigantic in stature, or for flames to be erupting from his eyeballs. After what had happened, she would have believed almost anything of him, of *it* really, she supposed since, like the monsters on the mountainside, nothing human could do what it had done. It was just standing there, however, silent, and unmoving, its head slightly bowed, and its face was hidden in the shadow of its hood. She shivered and looked away, deciding that she really did not want to attract its attention.

Something else was bothering Mira, something about the stories that had been told around the campfires of recent nights, brought in by returning scouts or work parties passing through on their way to some task or other. Stories about being attacked by monsters, about people being carried away in the night, and about horribly mutilated bodies being found along the road. Mira had discounted most of them as tall tales, probably born of boredom or humanity's natural tendency towards exaggeration. She was now rapidly revising that belief, but if the stories were true, that posed another question.

"My lord, if I may?" Ohtrad gestured his assent with a languid wave and Mira pressed on.

"From the reports I've heard, my lord, we've lost hundreds building this road through the mountains. Maybe thousands. Why were the Avatars not sent to defend them?" Ohtrad was silent for a time, his smile fading, and Mira wondered if perhaps she had overstepped her bounds. When he finally responded, however, he seemed unoffended.

"An *astute* question Captain, and one to which there are three answers. First, although powerful, the Avatars are yet few, and there are numerous demands upon their time. Second, there are other *powers*, that hide among the snowy peaks. We could not risk drawing their attention until it was absolutely necessary." He paused again, watching Mira's face to see whether she followed his reasoning. In truth, she did not, at least not entirely, but she was unwilling to push her luck by questioning him further.

"And the third reason, my lord?" she prompted politely, for all the world as though they discussed the finer points of philosophy over steaming mugs in a quiet coffee house somewhere, rather than being on the frozen side of a mountain, in the aftermath of an obscene show of force.

"The third reason, Captain, is perhaps the most *prosaic*, though you will find it somewhat heartless. More than thousands were lost, tens of thousands would be closer to the truth and probably still short of the true tally if you include the indentured and the slaves. But so what? We have plenty more soldiers and more slaves than we know what to do with. The simple truth is that protecting them would not have been worth the price it would have incurred. So, we let them die, but in the interests of the restoration of Rutik glory, of course. To have done so is an honour far past what most of them were entitled to.

Wouldn't you agree?" Mira was not sure that she did agree, but equally, she was not sure that she wanted to disagree with Ohtrad at that moment, with the Avatar standing over his shoulder.

"Yes, my lord," she replied quietly. "An honour indeed."

A short time later, they were back on their horses and headed back towards the previous night's campsite, expecting to meet the rest of the Expeditionary Army somewhere along the way. Mira spent the short journey silently, deep in thought. Until that morning, she had thought of the League as a political force, by no means benign but certainly no worse than the myriad other factions that fought for supremacy in the Kingdom of the Rutik. The courtiers in Rutiksborg, military headquarters in Harbrook, Northern Command in Magdeborg: the list was endless, and they fought amongst themselves with as much fervour as they did against the enemies of the Kingdom. Plotting and scheming in an eternal game of one-upmanship was a way of life amongst the Rutik and always had been. It now appeared, however, as though the League were in another league entirely.

That was only the first of such incidents that Mira witnessed during their journey through the mountains. On another occasion, she saw the Avatar dismount and walk casually into thin air, to cross a gaping chasm that lay to the side of the path. Once across the gap, he stooped low to pick up something off the ground, before returning to Ohtrad's side. There were other bizarre and disturbing moments too and after a while, Mira began to wonder if perhaps she was imagining them. Perhaps the cold had frozen her brain somehow and she was seeing things that were not there. Impossible things that made Mira fear for her sanity. Unfortunately, if that were not the case, and these things were really happening then that was even more disturbing to her. She had always been a practical person, believing that the world was at times hard and cruel but at least bound by certain immutable rules that at the least ensured that one could be certain of waking in the morning to find that up and down were still in the same directions as they were when one fell asleep. If the Avatars, and by extension the League, were somehow unbound by those simple, basic rules, what did that mean for the Kingdom? What did it mean for Mira, who was herself bound, by oath, to follow where they lead?

There was little time to worry about the future when the immediate present was so unrelenting and harsh but try as she might, Mira could not evict the Avatar from her mind. Despite her distaste, she found herself staring at it more and more as the days passed. What exactly was it? Where did these strange powers come from? What else was it capable of? Was it one of the ones she had seen in Magdeborg or were there more of these creatures running around the place? Question after question ran through her mind and she had answers to none. She considered challenging Ohtrad on the subject several times but was invariably put off by the Avatar standing nearby. It seemed the creature never left Ohtrad's side for more than a minute or two and watched over him silently at all hours of the day and night.

The scribe Waldebert, however, could often be seen scuttling from one end of their nightly camps to another, carrying messages, fetching water, and doing whatever small tasks Ohtrad needed to be done. It seemed he was more of a manservant than a scribe, although there probably was not a huge amount of writing to be done whilst crossing frozen mountains. Regardless, Waldebert was the weak link in Ohtrad's entourage. Ohtrad himself was too intelligent and too cunning to give much away. The Avatar was utterly, completely, and totally unapproachable. Besides, Mira did not know whether the creature could even speak, much less answer questions, even had she dared to ask it. The two bodyguards showed little inclination to speak with anyone, and by their appearance, they were more likely to stab a questioner than respond with any information. Waldebert was young and fresh-faced or had been before the Devil's Teeth took their toll. He was also treated as if he were dirt by his master, and his master's other minions and never looked terribly contented. Perhaps Mira could leverage his dissatisfaction to get some useful information for once.

Mira resolved to engineer a meeting with the scribe as soon as possible. It had to be done somewhere as far as possible from Ohtrad's supervision and the watchful eyes of the bodyguards and the Avatar. Her first opportunity came late in the evening, a couple of days later when she spotted him heading for the supply depot, presumably to collect some provisions for his master. Mira was on her way to inspect her horse at the time but immediately changed course and followed Waldebert towards the warehouse. It took her a few minutes to catch up and she felt obliged to pause at the doors and pass a few moments in conversation with the guards so, by the time she got inside the building, Waldebert was already amongst the stacks, head deep in a large crate.

As Mira approached, she could hear him muttering to himself as he rooted through the crate's contents. He seemed angry about something, giving Mira her opportunity.

"Is there something I can assist with, Waldebert?" she asked loudly. Waldebert straightened up quickly, cracking his head sharply against the propped-up lid of the crate. Rubbing his injury, he peered at Mira in the dim light and stammered a response.

"Captain Mira. I don't... I mean, I'm not... what are you... I mean..." He trailed off, then sighed heavily and seemed to recover somewhat.

"Apologies, Captain. The Lord Ohtrad sent me to find some dried meat to supplement his rations. I thought this was the correct area but I'm afraid I've come up short once again."

"It can be difficult to keep one's bearings in here, especially at this time of night," said Mira, sympathetically. The warehouse was huge and well laid out but labyrinthine and filled with row after row of near-identical crates.

"Come this way," she continued, waving to him to follow. "I believe you will find your supplies in the stacks along the western wall." Without waiting for him to respond, Mira headed off towards the far side of the warehouse. In truth, she had no idea at all where the dried meat was, she left it to the local quartermaster and his staff to take care of such details. She led the hapless scribe along a route that was unnecessarily long and winding and used the opportunity to strike up a conversation. At first, progress was slow and painful. Waldebert seemed intimidated, either by her station or her reputation and gave only short, unhelpful answers. Mira kept at it though, chatting away lightly about inconsequential matters and eventually he relaxed and began to engage more fully. Mira decided it was time to push a little harder.

"So how long have you been working for Lord Ohtrad?" she asked innocently. Waldebert paused for a moment to count on his fingers.

"Why, almost five years!" he responded, seeming surprised himself. "I joined his staff shortly after arriving in Rutiksborg, but it seems like only yesterday!"

"You enjoy the work then?" prompted Mira.

"Oh yes, of course. Lord Ohtrad is a demanding master but only because his work is so particularly important. Since joining his staff, I have travelled all over the Kingdom and even into Asfáleia. I love to travel, especially to places where there are different customs and traditions to be observed. It's fascinating."

Mira almost laughed at the little man's sudden burst of enthusiasm but restrained herself. She was conscious that she would not be able to drag the search for meat out indefinitely, and so the conversation needed to be brought to a point as soon as possible. The other option was to treat the conversation as an appetiser, to be followed by the main course at some future date. Mira was not keen on that option though, believing that once Ohtrad heard that she had been sniffing around, the scribe would be cautioned to silence.

"Not many traditions on display around here. Unless you count freezing to death, I suppose." Waldebert snorted a laugh.

"It is true that this has not been my favourite of our journeys thus far," he replied. "But I am looking forward to seeing Tarsus. Do you know it is the oldest extant city in Asfáleia? Save of course for Menos, but no one knows whether that's even there anymore. I'm told the walls alone are worth the visit."

"If you remind me closer to the time," Mira offered. "I can allocate some guards to escort you around once the city has fallen. It will be some time before the streets are safe for sightseeing alone. Lord Ohtrad, I imagine will be far too busy for such pleasant pastimes, as will I. There will be much work to be done in securing the city and such. Shame to have to go alone though, perhaps the Avatar will join you?" At the mention of the Avatar, Wilbert started, almost choked, then stopped in his tracks to stare at Mira in astonishment.

"I very much doubt it, Captain Mira," he replied hoarsely. "Those of us in the lower levels of initiation are privileged to see such a divine manifestation of our faith in a person, so to speak, but my little hobbies are unfathomably far beneath the notice of such a being."

"What does it mean to say that he's a manifestation of our faith, Waldebert? As you know, I am not initiated into the League at all, but I'm keen to learn more and perhaps consider my future in that regard."

"Captain Mira, that would be tremendous. I am quite sure that Lord Ohtrad would welcome you into our brethren with open arms. I should caution though that my understanding of such matters is little better than that of the common man, though I have picked up some more esoteric knowledge in the course of my work."

Mira smiled to herself at that last part. Waldebert was keen to impress his new friend and the conversation was going the right way. Now all she had to do was keep him talking a little while longer.

Mira's train of thought was derailed as they rounded a corner and came face to face with the Avatar itself. It stood there between the rows of crates, silent and unmoving and Mira almost staggered as she drew up sharply to avoid hitting it. Waldebert's eyes widened at the sight, and he began stammering again, seemingly torn between addressing the Avatar directly and walking back his last statement to Mira. The Avatar looked down at them for a moment longer and then, to Mira's surprise and shock, it spoke.

"Lord Ohtrad requires your presence in his lodgings immediately, scribe." The voice was low-pitched and slow, somewhere between a gurgle and a whisper and it forced its way through Mira's ears like a hot wire and burned itself into her mind. She suppressed a shiver as Waldebert obediently scampered away and the Avatar turned its attention towards her.

"Captain Mira," it continued. "Daughter of Alwina and Valamir, both of Norderhofschlag. Captain in the Northern Army and hero of the Drevenwood. Seconded to Lord Ohtrad's service, currently assigned to bodyguard duties. It seems you have your hands full and thus surprises me to find you in a warehouse, making small talk with a clerk in the dead of night."

Mira was torn between burgeoning terror and determination to make the best of this unexpected opportunity to question the Avatar itself. However, the Avatar had no intention of allowing her to take control of the conversation.

"I believe you are a troublemaker, Captain Mira. You are uninitiated and show no interest in aligning yourself with the League, yet you watch us constantly and seek opportunities to delve deeper into our affairs. Lord Ohtrad believes you have value to this mission. If it were my decision, I would reduce you to the dust from which you came and be finished with the matter before another moment passes but, for now, I shall abide by his wishes. I strongly suggest, however, that you stick to your duties, keep your eyes on the road and your tongue firmly in your head, lest something happen to change our minds." As it continued speaking, Mira felt the full force of its attention boring into her, lacerating her thoughts, severing her consciousness from her body, and leaving her paralysed and unable to respond. The Avatar regarded her for a minute longer before turning to walk away. Mira watched it go and then, as soon as it was through the door and gone, she collapsed to her knees and for the first time in years, bowed her head and cried uncontrollably.

CHAPTER THIRTEEN

The Royal Palace, City of Tarsus
15 of Euthaios 870M - Late Spring
Day ten of the siege of Tarsus

- Conqueror's City -

The origins of the League for the Restoration of Rutik Glory are shrouded in mystery. They first appeared on the streets of the smaller Rutik cities along the coast – Bremerhafnō, Cuxhafnō and Dillenhafnō so perhaps they came from the sea. More likely though, is that those cities were chosen for their large populations of the working poor. It was amongst the underclass of sailors, porters, stevedores, and labourers that they found their most amenable audience. The League gave them someone to blame for their woes, the Achaeans, and assured them that their lot would improve if only they listened and obeyed.

Acusilaus, "Peoples of Asfáleia", c. 900M

Chapter Thirteen

Although he did not realise it, Arion was perhaps the most sheltered person in the entire Kingdom of Tarsus. He was blissfully unaware that he enjoyed a measure of security that even the most wealthy and illustrious of the citizenry could not aspire to achieve. High walls and tall towers guarded every approach to his residence. The finest guards his father's armies could muster watched over his every move, from dawn until dusk and back again. The beloved son of a powerful father, he was protected, coddled even, insulated from the myriad vagaries and dangers of ordinary existence. Even so, with their greatest enemy at the gates, the savage truth of the wider world was asserting itself. Life in the palace continued almost as normal but the lethargic but tenacious tendrils of brutal reality were slowly working their way past all his defences. There was no change to Arion's routine, but an undercurrent of tension and fear now ran through the palace. The guards were more numerous and more vigilant. Visitors were few and carefully supervised. Servants huddled in corners, gossiping in hurried whispers, falling silent whenever he approached. Rumours of dire portents spread indiscriminately, spinning like sycamore seeds on the wind, taking root and growing wherever they found fallow ground.

Nor were all the signs so intangible. The clashing sounds of battle, for instance, that now echoed off the paved streets were audible even within the palace. They were a distant clamour that rose and fell sporadically, day and night. During large-scale assaults, they reached a discordant crescendo, before petering out once more into a low background cadence. Sometimes the ground beneath Arion's feet shook and trembled, reverberating in sympathetic harmony with the city walls as they stoically defied all that the enemy could hurl at them. Often, even the light southern breeze carried the dissonant tune of war: pungent overtones that contrasted sharply with the more subtle flavours of pollinating flowers and grassy fields. The rank odour of human bodies rotting in the sun drifted and mingled with the acrid stench of smoke from burning buildings. Even the miasmic reek of thousands of men and women fighting and pushing, straining and sweating, voiding and dying, percolated through the streets like a wicked rumour. Positioned in the centre of the city, the royal palace was undoubtedly the safest place in Tarsus, but war had come to its doorstep, and nowhere in the city was truly impenetrable to its heralds of suffering and death.

The Kingdom of the Rutik had come to settle a score that was a century in the making. Tarsus was the most venerable of the ancient Achaean cities, the august and majestic heir to a glorious history that stretched back a thousand years and more into storied antiquity. The Rutik, in contrast, were recent and unwelcome interlopers, scarcely a handful of generations removed from the first barbarous horde that had appeared on the plains of Asfáleia. They came from the far north, it was said, from a land ruled split into a mercurial patchwork of tribes and nations. Its people were raised to battle, the poets declaimed, each tribe at war with its neighbours and all continually raiding each other for plunder and excitement. The Achaean cities boasted high walls and strong defenders but in less than a hundred years, the Rutik had taken most of the western half of the country and set them to fire and ruin. The remaining cities, Tarsus among them, had formed a defensive alliance and for years had held their ground but almost no one truly believed that they could hold it forever. There was an ominous as an undertone to every poem recited and every saga written: *the Rutik are coming; the Rutik are coming.*

As a younger child, Arion had been, in equal parts, thrilled and terrified by the stories of the Rutik and their violent conquests. Even now, and despite his growing unease, he could not help but be enthralled. He had heard, for instance, that the enemy numbered in the tens of thousands, a horde so shockingly vast that he found it almost impossible to envisage. He imagined them marching in rank after rank, chanting their songs of war as they advanced on the city. Fearsome war machines had been assembled within range of the walls: catapults, trebuchets, siege towers and the like. The Rutik were masters of such things, builders as well as destroyers. With slaves, oxen, and mules they had hauled the fearsome contraptions hundreds of miles from their home in the west. Now they would test their might against the strongest walls in the world. Arion wondered how they worked, how they were put together and what incredible damage they could do. Then there were the famous Rutik cavalry formations. Arion could see them in his mind's eye: a stunning display of beautiful chestnut mares, charging into battle, pennants flying, their riders' armour and weapons glinting and gleaming in the late spring sun. The glorious magnitude of it mesmerised him, almost to the point of completely eclipsing their fundamental menace.

That afternoon, Arion's tutor struggled to keep his attention on the finer points of ancient philosophy as the boy's fertile imagination wandered to breathless visions of battle and glory. He tried and failed to engage his pupil's interest in a discussion of the difference between an act that is 'lawful' and an act that is 'just' and whether an act is by virtue of its being lawful, or whether being lawful but unjust means that the law itself is unjust. Such niceties, however, were a poor contender against cavalry charges and heroic triumphs over desperate odds. Finally, the tutor despaired of his task and dismissed him with a sharp word or two that were almost entirely unheeded. It seemed wildly unfair to Arion that the enemy was at the gates and the entire city was marshalling to their defence, whilst he was stuck in the palace playing with blunted swords and listening to old men drone on about dialectic method. He was self-aware enough to accept that he was not yet worthy of a place on the battlefield, his repeated drubbings in the training ring were evidence enough of that. Still, he should at least be allowed to go and watch, to see the excitement for himself.

Arion's bodyguards were waiting for him outside the tutor's rooms and fell into step behind him as he headed off down the corridor. The soldiers were attentive and watchful, one keeping his attention completely focused on their charge, the other constantly scanning their surroundings, her attention outward, always looking for potential threats. Guards had been a constant feature of Arion's life for as long as he could remember, of course. This was the royal palace after all, and Tarsus had never been short of enemies. Since the arrival of the Rutik, however, the constant supervision had become utterly stifling, closing off any possible avenue that might lead to mischief or excitement. At that moment, Arion began thinking of his guardians as captors and resolved to escape their custody as soon as humanly possible. A half-formed plan marinated in his head as they walked and he began to watch his surroundings as carefully as did the soldier, waiting for an opportunity to present itself.

Arion's moment arrived when they reached one of the palace's long portrait galleries, on their way to the back stairs. The room had only one entrance and one exit on the ground floor, each at opposite ends of the hall. Along either wall, massive paintings were displayed, each in its alcove and as Arion entered the gallery, he felt the weighty gaze of a dozen generations of ancestors staring down upon him from the age-darkened canvas. Above the paintings, a narrow mezzanine ran the length of the room on either side, decorated with a series of natural white Carrara marble busts — more gloomy ancestors, frozen in a different medium. There were no stairs in the room itself and the upper level was only accessible from the floor above but halfway down the gallery, Arion spotted a group of servants balancing on ladders to clean the dust from the tops of the paintings and his plan rapidly crystalised.

Stopping once again to greet the servants, Arion manoeuvred himself to a position where one of the servants stood between him and the guards, and beside a spare ladder that was leaning against one of the marble pillars supporting the mezzanine. The servant was leaning on a mop, waiting for the others to finish dusting so that he could clean the floors. A young man, only a few years older than Arion himself, the servant was keen to talk and chattered away mindlessly as Arion edged closer. One of the guards was still watching him but the other was watching the doors and glancing up towards the balcony. Arion made a joke that was at best half-humorous, but the servant seemed well amused and burst into loud laughter, letting go of his mop to clutch his sides. Arion stepped forward, ostensibly to clap the man on the shoulder but instead deliberately tripping over his bucket.

The bucket tipped and the mop fell with a crash as Arion staggered theatrically into the servant, knocking him off balance and sending him reeling back into the watching guard. The guard reacted instantly but his movements were confused between catching the hapless servant before he fell and fending off his sudden and unexpected approach. The second guard spun around at the sound of the mop hitting the floor, turning to see a wave of soapy water heading her way and jumping back smartly to keep her boots dry. With both guards momentarily distracted, Arion seized his moment and jumped onto the ladder, climbing the rungs as quickly as he could without looking back. The pillar was tall and perfectly smooth, and the ladder ended a little less than three feet from the top. The marble came from the royal quarries, in the foothills of the Devil's Teeth Mountains north of the city and was renowned for its uniformity of colour and perfectly smooth surface when properly polished. Arion knew his fingers would find no grip on the hard stone, but the top of the column was decorated with garlands of acanthus leaves, carved to appear that the balcony was perched atop a marble bush. Jumping from the top rung of the ladder, Arion was able to grab the nearest leaves and pull himself higher until he could swing his leg around and up to reach the railings above.

Ignoring the angry cries of his guards, echoing up from below, Arion scrambled over the railings and landed awkwardly on the polished floor of the mezzanine. Barely recovering his balance, he looked up to find himself face-to-face with the scowling visage of his grandfather's great-great-grandfather, Achaeus the Third, renowned in Tarsean history as being an inveterate gambler who squandered the greater part of the royal fortune on dubious ventures. Feeling unfairly judged by the long-dead king, Arion pulled a face and stuck out his tongue before darting off along the balcony towards the nearest exit. The guards were still shouting from below, but Arion knew that there was little they could do. In full armour, there was no way they could follow him up the narrow ladder and have any hope of making it to the floor above. They would be forced to run for the back stairs instead, then double back upon reaching the next floor. By the time they reached the mezzanine, Arion would be long gone.

Arion now had an avenue of escape that was narrow and perilous but still viable. Darting through the door, he made his way to an outer room and on out into the corridor beyond. From there, he slipped through the marbled halls like a diminutive but stealthy cat-burglar, dodging and hiding from guards and servants alike, cunningly evading capture until he reached one of the towers that stood watch over his father's kingdom. The palace itself was built on a low hill and its towers were tall. From their soaring heights, it was possible to see miles past the city walls on a clear day but as Arion emerged onto a balcony about halfway up, there was little to see. The surrounding houses were already well below his eye-line, so the city walls were in view in the distance, but the Tarsean soldiers on the walls were hard-to-distinguish blobs of shapeless colour that moved and mingled and the enemy beyond was, of course, completely hidden. Luckily the balcony was not Arion's destination and after a moment spent staring at the walls, he turned to look for his next objective.

Arion had been born inside the palace, and in the fourteen years since had spent much of his life within its walls. On occasion, he had been permitted to accompany his father on state visits to some of the more southerly city-states. They had travelled to the mighty Chalcis where the two rivers that descended originally from deep in The Devil's Teeth, met and merged before continuing their journey to the sea. He had even been as far south as the port city of Larissa where the merchants of many nations met and mingled, trading their wares, drinking coffee and liqueurs, and exchanging news of faraway places. From the docks at Larissa, he had been shown the brilliant aquamarine waters of the Arryal Sea, stretching out to meet the Endless Ocean to the west, with the Broken Islands in the near distance. In recent years, however, their visits had been curtailed as the war with the Rutik gained in intensity and made the roads unsafe to travel in anything less than very large numbers.

Arion's travels had been long ago in a child's terms and for most of his life he had resided within the palace and, as young children will, he had made a favourite game of exploring its winding corridors and hidden recesses. The palace at Tarsus carried the weight of centuries, repeated renovations and extensions, and dozens of masters, each with their own ideas, and each with the resources to make their vision a reality. In that context, it was inevitable that the building would have its share of secrets. There were entire wings that had not seen use in centuries, others that were inaccessible except via a maze of corridors, or small portals long overlooked. Some doors opened onto blank walls, others led to leftover spaces, the forgotten remnants of rooms divided and merged. The attics and cellars were cavernous and filled with the detritus of hundreds of lives lived within the walls. Between the two, miles upon miles of corridors ran back and forth and beneath even the cellars were tunnels and caves where even Arion dared not wander.

One such secret was that the balcony on which Arion stood was a later addition to the tower. Whether it was built for simple aesthetic value or as a position from which to look at some specific landmark, Arion did now know. He did know that if one emerged from the door and followed the balcony to the left, around towards the back of the tower, there was a point where there had not been sufficient room between the palace and the outer walls to complete the curve. On that side, the rounded edge of the balcony merged with the outer wall, marble disappearing into the heavier stonework only to reappear about ten feet further along and continue its circle around the tower. Whatever the balcony's original purpose, it had seen little use in recent years and thick ivy had been allowed to take root in the cracks of the stonework. The creeper was filthy and full of bugs but made a perfect ladder that Arion quickly scaled to reach the top of the walls.

The palace walls were sparsely patrolled, with every available soldier being badly needed on the southern city walls themselves so Arion was able to make his way along them without incident until he reached the junction with The Narrows Wall. Before raising the city, Arrias the Conqueror, the first king of Tarsus, had built an impassable wall across the full breadth of the Tarsean Narrows. The wall joined the eastern range of the Devil's Teeth to its western counterpart and served to close off the Narrows to anyone north or south of that line and were almost forty feet tall and punctuated regular intervals by towers that stood twenty feet higher again. At its base, the wall itself was some fifteen feet thick and composed of mortared rubble, reinforced with blocks of fitted granite and faced by layers of red brick. Even at its summit, the wall was almost ten feet wide and protected by ramparts to half the height of a grown man.

The foundations of the palace had been laid at the midpoint of The Narrows, on the southern side of The Narrows Wall. The palace walls stretched to two thirds the height of the outer walls, curving in semicircles to either side, forming another layer of defence and protecting the main thoroughfare between the city's two halves. The city walls, in turn, formed a concentric circle with the palace, almost the height of The Narrows Wall and heavily defended in preparation for Rutik attacks. Passing from one wall to the other, Arion was able to slip past a group of defenders, onto a staircase and down into the city. The streets were busy as citizens tried to ignore the danger at their walls and carry on their normal activities, all the while making way for troops of soldiery and wagons laden with materiel and supplies for the defenders. Arion's outfit was well made and expensive but not overly remarkable and he knew he could pass through the crowds without drawing attention.

CHAPTER FOURTEEN

Southern walls, City of Tarsus
20 of Euthaios 870M - Late Spring
Day fifteen of the siege of Tarsus

Tarsus was conceived and constructed as the ultimate stronghold: an impregnable fortification writ large into the form of a city. The Narrows Wall runs east to west, joining the opposing tips of the Devil's Teeth and closing the Narrows Gap against all comers. Tarsus sits at the very centre, guarding the only passage through. The outer walls of the city extend in rough semicircles, attached to the Narrows Wall like barnacles on a ship's hull. Within their circumference, the walls of the Royal Palace form a concentric circle, a fortress within a fortress, a last line of defence should the impossible occur and an enemy somehow penetrate the city limits.

Acusilaus, "The Eternal Glory of Tarsus", c. 850M

Chapter Fourteen

Arion hurried through a bustling marketplace and across a wide-open square, decorated with marble columns and dramatically posed statues. From there, he made his way to the southern wall and began looking for an opportunity to climb back up. After half an hour, however, it seemed that his plan was doomed to fail at the last step for his father's soldiers were everywhere and he could find no way to reach his destination without being caught. Finding a narrow alley between two buildings with a view of one of the stairways, he huddled back into the shadows to observe. It seemed the Rutik attacks had abated, at least for that moment and at least on that part of the wall and the Tarsean soldiery were going about their business with little haste. Arion watched them come and go with an increasingly glum expression.

"Arion." The voice was soft but came from directly behind him and Arion jumped and spun around in surprise. A diminutive figure bowed his head in greeting.

"Corraidhín! What… how did you find me?" Corraidhín ignored the question and stared at Arion with a raised brow. Even at fourteen years of age, Arion was a couple of inches taller than Corraidhín but there was a coiled strength to the man, and he was lithe, like the patterned cats Arion had seen brought out of the faraway plains on the southern continent. He had a catlike aura of preternatural calm too, perfectly still but seemingly ready to pounce at any moment. His clothes were dark and travelworn, his rapier strapped to his left hip, and his spear fastened across his back. He stared at Arion with dark eyes that glinted in the reflected light from outside the alley and Arion had the uncomfortable feeling that he was the hapless prey in this relationship.

"The palace is in an uproar, Arion. Your father has turned out the guard and every servant within the walls is out looking for you. I myself have far more important tasks to attend to than tracking down wayward children."

"I just wanted to see the walls. I didn't realise it would cause that much trouble!" Truth be told, Arion had expected to get in trouble for his exploits, but he had not for a moment considered the uproar that would ensue when his absence was discovered. He turned back to look at the soldiers on the walls so that Corraidhín would not see his cheeks burn with embarrassment. There was going to be hell to pay when he got home, he thought ruefully. With the Rutik siege now fully underway, his father would take a dim view of being burdened with one more thing to worry about.

"Out of curiosity, how were you intending to get onto the walls?"

"Well, I thought I could sneak up when there was no one looking." Arion watched the bustling soldiers ruefully. Corraidhín laughed.

"The city is at war, Arion – there's always somebody looking. Come on, first, we must find a courier and send word to your father. He will want to know you are safe and well. After that, I will take you up on the walls and we shall see what is to be seen. Agreed?"

"Yes! Yes, of course – agreed! Thank you!" Arion was unclear on how they had progressed from his being in trouble to his getting what he wanted but he was not about to question it. Corraidhín smiled and reached out to give Arion's shoulder a friendly squeeze.

"Come on then, let us be off."

Still not believing his luck, Arion trailed after Corraidhín as he took them to the nearest guard post to requisition a runner. His message to the king was polite but succinct and indicated that they would return to the palace before the afternoon waned. That duty done, he took Arion to the gatehouse that towered over the main entrance to the city and presented his papers to the officer of the day. The gateway itself was wide enough to permit three carts to pass at once and the fortifications that protected it were formidable. Essentially a small, self-contained fortress, the gatehouse was a rectangular block, six storeys high, with tall, round towers at each corner. The paved road ran beneath through a short tunnel, closed at either end by a steel portcullis that was inches thick. Between the two ends, the ceiling of the corridor was punctuated with murder holes and gaping iron spouts directed to belch jets of boiling oil on anyone unfortunate enough to be within the tunnel. The outer walls were peppered with loopholes and arrow slits, allowing those within to rain missiles on attackers. On the roof of the gatehouse, four massive ballistae waited, ready to bring bloody ruin to enemies by the dozen. In all, the gatehouse could hold two hundred soldiers in relative comfort and safety, allowing them to hold the position and continue to fight even if the gate itself should somehow fail. The ancient Tarsean architects had valued both form and function, however, and the lines of the gatehouse were perfectly proportioned and decorated with beautifully carved lintels, leering gargoyles and long, trailing pennants that fluttered in the breeze.

The Tarsean officer raised a sceptical eyebrow on taking in Corraidhín's less than military appearance and scrutinised his papers carefully. He asked a couple of questions but was eventually forced to admit that the documents were in order and permit them to ascend to the walls. Arion wondered what papers Corraidhín possessed that gave him such freedom of movement in the middle of a siege but filed the thought away for consideration later. Skirting the gatehouse itself, they followed a narrow stairway along the face of the wall that ended on a wooden platform about halfway up. At their summit, the walls were wide enough to allow for large scale troop movements at speed and specially trained horses were even used to communicate between one section and another. The wooden platform on which they stood was the equivalent of a backroad – a different path to take when the top of the wall was overcrowded or under direct attack. Large staircases ran from the top of the wall, all the way to the ground at regular intervals but there were also ladders between the platform and the top and it was by that method that Arion and his companion ascended to the heights.

The stretch of wall on which Arion and Corraidhín now stood had seen action recently, judging by the battered stonework and tired-looking soldiers. The soldiers looked up as the two approached but upon realising that they were neither enemies nor officers, they quickly returned to their duties. Staying out of their way as much as possible, Arion and Corraidhín stood in silence for a few minutes, staring out over the walls.

"Now Arion, what do you see?"

Arion continued to stare, a little baffled for there seemed to be little to see at all. At the base of the wall, the deep waters of the Spercheios River had been diverted to run from east to west, set out from the wall and lined with brick, to avoid damage to the foundations. It formed a fast-moving and treacherous moat and a formidable obstacle to attackers but immediately below where they stood, the river was already bridged. They had approached under cover of large, thick leather canopies, that were soaked with water to prevent the defenders from setting them alight. Long, heavy oak beams had been levered out across the flowing water, each almost two feet wide and three inches thick. Placed side by side, the beams formed a sturdy and effective crossing point. The ground to either side had been churned into the muck by the passage of booted feet. Broken ladders, fallen arrows and discarded weapons were everywhere, along with what Arion was horrified to realise were the bodies of the dead. Nothing moved in the field of debris except a flock of scruffy-looking crows, gorging themselves silly on the horrendous bounty of war.

"Where is everybody?" said Arion and Corraidhín reached down to pick up a small rock from the ground. Brushing the dust and dirt from the top of the nearest merlon he began using the rock to scrape a rough map onto the surface of the stone.

"Tarsus," he said, drawing a slightly jagged circle. "We're here, looking out onto the plains of southern Asfáleia. The Devil's Teeth Mountains protect our flanks to the east and the west." He drew two parallel lines, each a short distance from either side of the circle.

"The Narrows Wall stretches through the walls of the city and across to the mountains, like so." He drew a third line bisecting the circle, then drew three smaller circles to the south of the city.

"The main Rutik camp is here, and they have two others: here and here. We're three weeks into the siege at this point. For the first week, little enough happened at all: the Rutik spent their time fortifying their camps, assembling their siege weapons and so on. In the second week, they carried out a series of small attacks all along the fortifications. That was the Rutik getting the lie of the land: take note of that, you'll be a general yourself one day and there's no substitute for first-hand information on your enemy. This week they've been launching more determined attacks, here close to the gate but also still way off to the east and west."

Arion stared at the sketched map and frowned.

"But why are they attacking over there at all? Surely, it's the city they want so why not just attack here?"

"Two reasons: one, in normal times the city walls are open to anyone who wants to take a stroll and the Rutik have had scouts crawling all over them for years. The Narrows Wall is harder to access, only our own soldiers are allowed access, so the Rutik need to get a closer look. They're hoping to find a weakness. But more importantly, they're making a point: they have the numbers to attack us wherever they want, in half a dozen places at once if they so please. They're letting us know that we need to defend every inch of the city walls and the Narrows Wall," he indicated the horizontal line, then pointed to the circular city. "And every soldier we have out here is one less we have to defend the city. When the assault on the gate comes, they want as many as possible of our soldiers tied up elsewhere. Your father's armies are stretched thin, and the Rutik intend to stretch them even more thinly."

Arion nodded, understanding the point immediately. The siege now seemed not so much a matter of curiosity and excitement. Corraidhín's map was rudimentary, but somehow just seeing it all laid out made the whole thing seem much more real, in a way that even the scattered bodies and fallen weapons had not conveyed. Through the scuffed lines of the map, Arion now saw the Rutik path to victory and knew that they were a viable threat, prepared and determined to destroy everything he knew.

"Are we going to lose, Corraidhín?" he said, still staring at the map. Corraidhín took him by the shoulders, staring straight into his face before answering.

"The Rutik are fierce opponents, and they are many, but this is Tarsus: the greatest city Asfáleia has ever seen. Never in a thousand years have these walls failed, never once, not even when the menace to the north threw the ravenous spawn of his foul magic against them, not even then. I do not believe it will fall now either. Now. The day wears on and we had better get back to the palace." They walked back across the city in the warm spring sunshine and chatted about inconsequential things.

Arion returned to the palace with a lot to think about and found himself rapidly escorted to his rooms to change and clean up in advance of an audience with his father. With a heavy heart, he splashed water from a basin to rinse off the last of the dust and grime he had accumulated on the walls. His father was not a cruel man, nor was he given to shouting at his son or dispensing heavy punishments. It was far more likely that he would merely look mournful and a little disappointed and then brush the whole thing off as his attention was diverted elsewhere. Arion would have preferred to be yelled at, confined to his rooms, or denied his privileges for a period – anything, to get a hint that his father truly noticed what his son was up to. He missed his father as he used to be: kind, good-humoured, and always ready with a hug or a word of encouragement, and never letting the burden of his responsibilities get between him and his oldest son.

Not that Achaeus did not have good reasons for melancholy. First Arion's mother was taken by a fever, shortly before his third birthday. The king had taken it badly but eventually remarried, as much, Arion suspected, for the Kingdom's benefit as his own. His second wife, younger and fresher than he, had brought a spell of bright sunshine to the palace and a smile to his father's face, especially when the news came that she was with child. Then death struck again, and Arion's stepmother passed away in childbirth. The twin boys that she delivered with her dying breath were detached and distant. Even now, ten years later, they hardly spoke to anyone but each other, rarely made eye contact and did not seem to understand what the world was about. Arion liked the twins, even though they were never the playmates and partners-in-crime that he had fervently hoped for. They were quiet, it was true, but when they spoke it was usually to say something worth listening to and in all their lives Arion had never heard either of them utter an unkind word, nor so much as a half-truth, never mind a lie. They were also highly intelligent and far more diligent about their studies than their older sibling. Whatever the subject, Arion could always rely upon his brothers for assistance when he struggled. His father seemed to see things differently, however, and maintained only a passing relationship with his younger sons, throwing himself into his duties instead.

That, of course, was another likely source of the king's malaise: the war with the Kingdom of the Rutik had not come out of the blue but was rather the culmination of decades of friction and low-level aggression. His term as king had been one of constant strife and Tarsus was the greatest of the remaining Achaean city-states. If Tarsus fell, it would take with it the battered remnants of hope amongst all Achaeans, dashing it to fractured pieces on the jagged rocks of Rutik aggression. If Tarsus was the cornerstone of Achaean resilience and resistance, Arion's father was the foundation of it all. On his shoulders rested the fate of not only his kingdom, and not only his people but all that remained of free Achaean society. The weight of such responsibility would have broken a lesser man, but Arion knew that even his father was struggling to bear the load.

Arion arrived to find his father seated on his throne as usual, but even as he approached, he was immediately struck by how tired and drawn his father looked. A man in his early fifties, tall and strong from a life spent as a soldier and a general, Achaeus appeared to have aged a decade in the mere weeks that had passed since the arrival of the Rutik. An intelligent, capable man, he had taken the throne some fourteen years prior and now occupied the same seat as his father, his father's mother and almost thirty generations before that. He found himself the inheritor of a kingdom long neglected, a treasury depleted, and hundreds of years of accumulated power and glory squandered and lost by venal kings and feckless queens. Upon taking the throne, Achaeus had immediately begun a programme of reforms – restructuring corrupt institutions, rebuilding the army, and providing vital succour to the weakest and most vulnerable of his subjects. In parallel, he began a programme of diplomatic outreach, reaffirming and restoring relationships with the other Achaean cities and forming the King's Rangers to travel the Narrows and further afield, offering military support to anyone who called for it. In a little over a decade, he had succeeded in halting the decline of his nation and set his people back on the path to greatness but all that had come to a shuddering halt with the resurgence of the war with the Kingdom of the Rutik. For the last three years, all of Achaeus's efforts had been directed towards a single goal: survival. Pivoting masterfully to his new role, Achaeus built a coalition of Achaean armies that held the Rutik at bay for months and years on end.

In short, Achaeus the Fourth, King of Tarsus and heir to Arrias the Conqueror himself, was a man of both ability and vitality. He had always appeared to his son as an invincible, yet kindly giant but now he seemed not even to register his arrival, his weary gaze locked blankly on a wide tapestry that covered one of the walls. Arion stepped forward and coughed politely, expecting his father to start in surprise but the king scarcely seemed to notice and continued to stare at the wall hanging for a while before slowly looking up. As his eyes found Arion, a little of his old energy seemed to return to his face and he smiled warmly.

"My son. Apologies, I am distracted."

Arion moved closer to sit on the steps below his father's throne and turned his head to look up.

"Father, no – I came here to apologise! I really didn't mean to cause so much commotion!"

"If intentions were a sufficient excuse, we would all be forgiven." Achaeus's smile faded, and Arion noticed that his hands were clutched tightly together in his lap, as though to prevent them from shaking. Arion was at a loss for words. His father had always worked hard and had been under tremendous pressure for as long as Arion could remember. Never had he seen him so despondent, so defeated. Was the situation so dire that even his father's indefatigable courage had failed?

After a long, awkward silence, the king finally spoke again, seemingly answering Arion's unspoken question.

"My generals tell me that we are holding the walls without heavy losses but how can I trust them?"

"Father?" Achaeus glanced around the room and then leaned down to whisper to his son.

"They conspire against us, Arion. They hide it well, but I see them: huddled in corners, whispering, plotting. They think me a fool, Arion!"

"Are you sure, father?" It seemed unimaginable to Arion that the Kingdom's generals, faithful heroes all, could be involved in any such nefarious activity. He felt it more likely that the statues in the hall would come to life and begin speaking than those stalwart men and women turn upon their king. Achaeus leaned closer.

"Quite sure. We can trust no one, Arion. No one at all." He paused for a moment, looking thoughtful, then sat up and blinked slowly.

"Arion?" he said, almost as though noticing him for the first time. "I have ordered an extra guard posted at the door to your rooms. Return there immediately and remain until I have time to deal with you." His eyes now blazed with anger and Arion felt tears welling up for the second time that day.

"Father, no! You cannot. I won't go! You can't make me."

"Can you not see that this is no time for your foolishness? We are under siege, Arion. The enemy is at our gates and clamouring to be let in. We cannot spare the resources to track down a wayward child."

"But you can't just lock me up, father. It's not fair. You just want me out of the way!"

"Stop this nonsense at once!"

"Father, I…" Arion trailed off under his father's ferocious glare. Achaeus rose to his feet and pointed to the doors.

"Go!" he shouted. Unable to process what was happening, Arion almost tripped over his own feet in his haste to turn and leave the room. Somehow, he reached the doors and slipped out without looking back, fleeing across the palace to the safety of his rooms.

Alone in the throne room, Achaeus sat unmoving, his hands now white-knuckled, gripping the arms of his throne. A grey fog seemed to have settled on the world around him, obscuring detail and twisting meaning. He tried to marshal his thoughts but dismissing one worry only made space for another to take root in its place, dragging him back down into the haze. He knew that there were things he should be doing: orders to be given and followed up, reports to be taken, plans to be made – but somehow, he could not summon the will to rise. In his absence, orders would go unissued, and the defence of the city would become fractured and weak as each of his generals and Captains tried to do what seemed best from their limited perspectives. Awareness and comprehension seemed to screeching for attention at the back of his mind, but the sound was dull and muted, easily ignored. His son needed him, his people needed him, and his kingdom needed him, but Achaeus found himself unable to act.

Thinking of Arion sent a pang through him that seemed about to pierce the cloying gloom, but the moment passed, and darkness descended once more. Arion was just a boy and Achaeus would not risk his life in battle, not yet. Bringing the boy on the hunt for the Vedi had been a mistake, he could see that now, and the injuries Arion had sustained that day could have been so much worse. Waking to find his eldest son, and the heir to the throne, unmoving on the ground, and not knowing in that moment whether the boy was alive or dead, was one of the worst moments of his life. Arion had acquitted himself well, it was true, and by all accounts had finished off the Vedi almost single-handedly. That news had made Achaeus immensely proud of his son, but not so much so that he would permit the boy to place himself in the line of danger again.

Besides, he reasoned, it was the War Spear that did most of the work. Achaeus glanced over at the weapon, where it stood on a purpose-built rack to the left of the throne, a tangible symbol of Tarsean might for any who might visit the throne room. For a moment, he would have sworn that it glinted, as though acknowledging his attention. Truth be told, the spear frightened him a little. There had been times, over the years, where Achaeus would have backed away from a fight, or would have spared a vanquished enemy but the spear, somehow, had other ideas. Once the power started flowing through it, the thirst for blood became almost uncontrollable and it was not a feeling that Achaeus was fond of. That said, it was a truly fearsome weapon and he suspected that its thirst would be well satisfied before the siege was ended. He should have gone to the walls days ago, should have shown his face to the soldiers, given them what encouragement he could, or at the very least shared in their struggles against the enemy. *Tomorrow*, he told himself, *tomorrow we'll go.* In his heart, he knew he was lying to himself, however, and tomorrow, like today, he would find some excuse to remain in the palace. The soldiers would just have to understand the burden that rested upon his shoulders – the weight of an entire kingdom and lives in their tens of thousands. He felt as though the siege had condensed it all down into a massive boulder that rested uneasily upon his back. The soldiers would just have to understand.

Behind the throne, three tall alcoves displayed ten-foot-tall marble statues of the first rulers of Tarsus – Arrias the Conqueror, his daughter Agariste, and his grandson, Achaeus's namesake whose fitting epithet had been "the Wise". The three looked down upon their descendent with eyes that were stony and blank but in the folds of Agariste's robe hidden from view to anyone below, something winked and glittered. What appeared to be a small, black pearl had been hidden there, perfectly round, unblemished, and somehow glowing with a dull, flickering light. Close up, the pearl seemed to exude a twisted aura of frightening menace, a sensation that would become almost palpable were one to touch the surface. Even as Achaeus sat brooding, the aura reached out across the throne room to wrap his mind in its grasping tentacles. Where they touched, all happiness withered, despair took root and the light guttered and died.

Somewhere in the darkness, but faint as if coming from a tremendous distance, something cackled.

CHAPTER FIFTEEN

Southern walls, City of Tarsus
20 of Euthaios 870M - Late Spring
Day fifteen of the siege of Tarsus

At their closest point, the Illyan Isles sit a mere eighty nautical miles off the coast of Asfáleia, across a sheltered and easily navigable channel. The Rutik ports of Bremerhafnō and Cuxhafnō both sit on the near shore of the same waters, waypoints on the busy coastal shipping routes. Raiders and reavers from the pirate city of Skibbrudpunkt pass by on their way to easier pickings in the south. Merchant convoys from the Achaemenid Empire sail close on their way to exchange spices and exotic wares for timber and metals in Rutiksborg. And yet, despite all that traffic, none make landing on the Isles.

Cleitarchus, "The Natural Wonders of Asfáleia", c. 675M

Chapter Fifteen

The Rutik army had arrived at the gates of Tarsus on the sixth day of Euthaios, as spring turned to summer and the last of the spring rains evaporated from the ground. A week later, Radomir stood his post atop the wall and watched as his followers sat with their backs to the outer rampart, sweltered in the heat and patched their wounds. Unlike the Rutik, who had developed a very complex and formal system of military ranking, the Achaeans still clung to the old ways, where authority was based on popular acclaim and the hard-won approval of the governed. Radomir thus commanded a body of soldiers that was two dozen strong, popular despite his short temper and total disregard for the softer skills of interpersonal relationships. Responsibility for their lives was not a privilege he had sought out, or particularly welcomed, but long years of experience had taught him that his own chances of survival were far higher with a loyal and cohesive body of soldiers behind him. Still, as he stood and listened to the soldiers moan and complain, he missed the quiet solitude of the Narrows and the freedom to act entirely without consideration of any other.

The mood amongst the defenders was grim, far more so than it should have been, in Radomir's assessment. Of the hundred and thirty-five soldiers assigned to that section, they had lost perhaps a dozen in the morning's fighting – four to disabling wounds, two severely injured and unlikely to survive, and six killed on the spot. The base of the wall was piled with Rutik corpses but although the enemy had lost a dozen for every one of theirs, the enemy could afford to lose ten times more, whereas Tarsus could not spare a single man. That said, despite their numbers and obvious determination, the Rutik had failed to gain any serious victories. The walls of Tarsus were unique in Asfáleia for their height, their thickness and their cunning layout that allowed the defenders a plethora of advantages over the attackers. The Rutik were strong and would keep coming as long as they were able, but their chances of success were vanishingly small. If the Tarseans stood firm, sooner or later the invaders would have to give up and go home. The Rutik were famous for their command of logistics and the campaign against Tarsus had been years in the planning but sooner or later the inexorable equations that governed the provision of reinforcements, supplies, and materiel's for an army of this size, so far from home, would start to tell against them. The western half of Asfáleia was densely populated and the Rutik would be bleeding the local farms and villages dry but even that convenient source of resupply would be exhausted eventually. When that happened, they would be forced to rely upon long trains of wagons, transferring food and other goods from further afield. There would be losses and wastage along the way, and both the wagon drivers and their beasts would literally eat into the supplies. The wagon trains would need guards too, who would also need to be fed and watered, further diminishing the stocks that eventually reached the investing army. Even the Rutik could not keep that up forever. Those facts were common knowledge amongst the Tarsean soldiery, and should have been enough to maintain their spirits, but for reasons that Radomir could not yet fathom, a pall of despair and disillusionment hung over the defenders, as though defeat were an inevitability they could only forestall.

As Radomir pondered the mystery, an enormous boulder, launched from a Rutik siege engine, hit nearby and a few of the Tarsean militia volunteers flinched at the crashing impact. The section was mostly manned by such volunteers, with a solid backbone of skilled warriors, including Radomir's Ranger comrades, Red and Ombly. Like Radomir, the pair had chosen to join in the defence of the city rather than remain in the north. Most of the other Rangers had taken the opposite decision, believing that their oaths were better served by attending to their regular duties. Red laughed derisively at the outcry, rubbing at his bristly red beard with a sneer.

"Scared of loud noises now, are we? Some use you lot are. You all should have stayed in your little houses, making pottery or whatever the fuck you did before signing up. You're useless."

"Leave them alone, Red, you old, hairy goat-fondler," snapped another soldier. The bearded man glared at him, more outraged by the interruption of his fun than the insult to his sexual proclivities.

"How about I throw one or two of them over the wall instead," Red growled. "And you too, Iappous, you old sack of shit. How would you like that?"

"I'd like to see you try, Red. You couldn't lift my dick without help." Red's eyes widened and he made to struggle to his feet when a dark shadow fell, and Radomir loomed over them.

"Shut the fuck up, both of you idiots," he snapped, giving Red a kick for good measure.

Red subsided against the stone once more and rubbed at his leg where Radomir had kicked him. Iappous, whose name meant "grandfather" in the old language of the Achaeans, smiled slightly, and closed his eyes, leaning his head back against the wall.

"Thanks, boss," piped up Ombly. "I was getting sick of listening to those two idiots, to be honest."

"You shut the fuck up too. And get your gear ready, they'll be back any minute."

The soldiers grumbled and moaned but gathered their weapons and put on their helmets.

"Here they come!" The shout echoed down the line. All along the wall bows began to sing out and arrows rained down upon the charging Rutik. The Rutik kept coming though, shields held above their heads for protection, long ladders carried between them. As they approached the wall a final barrage of siege missiles was launched over their heads and two massive rocks hit close to where Radomir and the others waited. The twin collisions were scarcely ten feet apart from one another and the soldiers were enveloped in dust and peppered with hundreds of fragments of razor sharp shrapnel. One rock landed directly in the middle of a clutch of volunteers, killing five instantly and throwing three others backwards off the wall and into the city. The second hit a relatively empty spot but still managed to annihilate one of Radomir's soldiers.

The tops of Rutik ladders appeared all along the wall and shaking his head to clear the dust, but otherwise seemingly unaffected by the bombardment, Radomir raised his axe and roared at his soldiers, calling them to arms. The sudden and gory deaths had more of an impact on the volunteers though, and those within sight of the impacts were badly shaken. A nearby group of three immediately turned and ran when the Rutik ladders appeared, their nerve lost utterly. Their departure left a gap in the defence, that widened rapidly as the volunteers to either side scrambled towards the relative safety of their fellows, further along the wall. Rutik soldiers poured over the ramparts to fill the void and within minutes, Radomir and the others were fighting for their lives.

It was almost an hour before they managed to clear the wall, and another hour after that before the Rutik assault finally subsided. At one point, Red fell in a tangle of bodies and was only saved from the enemy's spears when Radomir jumped across him and, with a couple of swings of his axe, beheaded one of the attackers and carved a second nearly in two from shoulder to waistline. Radomir followed up by using the haft of his weapon to stove in the head of a third soldier, then reached down and dragged Red to his feet with one meaty hand. As he wiped the blood from his eyes, Ombly appeared beside him, with Iappous and half a dozen of the remaining volunteers close behind and together they established a rough formation, with Radomir on point, Red and Ombly at his either shoulder and the others backing them up, and then charged at the enemy with a shouted battle cry. Radomir hit the Rutik line like a battering ram, driving through them and chopping left and right with his axe. Red and Ombly stayed close and widened the breach, their spears darting out to steal the life from one Rutik soldier after another. Iappous and the volunteers flowed into their bloody wake, finishing survivors, and fighting in pairs to protect their backs. Finally, they reached the nearest of the ladders and the formation naturally switched as the soldiers turned to face the enemy on the walls, while the volunteers moved to the relative safety of the ramparts.

Two of the volunteers grabbed the top of a ladder and tried to push it backwards off the wall but the weight of soldiers climbing from the bottom made it almost immovable. Red's spear found a woman's cheek, slicing through skin and flesh and bursting out the other side of her face in a spray of gore and shattered teeth. The Rutik soldier reeled back in shock and agony, her screams becoming choking gurgles as her throat filled with blood. Red knocked her aside with one brawny arm and pushed his way over to the wall's edge.

"Not like that, you fucking dung-lickers," he shouted, shoving the straining volunteers out of the way. "Like this!"

And with that, he grasped one of the ladder rails in each hand with a mighty roar, drove the whole thing sideways along the wall's edge until it reached a point where gravity took over. The ladder toppled, taking down the two adjacent ladders as it fell. Red peered over the rampart for a moment, admiring the long stretch of gory, mangled ruin he had created at the base of the wall, then turned back to the volunteers.

"That's how it's done," he laughed savagely. "Those fuckers won't be coming back up. Now, get your arses behind me and we'll go do it again."

With Radomir and the others providing protection, Red and the two volunteers moved further along the wall and repeated the process twice more, felling half a dozen ladders in total. By that time, the Rutik had had enough. Those still on the ladders slid down as rapidly as they could, falling over one another in their haste to retreat. Those left atop the wall were forced back or driven into corners and finally slaughtered. No mercy was expected or given – both sides had seen too much death already for such niceties to endure. An hour later, the Tarseans were back slumped against their ramparts, hotter, more tired, and more battered than ever.

"Reckon they'll be back today, boss?" asked Ombly, producing a rag from somewhere and wiping the blood off her spear's point.

Radomir shrugged.

"Doubt it. Reckon they've had enough of dying for one day. Maybe tomorrow." Ombly nodded, then looked around at her exhausted comrades.

"I suppose the fuckers are in no rush," she said finally.

"Yeah, that's right," put in Red. "Might as well kill us all tomorrow as today really." No one had a response to that and for a while, the only sound to be heard was laboured breathing, and the moans of the wounded and dying that drifted along the wall with the breeze.

Radomir looked around at his soldiers, judging them with the eye of a seasoned leader. Red and Ombly were solid, of course. They might bitch and moan a bit, but they would stand. Radomir had known them both for ten years or more and they had fought side by side in battles up and down the Narrows and into the southern plains. Funnily enough, it was Red, a southerner by birth, who had thrived in the north. The Bulġha, Radomir's people, were warriors of Red's own temperament. Their preference for charging straight in and slugging it out toe-to-toe with their enemies matched his aggressive style and he seemed to enjoy the small scale, brief but ferocious pitched battles that were the hallmark of Tarsean campaigns against the northern raiders. By contrast Ombly, herself a Bulġha, flourished in the more formal, rigid battle lines of the south. One on one, Ombly was a fearsome fighter but standing shoulder to shoulder with her fellows, she was almost unstoppable. The added security of having others to watch her back allowed her more freedom of movement, and when she stood the line her spear jabbed at eyes, slashed throats, and punctured armour without ceasing until all the enemy were dead or had run away. Their battles in the south had been mostly fought as allied contingents in the armies of other cities, sent by the king to fulfil treaty obligations or in the hope of earning future favours. To Radomir, it was all the same. He harboured no illusions about himself and knew that the only thing he was ever genuinely good at was killing. Whether he killed Bulġha and stray Vedi in the Narrows or Rutik on the plains made little difference to him.

Iappous was less of a known quantity to Radomir, though he seemed solid enough. Technically a civilian volunteer, he was an old soldier who had laid down his arms years before to go and raise cattle on a patch of land in the Narrows. He seemed to have some experience of battle and was handy enough with a spear that Radomir was comfortable relying on him to act as a de facto leader to the other volunteers. Unlike their Rutik opponents, the Tarseans did not adhere to a formal system of ranks and hierarchy. They preferred the old Achaean way of doing things, where every soldier was technically an equal, but some were more equal than others. A soldier who showed and aptitude for war, was a mighty warrior or a charismatic leader could assume command of any who would follow. A hero of enough renown might thereby find themselves leading an ever-larger number of troops. The system had its advantages and disadvantages. A member of the nobility with sufficient resources might build a following by the liberal distribution of gold and favours, but overall only the genuinely worthy would generally rise to the top

The volunteers seemed to take comfort in Iappous's evident survival skills and his calm demeanour was less intimidating to them than Ombly's caustic aggression or Red's belligerent thirst for battle. They had begun the day with six volunteers, not including Iappous but after the day's fighting and the unfortunate accuracy of the Rutik siege engines, were now down to two. One was a younger woman from the Tarsean slums, skinny as a rake but quick and vicious. The company jokers had named her Smudge, Radomir neither knew nor cared why. The other was an older man they called Cloudy because of a tendency to daydream when not immediately occupied. He was some form of a schoolteacher in his former life, but his lessons had evidently not included fighting skills. He was a complete disaster with a sword and only marginally better with a spear. Radomir was surprised to find that Cloudy had survived the first day and even more so to be told that he had managed to kill a couple of people. Uncharitably, Radomir wondered which side those people were on before Cloudy poked them full of holes. Odds were as good that they were friends as foes.

All in all, Radomir reflected, they were not in great shape for the coming battles, but it could have been a lot worse. With the three seasoned warriors stationed as a bulwark against the worst of the Rutik attackers, and the others pitching in where they could Radomir believed they could hold their position. Assuming, that was, that the Tarseans did not lose hope altogether. Again, his mind turned to the question of morale and the baffling lack of faith amongst the troops. It did not help, he thought, that the king had not been seen on the walls in over a week. That too was puzzling. Radomir had known Achaeus since he was a child, had travelled the world with him and fought beside him on dozens of occasions. He was a man who had never taken his authority for granted, despite being royalty and a direct descendent of the greatest of Tarsean heroes. Achaeus had always led from the front, first into every charge and determined to take his fair share of danger. Now, when the soldiers needed him the most, he was absent, hiding in his palace while they fought and died on the walls. In the absence of his overall authority, the defence was fractured, and uncoordinated as individual commanders pursued their own strategies and goals. Radomir frowned as he pondered, then, with characteristic pragmatism, decided that there was nothing he could do about the problem and let it go. His mind drifted to Corraidhín, who he knew was fighting another, equally desperate battle, elsewhere in the city. If the walls failed, that battle would be for nothing.

Just get your royal arse down here, Achaeus, he growled under his breath.

A short distance away, in a small room above a nondescript dockside tavern, Corraidhín sat amidst a world of stunningly brilliant colour that only he could see. The walls of the room glowed blue but were translucent, almost transparent, allowing him to see the rooms beyond and the city itself beyond that. Vaguely human-shaped blurs in varying shades of gold and silver moved to and fro across the hazy backdrop: eating, sleeping, talking, loving – all the things that humans do. In places they were gathered in groups: in the tavern below the barflies sat and drank the day away, out on the river docks a dozen stevedores waited to unload a grain shipment from the Narrows, out on the city walls mingled tones marked units gathered to the defence. In other places they were alone: a man eating a meagre meal in a house not much bigger than Corraidhín's lodgings; a woman lying on her bed, her colour fading as some illness slowly drained the life out of her; a small child playing in the dirt of a fenced-in back yard. Corraidhín could see and feel them all. Tension and fear on the walls, anticipation on the docks, misery at his meal, resignation on her deathbed.

The Oracle's power had allowed Corraidhín to extend his awareness across the city and thus become an unseen fellow traveller of thousands of people. The power allowed him to see something else too: the oily, black stains on reality that marked the presence of a creature not of the mortal plane. There were far more of those than Corraidhín had anticipated and although the Oracle had given him the strength to fight them, it was only barely enough. He focused on one such tainted blemish and winced as it turned a wrathful eye in his direction. The sense of evil was almost overwhelming. Its inherent wrongness jarred his conscious mind like a discordant note in a lofty and still soaring symphony. He felt contaminated by its foul corruption, infected by the mere brush of its regard.

Steeling himself, Corraidhín focused harder on exerting the Oracle's power and forcing the creature down. It resisted, bellowing in rage, its shadow coalescing into a thing of fangs and claws. Tendrils of near-corporeal strength swept across the city, aimed at the room in which Corraidhín sat. The Oracle's power swept them aside and dashed them to pieces, their force shattered and dispersed to settle harmlessly onto the city. Corraidhín continued to push, beating the creature back, capturing its shadowy essence and imprisoning it within walls of pure will. The creature's roars turned to panicked screeches, but its hatred seemed only to grow in strength as its defeat loomed. Corraidhín fought on, knowing that to lose control at this juncture would be to doom not alone himself, or the people of Tarsus but maybe even the Oracle herself. For all her ancient strength, he knew she was not without limitations and the power she had passed to him for this task might well have left her vulnerable.

Fierce love for the Oracle gave new vigour to Corraidhín's efforts and with a final burst of effort, he drove the creature deep into the earth, burying it beneath a million tons of soil and rock. In the real world, sweat was running down his brow and his muscles were aching from the tension and his jaw was clenched so tightly he felt sure that his teeth would crack. Forcing himself to breathe, he withdrew a little to recover, satisfied with his victory. The creature was not dead, of course, Corraidhín did not even know if it was possible to kill such things, or whether death was even a meaningful term in the context of something that was not alive by any normal definition of the word. Nor would its confinement last forever. Sooner or later the creature would find its way back to the surface to begin its work again but that was a problem for another day, and perhaps a better man. The most Corraidhín could do was delay the creatures, and he could only hope that would be enough for now. They were causing murder and mayhem all over the city, and the fallout from that was sapping the will of the Tarsean people, weakening their resolve when their fortitude was most essential.

Another shadowy smear caught Corraidhín's attention, and he gave a heartfelt sigh. For days it had been this way: one enemy defeated and another rising to take its place. He likened it to trying to smooth out a large sheet of thin paper – a bump disappeared from one place, only to reappear as a crease in another. He was exhausted, mentally, and physically, and had not slept in almost a week. In all the long years of his exceptionally long life, he had never spent so much time on the higher planes of being. Amongst his people, it was considered a perilous task to dip one toe in those waters, and here he was wading in up to his neck. There would be a price to be paid at the end of it, he knew, and it would not be cheap.

The creatures were spread evenly across the city, as though deliberately scattered to bring chaos and misery to as many people as possible. Only in and around the Royal Palace were they present in higher concentrations. For every five that arose in the city, two were within the palace walls, even though the grounds occupied less than one-twentieth of the city by area. There was something else too. No matter where the creatures appeared, they soon gravitated towards the palace, as though drawn there by some mysterious compulsion that only they could understand. Corraidhín had initially assumed that the presence of the creatures was intended to cause maximum disruption to the Tarsean defence in advance of the more conventional attack from without. As an explanation, it was perfectly logical but if that were so, then he would have expected their attention to be focused on the walls and the main strength of the Tarsean defence. He now believed that their main target was the King himself, and possibly the commanders and advisors that surrounded him.

Even as Corraidhín struggled to defeat the next of his foes, he continued to fret. He was by no means sure that he could continue this fight for long enough to foil the enemy's plans, whatever they were. The Oracle had gifted him the use of tremendous powers, but he was only a man and sooner and later he would tire, make a mistake, and falter. At the instant he did so, he knew, they would be upon him like wild dogs on a stricken farm animal. Being torn to shreds would only be the beginning of his torments. Even more worrisome, however, was the nagging feeling that he was missing something vital and that all his efforts, no matter how determined, might be directed at the wrong target. It was something to do with the palace, of that much he was sure, something there that he was not seeing, or not understanding. The demon attacked fiercely, whilst clinging tenaciously to its tether on the surface and Corraidhín could give no further thought to the matter.

Late that night, the silence outside Corraidhín's room was broken by a soft knocking at the rough wooden door. No one answered from within, and, after a moment's hesitation, a large figure pushed open the door and stepped slowly through. The room was in darkness, the windows shuttered and closed against the night. The figure tensed and began inching around the perimeter until it brushed up against a small sideboard where it stopped. Silence returned for a moment, and then was broken by the crackling snap of metal against flint. Sparks flew, illuminating small areas of the room in brilliant light, then instantly dying, until finally one caught, and a lantern leapt into life, revealing the craggy features of Radomir, a deep frown furrowing his forehead.

Raising the lantern in his right hand, Radomir turned slowly to survey the room in its light. There was little enough to see so it was only a moment before he spotted Corraidhín, lying on the floor, silent and unmoving. Radomir's expression showed not an iota of emotion as he hurried to the fallen man's side and, setting the lantern on the floor, knelt to place a massive palm on his chest. To his immense relief, he felt the tiniest movement there. It was faint and scarcely detectable, but Corraidhín's small chest was rising and falling slowly. Radomir growled and moved his hand to the other man's shoulder, shaking him with surprising gentleness.

"Wake up, you old fool. You're asleep on the floor." Corraidhín slowly opened his eyes and looked up at him, then smiled weakly.

"Radomir. I must get back to work. The King is in danger." He tried to raise his head and failed, slumping back to the floor a moment later. Radomir snorted.

"We're all in danger, my friend. The King will have to survive a little longer without you." Corraidhín attempted to object, but Radomir ignored him and, sliding one arm under his shoulders and the other under his knees, he picked him up off the floor and stood in one effortless movement.

Corraidhín spoke no more as Radomir carried him over to the room's only, single bed and set him down on the scratchy, straw-filled mattress. He was asleep an instant later and Radomir stood watching him for a minute or two before reaching to pull a blanket over him and moving to a nearby chair to sit down. He remained there, awake in the chair, watching over Corraidhín until the first rays of the morning sun filtered through the cracks around the shutters and cast patterns onto the rough wooden floor. Then he stood, yawning, and stretching, took a final glance at Corraidhín and left the room. He was due back at his post in an hour, but the other man's breathing was deeper now and the colour had returned to his face. Radomir had only a limited understanding of what Corraidhín had been doing before his arrival, but it seemed the worst of the danger had passed for the moment at least.

A twelve-hour watch lay ahead of him, tough to do without having slept but it was a price Radomir was willing to pay.

CHAPTER SIXTEEN

Western Devil's Teeth Mountains
25 of Euthaios 870M - Late Spring
Day twenty of the siege of Tarsus

It is my belief that the phenomena we now call "magic" in Asfáleia, is but the lingering remnant of power bequeathed, borrowed, or stolen from the Firstborn. As a corollary to that, I would strongly argue that it is a finite resource, which argument is supported by the gradual fading of magic from the world over the centuries of human ascendancy. In the time of Arrias, for example, his twin brothers were renowned as great sorcerers and manipulators of power beyond comprehension. We have not seen their like since, and the petty conjurors and common hedge wizards of modern times are little more than tattered jesters before their mighty thrones.

Polemon of Chalcis, "The Ancients Weep", c. 975M

Chapter Sixteen

After the episode in the warehouse, Mira made great efforts to avoid both the Avatar and Ohtrad. If they rode to the front of the column, she retreated to the rear, and vice versa. It was not a perfect system, she still crossed paths with them occasionally, but there was plenty to keep her busy on the road and that gave her an excuse to be as unavailable as possible. By that time, they were into the last leg of their journey, having left the final resupply point the previous morning. Ideally, they would have had one more resupply upon entering the Narrows but the risk of detection by the Tarseans was too high. Instead, a long caravan of wagons had left in advance of their departure carrying everything the expedition might need to complete their mission and reach Tarsus itself. There was still a risk of exposure, but the plan was for the caravan to hole up in a secluded spot in the foothills and it was decided that the benefits of a final resupply were sufficient to warrant the taking that chance. The reason that final resupply was so vital was that the final stage of their journey was expected to be the hardest.

The Devil's Teeth had two unique geographic features. The first, and most obvious was the fact that the twin mountain ranges, the eponymous teeth, ran north to south in almost perfectly parallel lines, curving slightly, and in almost perfect unison, towards the west. The second was that on the outside edges, the Teeth grew out of the plains in a prosaic fashion, the land beginning to rise, leading to low foothills, gradually blending into the much higher peaks at the centre. On the inside edges, however, the topography was markedly different. There were no gentle rises and few foothills. The towering, snow-capped behemoths continued to the edge of the Tarsean Narrows and then dropped away precipitously, turning to flat grassland in less than a day's walk. Mira thought that it was almost as though the two Teeth had once been one extended range of mountains, stretching from the northern Kingdom of the Rutik in the west, to the dry wastes of the Hinterlands in the east. Then one day, somehow, impossibly, a giant hand had swept out of the sky, scooping up the central swathe of mountains and casting it off into the sea, leaving the Teeth orphaned and separated. She knew how fanciful the thought was, of course, but there was no more rational, or natural explanation for such a curious formation.

Whatever the explanation for the Devil's Teeth, they ensured that Mira's route to the Narrows would be as difficult as possible, for as long as possible. The engineers and their slaves had worked for months on this last section, doing heroic work in horrifying conditions but despite their best efforts, the expedition slowed to a crawl as the forces of nature attacked them with every weapon at their disposal. Freezing wind and rain transitioned to driving snow, gave way to showers of hail the size of large pebbles, and then paused briefly for ferocious displays of thunder and lightning before raining once more. Crevices opened, running along and even across the frozen road, swallowing soldiers and workers alike, then closed again just as quickly sealing their fate forever. Avalanches of snow were chased down the steep slopes by landslides and waves of boulders. Whole sections of the road disappeared as the cliffs and slopes below crumbled and fell. Horses, driven wild by the punishing weather and howling winds, reared and threw their riders with such regularity that eventually Mira had to order the entire column to dismount, and the journey continued on foot, becoming ever more miserable with each exhausted step.

All the while clutches of misshapen Vedi shadowed the Rutiks' movements, snatching up any person foolish or unlucky enough to be become separated from the column. The presence and nature of the Vedi had formed part of Mira's briefings prior to the expedition setting out. In the safety and comfort of the fortified camp, she had found the briefings difficult to believe and had wondered if perhaps he commanders were exaggerating for effect, or out of misguided superstitious fear. Now, having encountered the creatures up close and seen for herself their hideous deformities and savage ferocity, she knew that, if anything, the briefings had been toned down.

Mira found the Vedi terrifying, but far worse creatures came in the night, sneaking and slithering out of the foul weather to tear people's throats out while they slept, dragging the remains away into the darkness. Twice they were attacked by much larger beasts that had, as far as Mira knew, neither species nor genus. They lost almost three hundred soldiers to the first such attack before Ohtrad reached the scene bringing the Avatar to turn the tide with its uncanny powers. The second time they finally got lucky, and the attack came at a point close to where the Avatar rode. That creature was driven away before too much damage could be done but still, it left dozens of shattered bodies in its wake. There were other attackers too, less massive but deadly on their own smaller scale. Soldiers awoke in the morning covered from head to foot in leeches, or with arms or legs swollen to twice or three times normal size from spider bites. On one horrifying occasion, an entire platoon was stripped almost to the bone by a swarm of winged beetles that settled upon them so quickly and in such numbers that the soldiers could not even cry out before the insects began to devour their living flesh.

The Avatar turned out to have other uses too. Each evening during that last terrible leg of the journey it somehow managed to ignite sodden, windswept campfires that burned through the night with exceptional heat, driving away the worst of the cold. It parted avalanches like a boulder thrown into a river, the stream of rocks and debris splitting and turning to pass a hundred yards to either side of it. After that everyone, even Mira, wanted to be where the Avatar was, and fights broke out amongst competing groups. Ohtrad watched them bicker and squabble with an amused smirk, then ordered the Avatar to ride up and down the column throughout each day's march. The Avatar seemed immune to the vicious weather, and just as immune to the relentless exhaustion that plagued the rest of the column. For those days where it ranged along the column, it rode perhaps four or five times as far as any of the soldiers, changing horses every so often but without showing the slightest sign of tiring itself. In all their weeks on the road, Mira never once saw it sleep, eat or do anything that hinted at humanity, except ride and stand guard outside Ohtrad's tent, its dark hood not even fluttering in the wind.

All the Avatar's formidable power could not fix Mira's next problem. Around midday on the second day out from the last resupply camp, the head of the column crested a steep rise, and then came to a sharp, disorderly halt as the far side of the hill became visible. The chaos in front rippled back through the lines until eventually the whole column stumbled and staggered to a stop. From her position close to the rear, Mira was a distance from the event that had triggered the disruption. It was well into the afternoon before she finally reached the scene, her progress slowed by the milling crowd of soldiers. As soon as she reached the crest of the hill, however, Mira instantly understood what had thrown the lead soldiers off their step.

The far side of the hill was strewn with bodies and debris for almost a mile ahead. Dead soldiers lay twisted and frozen on the ground, some missing limbs or heads, others beaten almost to a pulp. Shredded and mangled horses lay tangled in the broken remains of carts and crates. All manner of supplies from food and fresh water to weapons and spare pieces of armour were strewn about, crushed, and trampled into the filthy mud. The supply caravan was destroyed. From where she stood, Mira could see, here and there amongst the bodies of men and horses, the larger, more variegated corpses of the Vedi and even some of the more esoteric denizens of the mountains. Each of the monstrous bodies was surrounded by a ring of dead Rutik soldiers. The caravan guards had stood their ground for as long as possible, before being overwhelmed by their attackers. Mira supposed it was possible that some lucky few could have escaped the carnage, but it seemed unlikely to be many.

A moment later, the full implications of the disaster struck her in that they would no longer have the comfort of knowing that fresh food and water, dry blankets, replacement boots and other essential gear waited for them at the end of their journey. She could see that the nearby soldiers had come to the same conclusion by the looks of complete dismay on their faces, and she could hear shouts of anger and frustration echoing along the line. At that moment Ohtrad and the Avatar appeared at her side, surveying the damage for themselves. For once the League's representative was without his trademark sleazy grin, and Mira wondered if he too had been clinging to the hope of a change of clothes and a hot meal.

"The caravan was well-defended," he said grimly. "How did this happen?"

"They were ambushed," replied the Avatar, its low voice somehow carrying perfectly through the wind and background noise. "Several larger creatures hit the front and rear of the caravan simultaneously. Most of the guard contingent moved out to meet them, but by doing so they exposed the main portion of the caravan. A large body of Vedi was concealed in that canyon to the east, waiting for the opportunity to strike. The caravan was devastated in minutes."

"The Vedi don't travel in large numbers," replied Mira, wondering how the Avatar seemed to know so much. "Much less plot sophisticated ambushes. They're savages. A nuisance, nothing more."

"They don't coordinate with the Vedi either," put in Ohtrad. "And yet here we are." Mira frowned at him, wondering why he chose the Achaean term, Vedi, to describe the creatures, rather than the Rutik equivalent. The Rutik called them Wildermänner, the savage men of the mountains. She filed the question away for later consideration as the Avatar spoke again:

"There was another power at work here. I can feel its spoor on the wind. Someone wished to ensure that the caravan was destroyed."

"The implications of that are *disturbing*," replied Ohtrad, showing what Mira felt was a masterful level of understatement. The Avatar, however, simply shrugged.

"If that other had the power to challenge me, it would already have done so," it growled. "We had anticipated that my presence would draw attention and the risk to the supply trains was deemed acceptable. This changes nothing."

"Completing our mission should be our only concern," agreed Ohtrad, and he pulled his horse around to move away. The Avatar seemed to stare at Mira for a moment or two, perhaps, she thought, gauging her reaction to the loss of supplies, then turned to follow him.

Alone for a moment, Mira remained in place, staring at the ruined caravan. In truth, there was no cause for despair. The loss of the caravan would make the last leg of their journey more miserable, certainly, and perhaps impact their effectiveness but it was not a killing blow. They carried enough supplies with them to scrape through on short rations and effect temporary repairs to weapons and equipment. If worst came to worst, she would leave a portion of her force behind and redistribute their mounts and gear amongst the remainder. Morale would take a serious hit but the only way to mitigate that was to keep the troops so busy that they did not have time to dwell on their sorrows. Evidently the commander of the expedition felt the same as Mira was summoned to a meeting of all officers almost immediately after the Avatar left.

The commander's first order was to set strong pickets all around the ambush site in case any of the attackers still lingered in the vicinity. A large contingent of soldiers was given the unenviable task of clearing the bodies from the road. A second was detailed to comb the wreckage for usable supplies. Once those two tasks were complete, a third contingent would do the heavy lifting, using their horses to pull the wrecked carts off the road. The Rutik were numerous, but the road was only so wide, and so the work parties were smaller than might have been considered optimal. Clearing the road would not be complete before darkness and no one had any desire to spend the night camped in the middle of such ruin. However, they could not send a contingent ahead to find alternative quarters without leaving one or another group outside of the Avatar's protection and the commander was not about to risk a second ambush. Instead, the work parties were ordered to dispose of the bodies and debris on the west side of the road, where most of it would roll or tumble down the mountainside. They would set up camp to the east, as far as possible from the dead. It struck Mira then that there was one advantage to the freezing temperatures – at least the corpses would not begin to rot overnight, and they would be spared the fetid smell of decaying flesh.

When the work was done and the camp was finally settling into an uneasy silence, Mira sought out Ohtrad. The scale and complexity of the ambush had shaken her more than she cared to admit. If they were to make it through the next few days, she needed to know what they were up against and Ohtrad knew more than he was letting on. She found him outside his tent, hunched over one of the Avatar's fires, squinting at an old book in the guttering firelight. Of the creature itself there was no sign, which Mira counted as a blessing. She could hear a shuffling from inside the tent but assumed that to be Waldebert, preparing his master's bed for the night. Ohtrad looked up as she approached and smiled, closing his book carefully and setting it on the ground.

"Captain Mira, what an unexpected pleasure. You are well, I trust?"

"Passably so. What are you reading?" Ohtrad looked down at the book before answering.

"Travellers' tales. A collection of stories from those few brave or foolish enough to have come this way before. I found it in the Royal Library, thought it might contain something useful." He shrugged and looked down at the book again.

"And? Does it?"

"Sadly, no. About half of it is, I believe, completely fabricated. Most of the other half is made up of stories heard from a friend, who heard them from another friend. What remains may well be true, or true enough anyway, but the writers seem more interested in persuading the reader not to go, than in helping him on his way."

"Shame," said Mira. Ohtrad shrugged in reply. "Your… the Avatar, he said there was another power behind the ambush. What did he mean? Who is out there?"

"Ah, now that is an even bigger question, and one even more likely to lead to tall tales and thinly veiled warnings." He smiled benignly at Mira's frown.

"I can't keep the column safe if I don't know what I'm fighting."

"You couldn't keep it safe if you did know and keeping the column safe is not your concern anyway. Your concern is to keep me safe, and me alone." He paused and looked thoughtful for a moment before continuing: "We think of these mountains as barren and unpopulated, but the truth is that many things live here. The Vedi, for one. The Vedi for another, though some would say they are but different variations on the same grotesque theme. Then there are… the others. Long before the Kingdom of the Rutik, or even Tarsus, long before the first humans ever set foot in Asfáleia, others lived here, and these mountains were one of their realms." He noticed the incredulous look on Mira's face and gave a short laugh. "Yes, it doesn't look like much does it? I am told they lived mostly underground, however, so perhaps the miserable cold above didn't bother them too much. Or perhaps the weather was different in those days, who knows?"

"And these "others" – they are still out there somewhere?"

"I believe so. Not many, you understand. But almost certainly some few still *linger*, here and there."

"What do they want with us? Are we trespassing?"

"Perhaps. More likely we find ourselves in a predicament of our own making, however. The Avatar has certain vital functions to perform once we reach Tarsus. Until then, he was charged with *smoothing the way* for us. You have seen what he can do. We believed that with his *assistance*, the expedition had far more chance of success."

"And now?"

"And now, ironically, I believe that our desire to make the journey easier, may in fact have made it considerably harder. Considerably harder indeed. Whatever is out there, I believe that it does not take kindly to *competition*."

Mira stared at him, trying to fill out the blanks he seemed to include in every second sentence. That the Avatar had magical powers, she now knew for a fact, even though mere weeks ago she would have maintained that such things only existed in fairy tales. Was Ohtrad saying that these "others" had powers too? The world seemed like a strange and dangerous place indeed. Ohtrad was watching her closely, and she wondered if perhaps he were testing her, gauging her reactions. If so, she wondered what he hoped to discover.

"Where is the Avatar now?"

"North of here, somewhere in the higher reaches, I imagine. We felt it was best that he draw their *attention* elsewhere." Waldebert emerged from the tent at that moment, and Ohtrad rose to his feet. It appeared that their conversation was drawing to an end, so Mira decided to press for one more answer.

"Will it work?"

"Perhaps. Get some sleep, Captain Mira. Tomorrow will be a long day indeed. I have the utmost faith in the Avatar's *abilities*, but it would be best if we were a long way away from here before darkness falls again." And with that, he stooped to retrieve his book before stepping past Waldebert and into the tent. Waldebert was staring at her, perhaps wondering what they had been discussing but a moment later, he too turned and ducked through the tent's opening, pulling the canvas flap closed behind him. Mira was left alone by the fire then, pondering on what Ohtrad had said.

The mood amongst the soldiers was grim for the remainder of their journey through the mountains. They endured three more full days' march through the most atrocious of conditions before finally reaching the edge of the high peaks and emerging into the sparse foothills on the eastern side of the Teeth. In all, the crossing had taken almost three weeks of slogging over some of the hardest terrain imaginable. Days were lost picking their way along narrow paths, balanced perilously between rearing cliffs above and rocky gorges far below. More were wasted waiting for scouts to find an alternative path around particularly egregious obstacles, or unexpected landslides, sudden snowdrifts, and hidden crevasses. The distance from where they now stood to the foothills far to the west was probably less than twenty leagues, if one could but fly straight, above all obstacles but the clouds. Down on the ground, burdened by weapons and baggage, fighting the elements, the wildlife, and the landscape at every turn, they had at times struggled to travel a single league in a day, and the path had been anything but straight. Mira believed they had probably travelled three times that twenty leagues and more, most of it along steep and treacherous inclines and none of it easy.

In those three weeks, hundreds of fighting men, and women of the Rutik were buried under falling rocks, had tumbled over cliffs, or been attacked and carried off by savage beasts. Twice or perhaps three times as many again from the baggage train. Hundreds more were lost to the icy cold and thin mountain air, extremities black with frostbite, lungs collapsed and ruined by wracking coughs. Three weeks of travelling from first light to frozen dark, leading the horses down trails almost too narrow to ride, despite the best efforts of the engineers, and lying half-awake all night, frozen and wet. Often, heavy storms of sleet and snow would come swooping down out of the higher reaches, reducing visibility to an arm's length and progress to a crawl. Gusts of bitingly cold wind would burst from hidden canyons, sweeping all before them and carrying men and women screaming to their doom.

They did not see the Avatar again until they were almost out of the mountains. At first, this caused much consternation amongst the troops, since they had come to rely upon it for protection against the elements and the predations of creatures great and small. It soon became apparent to Mira, however, that Ohtrad had been correct in his speculations. Once the Avatar was gone, the attacks reduced in both frequency and severity. Parties of Vedi were occasionally spotted on distant ridges, but they showed no interest in approaching the column any more closely. Of the larger, more ferocious creatures, there was no sign at all. Even the landslides and avalanches seemed to have relented in their desire to torment the Rutik. The road was still treacherous, and the weather was still appalling but at least the environment no longer appeared to be actively trying to murder them. Mira wondered how the Avatar was faring, alone in the mountains. She even dared to wonder if perhaps it was dead, but that seemed a forlorn hope indeed. She strongly suspected that, wherever it was, the Avatar was unlikely to meet anything more unpleasant than itself.

And so it was that, despite the hardships of the crossing, and the loss of the supply train, a week later an ordered mass of riders emerged from the quiet shadows and drew to a halt. As one they stood, silent and watchful, while the stars dwindled, and the sky grew lighter. Morning came in a drift, leaving behind a thick residue of damp, clinging fog that twisted about the horses' hooves. The morning air was cold and plumes of steamy breath from riders and beasts lingered long in the air, clumping and dispersing, mingling with the fog. It made them seem almost a part of the landscape – the brooding, snow-peaked mountains, the damp grass beneath their feet and the high, drifting clouds, far above their heads. It was as though they were all but chance formations of air and water that might vanish from being at any second. Their armour glinted and shone but their boots were worn and cracked from days of hard travel, through terrain where horses could only be led, and not ridden. Their mounts were proud creatures, bred to be war horses, but their mighty heads drooped wearily, and their ears were flat against their scalps. Along their sides, dark lines of shadow marked deep depressions between their ribs.

Mira rode a dozen yards ahead of the rest, beckoning to a junior officer to follow. The Lieutenant was barely older than she, his face barely covered by a sparse and somewhat patchy beard.

"Don't worry, Captain," said the man with a grin. "Even that black-eyed devil can't see through this cursed murk." Mira spared a sour glance for the Lieutenant and shook her head in disgust as a dark shape materialised from the twisting fog. One day, perhaps, the Lieutenant would learn to keep his mouth shut – if he lived that long. Suppressing a sigh, Mira summoned her courage and rode forward to meet the newcomer.

"Greetings," it said. The voice was low-pitched and slow, somewhere between a gurgle and a whisper and it forced its way through Mira's ears like a hot wire and burned itself into her mind. She raised a hand by way of a return and suppressed a shiver. Her mount whinnied nervously and danced back a step. Steadying it with a touch of her spurs, she looked at the figure before her and understood the animal's unease.

"Make haste to the south while the light lasts," the Avatar said quietly, emerging from the fog. After weeks of travel, Mira now knew that the Avatar was the earthly embodiment of whatever dark power stood behind the League. What that meant in terms of practical reality, though, she still had little enough notion. The Avatar kept its secrets close and though it had haunted them throughout their journey across the mountains, never once had Mira even seen what lay beneath its cloak. It occurred to her that perhaps there was nothing there at all and that the creature was but a phantom. Almost against her own will, she leaned forward a little and peered around its hood as it turned away to observe the legion. Even in the dim light, the creature's pale skin could be seen and the two black pits that served for its eyes.

The Avatar turned back, and Mira straightened up guiltily. For a moment it stared directly at her, and she felt trapped by the endless dark of its eyes. They bored into her, but somehow slowly, painfully, and at the same time seemed to draw her inward, threatening to swallow her whole being. She felt as though her entire skin, flesh and bone were being stripped away to expose her naked self beneath. She knew then that there was nothing she could hide from this creature, nothing she could hold back or keep to herself. It saw everything and knew everything. In the face of the Avatar's scrutiny, Mira knew herself to be nothing, less than the merest flying insect – to be used or expended as convenient but otherwise worthless.

"Ride on at speed," it said. "When you reach the gates, a way will be prepared for you." With that, the creature rode off and Mira breathed a heartfelt sigh of relief. Soon their mission would be over and then, perhaps, at least for a while, there would be relief from the terrible eyes. The young Lieutenant appeared at her side, scratching at his scrappy beard.

"Gives me the creeps, he does," he said with a nod. "What about you?" Mira stared at him wondering if she could ever find the words to answer without terrifying the young man beyond any hope of recovery. The Lieutenant grinned.

"We off, then?" he asked brightly. Mira nodded and gave her horse the signal to proceed.

Some things, she reflected, *were better left unsaid.*

CHAPTER SEVENTEEN

The Tarsean Narrows, close to Tarsus
26 of Euthaios 870M - Late Spring
Day twenty-one of the siege of Tarsus

The *Tis Thálassas*, Firstborn of the Sea fled the cataclysmic destruction of the Broken Isles and disappeared across the Endless Ocean; the *Tis Erímou*, Firstborn of the Desert retreated into the deep sands of the Southern Continent where nothing human can survive; the *Tou Págou*, Firstborn of the Ice were always the least numerous and most reclusive of their kind – perhaps they wander the frozen wastes still. Perhaps only the *Tou Dásous*, Firstborn of the Forest; and the *Tou Vounoú*, Firstborn of the Mountain, are truly gone from this world, one having destroyed the other and then themselves.

Meton, "The Ancient World", c. 700M

Chapter Seventeen

The fortifications protecting the northern gate of Tarsus mirrored those in the south, a reminder to all who passed through that once, long ago, the greatest threat to the city's survival had come from the Narrows. Those days were long past, however, and the enemy in the north had not stirred in centuries. The land close to the city had been tamed in the meantime, crops and pastures covering the buried remains of ancient battles with a veneer of rustic tranquillity. Further north, of course, the Narrows still held dangers. Rogue Vedi occasionally wandered down from the mountains, driven by hunger, bloodlust or simple madness. The last communities of Bulġha, dispossessed and impoverished as they were, were generally peaceful if they were left alone, but some were more aggressive and less accepting of their people's exile. Outcasts and fugitives turned to banditry hid in the foothills, lurking in wait for easy pickings. Wild animals roamed the plains too: wolves and bears that sometimes preyed on stray livestock or lonely travellers. Further north, the Narrows was still a perilous place but its dangers, although diverse, were scattered and as much occupied with fighting each other as preying on the people of Tarsus. Should any of them forget their place or step a little too far across the invisible line that divided civilisation from the wilderness, the King's Rangers dealt with the threat with brutal efficiency.

The northern gatehouse, therefore, was seen by many in Tarsus as a relic of a bygone era, a stalwart but superfluous guardian against a threat that no longer existed. It was still garrisoned, of course, but with the Rutik now attacking in the south of the city, and all along the Narrows Wall, the best and brightest of Tarsean soldiery were required for the defence. The inconsequential duty of guarding the northern gatehouse fell to those judged too old or too incompetent to be of any real use elsewhere. Seventeen men and thirteen women formed the garrison, divided into shifts of ten, with one shift on guard duty, one shift in reserve and one sleeping at any given time. Sleeping quarters were within the gatehouse itself and those off duty were required to remain in the immediate vicinity, meaning that all thirty could be quickly roused or recalled to the defence, in the unlikely event that it became necessary. As for the guard shift, at any given time there were usually four on patrol, in two pairs, two guarding the inside of the gate, three in the guardhouse and one assigned to lookout duty, standing on the battlements.

Cteatus had been on duty as a lookout since shortly before sunrise and the warm sun was now beginning to soothe the pre-dawn chill from his ageing bones. His left thigh ached in the mornings, a perennial reminder of a long-ago skirmish, far to the south and close to Eresos and the sea. His patrol had been ambushed by a band of Rutik irregulars, out to cause carnage and collect booty. Outnumbered and surrounded, the Tarseans dug in and defended fiercely. Cteatus had killed his second enemy when one of the Rutik got behind him and drove her spear deep into the flesh at the back of his thigh, hard enough to break the bone beneath. He remembered the sudden, searing agony, blacking out for a moment as his leg crumpled under him and he fell to the ground, screaming. The Rutik withdrew her spear with a vicious twist and his vision cleared in time to see her coming at him again, ready to finish the job.

He had been ready to die in that instant, but it was not to be: the Rutik stumbled as she moved forward, her foot catching on something buried in the grass. It was a momentary respite, but Cteatus knew his business well enough to seize the tiniest advantage. Ignoring the pain even as it threatened to overwhelm him once more, he rolled to his left, pulling a dagger from his belt. The Rutik recovered rapidly and spun to face him but only succeeded in moving herself close enough for Cteatus to strike. Propping himself up with his left hand, he slashed with the dagger in his right, cutting the tendon in the back of her ankle, and she collapsed to the ground beside him. Scrambling forward with his good leg, he flopped down on top of her, and they were face to face, close enough to feel each other's breath on their faces. The Rutik snarled and tried to wriggle free, beating at his back with the butt of her spear but Cteatus had the dagger in her gut now, driving it deep into the gap between her breastplate and her belt. She screamed in pain and rage, inches from his face, spraying him with bloody spittle and making his ears ring but he kept stabbing. Again and again, he drove the knife home, feeling hot blood spurt across his hand and onto his arm. He passed out still stabbing, shock and blood loss ending the fight before he even knew whether he had won or lost.

Cteatus leaned on his spear and rubbed at his calf, trying to massage away the lingering memory of pain. He had regained consciousness hours later to find the battle over, the enemy defeated and a bloodstained sawbones leaning over him, trying to determine whether the leg could be saved. Cteatus had come up fighting once again and cursed the doctor to a thousand horrible fates, telling him to take his thirsty scalpels elsewhere. He smiled at the memory, remembering the ferocity and determination that had earned him his reputation, as well as a permanent limp. Atop the guardhouse, feeling the weight of his years but coddled in safety and security, the memories seemed distant and almost unreal. Turning away from the Narrows, he walked to the far side of the roof, leaning on the battlements to watch the smoke rise over the southern end of the city. A part of him regretted not being there, missed the rush of anger and fear that could drive soldiers to deeds of cowardice or bravery, depending more on how the dice fell than any definable trait of personality or will. As the pain flared in his thigh once more, however, the greater part of him was happy to be out of it. There were few benefits to being an old soldier, unfit for active duty, but the fact that he no longer had to risk his life in the roiling chaos of battle was one of them.

Cteatus coughed, hacked up a mouthful of stodgy phlegm, strung through with dark, glutinous strands, and spat it out over the battlements, watching it sail through the air to land somewhere in the streets far below. Favouring his good leg, he headed back across the roof, pausing to take a half-hearted glance through the narrow portal that overlooked the gateway below. Nothing to be seen – as usual. From far away the sounds of battle rose for a moment in a wave of clashing steel and screaming, yelling men, and then died down again to a low murmur. Cteatus sighed and rubbed at his leg again. *Let 'em have their glory and curse 'em all.* When the war was over, he at least would be still alive. He closed his eyes for a moment, waiting for the old ache to subside, then opened them only to start in shock at the sight of a hooded man standing by the battlements, staring at him with eyes of deep, fathomless blackness.

"Blue blistering fuck!" Cteatus started and swung his spear to bear. The rooftop was accessible only by a tiny, winding staircase that led up from the guardhouse below. No one could reach the guardhouse without passing through the gate unless they came from inside the city of course and yet somehow there was, not four feet away, a tall dark figure in a long, green cloak. That could mean only one thing – a Rutik, an enemy in the gatehouse. Cteatus recovered his wits and called out a challenge, but the stranger ignored him, stepping forward slowly and deliberately until the point of his spear was almost touching its chest.

The Rutik reached out with a gloved hand and gently pushed the spearpoint aside, stepping past it to grasp his wrist with terrible strength. With a whimper, the old soldier fell to his knees and looked up into endless, terrifying blackness.

Despite its age and almost-forgotten purpose, as Mira and the Rutik expeditionary force approached from the north, the gatehouse presented a formidable and daunting obstacle. For the first time since leaving their camp on the far side of the mountains, it had seemed as though things were going somewhat according to plan. Their ride down the Narrows had been uneventful, unnoticed until they reached the populated areas, by which time it was too late for anyone to run to the city with a warning. Now they stood but a short distance from their goal, on schedule but stymied at the last hurdle. The soaring stone towers that flanked the gatehouse loomed over them, casting long and intimidating shadows in the morning sun. A massive iron portcullis, inches thick and looking as immovable and impassable as the stone walls that surrounded it, blocked their entry to the city.

Mira and her troop were drawn up to the front of the main body of Rutik cavalry, acting as an honour guard to Ohtrad, who stood amidst the senior officers, staring at the city gates from atop a small, grassy rise. The commander's own guard waited on the far side of the rise and the two groups eyed each other suspiciously as their respective charges debated their position. Mira's soldiers had grown increasingly unpopular with the rest of the Rutik contingent. Not only were they exempt from the less glorious duties that the other soldiers had to carry out, but they were associated with Ohtrad and, by extension, with the Avatar. The Avatar frightened them as much as it did Mira, but they at least could think of themselves as entirely separate from its malevolent presence. Mira's troop, however, was tainted with its stench, whilst retaining little of its power to instil fear and respect, and the other soldiers treated them with distrust that was tainted by disgust. For their part, Mira's soldiers regarded their fellow Rutik with disdain, knowing that they were both better trained and better equipped than they. Mira's soldiers saw themselves as an elite, and acted accordingly, with the unfortunate side effect of distancing themselves still further from the other Rutik.

A short distance away, Ohtrad and the commander were engaged in a lively discussion. The commander was becoming increasingly agitated, almost shouting at the League's representative, red in the face and gesticulating wildly toward the city. Mira could hear his words clearly, but not Ohtrad's responses for the other man remained calm and quiet, unflappable in the face of the commander's anger. He seemed unperturbed at their situation, and Mira wondered what he knew that the others did not. Of the Avatar, there had been no sign for the duration of their passage down the Narrows. Despite her allegiance to the League's cause, Mira did not regret its absence but part of her was uneasy at not knowing where it was and would have preferred that it remain in plain sight, where she could at least keep an eye on it. It occurred to her to wonder how many more Avatars were concealed within the ranks of the League. Was it the only one of its kind – unnaturally powerful and decidedly evil but ultimately a one-off freak? Or were there more of them out there? A handful? Dozens? Hundreds even? Mira shivered at the thought. Ohtrad undoubtedly knew the answer, but he was unlikely to tell her.

Perhaps that was for the best though, she thought sourly. *Perhaps she would prefer not to know.*

The commander's voice rose further in pitch and volume and Ohtrad finally reacted. Turning away from the city, he addressed the commander softly but firmly, utterly unphased by the other man's agitated tirade. Whatever Ohtrad said, it instantly took the wind from the commander's sails, and he subsided into silence, eyes widening in what Mira could only assume was fear. Ohtrad was not the Avatar and did not project the Avatar's unsettling aura of dark menace, but he exerted a different form of power, drawn from political influence and his elevated position within the League. The commander was a senior officer in the Northern Army of the Rutik, a decorated veteran, and a wealthy and powerful man in his own right. He also had thousands of soldiers on his side, over his shoulder at that moment. In theory, there was no reason for him to fear a man who held no official rank and commanded only a handful. He could have Ohtrad arrested, tried, and convicted by military tribunal, and hanged before the sun rose on another day; or order him murdered on the spot. They were a long way from home and observed by no one save the commander's own forces, so repercussions were unlikely and yet, even so, Ohtrad advanced and the commander retreated in abject fear.

Then, with neither signal nor warning, the gates swung outward, revealing a short tunnel to the city within. An old man stood watching them, his uniform the pale blue of Tarsus, his eyes wide with terror. The man stood staring at them, and Mira stared back, unsure of how to proceed.

Attack, fool. The voice was a whisper in Mira's head, but she could no more resist the command than had the Avatar been standing before her. She drew her sword and behind her, soldiers lowered their spears.

'Charge!' the word was barely out of Mira's mouth when the main body of Rutik thundered past, galloping through the gates, trampling the unfortunate Tarsean into the paved road. Spurring her horse into action, Mira raised her sword and followed them into the city.

Mira's charge was a welcome release from the tension of their weeks on the road but other than ensuring that the Tarsean guardsman could not close the gates again, it achieved little. They passed through the gate at a gallop and found themselves in a large open space, which Mira remembered from briefings was the famous King's Square. The square was bordered on two sides by the fabulous homes of the wealthiest residents of Tarsus and on the south end, opposite the Narrows Gate, by the walls of the Tarsean Royal Palace. The square was entirely unoccupied, and the Rutik charge quickly faltered and then broke up as soldiers milled around aimlessly, waiting on further orders. Mira was conscious of the dozens of glass-paned windows that overlooked the square but there was no sign of anyone having raised an alarm so rather than stand around, she took half of her troop to secure the gatehouse, sending the remainder back through the gate to guard Ohtrad.

Strictly speaking, her orders did not extend to taking an active part in the attack: she was supposed to remain with Ohtrad until the city was pacified and under Rutik control. The Avatar *had* ordered her through the gate, however, and besides, the commander was ignoring the gatehouse and focusing on getting his troops through the gate and reorganised for the next phase of the plan. Mira, however, would be damned before she left a potential strongpoint vacant to their rear and risked the enemy cutting off her only path of retreat, so she took it upon herself to remedy the oversight. They entered with weapons drawn, expecting at least some resistance from Tarseans within but all they found was blood and death.

On the ground floor, two Tarsean guards were slumped against a wall, their necks ending in ragged stumps, their heads nowhere to be seen. Moving up the stairs to the first floor revealed further slaughter: six bodies scattered around the room in various agonised poses, the skin torn from their flesh in strips and decorating the walls like ribbons strung for some macabre festival. One of the Tarseans moaned, a low gurgling sound made through cracked and bleeding lips. Mira realised with horror that despite their condition, the soldiers were still alive. One of them moved at that moment, stretching out a denuded claw of a hand to scrabble on the stone floor searching for something only it could see. Mira felt bile rising in her throat and choked it back, reflexively stepping forward to stab the stricken Tarsean in the back with her sword, killing him instantly. Behind her, Sergeant Teja barked an order and two soldiers moved quickly to finish off the others. Most died with hardly a sigh, too far gone in pain and terror to even register the Rutik blades sliding home.

The next floor was the armoury and storage area for the gatehouse, with racks of swords and spears lining one wall, and carefully stacked helmets and other bits of armour on the other. At one end of the room, a single Tarsean soldier appeared to be standing next to the wall but as Mira approached, she could see that he was pinned in place, nailed to the wall by a dozen shaftless spearheads that had somehow impacted with enough force to drive their points into the dressed stone behind. Another Tarsean lay in the corridor beyond, slumped onto the bottom of a staircase, dead of no obvious cause and Mira pushed her aside before advancing cautiously up the steps into what appeared to be a recreational area on the floor above, somewhere the guards might go when they were off shift: a place to rest, chat with comrades and eat meals. Mira was familiar with such facilities and knew that in normal times it would have been a warm, comforting place of respite from the rigours of duty. At that moment, however, it resembled nothing so much as the aftermath of an almighty explosion in a butcher's warehouse.

Clotting, sticky blood coated every surface sticking the soles of her boots to the ground as she walked into the room. Stringy clods of flesh hung from the walls and the ceiling, oozing yet more blood onto the floors below. Body parts were everywhere: a leg ending in a ragged stump lying atop a similarly truncated arm; a head propped up on what appeared to be a ribcage; two feet standing in the far doorway, so neatly severed that it was as though the body above them had just disappeared. Staring around in horror, Mira could see that there was no way to tell how many dead there were in that room, a dozen or more probably – judging by the sheer number of separated parts. Behind her, she heard one of her soldiers choking up vomit and could not find it in herself to judge him harshly. In her years at war, Mira had seen numerous battles, had faced her own mortality over and over again and was comfortable with its fragility. Fear no longer held sway over her, and scenes of slaughter and bloodshed no longer alarmed her. Thus, she had thought herself hardened and immune to the awfulness of violent death and destruction but the carnage in the gatehouse was on another level entirely. The sheer, violent butchery of it cut through her defences and exposed the core of her humanity within with brutal force.

As Mira froze in place, Teja pushed past her and advanced to the next staircase with two soldiers in tow. When they returned a few minutes later, Mira was still standing in place, struggling to tear her eyes from the massacre and focus her attention back on the task at hand.

"More dead in the rooms above," reported Teja. His voice was steady and business-like, a reassuring anchor to a world before this madness and Mira stirred herself into awareness.

"Same as this?" Teja shook his head.

"No, it's sleeping quarters up there. They're all dead in their beds. Didn't look too closely but there's enough blood to be sure none of them are getting up again. What a fucking mess." A slight quaver in those last words indicated to Mira that even the tough sergeant was not unaffected by the blood bath around them, and she knew that she had to regain control of the situation or risk losing her followers entirely. Sheathing her sword, she straightened her helm and drew herself up into as commanding and purposeful a pose as she could muster.

"Very good sergeant. I think we can safely call the gatehouse secured. Gather up the troops and let's get back out there. There's still work to be done today."

"Aye, Captain." Teja obeyed with neither question nor hesitation and as he turned to pass her orders on to the troops, she was pleased to note that they too fell in without a murmur of complaint. Minutes later they were back outside watching the troops assemble and doing their best to put the gruesome horrors of the gatehouse behind them.

CHAPTER EIGHTEEN

The Royal Palace, City of Tarsus
26 of Euthaios 870M - Late Spring
Day twenty-one of the siege of Tarsus

There is a persistent notion that the Firstborn were all-powerful, all-knowing, and all-seeing, and yet were infinitely benevolent and lived in perfect harmony with each other and their world. This is clearly untrue. The *Tou Vounoú* carved mountains into weapons and slaughtered the *Tou Dásous* with genocidal thoroughness. The *Tou Págou* value their icy solitude and woe betide any who might disturb it. The *Tis Erímou* lurk in the desert sands like scorpions guarding their territory. And the *Tis Thálassas*, Firstborn of the Sea? Pirates and raiders, murderers, and thieves. Wherever they sailed to, may they never return.

Polemon of Chalcis, "The Ancients Weep", c. 975M

Chapter Eighteen

King Achaeus was true to his word and following the episode of his escape to the walls, Arion was watched more closely than ever and found no opportunity for further mischief. From that day on, he was confined to his rooms, only leaving for meals and supervised exercise. Guards were posted to his door to ensure compliance and Arion had found them less than receptive to any suggestion that they might turn a blind eye and give him a little latitude. It seemed his father's instructions had been both explicit and uncompromising: the king was not taking any chances with his son's life. Arion supposed that he should be pleased that his father was so concerned for his welfare. Given the king's attitude at their last meeting, however, he could not help but feel like he was being locked away to prevent him from causing any further inconvenience, rather than as a display of fatherly love and concern.

Less than a week had passed since his father's decree was issued but already it seemed like the walls of his confinement were closing in around him. There were no more sessions with Radomir, or indeed any other martial tutor since anyone able-bodied enough to wield a weapon was either fighting on the walls, or else on guard duty somewhere around the city. Even his ageing philosophy tutor had been recruited, though Arion found it hard to imagine that the mild-mannered, studious teacher even knew which end of a sword to point at the enemy. The ranks of the palace servants had also thinned considerably: amongst others, Beka had gotten her wish and joined the army. They had shared a moment of tenderness when she came to tell him the news and for a moment, he had forgotten all about the obligations of a crown prince and almost begged her to stay. Instead, they merely stood and talked for a while, before she slipped her hand into his and confessed to being deeply frightened, despite her determination to proceed. They held each other then, and the memory of her tight grasp was etched into his mind. On a whim, he asked her to wait while he fetched something from his rooms and returned with a short leather cord, strung with glass beads in a variety of colours. It had been made for him years before as something to amuse a small child, but she could use it to tie back her long, black hair and she seemed pleased with the meagre gift. Arion wondered where she had been posted to, whether she was even still alive but dismissed the thought instantly, unable to bear any thought of the alternative. Still, it seemed ridiculous to him that a chambermaid was allowed to go off and fight for the city and the kingdom, but he, the crown prince, was not. If anyone should be fighting, it was he, since he was part of what they were fighting to protect.

Arion realised that the book in his hands had lain open and unread for some time. Furious, he snapped it shut and tossed it onto the carpet. The situation was ridiculous! He was fourteen years old, not a child anymore, and he knew how to use a sword. Why was he not allowed to join the fighting? It was all his father's fault, of course – him and his sudden change of mood. Just because he was in a foul temper all the time, Arion had to pay the price. The king was doing it to spite him. He jumped to his feet and began pacing around the room, aiming a vicious kick at the fallen book as he passed. It wasn't fair! Stopping by a window, he could see smoke rising from the north, a grim cloud of blackness that was notable only in that most of the Rutik missiles had fallen well short of the Narrows Wall and dropped into the southern half of the city. If only he could get out there, he would soon show everyone what he could do. He might not be able to take Radomir in the training ring, but he could certainly poke a few holes in some Rutik.

Storming back across the room, he began dreaming up ways to escape. His room was on the northeast corner of the palace, four stories above ground level. There were no balconies on that floor and the walls were free of ivy or any other obvious way of climbing down. He remembered reading a children's book long ago, about a princess escaping from her captors using a rope made of tied together sheets. He glanced over at his bed, unmade since he had thrown a candlestick at the door when the servants tried to enter that morning. Knotting sheets together seemed simple enough but there were only two on his bed and that would not get him all that far. No, there was nothing else for it – he was going to have to fight his way out. The candlestick still lay on the floor beside the door: it would make a passable weapon. He imagined feigning illness or injury, the guards rushing in, him stepping out from behind the door and raising the candlestick in both hands. The candlestick rushing down, with all his strength behind it, smashing the first guard's head before swinging back up to catch the second under the chin. He imagined it so vividly that he could feel the impacts shaking through his hands, feel the blood spattering across his clothes and face. He could hear the guards screaming.

Good, he thought, *let them scream, they deserve it.*

Arion was about to head for the door to pick up the candlestick, when something caught his eye through another window, this one facing east and looking out across the city. The smoke was thicker now, and clearly rising from within the walls. That was his father's library burning, surely, and over there a mansion belonging to the King's Chancellor. More smoke was drifting along on the wind, coming from the northwest, somewhere out of Arion's view. His anger guttered and died as he recognised that this was more than the Rutik flinging balls of flaming, pitch-soaked straw over the walls. Looking closely now, he could see large bodies of soldiers moving amongst the smoke. They were yet too far away and too obscured by the haze for him to identify their uniforms, but they were not moving in orderly columns, which they would have been if they were Tarseans on their way to the walls. There was cavalry too, and Arion knew they could not be Tarsean since his father had long ago ordered all their horses north to pasture. Pressing his face against the thick, leaded glass he stared in horror at the scene below.

Arion stood unmoving by the window for what seemed like an eternity. All thought of violent rebellion, and all his pent-up rage and his frustration with his father was forgotten. For the first time in what felt like days or even weeks, Arion found that he could see entirely clearly, his thoughts no longer constantly diverted into hatred and circular recrimination. Even as the clouds of smoke settled onto the city that was his home and his birth right, he felt as though another cloud had lifted from his mind, releasing him from a dense fog he had not even noticed was surrounding him.

Corraidhín's lonely battle against the invading demons continued, day after day, night after night. Like a compelling nightmare, they came back again and again, each time the same as the last, leaving vile corruption and palpable terror in their wake. After a while, Corraidhín fought by rote, finding a strategy that worked for a particular set of variables, then using it every time that set presented itself. He remained unsure of whether each demon was even different from the last, or whether the same ones were being cast down only to rise again renewed. He was exhausted, having tapped every reserve of his strength, and had only avoided another collapse by drawing directly upon the power of the Oracle to replenish his precious resources. The Oracle's soothing light filled him now, suffusing his blood and bones, reinforcing him with her unfathomable force of will. Each time he drew upon her well of power, he felt renewed and ready to fight again.

The Oracle's strength was Corraidhín's only protection now, his own power and vigour long drained past the point of recovery. A steep price would eventually be exacted for the privilege, however. It would not be of the Oracle's doing, of course, as he now knew she bore him no ill will for his failings and the disappointment he had undoubtedly caused her. She was above such things as petty grudges and harboured ill feelings. It was a matter of mechanics, the way things worked. The Oracle's power was giving him the strength to fight on, allowing him the continued use of his body and faculties and staving off the consequences of meeting his own limits and sailing on past. If he continued like this forever, he would not reach the limits of the Oracle's power and he would never feel the ill effects of its withdrawal but sooner or later he was going to have to stop. Once that happened, the power would drain out of him leaving him stranded and isolated once again, but this time in a body that had long passed the edge of the cliff and was hanging, artificially suspended over the yawning depths of utter collapse.

There was no time to fret about consequences for Corraidhín however, for another demon was pounding towards him at breath-taking speed, its insubstantial and shadowy feet somehow shaking the immortal ether with its steps. From a distant corner of his awareness, he had watched it rise, somewhere in the east of the city, back in the material world. Now it was getting closer and Corraidhín turned to study it more closely. He watched carefully as it charged towards him, noting its aspect, and tracking its movements, trying to identify a particular individual combination of factors amongst the myriad of options. *There!* He spotted a unique aspect to the creature's mien and recognised it as one he had fought a hundred times before, or at least another that was identical in every way. Classifying his enemy gave him the knowledge he needed to prepare his response and he settled into position, knowing exactly how the coming fight would proceed.

The demon was almost upon him now and Corraidhín braced himself, feeling the power of the Oracle rising within him, ready, eager even, to meet the challenge ahead. He raised his hands and nodded in satisfaction as a simulacrum of his trusty short spear materialised in his grasp. The manifested weapon was difficult to maintain and would not last for long, but it would be long enough to complete the task ahead. The demon got closer, its foul stench spreading past him like a filthy, reeking cloak. He forced himself to ignore the tainted atmosphere and lowered the point of the spear in readiness to strike. Closer still, and the demon's aura was all around him, clawing at his mind and body, viciously assaulting his carefully prepared defences. Closer still, and Corraidhín drew back the spear to strike.

This battle would be a short one, he knew, a simple thrust to the creature's abdomen, followed by a step to the left, and then another stab into the side of its neck. Twisting the spear and withdrawing it would be enough to rip out most of its throat and the battle would be over. The moment to attack arrived when the demon was already close enough for Corraidhín to clearly see the more material shape within the swirling nest of shadows and smoke. Pushing off his back foot, he drove the spear forward with all his borrowed strength, then stepped away and pivoted to strike again. There he faltered, however, stumbling to a halt in confusion. The demon should have been a few feet away, rearing back and away from him, exposing its throat for the kill. Instead, it was gone.

Thrown by the sudden change in the pattern, Corraidhín froze in place, every fibre of his being now tensed in readiness for an attack that no longer had a predictable vector. Moments passed, stretching into minutes, however, and still there was no sign of the demon nor any others of its breed. Slowly, cautiously, Corraidhín relaxed his muscles, the physical action triggering a corresponding easing of his mind. Time stretched out in the strange, elastic, way that it did in the higher realms and still Corraidhín could find no sign of his enemy. He wondered if perhaps he had finally defeated them, sent them all howling into the void, but that made no sense since he had hardly had the time for a single strike against the last one, and had not done enough damage to drive it away, much less destroy it. He reached out further with his senses, searching the hazy scenery that mirrored the city below but as a faint, ghostly replica. He still found nothing.

The spear vanished from Corraidhín's hands, and he straightened out of his ready stance. He continued to scan the distant horizons cautiously but there was still nothing to see. He allowed his consciousness to drift gently back towards the world behind, the earthly realm of man and beast. Back in Tarsus it was bright and warm, and the sun had been up for some time already, making it sometime in the mid-morning by his reckoning. In that moment, there was no sign of the creatures anywhere within the boundaries of Tarsus. Fearing some new ploy, a change of tactics, Corraidhín cast his net wider and looked out past the city walls. He started at the south gates, where the fighting was most fierce and where the shining beacons of individual humans were crammed together in a roiling, mingling mass. Waves of emotion swept over him as he passed over the battle – fear and anger, horror and joy, triumph, and defeat, hope and despair. Where men and women fought and died in such numbers, every sentiment and sensation in the world was manifested a thousand times over, each individual bellow and whisper finding others of their kind, merging sympathetic harmony, and intensifying into screams of emotion that echoed into the void itself.

Corraidhín moved on, following the walls to the east, passing over a dozen smaller engagements and witnessing a hundred different scenes of struggle and strife, resisting the urge to seek out Radomir and make sure that the other man was still alive. Here the Rutik were scaling the wall with siege ladders, and he felt their fear as they approached the parapet, knowing that the defenders were waiting to kill them as they crested the wall. There the Tarseans had defeated a similar assault and were cheering enthusiastically, shouting, and jeering after their retreating foe. In another place, Rutik siege weapons had caused a section of the parapet to collapse into the city, settling into a pile of rubble on the inside of the wall. Corraidhín could feel the abject horror that seized the Tarseans trapped beneath the debris as heavy stone crushed their limbs and choking dust filled their lungs. They were soldiers, half expecting to die upon the walls, but he could almost hear their voices:

Not like this, they cried. *Not like this.*

Steeling himself, Corraidhín continued his circuit of the walls, the siege playing out before his eyes in a series of bloodstained snapshots. The Narrows Wall remained intact, brave Tarseans still buying time with their lives, hoping against hope that the siege would be ended before they were and Corraidhín increased his pace, scanning the area a hundred yards at a time. Moments later he was almost at the northern gates, having found neither sight nor sign of the demons anywhere. He was considering abandoning his journey and returning to the more active areas in the south when something caught his eye, within the gatehouse that protected the northern entrance to the city. It was a shadow of a sort, like the shadows of the demons but more concentrated, deeper, and more solid. He moved closer, feeling the same sense of wrongness and obscenity that had accompanied the demons but again, more intensely than before.

Focusing narrowly on the gatehouse, he watched as the dark shadow approached the bright light of a man. The two met and mingled and then the light disappeared, like a flickering candle flame snuffed out in an instant. The shadow moved on and another light fell. Corraidhín was seized by an sudden, vivid, premonition. Tearing his gaze away from the unnervingly fascinating shadow, he looked to the north, past the gates and into the Narrows, where his worst fears were immediately confirmed. Thousands of people waited there on horseback, their minds filled with thoughts of triumph and victory, their desires focused on the death and destruction of all within the walls before them. Corraidhín looked back in time to see another light disappear from the gatehouse, leaving only one remaining in company with the shadow. He looked more closely, straining his will to bring the lifeless matter of the gatehouse itself into focus.

Despite Corraidhín's best efforts, the wood and stone of the gatehouse remained stubbornly hazy, but the picture was clear enough for him to follow events. The surviving light, a Tarsean he presumed, had moved down into the tunnel below the gatehouse and was standing in the gates, beckoning to the riders beyond. A moment of stillness followed and then the riders surged forwards in a tsunami of released tension. The hapless Tarsean was battered into darkness as they rushed past, crushing him beneath the hooves of their mounts. Corraidhín's awareness withdrew from the northern gate, flew above the city, and snapped back into his body and the prosaic, material world of his room. Disorientation immediately seized him as his mind struggled to adapt to the sudden switch from one reality to another and he staggered and almost fell trying to get to his feet. He needed to rest, to allow his thoughts to settle and his body to readjust but there was no time. The Rutik were within the walls and time had finally run out for the city of Tarsus.

Struggling to regain control of his body, Corraidhín closed his eyes and bowed his head. His exhaustion was total now, his strength drained. His limbs were leaden and beginning to ache, and he was finding it difficult to hold on to a thought.

"It is time to go, my child." The Oracle's soft, warm voice came from nowhere, arriving at his ears by some mysterious application of will.

"I could not have done this without you, wise one," he said, his voice a pained whisper. "Your generosity humbles me yet again." The Oracle was nowhere visible but somehow Corraidhín knew she was smiling warmly.

"Are you forgetting why I sent you to this land, all those many years ago, my little spear?" She addressed him by the translation of his name into the Achaean tongue, a strange choice, he thought vaguely, as he prepared to answer her question.

"I may have neglected my mission for a long time, wise one, but I never forgot it. Your words as we parted are seared into my very soul: find the evil growing in the east, seek out its source and find a way to fight it."

"Indeed. And though you have taken a roundabout route, with many missed steps along the way, here you are. The first part of your mission is fulfilled, little spear, you have found the evil that we sought, and begun to fight even, but we have not yet found the source and thus your task remains. If you are willing to continue." At that moment, still touched by the comforting glow of the Oracle's power, Corraidhín would have done anything for her, but he hesitated to answer, feeling the inescapable drag of his sorely punished body. He would have done anything for her, but feared that he could do nothing only die, exhausted and broken.

"I am yours to command, Oracle, but I fear my usefulness to you is at an end. I am sorry, I can do nothing more." Silence for a moment, as Corraidhín felt her touch intensify, reaching into his soul, gently probing, and exploring.

"You are not wrong, little spear, this trial has taken much from you that was not mine to take. It is I who should be apologising. Not only have I greatly abused your loyalty, but I fear I am about to abuse it even further."

"I am yours to command," he repeated, bowing his head in supplication. In his battles with the demons, Corraidhín had felt the Oracle's touch throughout and marvelled at the inexhaustible strength of it. As he said the words, however, he knew that what he had been shown thus far was but the smallest wave gently lapping on the coast, its tender caress belying the colossal force of the mighty ocean. The power welled up and swept over him, through him and into him, sweeping away his pain and exhaustion, restoring his muscles and sinews, forcing its way into the deepest recesses of his mind, rebuilding and fortifying his strength and will. A sense of rejuvenation and healing overwhelmed him, matched only by the extreme, almost unbearable pain as his self was torn apart and wholly rebuilt. Throughout it all he felt her overwhelming love and compassion, and even through the pain it humbled him again.

"My lady," he managed to get the words out through gritted teeth, fighting against the paralysing agony. "I am sorry for what I've done."

"No, little spear, it is I who am sorry." And the pain intensified until it consumed everything that he was.

Corraidhín opened his eyes and braced himself against a pain that was no longer present. The lines of his room had once again faded into shadowy rumours of solidity and he was back in the other worlds, that place that was not a place, a reality that was paradoxically not real.

"You are well, my child?"

Corraidhín turned to find the Oracle a short distance away, seated in an old, battered wooden chair such as he might have seen in a peasant farmer's cottage. She looked tired, her beauty and grace as stunning as ever but tempered by a fragility that he had never seen before.

"My lady? What has happened?"

"I am sorry, Corraidhín. I have taken more from you than could ever be justified. I must ask now for your forgiveness, though I do not deserve it."

"My lady, I do not understand, I feel whole again." Even as he said it, Corraidhín understood that "whole" was a word nowhere sufficient to describe the absolute completeness that he now felt. Soft, golden warmth was coursing through his veins, suffusing his muscles and organs, filling and strengthening his mind. Looking down at his hands, he realised that they appeared to be glowing. Fascinated, he watched in silence for a moment as a faint patterned aura rippled and blurred around them. Clenching one hand into a fist, he gasped at the awesome new strength in his fingers.

"It will fade somewhat," said the Oracle quietly. "This is the first rush, the joyful surge of new life finding its way. In time, if we have time, your body will find peace with these changes, and you will, I hope, find a way to accept them."

"But what have you done, my lady?"

"Corraidhín, we have not much time, despite that here, in this realm, we should have all the time beneath the eternal stars. Your battles against the creatures of shadow were instructive. I now understand what they are, where they came from, and, more importantly, who sent them. I now pity them more than I despise them, but that cannot hold us back from this fight. We cannot permit ourselves mercy or compassion in this matter.

"The creatures you fought were sent here for a dual purpose. They were to sow the seeds of chaos and disorder in the streets and to sap the will of the Tarsean people, and their leaders, for their fight against the Rutik. That task is now done, and they have turned to the second: to prepare the way for the other who now lurks in the north of the city.

"For centuries, longer even, Tarsus has been protected by wards laid down by the brother of Arrias, the one they called the Conqueror. You will have heard of him – Menidas by name, son of the Emperor Chavdar of Menos and twin brother to Menicode, whose name is a curse throughout the land. Were it not so, the one that now approaches would not have adopted so subtle an approach to its attack on the city. It would have gathered its fellows and together they would have cast the walls into ruin and torn apart all those within. The wards linger still, but the sacrifice of the remaining demons has weakened them sufficiently to permit it enter the city and even now it wreaks havoc within the walls."

Corraidhín struggled to absorb what he was being told but then realised that the reaction was purely instinctual. Somehow, he understood everything that the Oracle spoke of, and more. Knowledge, some of it ancient and esoteric, some of it contemporary but up until now obscure, was flooding into his mind. He found that he could remember events that he had never witnessed and recall secrets that he had never been told. In that moment, it felt like he knew *everything*.

"Avatar!" he cried, knowing the word but not knowing how he knew it. The Oracle nodded grimly.

"Indeed. They are so confident in their supremacy that they do not even try to hide their nature. They are an incarnation of pure evil, Corraidhín, the embodiment of the power that drives them. They are the essence of selfishness, greed and a lust for power that has endured through centuries."

"Menicode," said Corraidhín, certain in his fresh insight. "The one they called the Sorcerer of Menos."

"Indeed so. The revolution in Rutik society, the rise of their new and more powerful kingdom, the sudden resurrection of their designs upon Asfáleia – it was all too neat, all too quick, and all too focused to have been the turgid manoeuvrings of mere humans. Menicode has returned and the Avatars are his scions."

"What would you have me do, my lady?" replied Corraidhín, without hesitation. The details of Menicode's cruel and voracious appetites for destruction were legendary in the folk histories of Asfáleia, tales told around flickering campfires and cosy hearths alike, but always with an eye to the shadows and a curse to ward off his evil eye.

"To an extent, Corraidhín, you have already done it by accepting my gift. I fear that one day you will realise what has been taken from you, and perhaps hate me for it, however. To fight the enemy, I have made you as the enemy is. You are now, by some definitions, an avatar also. My power is yours, insofar as it is within my ability to bestow that power upon another, and insofar as it is within the capacity of your human frame to contain it. You and I are now one, and I send you forth once more but this time, I hope, with the power to achieve our goals."

"My lady, I am humbled by your faith in me. But where do I begin?"

"You have had your problems, Corraidhín, and your path has not always been true, but you have always been, and still remain, a good man. I cannot give you much more in the way of guidance at this time, save perhaps to say that the descendants of Arrias remain somehow essential to Menicode's schemes. Find them, protect them, ensure that whatever their role may ultimately be, their loyalties remain to the side of good. I send you back with that advice, with my lasting love and with my complete faith. Go now, and we will speak again when we can."

Corraidhín opened his mouth to reply but found that the Oracle was fading from his vision even as he watched. All around him, the lines of his room were coming into focus and solidifying, and he felt the pull of reality on the anchor lines of his soul. A thousand stray lines of thought swirled around in his mind, fuelled by the Oracle's power, by the knowledge she had bestowed upon him, and by the power that now coursed through his veins. He could feel the Avatar slinking through the shadows in the north of the city and focused his attention upon it, felt it pause and hesitate, sniffing the air like a mountain wolf catching the scent of pursuing hounds upon the wind, distant but approaching.

"I am coming for you," he thought, pushing the sentiment out through the ether. The Avatar stood perfectly still for a moment and then nodded slowly.

"Come," it replied finally. "Bring your borrowed and dwindling power, your crumbling relic of a bygone age. Her kind are gone from this world, it is long past time she joined them. Come, and I shall make it so."

Despite all that he had gained, despite the Oracle's power that now filled him, and despite the conviction bestowed upon him by her faith and her love, Corraidhín heard the infinite menace contained in those few words and shivered. Pausing only to gather up his weapons and pull on his cloak, he hurried from the room, bound for the palace and a battle he had no idea how to fight.

CHAPTER NINETEEN

Southern walls, City of Tarsus
26 of Euthaios 870M - Late Spring
Day twenty-one of the siege of Tarsus

Arrias built Tarsus to defend itself on two fronts. To the north, his own brother the malevolent sorcerer Menicode still lurked in the haunted ruins of Menos. Arrias had defeated his sibling once but was not so naïve as to think that the threat of further wanton evil was thus ended. To the south, the other Achaean city states jostled and frequently clashed, all vying for a greater share of the same power and wealth. Arrias knew that to fulfil his ambitions and take their territory, he would first need to eliminate any threat to his own.

Acusilaus, "The Eternal Glory of Tarsus", c. 850M

Chapter Nineteen

Mira, Teja and the others had emerged from the blood-soaked northern gatehouse to find her commander in the middle of a whirlwind of activity. A third of his force he was splitting into groups of a few hundred each and dispersing them around the city to unleash chaos on the hapless citizenry. Their orders were to break any resistance they met, fire buildings, and kill anyone who came within reach of their spears. They were also given explicit permission to pillage, rape and torture as they pleased – an order Mira had never in her life expected to be given. She could rely upon her own soldiers to act honourably and fulfil their orders with the minimum of carnage. Most of the rest of the army, however, would throw themselves wholeheartedly into their sudden freedom from the restraints of normal, civilised behaviour. The screams had started even before Mira left the gatehouse, and she suspected they would continue throughout the day and into the night.

Another third of the army was broken into larger contingents and despatched to take and hold certain specific objectives around the city – major junctions, significant landmarks, and such. They were not given the same licence for anarchy as their comrades but strictly admonished to hold their positions until relieved and Mira wondered whether they would be able to restrain themselves once the real chaos started. Their role was pivotal, however, and she noted with some grudging admiration that the commander had chosen older, more experienced and generally steadier units for the task. By holding the junctions and certain strategic passages through the city, their orders were to prevent the Tarseans from moving freely in their city. If the Tarseans could not move, they could not gather and if they could not gather, they could not present a determined resistance. Holding landmarks and garrisoning large buildings was part of it too, denying the enemy anything that might serve as a muster point.

The final portion of the army the commander gathered into a single massive assault party and directed towards the south. Among them were the hotheads, the hard-chargers, and the glory-hounds – those men and women who could be trusted to attack and keep attacking until the enemy was dead or they were. Their role was to ride across the city, stopping for nothing and no one, to take the south gate and hold it open for long enough that the main force of the Rutik army might drive into the city. In a way, their role was even more essential to the Rutik battle plan. The Expeditionary Army was strong and highly motivated, determined to spill as much Tarsean blood as possible, to make their painful journey through the mountains mean something. At the same time, in real terms, it was small, and heavily outnumbered by the Tarsean defenders. If they could not open the Gates of Arrias, or if they failed to hold them long enough for the rest of the Rutik forces to enter the city, then sooner or later they would be defeated. The Tarseans would suffer, of that, there was no doubt, and the Expeditionary Army would make them pay in blood, but sooner or later the Rutik would be ground down, separated and isolated, surrounded and cut to pieces by the vengeful Achaeans.

At that moment, she heard her name called and turned to see Ohtrad being escorted through the Narrows Gate by her soldiers. If she ignored the escort, Mira thought he looked as though he was out for a stroll on a pleasant summer evening, without a care in the world. He moved without haste, with his hands clasped behind his back, and looking this way and that with casual interest. He smiled as he approached, a smile that touched his lips but not his eyes, she noticed.

"Lord Ohtrad." She greeted him as politely as she could and managed to keep her expression neutral.

"Captain. Splendid day for it, don't you think?" He paused only momentarily, not waiting for an answer before continuing:

"Everything appears to be going according to plan thus far." Mira thought of the tortured bodies in the gatehouse and wondered what manner of a plan involved that manner of violence, and what mind could conceive of such a plan.

"I suppose so, my Lord." Perhaps detecting a slight note of discomfort in her voice, Ohtrad glanced at her sharply before turning away to study the assembling troops.

"We've come a long way, Captain," he said finally. "And the path has proven… more perilous than anticipated. I would be interested in hearing your thoughts."

"I remain at your command, my lord." She maintained her carefully neutral expression, but Ohtrad laughed at her response.

"Indeed, Captain. And a very diplomatic answer, if I may say so. However, it does not address the point of my question. I would have your thoughts, please."

"I'm a soldier, my lord, I don't have thoughts, I just follow orders." Mira knew she was being evasive and knew that Ohtrad would know that too, but she suspected that her actual thoughts would prove even less pleasing to him. Better to irritate him a little by avoiding the question than provoke his wrath by answering. Ohtrad frowned and snapped his tongue in disgust.

"A soldier. Just a soldier, indeed. Very well Captain, if you are determined to be "just a soldier" you might as well go off and do some soldiering. You have my permission to take your troop and join in the assault on the city. I shall remain here and place myself under the protection of the commander's guard. Perhaps the break will… give you time to gather an independent thought or two."

"Yes, my lord." Deciding not to push her luck, Mira bowed and walked away, leaving Ohtrad to stare after her with his brows knitted. She had a feeling that she would pay for that little bit of obstruction in due course but at that moment she was happy to be let off the League's leash, even for a little while.

Mira's troop rode hard to catch up with the assault party, and although their leader seemed to resent her presence, he nevertheless grudgingly allowed them to join forces. She offered her thanks with enough of a hint of sarcasm to remain, barely, on the right side of the line of insubordination and fell in immediately to his left and only slightly to his rear. In doing so, she effectively occupied the position of second-in-command, not in the formal structure of officers, of course, but definitely in the more subtle hierarchy of practice and convention. Mira could hear the other officers muttering angrily behind her but there was little they could do about the implied insult: her association with the League still protected her insofar as that at least. Somewhere further back, Teja and the rest of the troop muscled their way into a gap and the party got underway again.

Mira studied the Tarsean architecture with keen interest as they rode through the streets. It was only in the last couple of centuries that Rutik builders had begun to favour dressed stone over the more traditional wooden structures. There were some fine buildings in Rutiksborg now, as well as in the larger Rutik cities but Tarsus seemed to have palaces on every corner and was dotted with statues, monuments, and beautifully carved arches everywhere she looked. When Arrias the Conqueror built the city, almost nine hundred years before, he did so with the assistance of experienced and talented masons and craftsmen from the other Achaean cities, virtually inexhaustible supplies of marble and granite from the foothills of the Devil's Teeth Mountains, and a treasury boosted to overflowing with the spoils of his conquests. Tarsus was a fortress when Arrias first arrived, surrounded by shabby tenements and the crumbling ruins of far older cities. The Conqueror, never a man to do things by halves had ordered the entire area evacuated and razed everything to the ground. That enabled him to lay out the new city virtually from scratch and it showed in the clean lines of the long, straight avenues that crisscrossed the city, and the uniform, orderly city blocks in between.

The logical and efficient layout of the city made Mira's journey from one gate to the other relatively straightforward. The palace was a walled city within a walled city, with its own fortifications and defenders. The assault party had neither the numbers nor the equipment to assault it directly, so they left King's Plaza by a south-westerly route, passing through one of the two gates in the Narrows Wall where it bisected the city from east to west. From there, they emerged onto The Westernroad, a relatively humble area of the city, which in practice meant that the houses were merely impressively large rather than palatial. There were no truly impoverished districts within the city walls anymore. Those without the power or the money to claim a place on the hallowed soil of Tarsus had all been relocated, centuries before, and now lived in the slums to the south of the city or, if they were lucky, in the farms and villages to the north. A half-mile from the end of The Westernroad, they turned off the main road and threaded a passage through the narrower streets that ran between the major avenues. It was not a pleasant journey for cavalry, hemmed in on both sides with no room to manoeuvre but the alternative was to try taking the last leg of their journey directly beneath the city walls, where they would be easy pickings for arrows and stones from defenders above.

For all that the route was relatively straightforward, Tarsus was still the largest city in the world, and the distance from one gate to another was a little over five miles. They met pockets of resistance along the way too. The small gatehouse covering the passage from north to south was occupied, although not heavily, and it took the better part of an hour to clear out the Tarsean defenders and secure the building. Further south, they almost collided head-on with a small column of enemy soldiers who emerged from a side street as the head of the Rutik column rode past. The Tarseans fought bravely, despite being wildly outnumbered, and managed to delay the column by another half hour or so. All in all, it took almost five hours to reach the Gate of Arrias and by the time they arrived, the Tarseans were well warned of their coming and had begun preparing a defensive line across the approach to the gate.

Stretched across the Avenue of Kings, a solid formation of Tarsean soldiers barred their way, three rows deep, with shields planted in the front row and long spears lowered to meet their charge. The formation was perhaps a little over sixty soldiers in breadth, so close to two hundred enemy soldiers all told. Despite their losses in the mountains, and despite having already dispersed two-thirds of their forces, the Rutik assault party still numbered almost three thousand cavalry, so the Tarsean resistance, whilst well-organised and undeniably brave was doomed to failure. Even so, in normal circumstances, Mira would not have driven cavalry into such a robust line. Indeed, she did not believe that normal cavalry horses would have obeyed the order if it were given, but these were not normal times, and their mounts were no longer normal horses. Throughout their harrowing journey across the mountains, their equine will had been beaten into submission and subsumed utterly into that of the Avatar. Mira now suspected they would charge into the roaring flames of hell if she so ordered. She wondered if her soldiers were any freer of will in the matter. She wondered if she herself could refuse her orders if she so chose.

The idea of her actions being under the control of another disturbed Mira greatly and she was glad to push it from her mind as the party leader ordered the charge. The Rutik cavalry hit the Tarsean line with a sickening crunch, a ringing clash of metal and a chorus of screams from both men and horses. A number of the charging Rutik impaled themselves upon the spears of the Tarsean front line, but the falling horses became rolling battering rams, crashing through into the second and third lines, crushing their riders beneath them, but shattering the Tarsean formation and killing dozens of enemy soldiers. The Rutik second line jumped or trampled over the fallen – friend and foe alike – and devastated what remained of the second and third lines of spearmen. Rutik casualties were heavy amongst that line too but by the time the third wave of cavalry hit, the Tarseans were broken, and the task became one of mopping up the fleeing survivors and running down what remained of their resistance.

Whilst the bulk of the assault party busied themselves with chasing Tarsean fugitives and slaughtering the wounded, Mira dismounted with her troop and a few dozen others and set to clearing a final path towards the southern gatehouse. She could see similar efforts being made to the left and right of her party, and other groups of Rutik forcing their way up the stairs that led to the walls on either side of the gate. It made some sense to split up, she supposed. Once the area in front of the gatehouse was cleared the only route left for the Tarseans to bring reinforcements would be along the walls so blocking them off was the best way to prolong the Rutik occupancy. Also, the doorways on this side of the gatehouse, and the passageways beyond presumably, were narrow and would at best could accommodate two soldiers side by side. There was no point in pouring too many bodies through them at once then since anyone further back would be of little help to those in the front line. She took down a Tarsean with a wild blow that sent shivers up her arm from the awkward angle of the impact and looked around to find Teja at her left shoulder.

"That door!" Mira tried to shout over the clamouring noise of battle all around them but Teja still could not hear, despite being only a couple of feet away. She pointed instead, and the man nodded, a wolfish grin creasing his blunt features. Mira grinned right back at him, feeling the sudden rush of exhilaration that came with combat, a side effect, she assumed, of potentially being moments from death.

Arrows were flying down from above now that most of the Tarsean forces on the ground had retreated closer to the building or were already dead. The defenders in the windows and on the balconies above had mostly withheld their fire while there was still a chance of hitting their own but now there was nothing to restrain them. Mira saw three of her followers fall in an instant as a particularly well-aimed flight of missiles found their targets. The surviving Tarseans outside the gatehouse were hemmed in now and packed in together against the gatehouse walls. They knew they were about to die but seemed determined to make the invaders pay for the privilege and put up a tough fight. Mira narrowly missed being skewered by a Tarsean spear, dodged sideways and barely recovered her footing in time to stab her assailant neatly through their side. Teja took a glancing blow to the head and seemed none the worse for it but two others from Mira's troop were less lucky and joined the Tarseans on the ground. The outcome was still a foregone conclusion, however, and step by bloody step, the Rutik forced their way over the broken bodies and across the blood-soaked paving stones.

The gatehouse doors were of strong, ancient oak but with axes to hand and strong arms to wield them, the Rutik soon broke through, and the fighting spread into the building like a flame through a neatly stacked campfire. It was a different sort of battle in the narrow corridors and cramped rooms of the gatehouse – claustrophobic and desperate on all sides. In the confined spaces, Mira found herself pushed from behind by impatient comrades, whilst in front equally determined enemies were screaming right in her face. There was no room to properly swing a weapon and fighters were using fists, feet and shoulders as much as swords and spears. It was more like a particularly aggressive tavern brawl than a battle, but it was quick and shockingly brutal for all that. No quarter was expected on either side, and none was given and although the Rutik eventually gained the upper hand, it was almost two hours before Mira found her way to the room containing the gate mechanisms. Teja was still with her, along with half a dozen of her troop and perhaps twenty other Rutik so she divided most of them into groups to hold the doors and set the remainder to opening the gates.

Once the gates were opened the battle for the gatehouse was effectively over, but the fighting continued for hours more in the narrow corridors and on the winding stairs. Mira and the Rutik around her were hard-pressed for a while as a large body of Tarseans made a last-ditch effort to regain control of the gate mechanism but it was doomed to failure and too late anyway. Within minutes of the gates opening the first Rutik reinforcements began arriving, made up of those who had been already engaged close to the walls outside. The trickle soon turned to a torrent as the Rutik reserve forces were marched from the rear to the gates almost at a run. Deep inside the building, smouldering embers of combat burst into violent flame as pockets of resistance were surrounded and stamped out but soon the Tarseans were driven sufficiently far back that Mira and her comrades in the gate room were left more or less alone. From outside the gatehouse, the mingled noises of fighting and dying grew ever louder as the main Rutik army flooded onto the streets and fought their way along the walls. Outside the storm continued but in the gate room, a tiny eye of calm developed in the centre of the maelstrom.

Leaning heavily on their spears or slouching against the walls, the Rutik in the gate room finally rested, for what seemed the first time since leaving the Expeditionary Force base camp, weeks before. Only a half dozen remained alive, including Mira and Teja, and all were wounded in a dozen places, battered, bruised, and scraped in a hundred more. Exhausted and slightly dazed, Mira took off her helmet, ran a bloodstained hand through hair that was once again filthy and tangled, leaned her head back against a wall and closed her eyes. Flickers of memory from the last few hours floated back into her mind, wavering afterimages from staring too long at a flame. She opened her eyes and tried to blink the images away, determined to recover her senses as quickly as possible. The fight for the gatehouse was won, and the mission of the Expeditionary Army had been completed but the battle for Tarsus was far from over and they would most likely be called back to duty soon enough.

CHAPTER TWENTY

Southern walls, City of Tarsus
26 of Euthaios 870M - Late Spring
Day twenty-one of the siege of Tarsus

Not a single person amongst the nations of Asfáleia can honestly claim to be a native of this land. The Bulġha wandered lost in the barren Hinterlands for years before fate brought them meandering onto more productive soil. The Achaeans beached their wooden ships on the southern shores having sailed from some other land, now forgotten. The Rutik were driven from their homelands to the north and journeyed long in the leafy shade of the Drevenwood before emerging, blinking in the bright sunlight, onto the plains of Asfáleia.

Acusilaus, "Peoples of Asfáleia", c. 900M

Chapter Twenty

Radomir and his band of soldiers waited with varying degrees of patience for another attack. They were all veterans now, even the volunteers. No school taught so fast and so well as one where the slightest mistake could be fatal. Those of the volunteers that survived the first few days on the wall were those who learned their lessons. In the weeks since the arrival of the Rutik, their section had suffered two full assaults with siege towers, no less than nine major escalades, innumerable enemy probing attacks and a near-constant barrage of rocks, stones and of more recent days human remains. Radomir and his soldiers were tired, weary almost beyond reason. Their movements as they prepared for yet another attack were slow and stiff, aching joints and a myriad of minor wounds demanding respite and getting none. One of the volunteers had lost a large chunk of his upper arm to a Rutik axe a week before. He fought on though, determined to stand his post on the wall for as long as he could. Iappous looked particularly depleted, his more advanced years finally beginning to tell against him. A glancing blow from a thrown spear had taken off most of his right ear in the early days of the siege. He had been lucky: had the missile turned a little to the left in flight it would have gone through his eye. On the other hand, Radomir supposed, had it turned a little to the right it would have missed him altogether. Such were the fortunes of war.

Radomir did not believe in luck unless he was playing cards or betting on horses. Those were simple games, limited in scope. When everyone played by the same rules, and the opponents were well-matched, the results often came down to luck. Who drew the right card, or the wrong card; whose horse threw a shoe or whose horse was in especially good form that day and romped home a clear winner. Battle was an entirely different game though. Despite what the poets would have you believe, there were no rules to battle, no honour and no code to moderate behaviour. Once two sides clashed, the only rule Radomir believed in was that battles were won by numbers, by ferocity, or by discipline or more often some combination of the three.

Courage, always a favourite of the poets, was essential of course but courage alone never won a battle. A brave man badly outnumbered or meeting a more ferocious or better-trained enemy, would die as quickly as a coward, though perhaps with less whining. Years before, Radomir had been a part of punitive raids against the Vedi in the Eastern Devil's Teeth. The raids were designed to discourage the foul creatures from descending to the foothills, where they might be tempted to prey on the Tarsean farmers and their livestock that lived in the Narrows. The Vedi had no discipline at all, but a massive surplus of ferocity and were a dangerous foe. One on one, the average human would struggle to stand against even the smallest of their breed. The Tarsean patrols could not beat their ferocity, so they had taken them on in numbers and discipline. The patrols were well-manned and numerous and highly trained to isolate individual Vedi from the pack, separate them and surround them, beating them down. They had lost soldiers on those patrols, of course, but the Vedi were suitably discouraged, the Tarseans had deemed them a success and Radomir had gotten paid. All in all, a good job, Radomir felt.

On the wall, the Rutik had the advantage of numbers but that was negated to a great extent by the strength and height of the Tarsean fortifications. The two sides were about evenly matched in discipline, Radomir believed. Their motivations were different, of course. The Tarseans were fighting for their homes and loved ones, the Rutik for conquest and glory. Still, they both fought with equal resolve, and determination to achieve their goals. That left ferocity as the only potentially distinguishing factor, so Radomir had taught his soldiers to fight like the Vedi did all those years ago and to throw themselves utterly into the fight. He drove them to hit the enemy hard and keep hitting them until they stopped moving or fell back off the wall. That ferocity was hard to maintain over time, but the Tarsean's spirits were boosted by their continuing success. In almost three weeks of fighting, without respite or relief, they had repulsed every direct attack on their section, even being seconded to other sections on occasion when theirs was quiet and a gap needed filling elsewhere.

Ombly and Red were a powerhouse, almost unstoppable in combination. Red barrelled in, swinging wildly with a heavy poleaxe he had taken from a dead Rutik. Like the man himself though, the swings were only apparently wild, swung wide for effect but targeted with lethal precision. Red used his superior height and weight to his advantage, barrelling into his enemies, terrorising them with bloodcurdling roars, forcing them back by sheer intimidation, sustained by ferocious physical power.

Ombly was an ever-present demon at his shoulder, calling out targets and backing his plays. She was no passive observer though – she used Red as a battering ram, following him into every breach, spear darting left and right. Often she left behind even more dead than he could manage himself. In the time since the beginning of the siege, Radomir had seen her lose a spear more than once. On one memorable occasion, the long shaft had shattered at a direct blow from a double-headed Rutik axe, leaving her with a foot or so of splintered wood for a weapon. Ombly did not hesitate for a moment and instead of falling back, and perhaps retreating to find another weapon, she had instead sprung forward, stabbing the broken shaft into the axeman's eye, gouging out the eyeball and driving on into his brain. Releasing the deeply embedded shaft, she pulled a long knife from her belt and kept on fighting.

Iappous and the remaining volunteers, whose names Radomir still had not bothered to learn, were now almost as inseparable as the other two. They fought as a tight unit, Iappous teaching the others the southern art of fighting in line, shoulder to shoulder, shields locked. Having had so much practice over the preceding days, they now moved almost perfectly in lockstep – Iappous calling the moves, the others falling in without question. If one of them fell back unexpectedly, the others stepped back to flank them without hesitation, or closed ranks in front of them if they were on the ground. If one saw an opening, they could press forward with absolute confidence that the others would follow. The small phalanx killed like a giant meatgrinder, crushing their foes without flashy moves or clever tricks, but slowly, methodically and without mercy.

On that particular morning, the main thrust of the Rutik attack seemed aimed at a point a few miles to the west of Radomir's squad. He could not see the full length of the wall in either direction but the clouds of dust staining the morning sky seemed to indicate at least six or seven additional attacks underway. Another tough day for Tarsus, he thought to himself. Then he shrugged and returned to the task at hand – repairing a leather strap on his breastplate that was close to snapping. Quiet moments were rare on the wall and not to be wasted and besides, if he was going to die it damn sure was not going to be because his breastplate fell off in the middle of a fight.

He was never to complete the repair, however, as shouts of dismay and anger started to rumble along the wall, spreading like an infection through the Tarsean army as more and more soldiers were distracted from the approaching enemy and turned to see smoke rising over the city.

"What the blue-balled fuck is that?" snapped Red, glaring at the billowing smoke as though offended by the mere fact of its existence.

"That's the market quarter," said Iappous grimly, pointing to the east side of the city.

"Never mind that," shouted Ombly, pointing closer to their side of the city. "That's the main fucking barracks. Where's the fucking guard?"

"All on the walls," growled Red, raising both hands to the top of his head in despair. Radomir said nothing and tried to make sense of what he was seeing. At a quick count, there were perhaps a dozen fires overall, though some were much more significant than others. Tarsus was built largely of stone, mined from the nearby mountains, but the danger was that if the fires were allowed to burn unimpeded, they would soon be hot enough to leave all those stone buildings nothing more than burnt-out shells. And with almost every able-bodied man, woman, and child of more than ten years old either on the walls or resting near the walls, who was there to rein the fires in? Even if enough free hands could be found to form bucket chains and start dowsing the flames, Radomir doubted they would be allowed to do it unmolested. The fires had not started all at once, so far apart, by themselves – an enemy or more likely a whole contingent of enemies was setting the blazes and Radomir did not think they would take kindly to anyone trying to undo their hard work. Then, deep in the city streets, he saw the tell-tale flash of light glinting off metal. He narrowed his eyes and tried to pin down the sudden flicker and caught another a short distance from the first, then more still moving in a steady line down the city's main avenue. Armour perhaps?

The chorus of yells on the walls grew in volume and pitch as the Rutik assault on the outer walls began in earnest. Robbed of the security provided by the city at their backs, and facing yet another massive attack from the front, the Tarseans were beginning to panic. As the fires spread, freakishly fast, the acrid stench of smoke was starting to pollute the air, tickling throats, and making eyes water. Desperate officers were trying to restore order, some all but beating their soldiers back into line. Few of them met with much success, however, and the Rutik ladders were being thrown up against the wall. As the first helmed heads popped up over the ramparts, some of the Tarseans regained their senses and turned to fight, to throw back the invaders as they had done so many times before. More of them surrendered to the futility of fighting for a city already lost, turned the other way, and ran. Whole sections of the wall were rapidly overrun and the Rutik were quick to reinforce their footholds, fortifying the immediate area and finishing off any Tarsean stragglers – those too brave or too slow to flee. Once upon the walls in sufficient numbers, they began forming ranks, eight to a line, the full breadth of the wall and soon dozens deep. Once that happened, any hope of turning them back was lost. The Rutik had vastly superior numbers, were well-disciplined and, sensing victory, their ferocity swelled enormously. Without the advantages of height and superior fortifications, the Tarseans were doomed.

From their still relatively peaceful position, Radomir watched the collapse of the Tarsean defence. Their section was rapidly becoming more crowded as soldiers pushed in from either side, pressed back by the Rutik attacks or running in panic, seeking some place of safety. Radomir ignored them for a minute and reached inside the neck of his breastplate, pulling out a leather cord to which was attached a small, amber necklace, shaped roughly in the form of an owl. He broke the cord with a sharp tug and clutched the medallion tightly in one bear-like paw. Then he fell still and seemed almost to be daydreaming.

Radomir, how goes it? He could hear Corraidhín's voice as clearly as though the other man stood right at his shoulder. Radomir had no idea how the necklace worked but over the years he had grown used to relying upon Corraidhín's mysterious abilities and did not grudge him his secrets.

It's fucked, he replied, knowing that Corraidhín could hear him but no other. Bastard Rutik are swarming all over us. The walls have fallen.

The Narrows Gate has been taken; large numbers of Rutik are within the city. I am for the palace; can you join me there? As Corraidhín spoke, Radomir's mind filled with scenes of Rutik cavalry charging around the city, setting fires, and killing anyone they came across. He assumed that the visions were Corraidhín's doing but the trick was a new one and he wondered where the other man had learned it.

I can try. Lot of Rutik between here and there though.

There's another way, abandon the walls and head west, I will direct you from there. Be careful, Radomir – if anything happens, I may not be able to protect you.

Don't you worry about me, little man, worry about yourself. I'm on my way.

I always worry about you, you big fool. Be careful out there.

And with that the connection was gone and Radomir was left with only a memory of his friend's voice and the fresh knowledge of a route through the tunnels beneath the city that led from a graveyard to an underground cavern. There was a distance to go, and plenty of peril along the way, but Corraidhín was waiting for him and he would not let the other man down.

"Time to go boys and girls," Radomir roared, cuffing one of the volunteers around the back of the head. Red and Ombly quickly gathered up their gear and fell in, never questioning his decision. Iappous and the volunteers, however, looked horrified and stood frozen in place. None of them dared speak for a full minute until Radomir turned his glare back in their direction.

"We can't just leave," stammered Iappous eventually. "We have to hold the wall; we have to fight."

"Why?" answered Radomir, turning to the old man. "You think you can make any difference here? No chance. Look around gramps, the walls have fallen, the city is burning, and we've lost. You can come with me or stay here and die, up to you either way." For the normally taciturn Radomir, that counted as a long speech, and he did not bother waiting for a response, turning back to Red and Ombly who were now joined by a clutch of perhaps a dozen other soldiers. The newcomers were not under Radomir's command, but they knew him by reputation and decided they were better off in his company than out.

"Let's go," snarled Radomir. Iappous hesitated a moment longer, but the other volunteers gave in more quickly and joined the small formation. Finally, the old man, with one last look at the bedlam erupting further down the wall, made his decision and fell in too. Radomir did not turn them away, but he hardly acknowledged their presence. Instead, he pushed his way through the crowd and began directing the company west along the wall headed for the nearest staircase.

A handful of exceptionally enthusiastic Rutik soldiers had already pushed far enough along the wall to try and block the progress of Radomir and his small group. Radomir killed two himself, hitting the first in the face with the pommel of his axe before stooping to grab another by the knee and tossing her over the wall. Even through the noise of battle and fire, it was possible to hear a sickening thud as the woman's body hit the hard ground at the foot of the wall. The third Rutik to approach was a large man but nowhere near as massive as Radomir himself. Radomir knocked his sword aside with a one-handed swing of his axe, grabbed his throat with the other hand and smashed his forehead into his nose. The headbutt connected with an audible crack and a spurt of blood splashed across Radomir's face. The Rutik soldier crumpled and fell to the ground without a word. Three more soldiers were close and might have managed to get past Radomir's guard but Red and Ombly were there to step into the breach. Ombly speared one man through the throat, then pivoted to swing him around, crashing his body into the woman next to him and sending them both tumbling off the inside of the wall. Red laid into the third with a large mallet he had picked up along the way somewhere, battering the hapless Rutik repeatedly around the head until his skull shattered, and his brain was crushed to paste. By the time they reached the stairs, the company had killed half a dozen more of the enemy and lost two or three of the newcomers.

Evidently, the stairs had already been contested, as broken bodies, Tarsean and Rutik alike, were scattered across the steps and blood ran across the paved surfaces to gather in turgid pools at the bottom. Radomir kicked a couple of corpses over the side of the stairs and ran on downward. The stone staircase led into one of the staging areas for troop movements to the wall. There Radomir called a brief halt and his soldiers rearmed themselves and grabbed some supplies from the stockpiles gathered around. There was no sign of the quartermasters, which did not surprise Radomir. If the quartermasters had been fighting men and women, they would not have been quartermasters in the first place, or so he assumed. More Rutik were approaching along the wall, and in greater numbers, so the company did not linger in the depot for long. Instead, Radomir lead them away from the wall, took a sharp left, and then followed an alleyway for some distance across the city.

Along the way they crossed over four major streets, two of which were packed with panicking soldiers and terrified citizens, running this way and that, screaming and shouting at each other. Radomir pushed through them without pause, shoving men and women to either side, creating a bow wave of tumbled Tarseans to either side, the rest of the company rushing in his wake. The last street they crossed was empty but, in the distance, towards the centre of the city, they could see Rutik cavalry milling around, nearby flames flashing off their armour and casting long, flickering shadows across the paved road. The company hurried past but were scarcely back in the relative safety of the alley when a large party of Rutik spearmen emerged from a side road. Radomir skidded to a halt and the others formed up around him, in time to meet the enemy charge.

The pitched battle that followed was chaotic and bloody and even the three seasoned soldiers were hard-pressed to break through. The remainder of Iappous's volunteers quickly found themselves isolated and surrounded, fighting desperately back-to-back along with a couple of the newcomers. More Rutik spearmen were now entering the alley and the company was hopelessly outnumbered. Radomir knew that the volunteers could not be saved and continued along the alley, less than a dozen soldiers now in tow. Iappous himself, however, was unable to leave his proteges to their fate and charged back into the melee, fighting to reach them and add his strength to theirs. The old man's display of courage and loyalty shamed Radomir for a moment, and he almost turned back himself but pragmatism and the will to survive won over and he ran on.

Sometime later, after another full hour of running and fighting, dodging sparks and flames, and detouring around enemy strongpoints. Eventually, they reached a small, relatively peaceful square, protected on four sides by tall buildings and still untouched by the flames. Even Radomir was starting to flag at that stage. The billowing smoke was choking him, and the immense heat was sapping even his mighty strength, so he called a halt. The company sank to the ground, panting and sweating, trying desperately to catch their breath. He knew they could not afford to linger long in one place but equally, he knew they could not keep running indefinitely without rest, so he gave them a few minutes of peace. Then he felt a hand on his shoulder and turned to find Red and Ombly crouched beside him, their smoke-blackened faces worried and tense.

"Where we goin' boss?" asked Red quietly, pitching his voice so that the others could not overhear. "Seems like we're headed in a big circle to me."

"Got to get to the palace," replied Radomir tiredly. "Got to find Corraidhín and the king." The other two waited for him to elaborate but Radomir closed his eyes and leaned back against a stone pillar, apparently having said his piece.

"You're gonna need to give us more than that, boss," said Ombly. "Seems like if you want us along, least you could do is tell us the plan." Radomir opened one eye and regarded them with a bloodshot glare. On the one hand, he was disinclined to share his secrets with anyone. On the other, his chances of escape were significantly better with the support of the other two, than without it.

"Fine," he snapped eventually. "When this city was built, they pulled down the old city and built on top of the rubble. Most of it is still down there somewhere. And below that, even older ruins are buried too. And below that again caves and tunnels, underground rivers and all that shit. Like a fucking rabbit warren down there."

"Not much for caves me," said Red, with a shudder. "You know the way through?"

"Yeah, I can get us there. Corraidhín showed me the way."

Ombly glanced over at Red, who just shrugged. They too had learned to rely on Corraidhín's abilities over the years and were willing to place their faith in the little man.

"Guess we've nothing better to do today," she said with a shrug. Red nodded his agreement and Radomir closed his eyes once more.

"Five minutes," he growled. "Then we move."

CHAPTER TWENTY-ONE

The Royal Palace, City of Tarsus
26 of Euthaios 870M - Late Spring
Day twenty-one of the siege of Tarsus

Arrias was the greatest hero Asfáleia has ever known. He laid the first foundations of Tarsus in the year 30M, five years after defeating the warped legions of the north. In the decades that followed, he brought the squabbling south into the fold, all to the greater glory of the Tarsean Kingdom. He was the conqueror, but also the peacemaker, for he brought harmony and reconciliation to all the people of Asfáleia. He was the builder, raising Tarsus from the ashes. He was the wise, for he saw the future laid out before him, and in his wisdom grasped it.

Acusilaus, "The Eternal Glory of Tarsus", c. 850M

Chapter Twenty-One

Corraidhín arrived at the palace early in the afternoon to find the Royal Guard mustering in the northern courtyard, King Achaeus in full armour, watching from a nearby platform. The tension in the air was so thick as to be almost palpable and he realised that his sense of such things was now greatly heightened. He understood now that the Oracle's strength had not only repaired him to his previous state but had taken him further still, making him somehow more than he had been before. He had no way of judging the extent of the gift, or what abilities it might have blessed him with but time, he supposed, would provide plenty of opportunities to find out. Gathering his things as quickly as he could, he had left the inn without a word to anyone and headed off across the city. The Oracle's gift had brought with it a new passion for his mission and he was eager to pit himself against the power of the but first and foremost in urgency was to bring warning to the King, before it was too late. He reached the King's platform and paused at the bottom of the steps, bowing deeply.

"My lord," he said, still bowing. "I bring grave news." Achaeus called him forward, then as Corraidhín approached took a step back and held up his hands to ward him off.

"Fate's touch, Corraidhín, you smell truly awful!" Corraidhín paused at the top of the steps, baffled for a moment, then understanding that his physical form had remained where it sat, on the floor of the inn, for however long his incorporeal spirit had been away. Looking down, he saw that that his clothes were wrinkled and filthy, stained and stinking with days of sweat and grime. Dirty brown flakes of blood crusted his left shoulder and chest where he had, at some time in the endless battles, sustained an injury to his face that was mirrored into the world behind. He reached up and ran a hand through his long, brown hair, finding it greasy and tangled.

"Apologies, Lord King, there has been much to do and little time to attend to matters of hygiene. I fear I am quite unsuitably prepared for this meeting." Achaeus laughed and waved off his apology good-naturedly.

"I believe we have better things to worry about at this moment, old friend. The Rutik are within the city, having somehow reached the Narrows Gate early this morning. Reports are frantic and confusing at this stage, but they appear to have spread out across the north of the city. I have ordered the Royal Guard to form up – we will have to plug the gap until reinforcements can be brought from the south." Corraidhín stared at him, his mind racing. His sense of time was still badly out of alignment, but he figured that the disappearance of the demons must have occurred at the exact moment the Rutik breached the Narrows Gate. The obvious implication of careful coordination between the two realms was deeply disturbing.

At that moment, a Guard-Captain arrived to inform the King that they were ready for departure. The officer looked worried, and Achaeus placed a fatherly hand on his shoulder to comfort him.

"Fear not, Captain. Tarsus is our home; the Rutik will not stand. Will you join us, Corraidhín?" The islander thought for a moment, wondering if his newly renewed fealty to the Oracle required him elsewhere. As far as furthering his mission went, however, he had no idea what to do next, so heading out into the city seemed as good an option as any.

"Yes, Lord King," he replied and Achaeus nodded before turning back to the Guard Captain with a smile.

"You see, Captain? Corraidhín of the Illyan Isles is with us! Wait until you see what he can do with that spear. We'll have the cursed Rutik on the run in no time!" The Guard Captain smiled, and nodded in acknowledgement to Corraidhín, before Achaeus dismissed him and he departed to make his final preparations. Not for the first time, Corraidhín admired the easy rapport Achaeus seemed able to strike up with almost anyone. It was one of the reasons his troops, and most of his citizens, were so enamoured of him.

"If I may say so, Lord King: you seem in good spirits today, considering the day that's in it."

"You may indeed say, and you're right, my friend. I can't explain it but today, for the first time in weeks, I feel… free. Since the siege began it has been as though a storm cloud rested above my head, blotting out the sun and constantly threatening. Early this morning, I looked up and it was gone. Perhaps it's the release of tension now that the end game has finally begun, I don't know, but I don't intend to waste the feeling! The only thing that could make it better would be a strong horse to ride, but alas…" He shrugged and laughed and Corraidhín smiled in return but behind the smile he was adding the King's curious malaise to the list of strange events that seemed tied to the departure of the demons. It occurred to him that he still had not told Achaeus about the demons and the threat posed to the city from within. There was nothing the King could immediately do with the knowledge, however, so Corraidhín elected not to spoil his mood. A few minutes later they headed out into the city, Corraidhín at the King's right-hand side, and wary Guards all around them.

Their first contact with the invaders was a brief and scrappy affair. Leaving the palace by the north gate, they emerged onto King's Plaza to find it largely clear of the enemy, save for a dozen apparently leaderless soldiers in green tunics, industriously engaged in toppling a large statue from its plinth. Heavy ropes had been thrown over the statue's shoulders and around its neck and the Rutik had broken into two teams, each hauling on a rope end for all they were worth. They were so engrossed in their vandalism that they failed to notice the contingent of Tarsean Guards until it was already too late. Even as they dropped the ropes and scrambled for their weapons, Achaeus called the charge, and the fight was over in moments.

They left the enemy's bodies where they lay and moved on, heading for the Narrows Gate. They had expected to find the gate occupied and defended, if the Rutik would want to protect their rear, and their avenue of escape. All was silent as they approached, and the doors lay open, swinging gently in the breeze, so Achaeus sent squads of Guards to scout out the interior. The soldiers were gone for some time but returned to report that there was not a single living soul to be found, anywhere within the building. They also reported the dead inside, however, and even the most hardened among them looked pale and horrified at what they had seen. The King's expression hardened as they told him of the mutilated bodies that decorated the blood-soaked gatehouse. Corraidhín had seen that look on his face before and knew that whoever ended up on the receiving end of the King's righteous fury was in for a hard time indeed. Achaeus might have been friendly and easy-going with his people, but he was a skilled warrior and a dangerous enemy to have, especially when angered.

Achaeus ordered the gatehouse closed and sealed and made plans to seek out the enemy elsewhere. As it turned out, however, the enemy found them instead as a large party of Rutik cavalry emerged into the Plaza in good order. With a curse, Achaeus unslung the great War Spear of Tarsus and began shouting orders. They had about twenty archers on their strength, and Achaeus sent them into nearby buildings, with orders to find windows that overlooked the gatehouse. The rest of the soldiers he formed into a large block and prepared to meet the Rutik charge. The Rutik cavalry wore only light armour of chainmail and a breastplate, however, and were not kitted out for a mounted attack against a solid formation of Tarsean spears. Instead of attacking directly, they dismounted and formed an infantry block of their own, before advancing. One of them had a large bugle, which he now held to his lips and blew with all his might.

Corraidhín did not recognise the signal being blown on the bugle but, evidently, it was a call to arms, or else an appeal for help. Either way, scarcely had the last, warbling note faded from the air then another contingent of cavalry appeared on the edges of the plaza. They too quickly dismounted and came on, approaching the Tarseans from the west along a line perpendicular to that of their fellows. Moments later, the Plaza rang to the sounds of battle, as Achaeus coordinated their defence on two sides. The Royal Guard wore armour that was ornate and highly polished and Corraidhín knew that the regular army often considered them little more than shiny baubles, good for making the palace look pretty but not a whole lot else. What he saw in the next few minutes left him utterly convinced that their reputation was ill-earned.

The Royal Guard might have been well dressed, but they knew their business. Closing ranks to defend the King, they met the enemy on both fronts and held the Rutik line without taking so much as a single step backwards. With their shields planted on the stone paving, they were unwavering in the face of attack, beating the Rutik back with a grim ferocity. At that moment however, a shout of warning rose from the Tarsean ranks as some of the soldiers spotted yet another party of Rutik entering the Plaza from the west. Another appeared beside the first, then another, then a fourth arrived from between the houses on the eastern side of the Plaza. The situation had become far more perilous as the Rutik now outnumbered the Tarseans and still more were coming, in twos and threes or more often in larger groups. Achaeus himself was now obliged to join the fighting, leading the defence on the south side of their formation, Corraidhín ready at his shoulder.

The War Spear of Tarsus began to sing its bloodthirsty chorus as Achaeus killed one enemy after another, rapidly turning that side of their formation into the area of the battle that the ordinary soldiers would go to almost any lengths to avoid. Corraidhín was moving quickly, ducking, and dodging around Rutik attacks, striking left and right with his spear, killing or wounding a dozen Rutik in the first few minutes. As the battle wore on, and still more Rutik joined their comrades, he was grateful once more for the new lease of life the Oracle had granted him. He was stronger and no faster than he had ever been, his limbs did not seem to be tiring as they once would have, and his breath was steady throughout, as though he was taking a gentle stroll in the countryside, rather than fighting for his life on a blood-slick city street.

The archers were getting in position now and arrows began to rain down on the Rutik. They were wary of hitting their fellow Tarseans, of course, but there were plenty of targets further afield and more and more of the Rutik were falling with feathered shafts sprouting from their bodies. An hour passed, then another, as the enemy attacked, fell back, reformed and attacked again. Corraidhín was hardly even tired, but he could see that the Tarsean soldiers were beginning to weary of the constant fighting. Killing a Rutik officer with a short stab to the neck, he found a moment of calm in the midst of the chaos and looked around to try and gauge the likely course of the battle. The Tarseans had lost perhaps a third of their number killed or disabled. The Rutik had lost more, but their numbers had only grown in the meantime. He turned to look for Achaeus, thinking to suggest that perhaps they should retreat to the safety of the palace when a flash of blue caught his eye from the far end of the plaza.

A small contingent of Tarsean soldiery was approaching from the direction of the palace but the Rutik had spotted them too and a large contingent was moving to intercept. Corraidhín shouted a warning to Achaeus, who looked around and instantly understood what was happening.

"Guard!" he bellowed, straining his voice to be heard in the crowded, noisy plaza. "Guard! On me!" The Guard quickly reformed to follow their King as he headed towards the approaching friendlies. The next few minutes were a frantic race as the newcomers hurried north, Achaeus led the Guard south to meet them and large numbers of Rutik charged to get between the two. The edges of the Guard formation were fighting and running at the same time, under constant attack but determined to protect Achaeus. The other Tarsean group had thrown caution to the wind and were running for all they were worth but the distance between them was just too far.

A group of about twenty Rutik managed to get between the two Tarsean formations, winded from a hard run but with weapons raised and ready to fight. They would not need to hold for long, more Rutik were rapidly approaching, and all they had to do was dig in and stall the Tarseans from meeting for enough time for reinforcements to arrive. Corraidhín shouted to Achaeus again, but the King had already seen the danger and did not hesitate. He barrelled into the Rutik without pause, allowing the momentum of his run to carry him into the middle of their formation and the mighty War Spear sang out again. Achaeus killed two in the first moments and knocked a third from her feet with the Spear's butt end. Coming in behind, Corraidhín darted past him and sliced the throat of a fourth with a quick, horizontal swipe of his own spear. The rest of the Guard piled in behind them and although for a moment it looked as if the Rutik would hold, the other Tarseans arrived in time to hit them in the rear and between the two groups they were quickly annihilated.

Achaeus shouted the order to form up and both groups of Tarseans quickly formed a protective square around him, the newcomers hurrying to fill gaps in the depleted Guard ranks. More Rutik were attacking now and the Tarseans were fighting defensively, those on the outside of the formation buying time for the others to get into position. The leader of the newcomers, a tall Major in her mid-forties with a vivid scar running along the left side of her face and down onto her neck.

"A close-run thing, Major, well done," shouted Achaeus, leaning on his spear to rest. He had taken several small wounds in the fighting but appeared mostly intact. Corraidhín moved to stand beside him, keen to hear the Major's report. She glanced around as a particularly aggressive group of Rutik attacked from the east, then, seeing that the Tarsean line would hold she turned back to the King and gave a courtly bow.

"Your majesty is too kind. Had it not been for your intervention, we would not have made it. I bring dire news though; the Gate of Arrias has been taken by the enemy and the city has been opened to the Rutik horde. The streets are filling with them, and large sections of the wall have been abandoned or overrun. We cannot hold them, my King." Achaeus took the news silently, his expression frozen, but Corraidhín could see the anguish in his eyes. He could not imagine how the King felt in that moment, having heard that everything he and his ancestors had built over centuries was now lost and would soon be destroyed. The silence stretched and still Achaeus did not speak. All around them, Rutik and Tarsean fought on with equal ferocity but still he did not move.

"Lord King," he said finally, as gently as he could whilst still loudly enough to be heard above the clamour. "Achaeus, we cannot stay here. More Rutik will come, we must retreat to the palace." Achaeus turned his head slowly to stare at him, looking vaguely surprised as though he had entirely forgotten that Corraidhín was there. He looked old in that moment, Corraidhín thought, tired and lost – unsurprisingly given the situation. Then he seemed to rally somewhat and a little of his previous vigour returned.

"Very well," he replied, before turning to shout the order to retreat to the Guard-Captain.

The Rutik pressed them hard as they tried to move towards the palace, gathering in ever-greater numbers on all sides. In minutes, the Tarseans had lost a dozen more killed and wounded, having gained less than a few yards of ground. Achaeus fought like a man possessed, with Corraidhín at his side and the remnants of the Guard doing their utmost to match his fervour but it was all to no avail. The enemy were too numerous and despite their losses, they were pinning the Tarseans down by sheer weight of numbers. One by one they were being picked off or pulled down by the Rutik, dying in a chorus of bloodthirsty cheers. The situation was beyond desperate and despite all he had gained, Corraidhín found himself despairing of their fate. It seemed so unfair, after all this time, to have finally regained his purpose, only to die at the hands of a baying mob.

The city is awash with death, little spear, and the flagged streets have forgotten their roots. But look deeper: beneath the stone and gravel, beneath the buried remnants of forgotten civilisations… the soil remembers…

The Oracle's voice was clear and distinct, held somehow aloof from the noisy chaos that surrounded him and for a moment, he was puzzled. His senses, although heightened, were swamped by the cacophony of emotions and savage intentions that swirled around him. Batting away a Rutik spear with his own, he stepped back into the midst of the shrinking Tarsean formation and tried to focus his concentration.

The roiling, agitated crowd of men and women fighting for their lives was a seemingly fathomless sea that crashed in waves upon his mind, battering the cliffs of his awareness and clamouring for his attention. With an extraordinary effort, however, he suppressed, and let his awareness sink gradually downward, through the churning currents of passions and feelings, towards the dark, silent ocean floor. The hard, compact stone of the plaza was pale and lifeless, utterly inert except for splashes of vivid energy where the life force of dying soldiers leaked into its cracks and pores. Deeper still, the litter and detritus left behind by a thousand years of "civilisation" was equally passive, buried and forgotten by the frantic haste of humanity. Deeper still, buried ruins and long-forgotten cellars turned to caves and natural passages, carved out of the clutter by rushing water, shifting ground and the weight of newer construction. Vaguely, as though now at an immense distance, Corraidhín could still feel the commotion of the battle above, and with it the spiralling desperation of Achaeus and his people but now it competed for attention with a profound silence that had remained undisturbed for centuries.

For a brief moment, Corraidhín almost believed that the Oracle had been wrong in her assessment, that the ground beneath the streets was as lifeless and inactive as the stone above. Then he felt it – life not living, but not gone either, hibernating almost. The feeling was faint and hard to pin down but as he focused all of his attention upon it, he realised that beneath the slumbering torpor, a sleeping giant lay. Far below the scarred and battered surface, the soil indeed remembered better days and, moreover, it knew that those days would come again. Time might pass, centuries – millennia even – but what was time to the immortal earth? One day, the surface dwellers would be gone, all of their works would crumble into dust, and life would re-emerge, blinking into the gentle light of a new, better dawn. All that life had to do was wait, and its time would come but he sensed an eagerness there, despite its glacial patience. The soil's energy was powerfully keen to emerge and Corraidhín realised that all it needed was a nudge. Stretching out with his mind, he gathered in the tendrils of buried life and channelled them upward.

Back on the surface, he returned to himself just in time to dodge the butt end of a Tarsean spear that otherwise would have caught him on the temple. A sudden, overwhelming sense of loss filled him as he separated himself from the life he had awakened below. Somehow, he knew that his choice was to either let it go, or let it swallow him completely but still it was not an easy decision and the world around him now seemed listless and dull. He could feel it coming, however, could sense the ground beneath his feet tremor and quake as a mighty geyser of life and energy forced its way upward. At first, the approaching upheaval was only evident to Corraidhín, and it took him a moment to register that what had been a purely ethereal earthquake was now emerging as something fundamentally more physical. A hundred individual battles and thousands of shouting voices petered out into confused silence as a gentle rapidly increased in intensity and frequency. Soldiers caught off balance were tumbled to the ground, and those better positioned were staggered and shaken. Further out from the group of Tarseans, surprise turned to fear and panic as the flagstones themselves began to crack and crumble, opening shadowed rifts that ran terrifyingly deep into the earth below.

In a perfect circle around Corraidhín, encompassing the entire Tarsean contingent and not a few of the closest Rutik, the motion remained a mere quivering shake. Outside of that radius, and stretching almost to the edges of the plaza, the world was in complete upheaval. Thrown from their feet, Rutik soldiers were desperately trying to regain their balance, with minds and bodies overwhelmed by the sudden upsurge of energy. Inches from their faces, and beneath their fallen bodies, a hundred millennia of erosion and decay crammed into tightly packed instants ground the flagstones into shards. Shards quickly crumbled into pebbles and dust, then pulled the shattered remnants down into the waiting embrace of the earth as fresh, fertile soil rose osmotically to the surface. Men and women alike were shouting in shock and terror as their bodies were sucked into the trembling movement and pinned to the ground by the earth's resurgent vigour.

Even as the last traces of humanity's dominion disappeared below the surface, new life sprang up in its place. Moulds and mildew turned the loamy soil into a thousand shades of green and brown, fungi sprouted in lumpy clusters, bursting into life, growing, and then falling into decay in moments. Scrubby weeds sprang up, grew rapidly towards the sun, and then fell back to be replaced by thorny brambles and creeping vines. Screaming Rutik soldiers vanished into fresh undergrowth as entire bushes burst into life, spreading and mingling, only for the tender stems of new trees to push through from beneath and claim the plaza for their own. Within the space of perhaps five short minutes, the Tarseans found themselves in a clearing, surrounded by lush forest that might have been growing there undisturbed for centuries. The Rutik soldiers had fallen silent and were nowhere to be seen.

Despite the relief the forest's appearance had granted them from their attackers, the Tarsean soldiers were shocked into silence and unable to process what had happened. Even Achaeus stood still, mouth agape, staring at the thick foliage with eyes that were almost wide enough to be called wild. Swallowing his own not-inconsiderable shock, Corraidhín tapped into the life force one final time, imploring it to be still and return to its rest. The energy resisted for a moment or two, and he had a sudden vision of the entire city being swallowed by its voracious appetite, but then, reluctantly, it acquiesced to his wishes and withdrew. The surrounding trees continued to grow but then almost all at once, shed their leaves, shrivelled, and began to rot. The air was filled with the creak and groan of cracking limbs and crumbling trunks and punctuated by the echoing crashes of dozens of trees felled by their own decay and falling to back to the earth that had birthed them. Almost as quickly as it had grown, the forest fell apart and disappeared, leaving only the bare soil and occasional desiccated branch as evidence of its passing.

Corraidhín released his connection to the life force, bidding it farewell and counselling it to abide in peace until its proper time came. Then he turned to Achaeus, swallowing down the pangs of bereavement that wracked his soul.

"My lord, we have to go!"

Achaeus tore his gaze away from the ruins of the plaza and stared at him as though seeing him for the first time.

"Corraidhín? What… I don't understand…" Achaeus was clearly struggled to form thoughts into words and despite being immensely sympathetic to the king's plight, Corraidhín knew that they had only a very short window of escape.

"My lord, more Rutik will come. We must get back to the palace."

"Yes. Yes, you're right. Let's… but… I don't…" Achaeus trailed off again, stealing furtive glances in all directions, as though expecting the mysterious forest to return at any moment.

"Now, my lord!" shouted Corraidhín, putting as much forceful command into his voice as he could muster. "We have to go!"

Achaeus frowned and glared at him and for a moment, Corraidhín thought he had overstepped. The frown quickly disappeared, however, and the king seemed to shake himself into action.

"Guard, to me!" he cried, waving the War Spear above his head like a banner. Much like their leader, the Tarsean soldiers were stunned and not a little frightened, but he still commanded their loyalty. Not giving them any more time to brood, Achaeus started towards the palace at a run, drawing them into his wake by sheer force of will.

They made it to the safety of the gates without interruption but by the time they had filtered through into the courtyard, more Rutik soldiers had arrived from elsewhere in the city and they were forced to fight a savage and bloody rearguard action before they could finally get the gates closed. The solid gates and high walls surrounding them effectively muted the baying of the mob outside and had it not been for their own wounded, it could almost have been any other day on the palace grounds. Even Corraidhín was starting to tire by that time, but Achaeus seemed indefatigable, his previous moment of weakness apparently forgotten, or at least forgiven.

"Guard-Captain!" The King snapped out the order, determined not to lose the momentum that had carried them through the gates. "Gather the rest of the Guard and begin the evacuation of the palace. We have planned for this day – see that those plans are followed. A dozen guards to follow me, please, we're for the caves beneath the city, and a dozen more to accompany Corraidhín." The islander started at the mention of his name, having been lost in thought, pondering the mystery of the demons.

"You have orders for me, Lord King?"

"I have a request, Corraidhín. One final task, though you owe me nothing more. I know you can slip out of the city if you want to, no one knows its secret ways better than you. Know that I will not judge you, should you choose that option now."

"I appreciate the thought, Lord King, but I will see this through to the end, no matter how bitter the taste."

"Very well then. The task I set you is to protect the two things most precious to me in this world, now that all is come to ruin. The lesser of the two is the War Spear of Tarsus. We head into unknown territory and the Spear is the greatest legacy of our house, forged for Arrias himself by the wizard Menidas. You know where the Royal Vault is?"

"Yes, my Lord, but I understood it to be inaccessible to any but you?"

"Any but someone with the blood of Arrias running strongly in their veins, to be technically correct but yes, normally you would be unable to get inside. However, as a precaution, I left it unlocked – a risk to be sure, but in all honesty, there is little else of value left inside. Too many of my ancestors were less than frugal with our wealth, and I spent heavily preparing for this day. Take the spear to the vault and seal it in, it will be safe there until someone comes for it."

"It will be done, Lord King, and the second part of my duty?"

"Arion. My son is in his rooms, confined to quarters you might say. I'm afraid we had angry words the last time we met. I would have you go there once the Spear is secured. Collect Arion and bring him to join me in the caves. You are the only one I can trust with this duty, Corraidhín, my only wish is that Radomir was with you too. Together the two of you are unstoppable. Do you know where he is?" Corraidhín looked down at the ground, reluctant to face a truth he had been studiously avoiding.

"He was on the south wall, Lord King, close to the Gate of Arrias." Achaeus looked dismayed, knowing as well as Corraidhín that the chances of anyone on that section of wall having survived were slim indeed.

"It will take more than a few Rutik to stop Radomir, Corraidhín, you know that. He will be alright; I am sure of it." The attempt to be comforting was weak but still appreciated by Corraidhín. He and Radomir had come through many dangers together, and the other man was certainly well able to take care of himself. That, of course, would never be enough to stop Corraidhín from worrying, and he resolved to make contact with Radomir as soon as the opportunity presented itself.

"Yes, Lord King, let us hope so. In the meantime, however, we should both get moving. We have much ground to cover, and the Rutik will not be far behind." Achaeus nodded and handed over the War Spear. Corraidhín was surprised at the weight of it in his hands, especially in contrast to his own much lighter weapon. He was even more surprised when Achaeus stepped forward to embrace him like a brother, holding him in a tight embrace for a moment before releasing him again.

"Fetch my son, Corraidhín, keep him safe and the line of Arrias will be eternally in your debt."

CHAPTER
TWENTY-TWO

The Royal Palace, City of Tarsus
26 of Euthaios 870M - Late Spring
Day twenty-one of the siege of Tarsus

Arrias was a great hero for Tarsus, there is no arguing with that. In a single lifetime he took the ruins of a burned-out border post and turned it into the capital of a powerful kingdom. Let us not sugar-coat the truth, however. Cutting through the stories and the legends, Arrias was no better than his father – a warlord, a killer, and a destroyer. The Achaean city states had endured for centuries, imperfect to be sure, but nevertheless proud and free. One by one, he crushed them, slaughtered their armies, and pulled down their walls, bringing them under his thumb with little regard for life or liberty.

Polemon of Chalcis, "The Ancients Weep", c. 975M

Chapter Twenty-Two

With the gate firmly in Rutik hands, and reinforcements now pouring into the city, Mira walked away from the action in search of a moment's peace and a good spot from which to observe. The steps that led upwards from inside the gatehouse were steep and tall and a wave of fatigue hit her as she emerged onto the fortified rooftop. Pulling off her gloves, she put out her hand to steady herself, leaning against the nearby battlements. Finding that the smooth stone surface of the merlon was warm from the sun and that there was no one around save a handful of dead Tarseans, she slumped against the wall and sank down to sit on the top step of the stairs. The feeling of relief was tremendous, for she had not relaxed in some time. Between the natural perils of the mountains, the constant threat of attack from their occupants and the strange and disturbing abilities of her allies, she had felt beset on all sides, and at all times, throughout their journey east.

As her strength slowly began to seep back, she raised her head and one of the dead Tarseans caught her eye. She was female, probably not even Mira's age and she lay slumped into a corner of the roof, her hands in her lap, her head bowed as though sleeping. The girl's helm had been torn off or removed and her long, black hair fell loosely to either side of her head, framing a dark-skinned, pretty face with deep brown eyes that now stared sightlessly into the ground. A leather thong, strung with beads dangled loosely from a snarl of hair, incongruously colourful and cheery. A single grey-fletched arrow protruded from her neck, a little off centre so that the feathers brushed gently against her left cheek. Other than the arrow, and the patina of hardened blood that glazed her chest and stomach, her uniform was pristine and appeared almost new. Her spear, assuming she had one, was missing but her sword was in its scabbard, undisturbed and Mira wondered if she had ever drawn it in anger.

From her appearance, it seemed far more likely that the young woman, hardly more than a girl, had barely arrived on the wall when the final Rutik attack began. Mira had a vision of the newly minted Tarsean soldier: fresh-faced and eager, taking up her assigned post with pride and determination to defend her city. She imagined that first watch ending, perhaps only moments later, a Rutik arrow sailing over the battlements, probably not even aimed at her, but pointed at her neck, nevertheless. One day she might have been a great warrior, or maybe she would have retired after the war and gone back to doing whatever it was she did before. She might have had a long, full life, a partner, perhaps children. Instead, her fate was to be shot through the neck and bleed out in defence of a wall that was lost before she even arrived. Mira shrugged and looked away: fate was cruel sometimes, and that was all there was to it.

She got to her feet, wincing as a cut on her side reopened with the movement, and walked across the roof to look down over the battlements at the streets of Tarsus below. It was a scene of noise and chaos, with the Rutik army showing little of the discipline and order that had carried them across most of Asfáleia. The Avenue of Kings ran as straight as an arrow from the southern gates to the gates of the palace and every inch of it was crowded. About half a mile past the gate, the Tarseans had formed a defensive line, cutting across the road behind pre-prepared barriers of piled crates and overturned carts. Behind them, more blue-clad soldiers were rushing to the defence whilst mobs of civilians ran this way and that. In front of them, the attacking Rutik were pushing in, their front lines directly up against the barricades. A desperate and vicious battle was underway, the Tarseans with nowhere to go, the Rutik with no interest in going anywhere except forward. More Rutik were arriving all the time, so that even the majestic avenue was not wide enough to contain them and they spilt out to left and right, onto side streets and into houses and shops. Glancing back over her shoulder at the hordes of Rutik still to enter the city, Mira knew that the Tarsean defence was doomed, but she found herself admiring their tenacity.

Further afield Mira could see the roving parties of cavalry still riding this way and that, bringing fire and death wherever they came. With an experienced eye, she counted the groups and estimated numbers, concluding that their casualties had been light thus far. There was no sign that they had met organised resistance anywhere within the city, which made sense Mira supposed since the last thing the Tarseans had been expecting was an attack from the north. Like the wasp that gets into the bees' nest, she thought, remembering a tale from her childhood: bees would defend their hive to the death but once a wasp managed to get inside the resistance stopped, and the bees seemed merely confused at the presence of an enemy within. The Plaza of Kings and most of the northern city was hidden from her view by the looming bulk of the Tarsean palace. In the east of the city, the fires were spreading rapidly, smoke billowing out over the wall and into the nearby mountains, making it difficult to see much of anything. In the west, the fires were more isolated and even the far wall could still be seen clearly. She watched as a large contingent of cavalry swept south along the Westernroad and could even hear their whoops and bellows of excitement as the Tarsean citizenry fell back before them in terror.

As much as she understood its necessity, Mira found the entire process of sacking the city utterly abhorrent. The Queen herself had ordered Tarsus destroyed — not only defeated, nor even merely conquered, but destroyed. Every living soul within the walls was to be killed or enslaved, every building burned or pulled down, every statue toppled, every flag trampled. The Queen had ordered it and so it would be — death would come to Tarsus and leave nothing living in its wake. Until that moment she had accepted that too as merely another twist of callous fate — unfortunate for the Tarseans but as unavoidable as the sunset. Now, looking down from the roof of the gatehouse with the smell of greasy smoke in her nose and the ring of terrified screams in her ears, she was not so sure. Something caught her attention, and she leaned a little further forward, straining her eyes to see. She leaned a little too far for comfort, however, and the battlements were only waist-high – intended to crouch behind rather than stand tall. Her balance shifted and she looked down, the sixty-foot drop filling her vision.

The moment passed but even as Mira was recovering her footing, a voice from immediately behind threw her back into instability.

"This is no time to tarry, Captain," it said, and Mira turned slowly to find the Avatar staring at her from beneath its dark hood. "There remains work to be done this day." Mira struggled to bring herself to attention and even managed a bow before the Avatar continued.

"Gather your troop. We are for the palace." For a brief, fleeting instant, Mira was tempted to argue the point. Her soldiers were exhausted, as was she. Fresh Rutik divisions were rapidly filling the city: could the Avatar not find someone else for this further duty? The inclination passed quickly, however, and instead, she merely bowed once more and hurried off to muster the unfortunate soldiers.

The Tarsean palace was plumb in the middle of the carefully planned city, atop a small rise that added to its towering height and cast long shadows onto the paved streets. By that time, Rutik forces had pushed the Tarseans through the palace gates and were bullying their way into the courtyards but that only left the streets outside even more crowded and chaotic, and Mira knew that there was no way her small troop would be able to force its way through. The Avatar had other plans, however, and led them through the massing Rutik with ease. She watched as hard-bitten soldiers turned pale and dropped back as it approached, rapidly clearing their path forward. She wondered for a moment whether the Avatar intended proceeding in that manner as far as the front line and on into the Tarseans beyond but about halfway along the avenue it turned to the east and headed into the side streets.

Once off the main road, their pace quickened still further and soon Mira's soldiers were half jogging to keep up with the Avatar's long, unhurried strides. After a while, they reached Merchants' Row, which ran parallel and to the east of The Avenue of Kings. There they stumbled upon a division of the Expeditionary Army heavily engaged with a large group of Tarsean soldiers. Finding herself directly behind the enemy, Mira made a snap decision and ordered a charge. The sudden arrival of more Rutik to their rear threw the Tarseans into disarray, allowing the other Rutik the chance to rally and push forward. The battle was short and decisive, with Mira's troop striking before the enemy had a chance to adapt to the new threat. Given a new lease of enthusiasm, the other Rutik fought with equal ferocity and the Tarseans were quickly crushed. Once the survivors were mopped up or had run off, Mira gathered her troop and cornered the officer leading the other group of Rutik, a slightly pompous looking Major with a carefully trimmed moustache. A brief battle of wills ensued, with Mira citing the authority of Lord Ohtrad and the League to co-opt the Major's command. For his part, the Major pulled rank and insisted that she would do no such thing. It seemed they were at an impasse until the Avatar arrived at Mira's shoulder and in its unsettling presence, a compromise was quickly reached. Mira's troop set off again with twenty additional soldiers added to their strength, whilst the Major went about his business with a force reduced by the same number.

They continued north along Merchants Row and eventually arrived at the Narrows Wall, where they found the gatehouse abandoned, with black smoke billowing from one of its two protective towers. The gates lay open and undefended too, and under the shadow of the archway, the Avatar led them through a small doorway and onto a winding stone stair. Climbing the stairs, they quickly emerged onto the top of the wall and headed west towards the palace. They had only to travel a short distance but a door at the far end of the wall slammed open and Tarsean soldiers came pouring out, looking tense but in good order. Spotting the approaching Rutik, one of their officers drew up sharply and began shouting orders. As the Tarseans formed ranks and prepared for battle, Mira looked to the Avatar wondering whether it would use its power to remove this obstacle. The Avatar seemed uninterested in involving itself, however, and merely waved Mira towards the enemy.

Not sure what to make of the Avatar's sudden show of restraint, Mira turned away to look for Teja instead.

"Attack formation, sergeant!"

"Aye, Captain! Rutik: form up around me, quickly now!" Mira's soldiers responded well despite their obvious tiredness and moments later they were charging down the stone surface of the wall, screaming their battle cries at the huddled Tarseans. The enemy soldiers stood their ground, grimly silent as the Rutik approached at a run. At the last possible moment, their officer shouted an order and in unison, the entire contingent took a single step forward before settling back into defensive stances. They made it look simple and a part of Mira's brain found time to admire the discipline of the Tarsean forces. A single step forward seemed such a little thing but to do it in perfect formation, in the face of a charging enemy and at the exact right moment to disrupt the momentum of the Rutik charge? That impressed her.

The two sides met in a crash of blades, armour and shields and an inharmonious chorus of yells and screams. Mira stumbled and hesitated when the Tarseans moved forward but Teja and a handful of other Rutik soldiers managed to keep going and were the first to connect. Bellowing like a maddened bull, Teja set about himself with his long-handled *bardische*, swinging the heavy weapon as easily as if it were a mere stick. Momentum carried him onward, and he shouldered another enemy aside before swaying back and bringing the axe across in a wide, horizontal arc that hit the unfortunate Tarsean in the neck, ripped out his throat and kept right on going. Another Tarsean dodged out of the way, but their officer was not so lucky and Teja landed a solid blow on her breastplate. The officer let out a strangled yelp as the air was driven out of her lungs by the impact, knocking her from her feet to the ground. Teja stepped smartly forward and reversed his weapon, striking downward to cave in her forehead with the steel-bound butt.

Spotting the gap created by her sergeant, Mira quickly changed course and darted in behind him, stabbing sideways with her sword as she moved. The blow was poorly aimed and scraped across a Tarsean's chainmail without penetrating but caused him to rear back, creating enough room for Mira to slip past and take up position behind Teja. Beuca had followed his Captain, along with another soldier, a thick-set former mercenary by the name of Berig. Berig had joined the troop a year previously, following a short but bloody assignment on the plains east of Harbrook. He was a scarred, and terribly ugly man but a canny fighter for all that and from the corner of her eye Mira saw him engage the Tarsean she had just passed, drawing him forward and around until his back was to the scout Beuca. Snatching the opening, Beuca leapt forward, throwing his right arm around the Tarsean's face from behind, pulling his head up and back, before slicing open his throat with a curved dagger.

Teja took down two more of the enemy with his bardiche and Mira killed three with her sword before the fight abruptly came to an end, the last of the Tarseans isolated and cut down by Mira's troop. Without even allowing them to pause for breath, the Avatar stepped over a soldier's corpse and disappeared through the door. Mira rolled her eyes and took a headcount before following. Four of her soldiers were down, two dead and one probably on her way, one with a nasty gash across his forehead and what looked to be a broken ankle. She herself had taken a solid hit to the head from a Tarsean axe, her helm softening the blow but deforming in the process. She pulled the helm off impatiently letting it drop to the ground and shouted to another solder to stay with the wounded before waving the others towards the door, hurrying to catch up with the Avatar. The door led into a tower and Mira followed the Avatar down the winding stair to emerge into the courtyard in front of the palace.

They crossed the quiet courtyard quickly and unopposed until they reached the main doors, where a few dozen Tarsean guards were huddled protectively in front of the entrance. Not liking the odds, Mira nevertheless paused and prepared to order an attack, but the Avatar swept past her without a word and walked right up to the enemy formation. Mira's breath caught in her throat as she waited for the soldiers to strike the Avatar down, surprised to find the thought not entirely displeasing. It was not to be, however, for the enemy seemed frozen in place by the Avatar's approach and did not attempt to fight or even flee. Stopping a mere six inches from the closest Tarsean, the Avatar slowly raised its right hand and then swung it sideways in a strangely gentle but deliberate sweeping motion. There was nothing gentle about the effect on the Tarsean soldiers, however. As though hit by a sudden and immensely powerful gust of wind, the soldiers were thrown to one side, following the trajectory of the Avatar's right hand. Screaming, they flew to the right of the door and across the courtyard, crashing into the far wall of the palace. Afterwards, Mira swore that she heard the crack of bones as the bodies hit the stone wall and the screams were cut abruptly short.

Not one of the Tarsean soldiers moved after landing, except to slide slowly into a jumbled, messy pile. The Avatar lingered a little longer, as though admiring its handiwork and then waved its hand again. The palace doors swung open without a sound and the Avatar stepped inside. With little choice but to follow, Mira tried to ignore the diorama of human carnage the Avatar had created in the courtyard and followed it through the doors, wondering bitterly if it could not have taken the same approach on the walls and saved the lives of three of her soldiers. Mira's contingent of soldiers continued to diminish as they followed the Avatar through the palace. Once inside, Mira was dismayed at how much resistance they met, having hoped that the majority of Tarseans would have joined the battle in the city. Even though the troop still had the numbers to brush the enemy aside, and the Avatar to make even that unnecessary, they lost soldiers as they were ambushed at junctions, sniped at from balconies and held up at barricaded strongpoints.

The Tarseans in the palace fought almost rabidly, savagely, and unheeding of their own safety. She assumed that this was a result of having effectively cornered them in the palace, leaving them no other option but to fight to the death. She wondered if perhaps it might not have been more sensible to maintain the cordon for a while, allow the situation to stabilise, and then sweep up the surviving Tarseans with overwhelming numbers once they were weak and disheartened. Certainly, her soldiers would have been spared casualties by that method, but she guessed now that the Avatar had no interest in such niceties and cared not a jot for the lives of her troop, or her own. Since the display at the main door to the palace, it seemed to be hoarding its power once again, content to let the soldiers clear the way, whilst leading them ever onward towards whatever destination it had in mind.

Despite the chaotic scenes on the Avenue of Kings, Mira was surprised to find that so many other Rutik within the building, and she wondered how they had gotten in so quickly. Either the northern gate to the palace had already fallen, she supposed, perhaps to a division of the Expeditionary Army, or else the other Rutik had come along the walls as she did and entered the palace grounds via a different tower. Either way, there were groups of green-clad soldiers scattered all over the place: fighting with Tarsean guards, hunting down the palace staff, or looting and vandalising the ancient building. Mira recruited a handful to replenish her numbers, but most were too happy to be let loose in the city and unwilling to submit to any authority that might try to rein them in. Some were making their way upstairs, perhaps in the hope that there was more valuable loot to be found in the bedrooms and higher halls, but the Avatar passed several staircases without so much as a glance. Wherever they were headed, it was not upward.

At the foot of one particularly wide and impressive staircase, they found themselves coming under fire from a party of Tarsean bowmen, positioned on the landing above. Six of Mira's soldiers died in the initial volleys, before a well-aimed Tarsean arrow struck the Avatar directly in its left eye, sinking deep into its skull until only a few inches of shaft and fletching protruded from under its hood. The world seemed to freeze at that moment. Neither Mira, nor her soldiers, nor the Tarseans on the balcony seemed able to move a muscle and they all stared in horror at the Avatar, as it reached up, grasped the shaft of the arrow, and gently pulled it back out of its eye with a horridly moist sucking sound. The Avatar inspected the arrow carefully for a few moments before discarding it, seeming none the worse for the experience but evidently irritated.

Turning its hooded face upward to look at the Tarseans on the balcony, the Avatar made a complex gesture with its right hand, while raising its left to hold up its palm, fingers splayed. The entire balcony, which was perhaps thirty feet in length began undulating wildly beneath the shocked Tarseans, throwing them from their feet. This continued for a few minutes with the terrified Tarseans being tossed this way and that, unable to regain their footing, then the Avatar clenched its left hand into a tight fist and the balcony appeared to collapse into itself, smashing itself to pieces and killing its occupants instantly. The remains of the balcony and the unfortunate soldiers clattered onto the stairs, broken wood and plaster mingled with shattered bones and crushed entrails. This time the Avatar did not pause to survey the remains but moved on immediately, leaving several of Mira's soldiers vomiting noisily in its wake.

A high-pitched squeal of dismay caught Mira's attention and she looked further back along the balcony to see a young boy looking down at her wide-eyed. Their gazes locked for an instant, the mingled brown and gold of her hazel eyes staring directly into the steely grey of his. The moment somehow seemed to stretch into infinity as the connection continued. She found herself wondering who this boy was, with his mop of curly brown hair and fine, almost delicate features. She saw his expression harden and frowned in return, perhaps as he remembered that she was the enemy, invading his home and bringing a monster into his world. She glanced around to see if any of her troop had a crossbow ready, but they were all busy scrambling back out of cover and looking for more enemies. She looked back in time to see the boy jerk away as someone grabbed him from behind and pulled him from the rail. He disappeared and she berated herself for standing gawping when there was work to be done. For once, she was glad that her troop had not been ready for action, however, and for some reason, a little pleased that no one had thought to take a pot shot at the balcony. The boy would still be lucky to escape the palace alive but for reasons she could not fathom, she was glad he would at least get the chance to try.

The Avatar stalked onward, seeming completely sure of its route through the palace, despite the impossibility of its having ever even been there before. Following the incident at the staircase, it increased its pace, somehow still without seeming to hurry, and Mira again had to switch to a half run to keep up. It led them the length of a narrow corridor, that ended in a second staircase, this one narrower than the first and winding downward at a steep angle. They descended, traversed another corridor, and then descended again. On and on they travelled, always heading downward. The décor surrounding them became more and more spartan and grey until eventually, they found themselves emerging into a rough-hewn tunnel that stretched into darkness in the distance. The Avatar allowed them a moment's pause then, to find and light enough torches that they could see their path and then strode on into the darkness.

The tunnel continued for what Mira estimated at nearly half a mile before opening out into a much wider space.

The space was in darkness, save for two pools of flickering torchlight and had a cold, echoing sense of emptiness that suggested they were in a large cave. There was a strong odour of musty dampness in the air but disturbed by a slight fresh breeze, suggesting an opening to the outside world somewhere nearby. In the background, Mira could hear the steady clamour of rushing water. One of the torches illuminated a cluster of armoured soldiers, including one whose attire was particularly striking. The other flickering glow was emerging from a second tunnel entrance to the right of theirs. There were a few soldiers there too, but for the most part, the crowd of figures appeared to be a mix of servants, elderly nobles, and terrified children. Mira's troop had now readied their crossbows and as they poured into the cave behind her, she pointed them at the larger group of soldiers. Rutik crossbows used a rolling cylindrical pawl called a nut to hold back the string, mounted on a metal axle that fitted into the hard oak tiller. They were sturdy and well-designed weapons, deadly against unprotected flesh even at three or four hundred yards. The range now was not much short of that, and their targets were wearing armour, but most were ordinary soldiers with chainmail shirts so with a bit of luck some of the shots would still do damage.

Soon the cave was filled with the twang of waxed hemp bowstrings snapping against yew laths and the whistle of rushing air as bolts sped towards their targets – fourteen inches of ash shaft with a wickedly sharp, pyramidal steel head. Mira saw at least two of the Tarseans fall in the first volley, and then their leader seemed to snap awake and shouted the order to charge. Mira hesitated, wondering if the Avatar intended to intervene but, once again, it seemed content to observe and stood silently by the tunnel entrance. Disregarding it, for now, she sent a dozen soldiers to intercept the group of refugees, then led the rest to meet the Tarsean charge. Once more the enemy was heavily outnumbered, and she did not expect the battle to last long.

CHAPTER TWENTY-THREE

The Royal Palace, City of Tarsus
26 of Euthaios 870M - Late Spring
Day twenty-one of the siege of Tarsus

In just a few short years, the League for the Restoration of Rutik Glory had established a solid base of support amongst the common folk and turned their attention to the higher strata of Rutik society. They began with the younger sons and daughters of minor houses, but once they had ensnared a few of those, they used them to access more illustrious families, repeating the process all the way to the most exalted and powerful of men and women. Soon they controlled most of the major houses of the Rutik nobility and no longer felt the need to hide their actions, or their intentions.

Acusilaus, "Peoples of Asfáleia", c. 900M

Chapter Twenty-Three

Arion was still staring out of the window at the flames and smoke when he was interrupted by someone banging on the outer doors of his rooms. The noise was so sudden and so loud that he jumped and spun around in fright.

"Arion? Prince Arion! It's Corraidhín!" Arion recognised the voice and hurried to open the doors, almost tripping on the edge of a rug in his haste.

"Corraidhín, what's going on?" he cried before the doors were even fully open. Corraidhín greeted him with a formal bow, looking calm and collected despite the chaos outside and Arion was a little reassured. Less comforting were the dozen wary-looking soldiers, that accompanied him: blocking the corridor in both directions, facing outward with weapons drawn.

"Arion, I'm sorry – the Rutik are within the walls, and I fear the city is lost. Your father has ordered me to get you to a place of safety. You must come, quickly!"

"My father?" Arion's anger flashed back into life at the mention of the king but then vanished again almost as quickly, only to be replaced with sudden, sharp fear. "Where is my father? Is he… well?" Corraidhín raised his hands in a placating gesture.

"He was unharmed when last I saw him. He will meet us at the rendezvous point, in the caves below the palace. Plans were made long ago and there should be a boat waiting to take us downriver – with a little luck, we can avoid the Rutik blockade, and reach Chalcis. We'll be safe there, for a while at least."

"Us? What about my father?"

"The king will be going north, Arion. His duty is to remain with his people and what remains of the Tarsean army is escorting city folk into the Narrows."

"Into the Narrows? But they'll be trapped!"

"There is no other option. We haven't enough boats to bring everyone down the river and we cannot get past the Rutik forces on land but enough of this – no one will escape at all if you don't come now!"

In the corridor outside, the soldiers were shuffling their feet and looking around warily, and Arion noticed for the first time how tired and unkempt they looked: their eyes were bloodshot and weary, their faces tense and pale. Furthermore, their tunics, usually a brilliant blue and neatly fitted, were grimy with smudges of soot and stained with smears of reddish-brown. Two of them sported filthy and hastily-applied bandages – one across his face covering an eye, the other around her left arm. A tall soldier, most of his face obscured by a bushy red beard, noticed Arion's examination, nodded solemnly in greeting, and then broke into a wide grin revealing a mouthful of yellow and broken teeth. Arion's eyes widened in surprise and then, despite himself, he returned the favour with a smile. The soldier winked at him and then turned away as Corraidhín snapped out a list of orders.

Moments later, the group was hurrying through the palace, passing a series of tall windows paned with expensive clear glass, that looked out over the royal gardens and across the city beyond. Knots of armoured soldiery could be seen rushing this way and that, meeting, mingling and then breaking apart amidst the fires and the chaos. Then, even as Corraidhín set foot on the top step of the next descent, the sound of booted feet and jangling armour came echoing up from below. Peering around the islander, Arion's sharp eyes caught the glint of metal moving up the steps. At Corraidhín's snapped command one of the other soldiers stepped past him and onto the staircase. She clutched her sword tightly and her expression was grim, but she did not hesitate for a second. Moments later, an angry shout echoed up from the stairwell followed by a clash of metal and a short, sharp scream. Not giving them a moment to rest, Corraidhín ordered the others back down the corridor only to come to a skidding halt once more as a clutch of soldiers in smoke-stained, emerald tunics emerged from a side passage a dozen yards ahead. Three of the Tarseans pushed ahead to meet them even as the remainder of the party cast about for another avenue of escape.

For lack of a better option, they were forced to backtrack, reclimbing the stairs to the third floor, and hurrying back down the corridor above. From there Corraidhín led them towards the main palace staircase, which wound back and forth from the ground floor lobby, all the way up through the building. They found the third-floor landing held by a large force of archers and Arion's heart seemed to freeze for a moment before he realised that they were blue-garbed Tarseans and not the enemy. The archers were firing rapidly down the stairs and Arion peered over the marble bannisters in time to see a large contingent of Rutik scattering for cover below. Half a dozen of the enemy soldiers had been pierced with arrows and were no longer moving. As Arion watched, another Tarsean missile found its target, hitting one of the Rutik solidly in the face, impaling him through one eye and burying the arrowhead deep in his skull.

The injured man wore no armour and appeared to carry no weapons, which puzzled Arion somewhat. The man was no soldier so what was he doing in the palace? Arion stared raptly at him, as an unaccountable feeling of overwhelming unease began to fill his mind. Stranger still, the arrow now embedded in his face seemed not to bother the Rutik in the slightest. As the soldiers scrambled backwards and dived behind furniture and statues for protection, the cloaked man remained still. Then, slowly, he reached up and pulled back his hood to reveal an entirely bald head and skin that was deathly pale and smooth as marble. With one gloved hand he grasped the protruding shaft firmly and then, without any obvious sign of pain or even discomfort, he unhurriedly extracted the arrow. The arrowhead took a chunk of his eye out with it, leaving behind a bloody, tangled ruin but even as Arion watched he could see the terrible wound quickly begin to close. Within moments, the

Rutik's eye was fully restored, and the only evidence of the arrow's impact was left in the crimson streaks of blood that stained his pallid cheek.

Arion tore his gaze away and looked up to see the Tarsean archers watching open-mouthed as the Rutik examined the offending missile, then dropped it onto the ground. Languidly, the strange man raised his hands and began a slow series of gestures with his right. Arion watched, transfixed with fascinated horror, as the ancient stone stairway and the landing immediately above seemed to come alive, large sections of marble floor somehow bucking and rearing: an unbroken stallion unexpectedly burdened with a rider. The Tarsean archers were thrown from their feet in an instant, then tossed into the air and dashed against the walls by the violent spasms. A moment later the entire landing collapsed into itself and tumbled with an ear-splitting crash onto the stairs below. If any of the archers had survived the fall, they were certainly killed instantly as massive blocks of shattered stone crushed their fragile bodies.

A cloud of dust rose from the broken staircase, blinding and choking Arion in the same moment and he cried out in fright, rapidly rising panic turning the sound into a high-pitched yelp. As his vision cleared, he found himself looking directly into the eyes of a Rutik officer as she stared up at him from the floor below. The Rutik was tall, striking-looking, and missing her helm, her long, dark hair cascading down over her shoulders. Her gaze seemed to mesmerise him for a moment, and he found that he could not look away as her eyes seemed to bore into him, making it difficult to think clearly. He searched her face for any hint that she was as horrified by events as he, but finding no such evidence, he grew angry. Whoever the officer was, however, attractive she might be, she was the enemy and shared the blame for what was happening to his city. He was about to call out, curse at her perhaps when Corraidhín grabbed him roughly by the shoulder and dragged him away from the rail.

Releasing his hold on Arion, Corraidhín once more retraced their steps and searched for another avenue of escape. Several of the group looked to be on the verge of tears, whilst others were ashen faced with shock, struggling to rationalise what they had seen happen. Only Corraidhín somehow managed to keep his head, goading and bullying them all back into stumbling movement. Every time they passed a window the walls were painted with the flickering light of blazing fires below. The halls of the palace echoed with the sounds of fighting, the roars of the Rutik soldiery and the screams of their unfortunate victims. Arion no longer knew what was going on, his world seemed to be coming apart at the seams, his reality torn into ragged pieces that were being left dangling in the wind, broken and probably irreparable. He could hear the steady tramp of the guards' feet, their breathing heavy and laboured as smoke began to filter through the palace. He looked up to see Corraidhín marching ahead in the lead, his expression grim and holding little comfort. Near exhaustion, Arion staggered to a dazed halt. One of the soldiers made to drive him forward but Corraidhín appeared at the woman's shoulder and waved her aside.

"Breathe, Arion. The day is a dark one, but we can survive it. Your father awaits."

"Tarsus is burning, Corraidhín, the city is on fire. And… the last time I saw my father… we argued. I was… so selfish." With the reality of Rutik victory now plainly set before him, Arion realised how much pressure his father had been under these past weeks and months, how much the massive responsibility of an entire city full of people, all looking to him for leadership, must have weighed upon his shoulders. A loud crash echoed down the hall from the direction of the stairs and Corraidhín's head snapped around to look. Arion followed his gaze fearfully, but nothing further followed, and the islander turned back to face him.

"A piece of the staircase collapsing, I would say. Your father loves you, Arion, you know that. Perhaps you will have the opportunity to tell him yourself before we leave but only if we hurry. So, come, let us make haste."

Eventually, and by a roundabout route, they made their way to the ground floor. Rutik soldiers were everywhere but mostly in parties of two or three, ransacking and looting, and they were easily avoided. They came across Tarseans too: soldiers, palace servants and other citizens unlucky enough to have been in the building at the time of the Rutik assault. Most choose to join their group, others clearly preferred their chances of escaping alone but by the time they finally reached floor level, they were a party of almost thirty in total, split almost evenly between soldiers and civilians. Corraidhín seemed to have an almost preternatural sense of direction, leading them along a winding path from corridor to room, to the corridor again but always, Arion believed, heading roughly towards the western end of the palace.

Some of the civilians were having trouble keeping up, and Arion fell back to assist an elderly couple that he did not recognise. They both looked exhausted, and the woman was limping badly, an old injury exacerbated by the pace she said, thanking him for his help. Trying to emulate Corraidhín's calm demeanour, Arion assured them that they were nearly there now and that there was only a little further to go. They seemed comforted by that and managed to pick up speed a little, but Arion felt a little remorseful at the lie: in truth, he had no idea how much farther their path would take them, or even if there was safety at the end of it. He told himself that the lie was justified in the circumstances, and the reasoning rang hollow even in his mind but there was little time to ponder right and wrong.

Arion had one arm around the lady's shoulders as they hurried through a banqueting hall, leaving her husband to fend for himself. The pair seemed determined to continue, however, and Arion thanked his luck that their path remained unobstructed. At that moment, however, a large group of Rutik burst through the doors at the far end of the room and stumbled to a halt finding themselves confronted by a body of armoured soldiers. Corraidhín swore ferociously and pulled his spear free of the sling on his back.

"Soldiers of Tarsus: defend your prince!" he bellowed, and Arion found himself at the rear of a solid line of Tarsean soldiery, all grimly focused on the enemy ahead.

"Ware behind us!" The soldiers in the rearguard were now forming up too, as more Rutik appeared in the corridor they had just left. Moments later, both lines were engaged as enemy soldiers charged in, baying and whooping with fervour and excitement, determined to wet their blades with Tarsean blood. Despite his fear, Arion could not help but feel pride as the lines held and the Rutik were driven back, leaving half a dozen broken bodies on the floor. For a moment he even thought they might win the day but the veterans amongst the soldiers knew better.

"We cannot hold here!"

"I know, damn it! We'll have to…" Corraidhín's response was cut short as more Rutik rushed in, leaping over the bodies of their dead to reach the lines.

Corraidhín killed one with a neat stab to the throat, then hit another with a slice across the belly that would have disembowelled her had it not been for her chainmail shirt. The swipe was enough to stagger the soldier, however, and Corraidhín pressed his advantage by driving forward with his shoulder and knocking her roughly aside.

"Stand firm. We need another way out!" Arion recovered his wits enough to look around and then his eyes widened, and he shouted in excitement.

"There, Corraidhín, there!" Corraidhín followed his gesturing hand and focused on the door Arion had spotted.

"That's it, good lad! Pivot and form rank behind me, soldiers!" Corraidhín led the way and the soldiers turned neatly to keep their backs to him and continue facing their enemy. He snapped off more orders and they began edging backwards towards the door Arion had spotted, fighting off sporadic Rutik assaults along the way. Just as Arion thought they might make it clear, however, the game changed again as a towering, broad-shouldered Rutik officer appeared in the room and began shouting orders of his own. The Rutik were obviously well trained because they responded immediately, forming lines of their own and engaging the Tarsean across a broad front. The Tarseans were hard-pressed and then the Rutik officer himself joined the fray, swinging a huge double-handed axe in wide, whistling sweeps, knocking Tarsean soldiers aside and crumpling them into ruin.

Without hesitation, Corraidhín rushed in, even as two more Tarsean soldiers fell to the great axe of the Rutik officer. Corraidhín attacked in silence, with none of the roars and bellows of the Rutik but making every blow count. Ducking under one wild swing of the axe, he dodged smartly to the left and buried the point of his spear deep in the Rutik officer's side, exploiting a narrow gap between his breastplate and his backplate. The Rutik roared in anger and pain and pulled his axe back and up, preparing to swing it down into a blow that would surely have split Corraidhín from head to toe. Corraidhín was too quick, however, and instead of trying to recover his stance, he allowed his momentum to pull him forward, turning around the still-embedded point of his spear to pull it free at the last possible moment and strike downward himself, finding another gap in the Rutik's armour and slicing through the tendons in the back of his left knee. The Rutik officer's leg crumpled under him, unable to support his weight, and he fell shouting in agony, then gurgling into silence as Corraidhín stepped up from behind to cut his throat with a short knife.

Dismayed at the loss of their champion, the remaining Rutik fell back, and Corraidhín did not waste the opportunity. Taking Arion by the hand and calling to the soldiers to follow, he made for the door. Once there, he quickly picked four soldiers and then ordered the rest to hold the rear. Amazement, pride, and horror warred for supremacy in Arion's thoughts as he saw the Tarsean soldiers once again obey without question an order that surely meant their deaths. Even as Corraidhín pulled the door closed behind them, Arion could see the Rutik charging once more into the attack and knew that there was little hope for the men and women they had left behind. Turning away from the door, Corraidhín noticed his distress and managed a half-comforting smile.

"There's no escaping it Arion, I'm sorry. They die so that we can live. We can't fix it or change it; all we can do is make it worth their while." And with that, he hustled their much-reduced group forward and Arion was carried along in the flow, his worries and fears once more almost forgotten in the frantic rush.

From the banqueting hall, they eventually found their way to the kitchens, normally a bustling hive of activity but blessedly empty and silent as they passed through. From there a series of larders and storerooms took them to a cellar entrance and there they paused for a few minutes while the remaining guards lit torches and moved ahead to ensure that the path was clear. For Arion, the cellars passed by in a blur of flickering torchlight and echoing footsteps until they found themselves in a long tunnel that led steadily downward before emerging into a large open space. The sound of running water echoed off distant walls and a short distance ahead a large patch of torchlight showed a small boat bobbing gently in the current of a narrow channel. Nearby, Arion could see a dozen Tarsean soldiers milling around anxiously, swords and spears glinting in the torchlight. Among them, two figures stood in close conversation. One of the pair was dressed in the uniform of a Tarsean general and seemed to be mostly listening as the other man spoke. The speaker was taller and dressed in mail filigreed with gold and both men looked up as Arion shouted a joyous greeting:

"Father!"

Arion pushed past his guards and ran ahead as his father moved forward; arms outstretched. From that moment, time itself seemed to slow and almost stall and events followed one another with a nightmarish combination of sluggishness and terrible inevitability. A cry from the soldiers behind him caused Arion's father to pause and look back across the cavern. Arion skidded to a halt, confused, then slipped from his feet as his father drew his sword. In the black further reaches of the cave, a new pool of light had appeared as torch-bearing, green-clad soldiers poured in through some other entrance. For a second more, Achaeus hesitated, looking first at his son and then back at the growing horde of Rutik. Some of the newcomers carried crossbows and a deadly volley of bolts cut down two of the Tarsean soldiers, even as their king wavered. The screams of wounded and dying soldiers mingled with yelled orders and crashing armour to fill the enclosed volume of the cavern with a deafening cacophony.

Still moving with an almost implausible lack of haste, Achaeus turned to him again and smiled. It was a brief, quiet smile tinged with sadness, full of warmth and love but tempered by the acceptance of opportunities missed and memories that would never be made. So much emotion was conveyed in a single glance and Arion's eyes filled with tears that rolled freely down his cheeks as his father turned away and, rousing his soldiers with a cry, charged headlong to meet the Rutik attackers. The ranks of the enemy opened to receive them and then closed again, surrounding the brave Tarseans, and hiding them from the horrified onlookers.

"No!" Arion's yell echoed the resounding scream of utter pain that now consumed his heart. His stomach clenched and twisted in his belly and his throat quickly filled with a solid, burning lump. His pulse throbbed and beat in his ears, faster and louder even than the ring of swords and clash of armour. The sudden arrival of Corraidhín at his room had alarmed him, their passage through the chaotic palace had terrified him and the incident on the balcony had surpassed both his understanding and his ability to cope. Now, filled to the brim with horror and fear he lay prostrate on the ground, his limbs unwilling to respond to commands as his mind struggled desperately to protect the remaining fragments of his reason.

A short distance away, he could see Corraidhín fighting desperately to get to him, his spear stabbing and slashing, killing with every blow. Only three Tarsean soldiers now stood with him. They fought with equal fervour, standing shoulder to shoulder in a thin line between the Rutik and the remaining civilians. An arrow took one in the throat as Arion watched, and then the Rutik came on in a rush, overwhelming the other two in moments. Corraidhín fought on alone but despite all his speed and skill was being driven back towards the river. A Rutik mace caught him a glancing blow to the shoulder, and he staggered backwards, disappearing from Arion's sight. Farther away, the crush of soldiery surrounding the king heaved back and forth as each side sought advantage over the other, but the Tarseans were having the worst of it, and Rutik reinforcements were pouring into the cave.

CHAPTER TWENTY-FOUR

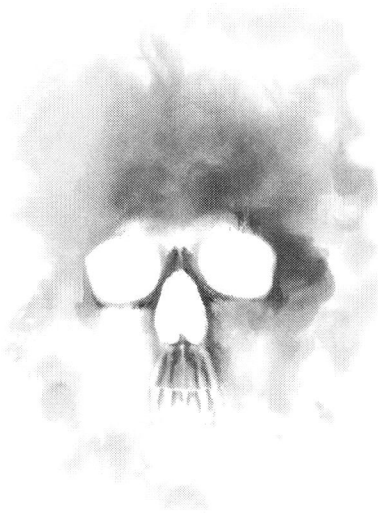

The Royal Palace, City of Tarsus
26 of Euthaios 870M - Late Spring
Day twenty-one of the siege of Tarsus

For the Rutik, and most of their fellow northern tribes, war was usually a brief, if bloody, affair. Even victories cost lives after all, and lives lost are lives that can no longer contribute to the tribe. An enemy defeated can often be recruited, or at worst enslaved. An enemy killed is just so much useless, rotting flesh. With the League in ascendance, however, the Rutik turned to the doctrine of total war. Once battle was joined, they would fight until none were left standing, execute the fallen injured and then move on to slaughter their families and burn their homes.

Acusilaus, "Peoples of Asfáleia", c. 900M

Chapter Twenty-Four

Corraidhín spun around, looking frantically for Arion amidst the flickering torchlight and lingering echoes of shouts and screams that gave the scene in the cave a surreal, nightmarish quality. Cursing himself for losing sight of the boy, he fended off a wild blow from a passing Rutik officer, catching the man's blade with the point of his spear and deftly turning it aside. Recovering quickly, he positioned himself for a counterattack, but the officer was gone, swept away into the press of shifting bodies. Corraidhín turned again, looking for a gap in the crowd, only to get knocked aside by a knot of soldiery, Tarsean and Rutik both, wildly swinging weapons at each other, as likely hitting their own side as each other's. Reeling from the impact of a badly aimed mace to his left shoulder, he ducked under a slashing sword, and stabbed one of the Rutik between the ribs. Momentum carried him forward and to the side, pivoting around the anchored spearpoint. Nearby, three Tarseans fell under a hail of crossbow bolts, leaving a momentary opening. There! He spotted Arion, face down on the rough stone floor of the cave, perhaps a dozen yards away, a Rutik soldier reaching down with a wicked looking knife in hand. Throwing caution aside, Corraidhín charged forward, brushing past enemy and friend alike, reaching Arion in moments and driving his spear straight through the Rutik soldier's exposed neck. Ignoring the screaming soldier even as her life blood splashed over him, he turned to check on Arion and then froze. A short distance away stood the mysterious and sinister Rutik that they had seen at the bottom of the staircase. Hood thrown back to reveal a shaved head, skin pale and scarred, the creature was staring directly at Corraidhín with eyes that were dark as the deepest pits and held nothing but hatred and death.

Mira led her body of soldiers into the charge in a tight formation, hoping to use their combined weight to force a way through to the Tarsean king. On the periphery of her vision, she saw the edges of her formation crumble as enemy soldiers attacked from the sides, but she ignored them, driving herself forward with all her attention focused on the prize ahead. If she could be the first to reach the king, if she could be the one to kill him, to take the crown and present it to her queen in triumph, the glory of this victory would be hers and a path would open to the heights of Rutik society. Their charge collided with the body of soldiers around the king, and she was forced to dodge aside as a Tarsean spear came directly at her face. Grunting with exertion, her face a rictus of determination and focused rage, she swung her sword up and to the left, battering the spear aside and driving her shoulder into the Tarsean's chest, knocking him aside. After that the fight became a riot of struggling bodies pressed up against each other, no room to swing a blade, but sharp points prodding from all directions, people pushing and shoving, faces close enough to feel each other's breath, everyone desperately fighting for an opening, a lucky break or room to move. The Tarseans were resisting with ferocious stubbornness, but Rutik numbers were beginning to tell, and Mira was getting nearer to the king with every moment that passed. An enemy soldier loomed up in front of her, thrown forward by a heave of the crowd, and as he roared in anger she could see every tiny detail of his features – a not unhandsome face, marred by an old scar across one eyebrow and a mouthful of blank and rotting teeth. His breath washed over her in a wave of decay and some unidentifiable spice, and she winced involuntarily. Her sword arm was trapped at her right side and her left hand was groping for a knife but in the press of bodies, she could not find one.

Rearing back as best she could, Mira threw her head forward to butt the soldier hard on the bridge of his nose, splitting skin, crunching bone, and driving a howl of agony from his throat. Sparks danced before her eyes as a spear came in from her right, aimed at her but missing by inches and catching her opponent in the upper arm instead. The Tarsean was pushed aside by the blow and Mira was through to the king, her sword arm came free, and she raised her blade to strike. The king was turned away, his back open and inviting to her attack. His armour was exquisite, beautifully made and obviously an ancient heirloom, protecting every part of his body but he had taken more than a few blows already and she saw an opening where a filigreed plate had been knocked out of place and hung loosely on a fraying leather strap. Shouting with the ferocious joy of impending victory, she pushed a Rutik soldier aside with her left hand and drew back her right to strike. The prize was hers to take!

∞ Þ ∞

Radomir burst out of the tunnel mouth with Red at his left shoulder and Ombly at his right, his body of co-opted soldiers close behind. They emerged directly behind a formation of Rutik crossbows, unnoticed as the enemy soldiers focused their attention entirely on picking out targets from the swirling mass of men and women. With a terrifying roar Radomir launched himself into their rear, swinging his great axe from side to side in tight, sweeping arcs. In moments, three of the Rutik were down: one almost beheaded, a second curled around a gaping wound in her side and a third holding desperately onto the stump of a severed limb, futilely trying to hold in his life's blood, eyes wide with shock and pain. Red hit next, now with a sword in either hand, chopping and stabbing madly in all directions. Two more Rutik died quickly as his furious blows cut deep. Ombly came behind in a far more measured rush, staying a little behind the two men, darting her spear through every opening they made, snatching lives away with quick, precise strikes. Even as the rest of the Tarseans piled in, the three were already through the Rutik formation, exploiting the shock of their sudden appearance on the scene to force their way through the crowd.

A shout from Red drew Radomir's attention and he followed the other man's pointed sword to see Achaeus and his guard locked in battle with a seething mass of Rutik soldiers. The Tarseans were holding the line for now, fighting with all they had to protect their king, but the numbers were against them, and the Rutik were pressing the attack with a ferocity born, no doubt, from the proximity of their prize. Sidestepping a charging Rutik soldier, Radomir swung his axe down and back, catching the man in the back of the leg and cutting through in a spray of blood. Knowing that he could not afford the time to finish the soldier off, he swung the axe back up and charged towards the king. Needing no instructions, Red and Ombly followed closely behind, protecting his flanks and preserving his momentum for the forward push. In minutes they were yards away from Achaeus, just in time to see a Rutik officer emerge from the press to the king's rear, his undefended back an open and inviting target. Radomir saw the next few moments play out clearly in his mind: they were still too far away to reach the king in time; the Rutik officer would strike her blow; and Achaeus would die; he saw it all happen with a staggering force of inevitability, but Radomir had never been a man to accept the inevitable. Judging distances and angles with an expert eye, he allowed the haft of his axe to slip down through his grip until his hand was at exactly the point of perfect balance between the head and the heavy shaft. Grunting with the effort and almost exposing himself to an attack from one side he flung the huge axe as if it were a spear, sending it flying through the air, directly towards the Rutik officer.

Achaeus was a strong and experienced warrior, and even without the bloodthirsty power of the ancient War Spear at his disposal, he was holding his own in the battle against the Rutik. Words could not have expressed the dismay and terror that had seized his heart upon seeing Arion go down. Ever since that moment, he had been fighting not for his life, nor even for his kingdom, but only to get closer to his son. His armour was beautifully crafted and tailored to fit his body with near perfect precision, but he was being set upon from two sides and had taken more than one blow solid enough to bruise and break bone, even through the heavy metal plate. Minutes passed and he was no closer to Arion, the Rutik were too numerous, and too strong. To his rear, one of his bodyguards fell, a Rutik halberd taking her in the shoulder and chopping down to bite deeply into her chest.

With his borrowed spear held tightly in both hands, Achaeus spun around and pushed forward to stab the Rutik soldier hard in the left side. The spear held no magic, nor did it have the glorious history and centuries of blood that would have driven the War Spear through flesh and bone, but it was a solid weapon, well made and razor sharp at the tip. Driven by a desperation that filled Achaeus utterly, threatening almost to overwhelm him, the spear point punched through the Rutik's chainmail and parted the skin and flesh beneath like a knife into an over-ripened fruit. Achaeus clearly felt her body's resistance change as the spear passed through muscle and organs before lodging itself firmly in her spine. She screamed, twisted, and fell back, almost pulling the spear from his hands and leaving him momentarily disarmed. Knowing that he had to keep moving at all costs, Achaeus instantly made the decision to let the spear go and swept his sword from its scabbard in a single, practiced movement, bringing it up and into a guard position in an instant. The Rutik soldier was still screaming but others were already stepping over and around her and Achaeus was forced onto the defensive, desperate in the knowledge that he was now moving further from his son instead of any closer. Another Rutik died at his hand and then two of his remaining bodyguard pushed past him and into the breach, determined to defend their king.

Achaeus had a moment to breathe but it lasted only long enough for him to hear a shout of victory from directly behind him. Knowing in his heart that it would be too late, he turned to face the new threat, coming around in time to see a Rutik officer coming at him, her straight, black hair flowing freely in the absence of a helmet, her face a mask of joy and bloodthirsty rage. Twisting his head around, he looked directly into her eyes and knew that this was the moment in which he would die. The officer's blade came forward in a perfectly aimed thrust, and Achaeus found himself absently admiring her poise and form, as though the whole scene was happening to someone else, and the sword was not about to steal away his life and crush what remained of his hopes and dreams. He thought about Arion for what would likely be the last time and a pang of sadness throbbed in his chest.

I have failed you, my son, I'm so sorry.

Arion recovered his wits and raised his head to see his father turning to face a Rutik officer who was attacking him from his rear. It was instantly clear to him that the king could not possibly bring his weapon around in time to stave off the approaching blow. He tried to scream, to shout a warning, to help his father somehow, before it was too late, but his throat was clenched tight with tears of heartfelt horror. The Rutik officer drew back her sword and was about to strike when something came flying out of the melee behind his father and collided with the Rutik officer. Arion was too far away to see exactly what the missile was but evidently it was heavy and coming in fast because when it connected with the officer's exposed side it knocked her sideways, sending her falling back into the crowd to crumple into a heap somewhere out of Arion's line of sight. His father completed his turn and even at that distance Arion could clearly see the surprise and relief on his face as he saw the mortal threat snatched away. Despite his fear, Arion almost cheered for the king's survival: it had seemed so unlikely, death so inevitable, perhaps there was hope after all?

He saw Radomir now, pushing through the enemy mobs towards his father with two doughty-looking fighters by his side. Turning his head, his eyes found Corraidhín, the islander only a short distance away after all and looking directly at him, his spear bloody and hanging loosely in his hands. Turning back, he watched as Achaeus rallied what remained of his guards and bellowed at Radomir, gesturing desperately in Arion's direction. Radomir charged forward with a roar, he and his companions barrelling through the Rutik, killing and maiming along the way, a veritable force of nature, unstoppable, or so it seemed to Arion. He looked back at Corraidhín, puzzled to find him still in the same spot, no longer staring at Arion but past him at something further back in the cave. Twisting to follow his gaze, Arion saw his father getting closer, moments from joining forces with Radomir. Together they would sweep all before them: Arion knew in his heart that nothing would stop his father from reaching him.

Then, seemingly out of nowhere, a fresh batch of Rutik soldiers arrived, keeping good order in close formation and inserting themselves between Radomir and the king. The formation broke apart, as the Rutik found themselves fighting on all sides, but by then it had done its job and Arion watched in rising dismay as his father disappeared into a scrambling melee. The king quickly regained his feet, only to fall once more as one of the Rutik smashed a shield into his face. It was not a lethal blow but a solid one and the shield had probably broken teeth and shattered cheek and nose bones. Achaeus was not allowed the opportunity to regain his feet for a second time. Like animals crazed at the smell of blood, the Rutik soldiers leapt on top of him, shoving aside the last of his bodyguard in their haste to reach him. Rutik blades rose and fell, chopping down and swinging back up, trailing showers of blood and gore that glittered and flashed, incongruously pretty in the flickering torchlight. A single Rutik soldier pushed clear of the roiling brawl, bellowing in excitement, and waving a plumed helm in one stained hand. From beneath the helm's rim, blue eyes stared sightlessly out into the patchy light of the damp cave and King Achaeus of Tarsus, the fourth of his name, direct descendent of Arrias the Conqueror and heir to a once-mighty kingdom, died in a filthy cave, at the hand of the lowest common soldier.

Corraidhín did not see the king fall, his attention fixed utterly on the grim visage of the creature before him. As their eyes met, he felt himself being dragged forward, pulled inexorably down into the endless dark of its eyes. In that instant he knew that he was lost, whatever this thing was it was filled with the same foul power that he had felt in the mysterious demons, only in more concentrated, more focused form. His vision began to blur, his thoughts falling apart even as he tried with all his strength to grasp hold of them and find some way to fight back. A rank contamination swept through his body, polluting every fibre of his soul and reaching unstoppably towards the core of his being.

Then, like a spark flickering into a bright flame, another power rose up to meet it. Corraidhín felt the boundless potency and fundamental goodness of the Oracle burst into a raging fire inside him that burned the blackness into nothing and drove the corruption back and out. His mind and vision cleared and as the last of the horrid infestation was vanquished, he felt a strength that resembled nothing he had ever experienced before. The Oracle's fire still seared through him, but it was purifying and cleansing, not scorching and burning. The pain was incredible, but it was the pain of sudden rebirth, bringing fresh life and new vigour. Corraidhín had no idea what force this transformation would bring to bear but he knew that it was enough, and he raised a hand, palm outward, pushing back with all his newfound might.

The creature across from him staggered but seemed otherwise unharmed and attacked again with renewed intensity. It's power hit Corraidhín as a mighty storm wind, a hurricane gale with the force of ten atmospheres behind it. For a moment, he was almost overwhelmed and then the Oracle's power surged once more, and he was fighting back. Gritting his teeth, he took a step forward, then another, his short spear held in a white-knuckled grip. The creature staggered again but held its stance and he felt it bending its will to the task, but still he pushed forward. One step, then another, and the creature was forced back against the cave wall. Another step, two, and Corraidhín felt it begin to weaken. He was inside its mind now, somehow, and could see its wicked, savage thoughts, feel its identity, sense its malevolent ruler lurking in the wings. The breath-taking scale of a plot in which the Avatar, the League and even the Kingdom of the Rutik were only bit players, was laid bare before him and he gasped at the audacity of it, recoiled in horror at the path it laid out for humanity. The Avatar was fighting back again but now the Oracle's power was reinforced by a cold, steely rage that was all Corraidhín's own. Still moving forward, he threw blow after blow of pure energy at the creature, knocking it hither and tither, battering it into submission.

Mira did not see the missile coming but felt it hit with a sickening crunch, snatching the breath from her body and throwing her sideways. She had not the wind to cry out but in her mind, she screamed in pain and outrage. To have come so close, to have so nearly gotten everything she had desired for so long, only to have it snatched away from her at the last moment – it was unbearable. Crashing to the ground after what seemed an improbably long time in the air, she hit her head sharply on a stone and lost consciousness. Whether she was out for seconds or minutes she had no idea but when she recovered her wits and managed to raise her head high enough to look around, there was no sign of the king, and no sign of whatever it was that had hit her. All she could see were men and women fighting and dying and she feared that the prize, her prize, was gone and lost to her forever. No! If she could get to her feet, perhaps it was not too late.

The entire left side of her chest was a mass of pain, most likely ribs broken from the missile's impact. Pulling her knees under her, she tried to push herself up on her hands, only for a blinding agony to shoot up her arm and into her shoulder, knocking her back onto the floor and almost into unconsciousness once more. As her vision cleared, she looked down at the arm, staring with a detachment born of shock, at the strange angle between forearm and elbow. Broken, and badly. *Fuck.* Holding the damaged limb gingerly to her body, she twisted onto her other side, and propped herself up on her good arm. One of her eyes stung and was blinded as blood from a gash on her forehead seeped down her face. She was facing in almost the opposite direction now, having somehow gotten turned around while rising and falling. The short, lithe figure of a man stood a few yards away, moving slowly forward, step by deliberate step as though into the teeth of a gale. Perhaps it was an hallucination from the pain, or the lingering effects of a concussion but in that moment, she could have sworn that the man's body was surrounded by an aura of softly glowing, warm golden light.

Ignoring the agony that threatened to overwhelm her, she turned her head to follow the man's path, and, to her shock, her remaining eye found the Avatar pinned against the cave wall and clearly struggling. A moment of grim humour struck her then – *Finally met your match, did you? Good enough for you.* She still had no clear idea of what exactly the Avatar was but could not find it within herself to take pity on it. The creature was evil and deserved to die, of that, she was sure. At the same time, Mira had been a faithful soldier of the Rutik for years though, and despite her personal feelings, she knew where her duty lay. Casting around, she spotted a fallen crossbow, mere feet away but it might as well have been a mile for how hard she knew the journey was going to be. Inches at a time, she pulled herself across the floor, every slight bump and scrape sending pain coursing through her, until the weapon was within reach.

Easing herself back down to the floor, she stretched out her one working arm to take the crossbow by the stock and pull it closer. *Finally, some luck!* It was loaded and the bolt had not come unseated when the weapon was dropped. The vision in her other eye was becoming blurred now too, though whether from blood or from the pain, she could not tell. Clinging desperately to consciousness, she raised the crossbow as high as she could manage, able to see the point of the bolt wavering in the air, pointed vaguely in the direction of the glowing man. In the instant that consciousness abandoned her once more she released the catch and vaguely registered the sharp snap of the string launching the bolt. Completely blind, she dropped the crossbow and instantly forgot about it as her mind drifted away into blessed nothingness and she collapsed.

∽ Þ ∽

Radomir roared in rage and frustration, knowing that their opportunity to reach the king had passed. Missing his axe, he set about him with his long knife and a sword he had pulled from the hands of a Rutik soldier moments before. He was killing one after another but there were always more and even his prodigious strength was beginning to fail. Glancing around he saw that Red was hurt, perhaps badly, but still fighting, and Ombly was slowing with tiredness, her stabbing strikes now much less sharp and far less precise. Through a gap in the crowds of enemies, he saw Achaeus go down, rise, and go down again. A moment later, a great roar of triumph rose from around the fallen king and Radomir knew that it was all over. He was not a sentimental man by habit, but Achaeus had been a friend and comrade for years, as well as being his king and one of the few people in the world Radomir truly admired.

There would be time to mourn later, however, and he pushed the melancholy ruthlessly aside as he tried to figure out an escape route. Their passage back to the tunnel by which they had entered was blocked by a mass of Rutik spears, who had worked their way around the edge of the cave in an effort to get behind the remaining Tarsean forces. He drove forward instead, battering his way through the crowd, heedless of any who foolishly got in his way. Spotting Corraidhín through the press he changed direction slightly to move towards him, in time to see a crossbow bolt somehow flying at an upward angle lodge itself in the islander's armpit, causing him to jerk sideways with the impact, and stagger to his knees. Radomir reached him a moment later, catching him by the shoulders and preventing him from falling. Ombly and Red moved past and to either side of them, facing outward, ready to protect their comrades.

"I'm here," he said, almost having to shout over the rolling noise around them. Corraidhín looked at him, his eyes filled with pain.

"No, not me. We have to stop it." He pointed across the cave with his good arm, shaking with the agony of his wound. Radomir followed the gesture but other than a section of wall that looked as though it had been battered with sledgehammers, there was nothing of note to be seen.

"It's gone, Corraidhín. Whatever you're pointing at, it's gone. And Achaeus is dead: we have to go too."

Corraidhín stared at him in seeming disbelief for a second or two, then looked around again. He looked confused and as if he was struggling to get his bearings.

"Arion? He was right over there!"

"I can't see him," replied Radomir in his usual blunt manner. "We have to go Corraidhín. They're coming."

""Find somewhere to lay low," said Corraidhín, through teeth that were clamped tightly together against the pain. "I can hide us."

"Got it. This is going to hurt though." With one mighty heave he picked Corraidhín up off the ground and swung him over his left shoulder. Nodding to Red and Ombly to follow, he headed towards the quietest corner of the cave he could find and then they were gone.

Arion's mind recoiled once more, utterly overwhelmed by stark and relentless horror, the image of his father's blank, staring eyes imprinted on his mind like a gory tattoo. The idea of his father's death was almost impossible for him to process: it seemed implausible. In one part of his mind, his father sat on the ancient Tarsean throne in all his royal finery, effortlessly dispensing justice and wisdom, personifying all that was good and right in the world. In another, his father was torn to pieces by a screaming mob, his armour battered and bloody, his weapons fallen and broken, his head separated from his body. The two versions of reality warred for dominance of Arion's understanding, leaving him dazed and utterly confused. He looked around for Corraidhín but of the islander, there was now no sign. Whether he too was lying dead in the cavern or had somehow managed to escape, Arion had no idea. All he knew for sure was that he was now alone in the dark, beset by terrible foes, lost and without hope of rescue. He was surrounded by savage giants, their voices braying and harsh in victory, their eyes glinting cruelly in the torchlight and his mind was a roiling sea of terror and heart-breaking sadness. His last memory before blackness claimed him was of gauntleted hands grasping at him from the darkness, cold steel fingers closing around his arms and legs.

CHAPTER TWENTY-FIVE

The ruins of Tarsus
30 of Euthaios 870M - Last days of Spring
Four days after Tarsus fell

The vultures circle
The worms prepare to feast.
An end comes to all things,
More often sooner than later

The poet Epinicus, c. 815M

Chapter Twenty-Five

The Achaean city of Tarsus finally fell on the twenty-sixth day of the month of Euthaios, in the year eight hundred and seventy by the Menosan calendar. On that date, centuries of history, culture and progress came to a sudden crashing halt, withering before the incandescent wrath of the Kingdom of the Rutik. Thousands of enemy soldiers swarmed over the walls and down into the paved streets below, sweeping all before them to ruin. At the same time, the steel-reinforced Gate of Arrias was flung wide, and the Rutik poured through in still greater numbers. The soaring towers were toppled or burned; the remaining defenders cast screaming to the rocks below. The majestic Royal Palace, ancient, beautiful, and long a shining beacon of Achaean civilisation, was stormed, ransacked and set to light. Within hours, the invaders were everywhere – the city gates garrisoned and held; major junctions blockaded with spears and pikes; crossbows on the rooftops picking off Tarsean survivors with no more mercy than a farmer might shoot the vermin that plagued his fields. As the noon sun passed unseen overhead, its summer heat smothered and obscured by clouds of smoke and dust, the last pockets of resistance were surrounded, isolated and obliterated. By mid-afternoon, few amongst the Tarseans had any fight left in them and still the Rutik hunted them as they fled. By nightfall, what was left of the city was entirely, and securely, in Rutik hands.

In a single, bloody day, Tarsus died.

Although the fall of Tarsus was as precipitous as it was violent, and the only small mercy was that death came quickly and moved on, leaving little time for gratuitous cruelty. What followed was a far slower and more painful torture: an obscenely wanton festival of destruction. Once night fell across the city, large swathes of the Rutik army seemed to lose all reason, and rampaged through the city burning, looting, torturing, and killing as the mood took them. The Rutik raged as if possessed, revelling in the screams of their victims, drenching themselves in the blood of men, women, and children alike. Fires soon burned in a thousand places around the city, entire quarters were consumed and the bodies of thousands committed to ashes.

In the ruined palace the flames leapt higher and higher, reaching into the smoke-filled sky, spreading greedily to consume nearby buildings and feed upon their shattered timbers. A thousand Tarsean soldiers were crucified along the Avenue of Kings. Ten thousand more were beheaded on makeshift chopping blocks made from scorched timbers or shattered stone. Their heads were impaled on spears or piled into gory pyramids around the remains of famous landmarks and fallen statues. Their bodies were cast aside, thrown into wells to poison the watercourse, or piled against the sides of houses. Blood ran through the gutters like floodwater, sloshing over discarded weapons and the assorted grim detritus of war. There was no point to any of it, no goal except the destruction itself and no reward save the pleasure of an enemy's screams. The common soldiers of the Rutik were unleashed unto mayhem and their masters did nothing to restrain them. Indeed, most of the officers were seized by the same madness and enthusiastically cast aside the shackles of responsibility, leading their subordinates only insofar as they inspired them by example. The sacking of Tarsus was less an occupation by a conquering army than a prolonged and utterly mindless riot.

Mira could only count two full years into her military career but in that time, she had seen her fair share of violence and brutality. War, by its nature, was never pretty. People died screaming, died crying, and died soiling themselves. Sometimes merciless slaughter was the most merciful solution to a conflict – an enemy met with uncompromising destruction was far less likely to return for a second helping. Often it was necessary to act without scrupulous morality, to murder in cold blood and achieve a goal that would otherwise require open warfare. Occasionally, it was preferable to torture a person on the other side, so that the information obtained could save the lives of your own people. Mira had done all those things, some of them more than once, and whilst she was not overly proud of the acts themselves, she recognised their necessity and took pride in the accomplishments they had enabled. Above all else, Mira was a professional soldier, and she took a professional soldier's pride in following her orders.

Now, at the grand old age of eighteen, Mira found herself sickened by the pointless, sadistic cruelty on display in Tarsus. She did not participate in the excesses of her fellow Rutik, nor did the men and women under her command but still, she felt soiled by them: she shared a uniform with them, and thus also shared their guilt. Once the initial fighting died down, Mira led her troop to a small, cobbled square in the northwest of the city and set up camp amidst a smattering of other small companies that stood aloof from the chaos. As the hours passed, they were joined by other such groups and even soldiers arriving alone or in twos and threes, separated from their units and lacking the stomach for further violence. Shortly after midnight, a group of senior officers arrived, accompanied by a wild-looking pack of followers and most of the stray soldiers were rounded up and forced back into the fray. When they approached Mira's small encampment, she met them with her hand on her sword hilt, her burly sergeant at her side and her soldiers in a neat double line formation behind her.

Mira was probably the most junior officer present but she stood her ground without wavering and refused to leave camp. Operating as she did, outside of the normal chain of command, afforded her that luxury since there was no one present with authority to question her restraint. She was within her rights to refuse but the other officers were excited, almost frenzied in their insistence that she join them. Behind the officers, a raucous mob of soldiery quickly assembled, most of them with weapons already in hand. Mira's troop held their formation, but she could sense their nervousness. They were wildly outnumbered with little chance of escape, and if tensions were to escalate to violence, it would surely go badly for them. One of the officers stepped closer to bellow an order directly into her face, arrogance dripping from his every move, his mouth scarcely an inch from the end of her nose. As he leaned in, the smell of stale liquor on his breath, filthy sweat from his body and dried blood from his uniform washed over her in a sour and sickly wave.

Mira might have permitted the man to shout at her, he was a Major after all if that even meant anything in the ruins of Tarsus. A moment later, however, he followed up by placing his free hand on her shoulder, perhaps seeking to detain her or to emphasise his point but either way, it was more than she could bear. Her left hand snapped up to grab his wrist, fixing him in place as she darted forward with her head, catching him solidly in the nose. She was wearing her helm and if the metal was less shiny than parade standard, it was certainly no less solid. Cartilage crumpled, and bone shattered as the blow connected. With a sound best described as an outraged squawk, the officer staggered back, and she released her grip on his wrist. Blinded by pain and anger, he pulled his sword and moved to attack only to find Mira's own blade resting on his throat and a look in her eye that clearly declared her intention to use it should she be provoked any further. Two more officers stepped forward to back up their comrade only to find themselves at the point of her sergeant's massive axe. Behind them the mob surged, baying for blood and Mira's troop spread out to her either side, shields raised, weapons drawn and ready.

A long, tense moment passed as the two sides faced off across the blood-spattered slabs of granite paving. Mira could feel the aggression peaking in the furious mob, jeers and insults peppering a constant angry murmuring as they encouraged and goaded each other into action. In contrast, Mira's soldiers were deathly silent, waiting in ready stances exactly as they had been trained but she knew they too were spoiling for a fight, despite the odds. It seemed that a violent confrontation was inevitable when a roar echoed across the square, coming from the south. The mob hesitated and turned to look and then, driven by the strange collective consciousness that guides such gatherings, decided as one that there were better and easier pickings to be found elsewhere. The officers held their positions a little longer but when it became clear that they no longer had the numbers so firmly on their side, they too retreated and walked away. Mira breathed a sigh of relief and turned to commend her troop on their discipline and restraint. Looking at them, she understood then how tenuous that restraint was. Her soldiers were moments from breaking: she could see it in their darting eyes, in their unsettled, fidgety movements and their white knuckles where they gripped their weapons too tightly. Their behaviour was equally as baffling to her as the other side's – neither such extreme savagery, nor such intense nervousness were characteristic of the common Rutik soldier. Her troop had been in worse situations and never flinched. The Rutik army was near-legendary for its discipline. Now her soldiers were acting like startled sheep and the rest of the Rutik had seemingly descended into uncontrollable frenzy.

What is happening here?

Mira knew that a certain amount of disorder was to be expected at the end of a siege. The sacking of a city was always an opportunity for soldiers to revert to their most base and murderous instincts: it was human nature, no matter what uniform you wore. In an ideal world, the attackers would have marched into the conquered city, raised a flag, and called it a day. Prisoners would have been taken, the city would have been garrisoned and everyone else would have gone home. In an ideal world, the rules of society and decency would have been remembered and respected but in an ideal world, there would never have been a siege in the first place. A certain amount of chaos was to be expected but what had happened in Tarsus was a level of excess that was almost incomprehensible to her.

After three full days and nights of unrelenting anarchy, the remains of the city finally began to quiet. Large numbers of the Tarsean population were in chains, most destined to work out their lives in slavery. Even larger numbers were corpses, scattered around the shattered city streets, buried under the rubble, or mixed into the ashes of the great fires. Some precious few had escaped the slaughter, fleeing through tunnels or by scaling the city walls and dashing into the night but they were few indeed, and most would be rounded up by the patrolling Rutik cavalry long before they reached anything approaching safety. The Tarsean palace was a smouldering ruin, as were most of the larger buildings around the city. Every statue was broken, every well and fountain soiled with bodies, blood or faeces, anything of value that could be carried away was in a soldier's pack somewhere. Anything that could not be carried was broken up or otherwise destroyed. A thick pall of greasy, foul-smelling smoke hung over everything, lingering in the still air.

As the fourth day dawned over the devastated city, Mira collected a breakfast of stale bread and hard cheese, along with an earthen jug of watered-down wine and retreated from the bustling noise of the Rutik camp. Skirting the various tents and campfires, she headed for the Narrows Gate, carefully skirting the eerie devastation of King's Plaza, and walked in the shadow of the walls for a while. Along the way she stepped over or around more bodies than she cared to count, soldiers of the Rutik or Tarsean armies and civilians alike. Although largely obscured by smoke and dust, the sun had been shining brightly for the last three days, with little in the way of wind to stir the air. On the city streets, the still, stifling conditions had only accelerated the inexorable march of decay and putrefaction. Most of the bodies were now bloated with noxious gases, their proportions swollen and gross. The fetid stench of corruption hung thickly in the air, and fat, black flies swarmed on every surface.

Finding her way barred by the smouldering remains of a Tarsean barricade, she headed down an alley and into the backstreets, in the hope of easier travel. There, in a small, cobbled square, hemmed in by shattered, smoking buildings she found an entire crucified, one alongside the other, pinned to walls and trees with heavy, iron nails. The adults showed signs of having been tortured before they were put to death. The children did not, but she could see from their contorted bodies that they were still alive when they were nailed up. Mira could normally ignore such things but the swollen, staring eyes of the children haunted her and she hurried on. In another smoke-blackened alley, she found lingering bonfires, the charred ends of human bones visible amongst the ashes. Mira paused there for a while, stirring the warm ashes with the toe of her boot, and pondering. Eventually she moved on, passing the mouth of a rubbish-strewn alleyway, where she saw what appeared to be an entire platoon of Tarsean soldiers left to rot where they had fallen. Presumably the unfortunate Tarseans had been fleeing pursuit and taken a wrong turn. The poignant significance of that momentary decision – turn left or turn right – struck her hard with the realisation that she had made similar decisions a thousand times before.

By the time she reached the walls again, Mira was sickened but thankfully she was blessed with a strong stomach and a stronger will. Even amidst the horror, she was determined to eat her breakfast in something approaching peace. She followed the walls to the east again for a short distance before reaching one of the soaring towers that punctuated the walls' length. The tower's door was broken and hanging off its hinges but otherwise it seemed to have escaped the worst of the destruction and she slipped inside. A single corpse lay crumpled at the foot of the stairs: a Tarsean soldier, armoured and helmeted but hardly looking old enough to have shaved even once. Protected in the shade of the small hallway, the body was in better shape than most of the ones she had seen outside but still starting to smell a little rank.

Mira had to stretch to step across the fallen soldier and onto the second step but from there the way was clear and she followed the winding stair to where another broken door opened out onto the top of the walls. The stair continued up, but Mira had no desire to follow it further, knowing what she would find. The towers boasted a single small room at the upper level, with balconies and loopholes to allow defenders to launch arrows and stones at enemies below. Some were equipped with heavier weapons: ballista, catapults and the like, and others with heavy cauldrons to pour boiling oil. Either way though, each and every one of them had been defended to the last by the Tarseans and Mira knew that ascending further would only offer yet more views of blood and death.

The stretch of wall onto which she emerged was some distance from the Narrows Gate and, spotting a relatively comfortable looking spot, she turned her back on the ruined city to look out over the Tarsean Narrows to the north. In the days after the fall of the city, some of the Rutik had abandoned the crowded streets and headed into the Narrows, looking for more plunder amongst the farms and villas. Thus, even the grassy plains and fields of crops had not escaped the plague of destruction that had befallen Tarsus. Mira was too high up and too distant to make out any details but some of the buildings were clearly still smoking and the corpses of citizens and livestock were scattered across the view.

A little to the east, the Bisaltes River flowed towards the city walls: sparkling, majestic and utterly untouched by the chaos it passed through. A flock of pheasants winged their way towards the horizon whilst high above some breed of falcon circled lazily, perhaps trying to decide whether the game birds below were worth descending for. In the far distance, she could make out the walls of Dobrich, nestled in the foothills of the Devil's Teeth. Seeing the mountains again sent a shiver through Mira as she recalled their long journey beneath the snowy peaks. At that distance, however, the slopes looked quiet and peaceful, almost serene in the morning light.

Mira's breakfast was wrapped in a few sheets of parchment, torn from some ancient book or other in the Tarsean palace. As she folded back the stiff material, she was vaguely amused to realise that it had previously served to present some ancient academic's assessment of the Tarsean Kingdom. Her grasp of the Achaean languages was not perfect, and the dialect was unfamiliar, but the opening passage appeared to read: "The great Kingdom of Tarsus shall last forever" – so *much for that idea*. Smoothing out the parchment to serve as a tablecloth, she made no effort to decipher the rest of the author's insights, instead breaking off a lump of cheese and popping it into her mouth whilst returning her gaze to the peaceful countryside.

The fate of kingdoms was nothing of Mira's concern: she was a soldier and that was enough. The last days of the siege had been, by turns, exhilarating and terrifying but she had played her part. There were bodies down there in the streets that had lost their lives to her sword, and she felt no shame in that. Those she had killed were all soldiers, and would all have killed her first, had she given them the chance. That was just war: fight and live or fight and die, those were a soldier's options and neither made much difference in the end. She washed the last crumbs of cheese down with a swig of wine and wiped her mouth on her sleeve. The needless slaughter of innocents that had followed the siege was not her doing, she assured herself, and not a weight she would carry upon her conscience but even in her mind, the words rang hollow. Mira could hear birdsong now, though she could not spot the singers, and the soaring melodies soothed her heart for a while. Soon, she knew, she would have to descend from her perch and return to the bloodstained atrocities in the city below; but not yet.

Mira remained atop the walls for longer than she had intended and by the time she finally descended, the sun was inching towards its apex and noon beckoned to any who remained alive in the ruined city. Technically she was late to her post, unacceptably late, but it seemed unlikely that there would be much concern for punctuality on such a day. Upon reaching the ground, she paused for a moment to brush the dust and crumbs from her uniform, straighten her hair somewhat and to check the straps and buckles of her armour. Although she was hardly fastidious in attending to her appearance, she keenly felt how grubby and unkempt she was at that moment. She was tall and slim, and although she would never describe herself as beautiful, she knew that she had a look that turned heads when she passed. *Heads would certainly turn if I passed now*, she thought wryly, though perhaps not in awe at my exquisite beauty. Angrily, she told herself that she had no reason to be ashamed of her appearance since she had earned every scratch and bump on her breastplate far more honourably than most. Frowning, she rubbed at a particularly egregious tear in the right sleeve of her jerkin, carefully sewn back together but still obvious and unsightly. Beneath the crease of stitching, she could feel the rough edges of the long scar that marked a line from her elbow almost to her wrist. She explored it with the tips of her fingers, the movement taking her mind back to a time two years earlier, and a place deep in the shadows of the Drevenwood. The place where she had started out on the long, bloody road that led to Tarsus.

Mira's head snapped up as two Rutik soldiers stumbled noisily out of a nearby alley. The two men were rollickingly drunk, talking and laughing loudly, then falling silent to stare balefully at the officer that now stood poised to spoil their fun. Neither showed much sign of having been in battle but one carried a large sheet, tied at the corners into an improvised sack that looked to be heavy, she presumed with loot from the dead and dying. Her lip curled as she took in their dishevelled appearance. The Rutik were descendants of a long, proud warrior tradition, stretching back to the old country, a tradition that valued courage and honour above all else. The two men offended her, and without thinking, she put her hand on the hilt of her sword as she snapped out an order to return to quarters. The men continued to stare, perhaps gauging their chances against the lone officer. Mira tightened her grip on the sword and cocked her head to one side, smiling grimly.

"Do it," she said, flicking a glance at one man's hand where it crept slowly towards his belt. "Draw your sword and you won't live long enough to be hanged for assaulting an officer."

They two men continued to stare for a moment before slowly raising their hands in acquiescence. Without a word, they turned and walked away. Mira grunted and released her sword, knowing full well that the men had probably gone in search of a route around her, rather than a route back to quarters but finding that she did not care as much as she probably should have. What difference did it make, after everything that had happened in the preceding days? Their activities were unsavoury and disheartening but would hardly even register on the scale of atrocities that had befallen Tarsus. Once they were out of sight, she dismissed them from her thoughts and went upon her way, allowing her mind to drift back to the Drevenwood as she walked.

What struck Mira most in the days that followed was the silence. As the fires burned out, and the Rutik horde collapsed, exhausted into corners, and abandoned homes, there was scarcely a sound to be heard in the ravaged city. Even the birds and animals whose cries would normally have drifted across the air seemed to have fallen quiet. The entire world held its breath, horrified at the apocalyptic scene. And yet the League were still apparently unsatisfied. The Avatar had disappeared once the initial conquest was complete, and the fighting had died down. Now it returned, along with a dozen of its brethren, walking in lockstep and accompanied by a small legion of fresh, grim-faced soldiers. Orders were rapidly distributed to the Rutik officers, giving them until the following morning to restore order and gather their troops. Another sort of chaos followed, as Captains barked at Lieutenants, Lieutenants shouted at sergeants, and sergeants found their corporals and began the difficult process of reconstituting their units. The process involved a lot of bellowing, a lot of threatening and cursing, much kicking and not a little beating with fists, feet, and even wooden truncheons. Eventually, the soldiers began to coagulate into something resembling coherent units and divisions and by the fifth day following the fall, they were on parade in the main square of the city, awaiting their new orders.

The army was to divide into sections, each led by an attachment of sappers and engineers, and what remained of the fortifications of Tarsus were to be dismantled. The soaring towers would be undermined and collapsed, and the great walls tumbled into the dirt. The League seemed utterly determined that Tarsus would forever be wiped from the map of the world, never again to rise to any prominence or reclaim its place in the world. As the soldiers toiled to complete the work around the walls, Avatars were seen stalking through the ruins inside, pausing at times to stand heads bowed. No one knew what they were up to amongst the rubble, but rumours and wild tales flew amongst the troops, becoming ever more fanciful with the retelling. Mira, who had seen their obscene power firsthand during the fall suspected that they were now spreading their curses around the city, salting the earth so to speak, poisoning the land against any future occupation by anyone vaguely human.

Thousands of Rutik soldiers were set to work on the demolition but still six long, exhausting weeks passed before the walls were substantially levelled. Further orders came then: a small division would remain to garrison the city, cautioned sternly to remain in the vicinity of their headquarters outside the ruined gates, and not to venture any further into the city itself. Large contingents were sent south to swell the forces already set to threaten the other cities of the plains. Others were sent back towards Harbrook and Rutiksborg to reinforce garrisons stripped bare to build the conquering army. Awards, honours, and promotions were distributed liberally amongst those of the officers who had distinguished themselves in the fighting, as well as those well-connected enough as to be impossible to pass over without causing massive political turmoil.

Mira was commended for her service, and awarded promotion to the rank of Major, with a bag of gold thrown in to sweeten the pot. She was also given permission to recruit enough soldiers to replenish her ranks and expand the troop to a size appropriate to her new command. It being the army, however, there was also a catch: her orders were to return to the north and pursue vengeance against the remainder of the Baimoi. It was not a glamourous or prestigious posting, being essentially a mopping-up mission following an already successful campaign. Nor was it one likely to earn her much in the way of further honours or glory, being far from the watchful eyes of the hierarchy. Still, Mira accepted the role with relish, eager to finally meet the Baimoi on her own terms, and keen to match their riotous savagery with her own cold resolution.

Truth be told, Mira would have gladly accepted any commission that took her away from the *League for the Restoration of Rutik Glory* and its so-called *Avatars*. She remained shaken by the things she had seen both during and after the fall of Tarsus. Her aspirations for honour and glory that had induced her to join their cause in the first place now seemed childish and naïve. Whatever evil the League represented, and whatever power they had bestowed upon their Avatars, she wanted nothing further to do with it. She would put some distance between herself and the vile horror that the League represented. She knew she could not forget them and suspected she would never truly be free of their influence but, for the time being, at least, she could be free and another of her father's oft-repeated aphorisms lingered in the back of her mind.

Fate brings fresh sorrow, soon enough.

- THE END -

Mighty Tarsus has fallen, its soaring towers toppled & broken. King Achaeus is dead, Arion a captive, alone & afraid. The Rutik will march to their next conquest and Mira with them, leaving the scorched ruins silent & empty. But stories never really end, they just... move on.

To be continued...

Book Two in "Histories of Asfaleia" is coming soon

People, Places & Languages

People, Places & Languages

Throughout *Conqueror's City*, I have borrowed liberally and shamelessly from ancient cultures to build the people and places of Asfáleia. Some brief extracts from Wikipedia follow, for information in lieu of formal historical references.

I will freely admit to being neither an historian nor a linguist. With all sincerity to anyone properly educated in those dark arts, I hope that my amateurish bastardisation of culture, grammar and vocabulary has not completely prevented you from enjoying the story.

The Achaeans (wikipedia.org/wiki/Achaeans_(tribe))

The Achaeans (/əˈkiːənz/; Greek: Ἀχαιοί, Akhaioi) were one of the four major tribes into which the Greeks divided themselves (along with the Aeolians, Ionians and Dorians). According to the foundation myth formalized by Hesiod, their name comes from Achaeus, the mythical founder of the Achaean tribe.

The Rutik (wikipedia.org/wiki/Rugii)

The Rugii, Rogi or Rugians (Ancient Greek: Ῥογοί, romanized: Rogoi), were a Roman-era Germanic people. They were first clearly recorded by Tacitus, in his Germania who called them the Rugii, and located them near the south shore of the Baltic Sea. Some centuries later, they were considered one of the "Gothic" or "Scythian" peoples who were located in the Middle Danube region.

The Bulǵha (wikipedia.org/wiki/Bulgars)

The Bulgars (also Bulghars, Bulgari, Bolgars, Bolghars, Bolgari, Proto-Bulgarians) were Turkic semi-nomadic warrior tribes that flourished in the Pontic–Caspian steppe and the Volga region during the 7th century. They became known as nomadic equestrians in the Volga-Ural region, but some researchers say that their ethnic roots can be traced to Central Asia.

It was not my intention to appropriate anyone's culture or history. The people of Asfáleia are inspired by history, but nothing that they do or say should be taken as a criticism or indictment of historical people, places, or civilisations.

Author's Postscript

Conqueror's City began as a very simple story, over twenty years ago now. At some point, I don't remember exactly when, I put it aside to focus on family, work, and all the other things that go along with real life. By the time I picked it up again the world had changed, and I had changed with it. Somewhere along the way, I discovered a new approach to character writing.

My original characters were deliberately crafted to fit a predetermined storyline, little more than walking, talking plot devices. Instead, older but perhaps not all that much wiser me, decided to drop them into the story at a particular place and time and then just wait to see what they did next. Left to their own devices, they made their own choices and decisions, changing the story as they went. Where backstory was required, I filled it in by asking myself: how did this person get to be who they are? Over time, personalities emerged, along with preferences, prejudices and points of view that were very much theirs, rather than mine.

For that reason, most of the characters now bear little resemblance to their original forms. Some have retained their names but most not even that. Corraidhín was once Kireen, and Radomir was once Beriad, and so on. Some quite beloved characters have fallen out of the story altogether. Bethen, for example, devoted nurse to Arion and his brothers, now resides only in a forgotten draft somewhere. I like to think she still sings softly to herself while she knits, the faint melody drifting comfortingly across her sleeping charges. Some equally important names lost their place in the story for now but wait in the wings for their cue to return. Be patient, Eres and Petya – your time will come.

Conqueror's City is no longer the story that I wrote two decades ago. I suspect that were the same period to elapse again and the story remain unpublished, the 2050 version would be as different again. At some point though, a writer must draw a line and say to themselves: "imperfect as it may be, this story is ready to be sent upon its way".

If just one person enjoys reading my book as much as I have enjoyed writing it, I'll be delighted!

Until next time,

Printed in Germany
by Amazon Distribution
GmbH, Leipzig